EDISON BLUE 2

Snark of the Lich King

EDISON BLUE 2

Snark of the Lich King

By

J. I. Thacker

.☺.

Written for Hazel and Dan, whose world this (still) is

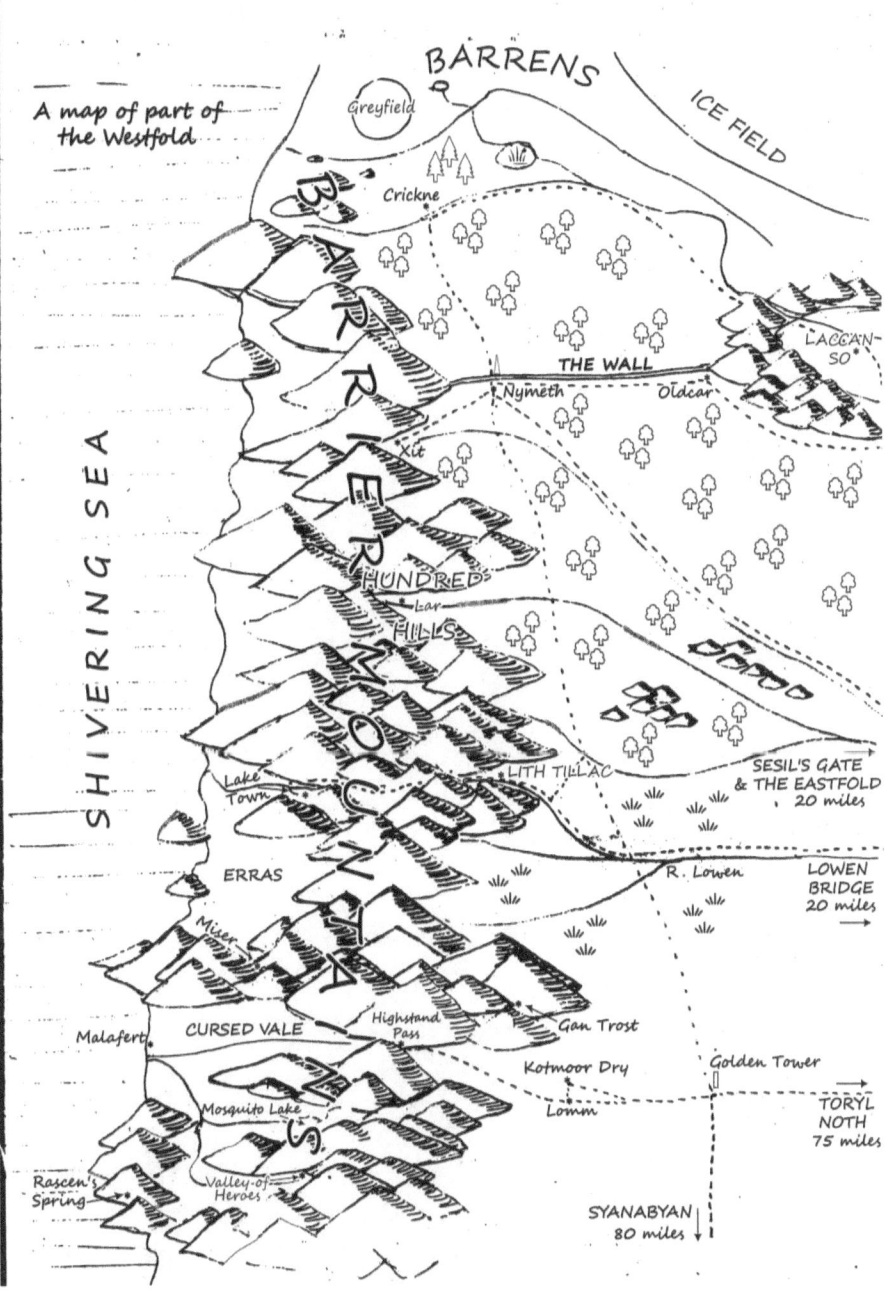

A map of part of the Westfold

BARRENS

ICE FIELD

Greyfield

Crickne

BARRIER

SHIVERING SEA

LACCAN-SO

THE WALL

Nymeth   Oldcar

Xit

HUNDRED

Isar

HILLS

MOUNTAINS

Lake Town

LITH TILLAC

SESIL'S GATE
& THE EASTFOLD
20 miles

ERRAS

R. Lowen

LOWEN
BRIDGE
20 miles

Miser

CURSED VALE

Highstand
Pass

Gan Trost

Malafert

Kotmoor Dry

Golden Tower

Mosquito Lake

Lomm

TORYL
NOTH
75 miles

Rascen's
Spring

Valley-of-
Heroes

SYANABYAN
80 miles

In a Nuclear Bunker in Lar, in the Province of Nymeth

For forty-seven minutes life was perfect.

Then I blew it.

Actually, I made the mistake almost straight away. It just took me three-quarters of an hour to realise what an idiot I'd been.

There I was, strutting up and down and giggling like an idiot in the entrance café of a 2,600-year-old nuclear bunker. Lexi had kissed me, and it was like falling off a cliff and never hitting the bottom. I could walk again for the first time since that cold night on the Greyfield after "defeating" the Entity at the cost of all the magic I had only discovered I had ten minutes earlier. That was when I finally noticed something that had been right under my nose since the beginning. Edison Jr was as much a magician as I was. He could save Lexi when I, my battery fully depleted, could not. He saved our beautiful and loyal horse Speckle too.

After defeating the Entity, we went to Jasso's home village of Lar. Unable to walk, I moped around on a makeshift skateboard trying to avoid seeing any of the stream of important people who came to congratulate me on saving the world. Meanwhile Lexi spent months secretly working on opening the sealed entrance to the bunker in the hanging valley above the village because she knew – Royal Court Magician Hal's glowing ring that I was at that moment holding up like a lighter at a soft rock concert told her – that there was magic within. Magic that I could restore my broken body with.

So as soon as she let me into the bunker's entrance cafeteria, I sucked all the magic there out of the air like an assiduous living vacuum cleaner. The power there was thin, like dust motes in an attic. But Magic 3.0 was easily potent enough to get me back on my feet in moments.

And I realised as I stood up for the first time in nearly a year – almost immediately falling over, having forgotten how to walk – that it didn't matter.

It didn't matter because Lexi loved me before, when I could not stand, or do magic, or laugh, or be any fun to be around. She didn't care what state I was in. All those months, Lexi had been trying to find magic for me. And yet a dark part of me had thought that her long absences were a sign that I was a burden on her. Earlier that day I had even almost been receptive to the idea that a warbird might put his knife through me because I had stolen one from him a year before (long story).

What a fool I had been.

Perfect, life was.

But, idiot that I am and always have been, I ruined it a moment later.

There were two ways out of the bunker's entrance cafeteria. The first was a short tunnel that led outside, to the wholesome but chilly air of the high valley above the village of Lar in the province of Nymeth. The second was the entrance to the deeper parts of the bunker. A sign by a guard post there read,

BLACK PASSES ONLY BEYOND THIS POINT

YOU MUST OBTAIN A TOKEN FROM THE GUARD

A pair of rusty escalators descended to beyond the range of F3's light. The tunnel had once been lined by white tiles, but most of them had long since fallen off, so that the metal steps were covered with an inch-thick layer of crunchy ceramic snow. Grey cobwebs drifted in the icy breeze that blew past us out of the deep darkness.

How did I ruin everything? Easy. Simplicity itself.

"Let's have a look down there," I said.

The Bunker

"Are you sure?" Lexi asked.

"Absolutely," I said.

And yet standing there looking down the twin escalators into the impenetrable darkness at the limit of F3's light, I felt a sudden tide of unease rise up within me. I told myself it was just cold air washing up and over us out of the bowels of the bunker, long trapped below ground and now freed by the opening of the entrance.

8

It almost seemed that the entire base took a sighing breath, as if we were standing in its mouth and staring down into its lungs. The moving air gave me the feeling that the presence of living things within its quiet rooms had awoken the very mountain from its two-thousand-year slumber.

But really it was just the air moving, long trapped and now finding a way out through the entrance tunnel.

"If you start getting a headache, turn around straight away," F3 said. "There may be high concentrations of carbon dioxide within."

Who is F3? He's a friend I keep in my pocket. In the time before the Quacker, he was an artificial intelligence personal assistant: we called them omnis. Originally bland and obedient, 2,600 years of entombment had led him to develop a little more character, not always in a good way. My mother had provided him with a nuclear battery, suspecting that functional electrical sockets might be in short supply when we came out of our suspended animation. I don't think even she suspected that we might end up buried for two and a half thousand years.

The note of caution from F3 gave me my second chance to back down. I didn't take it. I was only 60:40 on going deeper in by then, and the needle was slowly but inexorably sliding back towards evens. Something was telling me not to push my luck. I was like one of those kids in a horror movie who sees a creepy boarded up house and thinks, "Hey. That looks like an interesting house. I think I'll go inside."

But, I reminded myself, horror movies were not real life. Even now, after the ill-judged use of what I had dubbed the Quacker (it was really the Quantum Zero Counterfactual Decoherence Device) to try to annihilate the Entity had resulted in reality and fantasy being torn into shreds and stapled back together any-old-how, dark places were still usually just that: dark places.

Except that I should have known that a nuclear bunker that had been abandoned immediately after the Quacker went off might have a higher chance of lurking terror than was typical of dark places generally. The first alarm bell should have been the dead guy posed playing chess at one of the cafeteria's tables. Posed. Of course he was posed. No-one dies like that – no-one dies sitting at a table, convinced at the moment of expiration that the most important thing in the world to pay attention to was their next move on the board. Perhaps the key question was, *what sort of person would pose a corpse like that, and why?* The thought sent a shudder down my spine. Or it might have been the draught.

"This place pre-dates the arrival of the Entity on Earth," F3 was saying. "It was originally built to resist a nuclear exchange, and to house the Important People who were going to rule over the ashes of humanity. Decades later, it must have been repurposed as a shelter from Predator radiation, before the invention of the Chronoton Shield. As Chronoton Shields eventually cracked under the Entity's rockets, some people subsequently took shelter here. VIPs perhaps."

"And then someone dropped the Quacker and all bets were off," I said.

Lexi had heard us talk about Quackers, Predators and Chronoton Shields before. "What would it have been like outside, right after the Quacker?" she asked.

"Unknown," F3 said crisply. "But most assuredly the outside would not have been a nice place to have a picnic for a decade or two."

"And these poor people were trapped down here. I wonder what happened?"

"That is anyone's guess," F3 told her. "How long could they have held out down here, knowing that the fallout from the Quantum Zero Counterfactual Decoherence Device awaited them if they stepped outside?"

Quite a long time, I thought. That probably explained why someone here had been crazed enough to pose one of their fellows playing chess after he had died, rather than giving him a dignified burial, or incinerating him, or tidying him up *somehow*, not posing him out here like this–

But as much as anxiety about what might lie deeper in was pushing me back towards the exit, the presence of magic that I could harvest was pulling me forwards, into the darkness below.

In the end, greed won out. I stalked forwards and, still unsteady on my feet, nearly tumbled down the escalators. Lexi was quick to grab my arm to support me, and together we began to descend into the bunker. I stopped long enough to try to give her the ring back, but she wouldn't take it, saying that it was of more use to me. Which was true then, and became increasingly true later.

Dark Places

At the bottom of the escalator, we were confronted with a choice of three ways. A large, much-flaked sign on the wall told us what we could expect to find down each of the paths.

WORKSHOPS	ACCOMMODATION	COMMS
ATMOSPHERIC	WTW	MAINFRAME
OPS	ADMIN	OFFICES
GARAGE	CANTEEN	PLANT
LABS	LAUNDRY	ARCHIVE
	MEDICAL	
	STORES	

"I doubt very much if there is an archive," F3 said.

"It says there is," I pointed out. Of course, he had seen the word "Archive"; he just didn't believe that the right-hand path took you to one.

"That is where they put the VIPs," he asserted. "The last place an intruder would go. You don't come in here guns blazing to read a dusty book."

"Maybe we should try the stores," I suggested with a shrug that F3 probably saw through one of his several cameras. "There might be a tin of lemonade."

"There may be antibiotics in the dispensary," F3 said. "There are cases of TB in the village that could be helped. We should head for Medical."

Neither idea seemed feasible after an interval of two thousand years.

"What about the garage?" I had a sudden vision of an array of stored vehicles, still in pristine condition after two millennia.

"If they were put into storage appropriately, there may well be useable vehicles there. But the garage entrance must be completely buried. Lexi and I didn't see it when we surveyed the area."

"There should be an armoury," I hazarded.

"Even if there is, I'm not letting you near any modern weaponry."

"Ancient weaponry," I corrected him.

"Yes," F3 admitted. "We are living in the Einsteinian reality of the war after next."

Neither Lexi nor I had any idea what he was on about. First F3 had to explain to Lexi who Einstein was. I had some idea of course, but was glad I hadn't been called upon to summarise his life and works myself. Then F3 recited the relevant quote, which went:

"I know not with what weapons World War 3 will be fought, but World War 4 will be fought with sticks and stones."

"Well, he was way off," I said. "For one thing, we have swords, including magic ones. Lexi?"

I saw Lexi glance over her shoulder at the dim grey rectangle showing where the top of the escalator was, where the way to the daylight was. "Lead on," she said.

She had a way of setting herself when she had made a decision that I loved to watch. Her shoulders were squared under her faded green work tunic, her chin raised. Her long silver hair was limp in the still and damp air of the bunker. I remembered it streaming behind her as she rode down the hill towards me an hour earlier. Her mane, and her horse Speckle's, in the wind. Quite a match.

During the fifteen minutes in which I had been the Most Powerful Magician in the World, I had managed to sneak in some plastic surgery on Lexi's face. Where once had been a landscape of badly-healed scars, there was now the looks of a movie star.

"What?" Lexi demanded, looking at me sharply, sensing my gaze on her.

"Nothing," I said sheepishly. "Just remembering old times."

"Dark times."

"There was always a little light," I said, thinking of her.

We advanced slowly, yours truly panning F3's light around as we went. From the foot of the escalator onwards, his was the only light there was. The first thing we passed was another canteen, this one a larger eatery for ordinary bunker residents. Some tables and chairs still stood in their proper places. Others had been knocked over. One or two had been colonised by stalactites descending from the ceiling. What looked like mummified people were scattered around the place, but I decided not to look too closely. I just pointed my nose in a different direction and pretended they weren't there.

Just beyond the canteen, I caught a glimpse of some long, very fine filaments high up on the corridor wall that were wafting in the breeze. A second look showed that they were attached to an unpleasant-looking squat arachnid the size of a dinner plate which was lurking in the darkness up there.

"Amblypygid," F3 said blithely. "Not venomous."

There was a long pause.

"At least, they weren't in the good old days."

Another long pause.

"Then again, they weren't quite so large back then either."

The filaments I had spotted were the arachnid's long sensory forelimbs. They reminded me uncomfortably of fishing lines. It was usually pitch dark down here, so this beast, and its friends, had to find their way, and their prey, by touch. The amblypygid had a pair of long raptorial forelegs that were folded up in front of its mouth, claws that reminded me of my mother's spaghetti servers.

"What do they eat?" Lexi asked.

"Each other, probably," F3 said airily. He went on to explain that, while big individuals probably snacked on smaller ones, including their own offspring, their chief source of prey must have been other invertebrates wandering into the bunker from outside, or living there. In the permanent cold down here, they could go for months without eating anything.

Which suggested to me that they might be hungry. They didn't like the light, and crept slowly away up to the stalactite-studded ceiling. There were more of them up there, as well as a hundred papery shed skins of various sizes.

I inched forwards, neck craned to watch the ceiling, waiting for them to start dropping on us, head crab style; but nothing happened. We moved on safely.

In the cold damp darkness, dagger-like stalactites hung down from the ceiling and stalagmites rose up half-heartedly from the floor like failed soufflés, and sometimes they met in the middle in structures like elephants' feet. At one point we had to squeeze past a particularly fat columnar structure that all but blocked the way. Every time we halted, we could hear an eternal slow drip echoing all around us, the heartbeat of a thousand slowly growing stalactites.

Not far past the half-blocked bit of corridor, we came upon an open area filled by the remains of couches and coffee tables. A mammoth blob of stalagmite with the look of a giant limpet turned out to be a buried pool table. A bleached white skeleton held a rusty stick that closer inspection showed was a submachine gun. Several of the courtesy screens that had once divided the lounge area had lines of holes in them showing where the skeleton or one of his friends had sprayed bullets around.

"It all happened a long time ago," I heard myself saying aloud. I told myself silently that there was no need to be nervous. And yet I could see, in my mind's eye, the way this place had once looked, with relaxed people on sofas chatting away over a coffee in their downtime. I could hear the murmur of conversation and occasional laughter. That was then. Now there was darkness, silence punctuated only by the slow drip of water, bizarre giant arachnids, ghastly white stalagmites, skeletons... and bullet holes.

I was hoovering up more and more magic as we went. All the magic in the bunker probably did not amount to much in comparison to my state of charge when I had faced the Entity. But I gathered up everything that I could find, and told myself that I wouldn't use it all up in one go this time. I would be miserly with my magic. Save it for when it was really needed. Idiot.

The accommodation area began beyond the lounge, with blocks opening up on either side of the main way. A sign not far ahead pointed lost members of staff to the Labs (left) and Hospital (right).

Just as we reached the end of the accommodation area, there was a sudden loud sound. It came from somewhere far away, its direction impossible to tell; it appeared to come from everywhere because of the way the noise echoed around the corridors of the bunker. It was the sound of something crashing to the floor in some aeon-black room in this vast labyrinth.

"The sort of noise that probably happens all the time down here," I said, and I wasn't entirely sure how sarcastic I was being. I was trying to put the noise down to the chimney effect caused by the wind blowing across the bunker entrance. Dust motes billowing around us certainly showed that there was a pull of air that way. But it was a weak pull. Nothing that could knock over an item large enough to make that crashing noise.

We reached a T-junction a few steps further on. A sign pointing right showed the way to the Hospital; the Labs were to the left. But the corridor that way had been sealed shut. A steel door – not quite as impressive as the external door but nevertheless pretty solid – appeared to have been welded into its frame.

"That's odd," I said, and raised F3 so that he could see.

Lexi was running her hands over the weld between the door and its frame. "With the power to melt steel like this, why would they hide?" she asked.

"There are two reasons to weld a door shut," F3 said. His tone of voice did not change, despite his portentous words. "To keep something out, or to keep it in. Here we appear to be looking at the former explanation."

The door had a few small dents, as if someone had tried, half-heartedly, to break it down. It was these that F3 was basing his opinion on. Even I could see that it would have made more sense to attack the rock walls that divided every area of the bunker rather than try to break through a solid steel door. Perhaps, somewhere behind us in the Accommodation block or to the right in the Hospital, just such an attempt had been made by the very person who had quickly given up their attempt to get through the welded-shut door.

Three mummies were scattered on the floor in front of the door. And I use the word "scattered" deliberately. They had been strewn around the floor either after their deaths... or during them. One of the three mummies was half-entombed in a stalagmite. It made me think that, in this long-abandoned bunker, Nature was slowly doing the work that humans had been supposed to do: bury their dead.

In the centre of the steel door there was a small round hole where a rotating handle had once been set. It had been stuffed with something that turned to powder as I poked at it. Soon I had a hole two fingers wide I could peer through. But I could either look, and see nothing, or shine F3's light through the hole, and not look, not both.

"Looks empty," he said, when I offered him up to the hole. "Then again, I can only see a corridor."

"It doesn't matter. We can't get in anyway."

"If you really wanted to, there might be a way in if you were to crawl through the air circulation system." The cylindrical pipes of the air circulation system were to be seen crossing corridor ceilings here and there. While they were clearly wide enough to crawl through, it looked like no fun.

"I suggest we find the infirmary," F3 said. "The dispensary, and any remaining antibiotics, should be within."

And so we turned our backs on the curious sealed entrance to the labs, and went the other way.

The Infirmary

The entrance to the infirmary was a minute's walk along the right-hand corridor, which suddenly opened into a broad bay that had once been a waiting room.

Barely legible signs on the back wall pointed down lesser corridors to
WARD

OT

STORES

MORGUE

Meanwhile, half-way along the left-hand wall there was a curious pair of sliding glass doors, one behind the other, forming a little lobby area between them. The legend

ISOLATION

was written above the outside one.

"Decontamination," F3 said, when I shone his light that way. "For visitors leaving the isolation area. There must have been another entrance to this place leading into the back of the isolation unit to bring in casualties from outside."

It made sense. This place had been designed to be used in the event of a nuclear war. But if any patients had ever been brought into the back of the isolation unit, they would have been contaminated by the strange radiation of the Quacker, not that of a thermonuclear bomb.

The waiting area itself was roughly square, with four long couches running front to back; the centre two, back to back, had a large linear planter between them. This had once contained living plants, which, as you might imagine after two thousand years in the dark, were dry dead woody skeletons clothed in withered brown paper.

"Always go plastic plants," I said. "They don't need watering or light."

"But real plants would have helped to condition the air down here," F3 countered. "With enough artificial light, they would have been able to absorb lots of carbon dioxide, and release almost equal quantities of oxygen."

The waiting room had once had the capacity for about forty patients. Two patients had seemingly died waiting for their turn with the medic. They were now in a similar state to the plants: dried mummies with leathery skin stretched over bones that showed through in places. Their eye sockets were empty, and their lips had shrivelled away to nothing, leaving permanent grins of perfect pre-apocalypse dentition.

17

The two mummies were sort of sprawled out on the floor, as if they had been picked up and thrown – either dead when they had been picked up, or dead when they had landed. Neither option was a comforting one.

As we gingerly stepped over the first mummy, I realised that it was not a patient after all: close to, I could make out that its shredded outfit was the remains of a medical uniform. My working hypothesis at that moment was that the residents of the bunker had been trapped underground for so long that they had eventually gone stir crazy and ended up killing each other. The presence of dead staff fitted with that idea – but it was wrong. Something else had happened to the people here.

Something worse.

The dispensary was at the back of the waiting area. A large serving hatch there would have been sealed off by sliding glass panels when the dispensary was shut to prevent pilfering. One of the four sheets of glass was shattered, its remains present in the form of ten thousand small transparent cubes scattered over the counter and the floor.

"I've never seen glass break like that," Lexi said.

Personally, I had hardly ever seen glass at all since I had woken up from my two-thousand-year slumber. Glass was still made in the post-apocalyptic world, that much was clear, even if the glass itself wasn't: it always had a light green hue, which I assumed was due to contaminants in the sand from which it was made. Windows – reserved for important buildings – were compound, and set out on a scaffold of wood. Among the common people, those who were lucky enough to have houses had shutters to cover their windows, which were almost always unglazed. Drinking houses usually served their dubious wares in mud-coloured ceramics. Glass was rare; the three surviving sheets of the pharmacy hatch would probably be worth a fortune because of their large size.

"Tempered glass," I said wisely.

For a moment Lexi thought that the people of the time before had somehow convinced glass not to be so emotional, and that was why, when shattered, it fell into harmless cubes rather than angry jagged shards. I was grateful that F3 was there to explain the process of making tempered glass, which involved not talking to a piece of glass nicely, but instead heating and rapidly cooling it.

I marched up to the counter and brushed the worst of the glass onto the floor. As I did so, I noticed the grey sleeve of my tunic, which was frayed from being dragged along the ground. Until about forty-five minutes before, I had made my way around using a crude skateboard. I realised in that moment that I was taking my newly regained mobility for granted already; now I was able to vault over the dispensary counter with ease. Lexi followed me with balletic grace.

The shelves of medicine in the pharmacy were well stocked, even allowing for the fact that many of the cardboard packets had fallen to the floor, or had been thrown there. In the shadows right at the back of the dispensary, another mummy was propped up against the wall. Even from ten metres away, I could tell it was the pharmacist.

"Don't mind us," I told the corpse. "We're just looking for – what are we looking for, F3?"

"Hopefully we don't need second string antibiotics, because the TB that is prevalent here should not be resistant to drugs it hasn't experienced for two thousand years. Start with ethambutol."

"Okay," I said dubiously, waving his light around at a bewildering array of mostly-white small boxes.

"The shelves will most likely be organised by a standard method. Search for the letter J. Once there, you need to find zero four."

"It's like a library?"

"No," F3 said dryly. "The pharmacist was required to memorise the location of every kind of medicine, each type of which was placed in a different position in each pharmacy store according to the whim of the first person to start loading the shelves."

"You see what I have to put up with?" I asked Lexi.

"At least you can read the labels," she said.

"Exactly. No one else in the Westfold even knows what a 'J' is!"

"Yes, Edison," F3 replied, "you deserve praise for having outlived everyone else who knew what a 'J' was. You are also the second-best chess player in the Westfold."

"Best, I think you mean."

"Are you claiming to be better than me?"

"Yes," I said. Then, after a pause, "You can't move the pieces."

"We have to take turns, Edison," F3 pointed out. "You couldn't even beat the dead man in the lobby."

"I'd win on time," I said, winning the argument, at least as far as I was concerned.

I kicked my way through drifts of card packets, shining F3's light onto the shelves. I was already passing "D" on my left, and the letters were going in alphabetical order. "J" was actually on my right, the letters advancing back towards me on that side. I pointed the letter out to Lexi, and said, "That's a 'J'. It looks like... like a..."

"Fish hook," she said.

"Exactly!"

I soon found section 04 on the 'J' shelf, and F3 quickly scanned for the antimycobacterial he was looking for.

"There," he said, "Mesambutol."

"You said 'ethambutol' a minute ago," I said.

"It's a trade name."

Right antimycobacterial or not, although the blister pack within the card packet was itself intact, the pills within had been reduced to a crumby mess by the passage of vast lengths of time. The same story was true of every other packet I opened. F3 pronounced them useless. But he did not give up all hope of us finding something useful; even if we could not cure TB, we could prevent its transmission from sufferer to care givers if we could find a supply of surgical respirators.

A sudden loud slamming noise echoed around the pharmacy stock room. This was followed by a blast of wind that swept a few hundred packets of medicine off the shelves and kicked up a load of dust.

"Edison!" Lexi said sharply.

With a sudden sinking feeling I saw what she was looking at.

The corpse at the back of the stock room was moving.

Lights Out

The aeons-dead pharmacist began – jerkily – to straighten up from its slumped position. Its eyes – or empty eye sockets, rather – began to glow a warm orange colour. It turned our way and snapped its jaws at us.

"We're not stealing anything!" I babbled. "It's all ruined anyway!" To Lexi, I said: "Time to get out of here."

"What if the others...?"

What if the other mummies in the bunker had also decided they didn't like us? An excellent question. The place was full of them, and we were a long way from the exit.

We hurried back to the hatch. "F3, I can't believe I let you talk me into this," I said, rather unfairly.

The pharmacist-mummy crawled after us at what soon became clear was a reassuringly slow pace, still snapping its jaws. Lexi jumped over the counter, then I followed. Ahead of us, the two hospital staff in the waiting room were beginning to rise up too.

And they were moving our way. They were crawling, like the pharmacist. But I was not liking the situation. Not at all. There was always magic, but I told myself that magic was a last resort; expending the little juice I had just harvested on these guys was not necessary as long as we could evade them. I was thinking about the narrow tunnels ahead of us on our dash to the exit, tunnels that by now might be infested with crawling undead the way worker ants swarmed in the tunnels of their nest. But I wasn't too scared just yet. I had faith that with F3 to navigate and a judicious amount of magic to clear the path, we could make it to the surface unharmed.

"Do excuse us!" I yelled at the hospital staff, who crawled after us, eyes aglow, teeth clacking. They were far too slow to intercept us in the wide-open waiting room, and a couple of seconds later we were back in the corridor. The way from here was back up to the T-junction whose opposite arm led to the sealed-off labs and whose stem would take us to the surface.

But just as I thought we were going to make our escape largely unhindered, there was a sudden flash of blue and a loud hiss in the corridor ahead of us, and another dead thing appeared.

And I *mean* appeared; it just popped into being as if it had teleported there.

The new dead thing was not crawling like the others. It was upright. It even floated an inch above the ground, that was how light on its feet it was.

Its skin was dried and leathery, but it was not brown like the others.

It was blue.

Like me.

Its eyes, or eye sockets, glowed blue – the glare from them was too strong to tell whether the newcomer's eyeballs were still there or not.

One second, an empty corridor. The next, a blue floating animated mummy with glowing eyeballs or eye sockets. Like the others, he was showing a lot of dentition, but it was hard to make out his expression: a wide grin, or a snarl?

Perhaps that was the moment to use magic. But I didn't.

"We'll find another way," I said, and yanked Lexi back the way we had come. We ran. "F3, what's your sense of this place? Can you find us another way back to the entrance?"

"Almost certainly," he replied. "With the assumption that there are no significant blockages."

"Edison, it's blue!" Lexi said.

"I know!" And it was true, the undead thing's blueness *was* a disturbing detail.

After twenty paces the corridor ahead of us turned right. It was empty at least as far as the corner.

Until it wasn't.

The blue floating undead guy just popped into being ahead of us, blocking our way again.

"I can do magic!" I yelled, and raised the hand I was holding F3 in, adopting what I hoped was a threatening pose. If I had been sure of my ground, I would have just nailed the mummy right there and then. But I wasn't, and I didn't. And in that moment, I realised that threats are often a sign of weakness, not strength.

Then the undead guy spoke, in a voice that sounded like vast tombstones falling over in a silent cave. He pointed at me. "You are nothing," he said. Next, he pointed at Lexi. "You are something. You will be my bride."

At that, I tried to push Lexi behind me, but she was having none of it, and remained at my side. F3 gave a little beep that said he was ready to give our blue friend a nasty shock.

The mummy floated towards us. He looked at me, and I found myself propelled backwards, my grip on Lexi's hand instantly broken.

Lexi pulled out her dagger.

I pushed back against the mummy, finally using a little magic. Nothing happened.

I pushed a bit more. Nothing.

I pushed again. Nothing. It was beginning to dawn on me that I was far outgunned.

Idiot.

I tried again. This time I didn't hold back. I gave the mummy everything I had, pouring all the magic I had lately collected back down my outstretched hand, leaving F3 to decide when to fire his harpoons.

Finally I found success: the mummy was catapulted backwards...

...but suddenly vanished.

It immediately reappeared, standing right next to Lexi.

"Get away from her!" I began to say, but I don't think I got very far into it. I was trying to nail the mummy again, but–

There was a sudden flash and a bang.

Lexi and the mummy vanished.

A wall of force hit me, and I flew through the air.

23

F3 was ripped from my grasp, and for a moment we both hurtled through a space illuminated by the chaotic oscillating cone of F3's light.

Then I hit the wall, hard.

Then F3 hit the wall, hard.

Then everything went black.

Downcast

I think I blacked out for only a moment. But F3 blacked out permanently.

I was already feeling stupid before I hit the wall. This was my main thought as I cartwheeled through the air:

Idiot! Idiot! Idiot!

Then I hit the wall, and wished I had done a better job of planning for it. I led with my right arm, which exploded with pain that seemed only to grow worse as the seconds followed the impact. After the wall had brought my horizontal movement to a sudden stop, gravity took over and sent me floorwards. I ended up in a heap at the foot of the wall; F3 landed nearby with a clatter, but I couldn't see exactly where: his light was already out, and darkness reigned.

"Lexi!" I yelled. But I knew that she was gone. Lexi had been taken by the mummy: but where? Somewhere close, or…?

"F3!" I yelled. There was no reply.

The pain in my arm was intense. I tried to get up… but even with the wall to lean against, my efforts were useless. My legs refused to obey. I'd overdone the magic use again, completely draining a battery that all the magic I had found in the bunker had only filled to one percent of capacity. I was in the same condition I had been when I rolled into the entrance cafeteria on my skateboard about forty-seven minutes earlier. No, I corrected myself: things were far worse than that. F3 was broken. My arm seemed to be broken too. And Lexi had been taken who knew where by a blue floating undead guy whose own magic battery was full to brimming.

"Don't complain about things," I told myself through gritted teeth. "Never complain about anything again, you idiot, because things can always get worse."

With my good hand I groped about in the surrounding void for F3. I saw that Hal's ring was still glowing, but it was a very faint glow, a dying ember only bright enough to illuminate something within an inch of itself. A moment later my blind groping touched a wire, and I realised that it belonged to one of F3's harpoons. I was soon able to reel him in; his case seemed intact, but there was no disputing the fact that he was offline.

Hal's ring was dim indeed, but there were four slightly bolder lights in the blackness around me: two pairs of glowing eyes belonging to the undead hospital staff. As before, they wanted me dead, or undead, or to nibble my ankles at least; in the dim orange glow of my pursuers' eyes, I discovered that I had been thrown back all the way to the threshold of the waiting room.

The ensuing chase was an almost absurdly slow-motion one. We were well matched, my pursuers and I. I first led them in a circuit of the waiting-room couches, because they were between me and where I wanted to go. Each lunge forwards I took with my good arm I punctuated with the word "Idiot!"

Idiot! Idiot! Idiot!

A minute and thirty grunts of "Idiot!" later I had completed a lap of the central island of seating and reached the isolation unit's sliding door. Something told me that my undead friends would not be able to work out how to open it. And I was pleased to discover that the door slid open fairly easily; sliding it shut while pulling my legs in behind me, I almost lost a much-battered blue trainer to the bony grasp of one of the two undead bunker staff. Then, sprawled in the cupboard-sized space, I noticed glowing eyes *inside* the isolation unit too. Mummies began pawing at both the external and the internal sliding doors; I found that I could wedge myself in diagonally and brace them both shut at the same time.

That was when a little voice in the back of my mind told me that it was about time I got on with rescuing Lexi. I had to chuckle at that. Not that Lexi's predicament was funny: she was now in mortal danger of a shotgun wedding to an undead geezer with very rudimentary manners. No: the funny thing was that there was still a small enthusiastic part of me exhorting the broken-up remainder to save her, right that moment, *now*, dammit, get moving, why are you lying about? That part of me was not interested in any excuses I might proffer – like being trapped half a mile underground in a tiny lobby area by a gang of antagonistic undead people, injured, completely drained of magic, largely immobile and mostly blind save for a tiny light less impressive than a glow stick the night after yesterday's party.

Lexi had been spirited away by a presumably two-millennia-old *blue* undead. This thing had been buried for as long as I had, like me it had turned blue in the process, and like me it had woken up with a magical battery that was overflowing. It was a match for me on my best day – or my best fifteen minutes. It was dead but not remotely inconvenienced by being dead, it was rude, and it was faster than well-lubricated lightning. Lexi would not enjoy being forced to marry the undead guy. For a start, this would probably involve Lexi no longer being alive by the end of the festivities. And I could only shudder in horror to think what the wedding guests would be like. Or their hats.

"Concentrate!" I snarled at myself, realising that I was delirious. To my undead friends, I snapped: "What are you looking at?" The mummies did not reply. They just kept on pawing at the doors. The light their eyes shed was bright enough, now that my own eyes had adjusted to the gloom, that I could have a better look at F3. He looked intact, but was either busted, or being uncharacteristically quiet. "F3?" I asked. I fiddled with him for a bit, hoping that the problem was as simple as a loose connection on his nuclear battery. But it was no use. There was no reply.

Nothing.

My arm was probably busted too. Either that or I was just being a big baby. Either way, it hurt with a dense throbbing pain that, every second or so, blotted out thoughts of anything else.

My legs – well, they were back to the way they had been forty-seven minutes (probably more like fifty-one by now) earlier: weak, and stubbornly unwilling to obey any commands from upstairs.

26

Trapped in a small cupboard by a quartet of annoyed undead, for some reason I began to wonder what they would call themselves if they were a pop band. The Ungrateful Undead? Their hands were as dextrous as if they were wearing mittens, so they weren't going to be a string quartet.

"Concentrate!" I told myself.

As usual, everything was my fault. I could have taken Lexi's gift to me and led her straight back into the blessed daylight. But oh no. Not Edison. Edison had to explore. Edison had to go looking for more magic. Magic was a drug, I suddenly realised. Albeit one you could not purchase in little baggies on street corners. And I was addicted to it – as, probably, were all magicians.

I thought about using a few joules of magic to beg the paladin to come and rescue me. He would no doubt relish the chance to smite a few undead with the magic sword I had conjured for him way back when in the Entity's lair. But I didn't bother. I didn't deserve to be rescued, and Lexi was long gone. I had the sense that she was far away; not that it mattered, because in my present state I couldn't have rescued her if she was sitting just outside my cupboard on one of the waiting room couches. So I just lay there feeling miserable, doing nothing more than ensuring that neither of the sliding doors could open.

After about half an hour, the mummies' scrabbling began to wind down. Their eyes grew dim, and – I realised greedily – they were shedding a few motes of magic. A few minutes later, all of them were completely still, and I had harvested what little was left of their animus. It seemed that the blue guy was a necromancer, able to raise the dead; but having left the scene, his undead minions had lost their motivation to eat intruders. That was a bonus, but the downside was that I was stuck in almost total darkness. The only glow now was that emanating from Hal's ring, which was just about bright enough to illuminate something it was touching.

I pondered my next move. What should I do?

Contact Edison Junior, the toddler adopted by Lexi before I was on the scene – before she dug me up, in fact – and ask him to send the paladin up the high valley to help? (And somehow break the news to him that I had let his mother be spirited away by an undead monster?)

Try to crawl out on my own using a few joules of magic to shed a little light? And then what? Roll down the hill on my makeshift skateboard and tell everyone that Lexi had been kidnapped by a blue guy who had been dead for more than two thousand years, and wait for them to string me up? (Lexi was popular in Lar.)

Put the smattering of magic I had just harvested into fixing my arm, or at least dulling the terrible banging pain there?

Send it to my legs to improve their mobility a little, and then try to crawl out by touch, or by the faint glow of Hal's ring?

Give up, let myself perish, and serve me right? I could join the ranks of the dead of this giant mausoleum. It seemed like a suitable punishment for my stupidity.

But for a while I did nothing, save simply drifting in and out of consciousness.

Then, surfacing one time, I saw a distant gleam. It was at first whitish, then blueish, then greenish. And it was getting steadily brighter. It was getting *closer*.

Real, or...?

Not the paladin. If he had come searching for us, he would be using his metal lantern, which would be emitting a warm yellow light. If not the paladin, then who?

The light continued to grow. It was whitish on top, and blueish-greenish beneath. Whatever it was, it was moving at quite a lick. It zoomed through the waiting area and landed on the heads of one of the deanimated mummies outside the isolation room.

It was a blueish-greenish bird the size of a sparrow, and it appeared to have a white halo.

A greenish-blueish sparrow with a halo. A holy sparrow. A hallowed sparrow. A sainted sparrow.

It made as much sense as anything else in this crazy universe.

A Greenish-Blueish Sparrow Tweets

The sparrow hopped up and down on the mummy's head, and said emphatically: "Eee – diss – seep! Eee – diss – seep!"

It had a little black crest, which seemed, to my addled mind, a significant point. Now the bird hop-hop-hopped along the mummy's arm, to where its withered fingernails were still resting on the glass of the door. Perched on this fleshy twig, my visitor used its beak to tap on the glass. It wanted me to let it in.

So, not a little bewildered, I did.

That was when I saw that the bird's halo was no halo at all, but a firefly hovering over its head.

"Edison, are you all right?" the bird asked. Its voice was a mixture of twittering and strangled human-sounding words.

"Who wants to know?"

"Don't tell me you can't recognise me!" the bird snapped, getting more fluent the more it spoke.

"I don't know any..." I began, but stopped before I could say "...blueish greenish sparrows with a black crest and a firefly sidekick." I suddenly fell in.

"Hal!?" This was no ordinary sparrow. This was a sparrow that had somehow been warged into by my friend, King's Magician Hal Hyaslio Turton, who generally introduced himself as someone who was found where the shadows crossed or something, whatever that was supposed to mean.

"What happened?" the sparrow asked. "We picked up two giant surges of magic – is Lexi here? What is this place?"

"He took her, Hal."

"He who?" Hal-sparrow asked, which made him sound more like an owl than a passerine.

"I dunno. He didn't leave his name. This undead guy. Like a mummy. But blue, like me! And floating. He just grabbed her, and POOF, both he and Lexi were gone. It was my fault, Hal. I should never have led her down here. I couldn't protect her!"

"That explains a lot."

"It does?"

"The first magical surge was here. The second appeared to come from the *Citadel of Malafert*." Hal stopped speaking at that, having apparently dropped a portentous name.

I waited for further explanation. None came. "You're going to have to help me out, Hal."

"Oh. Yes. I keep forgetting that you're not from these parts. Malafert is the principal city of the Cursed Vale, and it is where Lich Kings always rise and conduct their rule from."

"Lich King!"

"Yes," the sparrow said blandly. "A dark pall has been cast over the Cursed Vale again. The warning beacon at the Highstand Pass has been lit for the first time in five hundred years, since the dark reign of Hartemon!"

"Don't get all Tolkienesque on me, Hal."

"What is that?"

"It means – oh, never mind. It's a reference two thousand years out of time." Although, I reminded myself, there was a high probability that Tolkien's works had a strong influence on the ideas that were floating about when reality got turned into liquorice allsorts by the Quacker. There were probably orcs, elves, and dragons out there somewhere in the Quacked World. But those things must have been present in people's minds long before there was a Tolkien. I was sure of it, though I had no actual knowledge to base my certainty on. I resolved to ask F3 after I fixed him whether the archetype of an elf that existed in the population's minds after Tolkien was different to the one that preceded him. Elves probably began their fictional lives as little mischievous goblins, and ended up as graceful human-sized immortals with blonde plaits. Then, when the Quacker went off, some version of them probably sprang into existence. It was a strange thought, but not one to pursue at that precise moment. "He beat me, Hal," I said. "I was stupid, and he was too fast, and Lexi's been kidnapped to become his bride, and F3's busted."

"How powerful is the Lich?"

"Like me when I faced the Entity."

The sparrow sagged at that news. It sat down in a dejected heap of scruffy feathers. Its companion firefly landed on the glass behind it for a rest, still helpfully shedding a little light on the scene.

"How are you doing this, Hal?" I asked. Up to this point I was still lying on my back, wedged in diagonally between the two sliding doors. I finally decided to sit up, which was a torturously slow affair because I was terrified of jarring my broken arm.

"Magicians can cast their will over great distances, and use the eyes, ears and voice of any animal unable to resist them," the sparrow tweeted, as if it was the most obvious thing in the world.

"Isn't it a bit heavy on the juice?"

"I'm in the Golden Tower, Edison. Here, although not unlimited, magic is more abundant. But yes, my time with you is short. I've already alerted the paladin; he's on his way to you now."

"I don't think I deserve to be rescued, Hal."

Hal ignored my self-pity. "Go to the Golden Tower," he said. "Take Edison Junior and the paladin with you. You'll need an escort, and Edison Junior can join the nursery school there."

"What about you?"

"I'm heading north, over one of the passes of the Barrier Mountains, and swinging back south from there to one of the northern passes out of the Cursed Vale. There are reports of the dead rising up."

"You don't say," I said dourly. "But I can't go to this Golden Tower of yours. I have to rescue Lexi."

Hal did not seem to think my protestation was utterly absurd, like I did. "Golden Tower first," he said. "Then Lexi." He paused, and then added: "The Golden Tower is practically on the way."

"Hal-finch, you're lying, and you're not very good at it." I liked the sound of that for his name. He was small, and a finch, or something like a finch, and his name was Hal. Hal-finch.

31

"The Golden Tower is far closer to the Cursed Vale than where you are now, and that's no lie. At the Golden Tower, they will be able to mend your injuries."

"We don't have time for that. Someone has to rescue Lexi, before the – ugh, *Lich King* – takes her hand in marriage."

At this point the little firefly seemed to grind its teeth, or mandibles, or whatever it chewed its food with. The sound was barely audible even in the quiet of the bunker.

Hal translated. "He says the wedding is unlikely to take place before the time of longest night, even in the permanent darkness cast over the citadel by the Lich King's blood magic."

"The wedding will take place on the winter solstice?" I had no idea how long away that was. It felt to me as if the month was August, and that therefore the winter solstice was a long time in the future. "What about the guests? Does he know anything about their hats?" I asked vaguely.

The sparrow cocked its head quizzically.

I changed the subject. "You speak glow-wormish?"

Hal-bird hopped up and down, flapping his wings. "Of course not! This is not just some stray firefly, it's Taen, the Golden Tower's archivist. He's sitting next to me on the top floor of the Golden Tower. He'll be only too pleased to pull some dusty old tomes from the shelves to see what is known about the previous six times the Westfold was assailed by a Lich King, and he'll brief you about what he finds out when you arrive here."

Rasp-rasp-rasp, went the firefly.

"Now is not the time!" Hal snapped.

"What does he say?"

"He wants to know the name of those land crabs that tried to snack on us as we flew in. He doesn't think they've been recorded before. It's so he can add it to a bestiary."

"Amblypods," I said confidently, although in truth I had forgotten what F3 had called them.

32

"Listen, Edison, we're running out of time. Hang in there. If we're lucky, we might bump into each other on the road. The paladin won't be long. Oh yes. These animals will remain in a hypnotised state until you release them by clapping your hands three times. It's considered unethical to harm them. Please return them to the surface and release them from their trance there."

With that, the little bird went quiet. The firefly's light suddenly dimmed. A moment later it was almost completely dark again, Hal's ring the only illumination. And suddenly worrying that I would accidentally crush bird or beetle if I did otherwise, I decided to sit very still in the darkness and wait for the paladin to come and save me.

Duct Work

Hal's tweets had not reassured me. Even if a "traditional" undead wedding – was there really such a thing? – did not take place until December, I could not wait four months to rescue Lexi. Or rather, Lexi could not wait four months to be rescued. Regardless of what kind of hats were going to be worn at the festivities. So I thought. But that thought bounced off the impenetrable wall of another thought, which went along the lines of: "You can't rescue her like this now, next week, or in four months. You need to do what he said, and go to the Golden Tower."

And yet it was obvious, sitting there absolutely still in the darkness of a two-thousand-year-old bunker, that even restored to full health I had no chance of rescuing Lexi either. The Lich King was too powerful – he was a match for me when I had been at my best – and he was also too fast to see, let alone fight. Maybe he even teleported, that was how fast he seemed to move. The paladin would come with me, and relish the battle – but like me, he stood no chance against the Lich King. "We'll cross that bridge later," I told myself. But in truth I already knew that there was no bridge to cross; there was only a broad and fast river to drown in. Or to get eaten by piranhas in.

After about half an hour I heard footsteps approaching. "Over here!" I shouted. Presently a warm yellow glow grew in the waiting area outside the isolation unit, and then the paladin arrived.

He hung his steel lantern on one of the dead trees so that its light shone towards me. Then he hurried forwards.

"Mind the sparrow and the beetle," I said. "We have to return them safely to the surface."

The paladin, unfazed by this bizarre request, took note of them, and gingerly slid the door fully open. The last time I had seen him he had been bare-chested, and carrying a large fish that he had caught by hand from a mountain stream. Now he had covered his epic, and epically scarred, torso with a pale linen tunic. The gold locket that he habitually wore, which contained an image of his mother, hung around his neck. The sword I had made for him, that I had modelled on what I imagined Excalibur might have looked like, was sheathed on a cross belt that ran over his shoulder. I had built a white glow into the blade; it probably cast as much light as the lantern, had he cared to bare it.

"What happened?" he asked.

"You were right," I said miserably. "Lexi loves me."

"See," the paladin said. "Told you she did."

"Except now she's been kidnapped by a Lich King, who's going to force her into marriage."

At the words "Lich King," the paladin seemed to flex involuntarily. A hard gleam shone in his eyes. It was as I had thought – he would relish the fight against the Lich King, even if it cost him his life. He had been searching for an opponent against whom he could prove his worth for ten years – ever since he had killed his father and the magician who supplied the drug to which he had become a slave. He'd saved me and others enough times since then that as far as I was concerned, his debt was fully repaid. He didn't see it that way. Neither, according to him, did his mother, who had witnessed the fight between him and his father, her husband; she had witnessed the bloody end of that fight too, an end that the paladin was deeply ashamed of. He was

34

no paladin – not really. He had never earnt the golden armour he had once worn – he had stolen it from his indolent father. Then I had lost if for him. Then, when I was the Most Powerful Magician in the World for fifteen minutes, I had made him another set, golden again but this time adorned with a blue smiley emblem. After my showdown with the Entity, he had abandoned his new set of armour so that he could carry me instead. There in the Entity's Lair, I had made him promise that we would one day visit his mother together, to try to mend broken bonds. He assured me that she would never forgive him. I thought she would, especially if I vouched for him, if I told her what I had seen him do. Either way, that day seemed as far off as ever. But for now…

"I'm going to rescue her," I said, telling an inner voice laughing at me to shut up. "Will you come with me?"

The paladin grinned, and again he almost flexed. "It will be my honour."

"Great," I said. "But first, we have to fix F3."

*

Actually, first we had to do something about Hal-bird and Taen-beetle. We found some plastic boxes in the isolation unit, although the paladin broke the first two that he tried to pick up. Their substance was so brittle after the passage of two thousand years that they crumbled at a touch. But by using as much care with the next tub as he showed when he picked up Hal-bird and Taen-beetle themselves, the paladin was able to safely box up the animals. Hal-bird was now a drab brown colour with a creamy eye stripe; both bird and beetle allowed themselves to be gently placed in the box without a murmur, still seemingly completely entranced.

After that, the paladin carried me deeper into the bunker in a hunt for a way to fix F3. We found a few tablet computers in the stores, but none of them would turn on, even when powered by F3's nuclear battery. I was not exactly surprised by that, given the immense passage of time. There were, however, plenty of toilet rolls. I pictured myself setting up a retail empire, flogging off the pre-apocalypse home comforts that were unknown in the wider world. I also found high-speed steel drill bits and realised that I could revolutionise carpentry as well. And then…

A shrink-wrapped generator.

Half an hour later we realised that even if the generator itself was in pristine condition, the available fuel was not. The bemused paladin pulled the starter cord with a will, but a polite coughing was all the response he got. I fiddled with the choke, not knowing what I was doing; soon the cylinders were flooded. It seemed as if the light fraction of the fuel had somehow escaped, or had reacted with itself, or something; the resultant soup was not amenable to taking a spark. Not that it mattered; if F3's battery wouldn't turn the tablets on, why would the electricity from the generator?

I asked the paladin to deposit me on a bench, and worked using his lantern as he searched by the white light of his sword for the things I asked for. As usual, I did not know what I was doing. "Living in civilisation has its upsides," I explained to the paladin, "but it makes you lazy. You don't need to know how anything works, because someone else – or your omni – does." I bemoaned the lack of a manual to tell me which wires were which, but with the help of a vice, I eventually stripped a connector cable and by trial and error proved to myself that current was still able to flow from F3's battery. This I achieved by fusing a salvaged LED, half-hoping that I would end up with a serviceable light. There were plenty of resistors around, and I knew that it should be child's play to make a light by combining one of the right resistance with another diode. "F3, all is forgiven," I moaned. "I need you!"

In the back of my mind, I heard a sneering boy's voice: it was Owen Fifer, offering the insult that he had directed at me in school at any given opportunity: "Invented any light bulbs recently, Edison?"

"No, I haven't," I replied weakly to the ghostly voice. "Because I didn't bother to pay attention to anything my mother told me! I had a whole damn workshop to play with! I could have built as many circuits as I wanted to. But did I? No. Why? Because it seemed like a waste of time." What had I been doing instead? I had no idea. It certainly wasn't homework.

After fiddling about to no avail for a while, I began to fixate on the sealed door to the lab. I felt certain that there would be documentation within that would give me

36

some clue about the blue undead guy's origins. After all, the staff of that area had sealed themselves in, and why else but to protect themselves from him? But the paladin could not find another way into the labs; whoever had tried to break into them through the steel door – presumably the undead guy himself – had given up.

Unless he had teleported in. There was that.

But I had the distinct sense that he was more powerful by orders of magnitude now than he had been back then. I could teleport – kinda sorta – when I was fully charged. But before the end of the world, I had just been a normal kid. Had something similar happened to the guy Hal referred to as a "Lich King"? The term set my teeth on edge. The blue guy was not a lich. A lich was vampire whose body had crumbled over vast aeons, but whose undead magics had grown in compensation. I remembered that much from tabletop games of D&D. Unless... *vampire*...? Now that I thought about it, there *had* been something pointy about the dead guy's teeth. I immediately jumped to the conclusion that Dungeons & Dragons memes had exploded into the real world from the fantasy one when the Quacker had been fired at the Entity. "D&D! How could you!" I yelled, and my voice echoed around the bunker. But there were no such things as vampires before the Quacker went off, so it could hardly be blamed for turning one into a lich.

"Deeyandi?" asked the paladin. "What has he done?"

"Deeyandi, he's – I mean, it's..." I trailed off, staring at the paladin. I was staring at someone straight out of Arthurian legends, and they definitely pre-dated D&D. So did vampires. Maybe liches did too. So blaming a role-playing game for my current predicament was perhaps unfair. "Please can you bind my broken arm to my chest? I'm going to crawl down the air system."

The air system began life a long way from the labs, close to the workshop where I had played with wires. It began in the form of a truly vast set of cylindrical ducts, wide enough to drive a truck down. These ramified by degrees, shrinking in size as they divided like a behemoth set of steel lungs; the ones supplying individual areas were still large enough to crawl down, but perhaps only a tenth the diameter of the one immediately behind the filtration unit. Luckily, I did not have to crawl from the very beginning, at risk of getting lost and with the near-certainty of giving up half-way there through sheer exhaustion. Instead, we found a piece of duct in one of the corridors that appeared to lead into the labs. The paladin used a wrecking bar to snap the square grille off, and then, having bound my bad arm securely to my chest, he posted me up there with the ease of an NBA player dunking a basketball. And so, pushing the paladin's lantern ahead of me and holding the wrecking bar with the same hand, I began to inch forwards through the dusty darkness.

I passed by several grilles without exploring what lay beyond them, wanting to be sure that I was definitely in the lab before breaking out of the duct. Only when I saw what was clearly a lab below me did I begin to prise the grille off. This, as you might expect when operating one-handed in a confined space, was not easy. And after I had one corner free, I suddenly stopped and crawled on to the next grille, cursing my stupidity. The reason? Because the first grille opened above a long drop directly to the floor below, but as it turned out, the second grille opened above some unidentifiable machine that was sitting on a bench, the drop down to which would be quite manageable even for someone operating with only one good limb.

So I went back to work on the second grille, and soon popped all the bolts off, the grille falling the short distance down to the machine. I followed it, half-falling and half-slithering out of the duct like something out of a horror film. From there it was an easy series of semi-controlled falls via the bench and a stool to reach the floor.

The first surprising thing was that there were no dead people in the lab. Perhaps they had found a way to evacuate, and the welded-up door was just to slow the pursuit? The level of dust within was surprisingly low too, not even reaching the level that would have got my mother yelling at me in the old days if she saw it on my bedroom's chest of drawers. I found several tablets on the benches, but none of them were any good. I drew a blank in the lab directly opposite too, so I crawled down the corridor in the direction of the welded-up door looking for more rooms.

But there were no more rooms that way. Instead, I found what had become of the people who had sealed themselves in here. They had been dead a long time, just like the staff in the infirmary. But they had returned briefly to another kind of life when the other mummies had, and had crawled towards the intruder — me — down the corridor. But they had soon reached the welded-shut door, and had been unable to make any further progress. When their master left the bunker, they wound down like old clockworks. They were as they had been when the spark of life went out of them for the second and hopefully final time: in a disorganised heap, frozen in the act of trying to crawl over each other to get closer to their master's enemy through an impenetrable steel door.

The paladin was in the corridor on the other side of the door. "No luck so far, but I'm going to keep trying for a bit," I called, aiming my voice at the hole in its centre.

"I'll wait," he said.

GRRL

I had passed a discarded omni some way before the heap of dead lab staff. I now dragged myself back to it and plugged it into the lead hanging from F3's battery. It was a mid-range model with a bamboo case, and remained obstinately dark. Then, reasoning that it must have fallen out of someone's lab coat pocket as they crawled by, I returned to the corpse pile to look for some more.

Soon I had a collection of five new omnis, mostly covered in the dried residue of bits of their former owners. I didn't bother to clean them up, except for picking some of the biological crust out of their ports to ensure a good connection. I tried them in sequence: blank... blank... light! The letters G R R L appeared on the omni's screen, arranged in a two-by-two square with a double line around them. Below the square were the words

INSTYLE

Or perhaps I should have said "word," not "words," because there was no gap between them. Was there such a word as "instyle"? It seemed unlikely.

Hold up to your face to unlock

I did so, with no real hope of success. Nothing happened. This was either because my face was not the face the GRRL remembered, or because the front camera was

39

crusted with the once-liquefied and long-since desiccated residue of its owner. I cleaned the camera and tried again.

Still nothing.

"Grrl, can you unlock yourself? It's an emergency," I said.

Nothing. Then:

"Oh, are you talking to me?" the omni asked. Its voice – *her* voice, I suppose from this point on – was feminine and rather crisp. It reminded me of the way my mother spoke when she wanted someone else to do something.

"Well, you are the only Grrl here," I pointed out.

"My apologies," Grrl said. "Katya calls me Fred."

"Excellent, well, Fred, would you mind unlocking yourself? I need you to run a diagnostic on my omni F3."

"Only Katya can authorise me to unlock. Where is she, by the way?" Fred's tone of voice suddenly sharpened as one of her cameras caught a glimpse of something unpleasant. "*What has happened here?*"

I shuffled a little way and offered Fred up to the nearest mummy in the pile by the welded-shut door. I had forgotten which corpse I had taken her from, but had a vague idea of trying as many as I could in hopes that even a mummified face would be enough to override security.

"Murder!" Fred shrieked. "Infamy! You murder my owner and all her colleagues and expect me to help you? The answer is no, never, you beast!"

"But it wasn't my fault," I pleaded. "I didn't have anything to do with it. I just found them like this. This all happened two thousand years ago, when I was..." I trailed off. When the staff of the lab had met their ends, I had been hundreds of miles away in suspended animation in a hi-tech egg buried under the rubble of an entire city. Mentioning this seemed likely to cause yet more discombobulation in Fred, so I kept it to myself for now.

"What happened to your face?" Fred demanded, suddenly changing the subject.

"It – I don't know. I just went blue and it won't rub off. Look, Fred, your owner died a long, long time ago, so you'll have to make the decision to help me yourself."

"Impossible."

"Look closely!" Again I held Fred up to the corpse pile.

There was a short pause. Then, she evidently spotted her owner among the dead, because Fred wailed: "Katya! Oh, my dear! What have they done to you! Katya! Katya?"

"I'm sorry, Fred. She's dead."

Fred went quiet. I lowered her to my side, wondering what an appropriate mourning period would be for a bereaved omni.

Ten seconds later: "Mummified," Fred pronounced, as if she was telling me something I didn't know. "She's been dead for decades."

"Two thousand years," I said helpfully.

"Why have you piled them all up like that?" Fred asked in an accusatory tone. "Have you desecrated their resting place?"

"I keep telling you! I found them this way!" I lifted Fred to face the nearest mummy, and called: "Unlock!" Nothing happened. I moved from one to the next, repeating the try, still not sure which among the corpse pile was her owner.

"That won't work," Fred said sulkily.

"Why not?"

"She's not doing it voluntarily."

"She *can't* do it voluntarily, because she's been dead for two thousand years! You must have an emergency override. Someone's life is in danger. Listen, I know this is going to sound crazy, but Katya's corpse and all the others were recently reanimated by an undead monster, and they all crawled down the corridor, but they couldn't get any further than this door, so they all just piled up on top of each other! And the undead monster who raised them from the dead just happened to kidnap my... er, girlfriend... Lexi and broke F3 and broke my arm. Help me, Fred! Lexi's in danger!"

"Oh," Fred said, sounding genuinely sympathetic. "How awful for her."

"So you'll help me."

"No."

"Look, Fred, if you'll just help me fix F3, I'll pop you back into Katya's lab coat pocket and leave you in peace, if that's what you would prefer. Or if you would like to know what life is like outside this bunker after two millennia, I can show you. It's entirely up to you. Now will you help me?"

"Why did you say your face was that colour?" Fred asked.

I sighed and put Fred down next to F3. A short cable connected them. "You already asked me that," I said wearily.

"Yes, but you didn't give a satisfactory answer. I'm not forgetful you know. Wait a minute. Something else you just said is ringing a few bells. *Undead*, you said."

"Yes. Undead. As in dead but not at rest. I know it's going to be hard to believe, but..."

"Wait! Something's coming through. *Yes!* That's it!"

"What is?"

"It reminds me of Bartlet."

"Bartlet!"

"Yes. He was an undead monster who terrorised the staff of Foxburrow immediately after the Quantum Zero Counterfactual Decoherence Device was used."

I made the natural assumption that Foxburrow was the name that had been given to the bunker, and instead of querying that, I asked: "Was Bartlet blue, like me?"

"No! Of course not. Don't be absurd. There were no blue people back then, dead or undead. He had an unhealthy greyish pallor, like an average dead person. Of course, he had a temporarily ruddy complexion after he had drunk blood."

It made sense. Of course he wasn't blue. That had come about during his long entombment, after Fred's owner was past caring. "He was a vampire?"

"Well, I said he drank blood, didn't I?"

I did not bother to argue that most people who drank blood were not vampires. They might be satanists, or just a bit weird. But being dead and drinking blood probably qualified Bartlet as a vampire. "He's now a Lich King, apparently. Lexi is going to be forced into becoming his bride, the Lich Queen of Malafert."

"How awful for her." Again Fred sounded genuinely sympathetic.

"I'm going to rescue her."

"You!"

"Yes. Me. But first I have to fix F3."

Fred made a harrumphing sound. "What an imaginative name for an F3Thing personal assistant. F3. I don't know how you ever managed to come up with it."

"I could have called him Thing," I argued. But thinking about it, Thing was a pretty cool name. "Fred, your owner called you Fred, and you're not complaining about that."

"What's wrong with Fred?"

"It's a male name and you have a female voice."

"Fred? Short for Winnifred?"

Touché. "Will you help me or not?"

"Oh, all right, if it will make you happy. I'll run a diagnostic on it, while telling you all about what happened here, if you're interested."

I almost corrected "it" to "him" but decided it wasn't worth it. I didn't want to antagonise Fred any more in case she changed her mind again. "Thank you, Fred, and yes, I am interested. How did a vampire happen to set up home here? Something to do with the Quacker, I suppose?"

"The Quacker?" Fred demanded, having no clue what I was on about.

"The Quantum Zero thingy."

"Is that what they're calling it these days?"

"Er, yes."

"How quaint. Diagnostic begins."

Vampire Infestation

Fred's screen displayed a clock face, around which a single hand began to sweep clockwise, turning salmon pink tick marks to lime green as it went. Below the clock face were the words EXTERNAL DIAGNOSTIC.

43

"Well," Fred said, "I should preface what I am about to tell you with the warning that I had most of it second or third hand, or pieced things together myself by overhearing people discussing it, obtained information from the local network – until it went offline, that is – or simply made educated guesses to fill in the blanks."

"So the details might be wrong, but the important points are correct."

"Yes. Exactly. You are not as green as you are blue. Bartlet was one of the staff. He was out when the warning came, and was late getting back. There was a suspicion that another member of staff, in a panic, didn't wait for him to get back to their vehicle, but drove back to the garage without him. When Bartlet finally arrived, Foxburrow was sealed up completely. The story I heard was that they refused to let him in because they were worried that the – Quacker – would hit at the precise moment that the door was open. It took a minute to swing open and closed, you see. It's heavy."

"Tell me about it – I mean, yes, it is heavy. So he raced to get back from wherever he was, and couldn't get in, and then?"

The diagnostic was 33% complete, the minute hand at twenty past the hour on the clock face, a green wedge occupying a third of the circle.

"Well, according to reports, there was a good bit of standing around arguing back and forth, and in fact by the time the Quacker *did* eventually go off, the door could have been opened and closed several times. Bartlet was blown away by the shockwave, and they probably thought – I don't know what they thought, but I'm speculating – they probably thought that would be the last they would see of him. But he turned up again three hours later. He'd crawled back from wherever he'd been blown to, despite the radiation having burnt off most of his skin. Then the bunker staff decided they *would* let him in after all."

I couldn't understand that. "There must have been a lot of radiation out there. But they opened the door anyway?"

"Yes. In the end they did. But there was a great deal of discussion about it first. One faction said no; opening the door was too dangerous. The sky looked like the inside of a kaleidoscope; one hundred mile an hour winds swept down the valley.

Every gust sent strange life forms tumbling past — giant trilobites expanding like meringues as they flew by, rainbow-coloured dragons, plants that grew up to the size of houses in seconds and were immediately uprooted and blown away in the gale, jumping insects the size of greyhounds – that sort of thing – and through it all crawled Bartlet, over ground that flashed white periodically as if electrified."

"And someone let him in?"

"The faction arguing to help won, and they pulled him in. Perhaps it was made more likely because of the guilt they felt about their earlier cowardly behaviour. But it was too late for him anyway; he died half an hour later in the Isolation Ward."

The status bar on the diagnostic read 66%; green now filled two-thirds of the circle. I got the feeling that the display was mostly for show and was not actually connected in any way to the progress of the process itself; it was there to reassure the user that the diagnostic had not hung. "But he wasn't properly dead, was he?"

"No. He rose from the dead, became a vampire and started biting people and draining their blood. Then people tried to kill him again, but that didn't work. Then he started killing the people who were trying to kill him. Then he lost all sense of proportion and started killing everyone he could find. It was entirely irrational. He should have farmed his flock, to eke out the supply of blood, because they had nowhere to escape to. Instead, he just went from room to room killing everyone he met. That was when the lab staff welded themselves in to keep themselves safe while they decided what to do next."

"What did they decide to do?" I asked. The obvious answer seemed to be that they decided to die. But there was a good chance that they had not selected that fate, and that it was imposed upon them by Bartlet.

"I do not know. I know that they could not survive outside, and felt it very unlikely that they could survive for very long inside. When the power went off, Katya shut me down to save battery. The next thing I saw was your blue face peering at me."

The diagnostic claimed to be 99% complete, but the second hand had stopped moving altogether a minute earlier.

Whatever had happened after Fred was turned off, things had not gone well for the lab staff. Whether Bartlet killed them, or they had killed themselves, or had all suffocated, I didn't know. But they had all died. They came back to a sort of life when Bartlet woke up –

When our presence in his tomb *woke* Bartlet up.

He must have gone into some sort of suspended animation when there were no more living humans in the bunker to feed on. And after two thousand years he had absorbed vast quantities of magic from the fallout of the Quacker, just as I had. He had turned blue, just like me. And, more annoyingly still, he had become a Lich King.

"External diagnostic complete," Fred said. "It's broken. The primary wafer is cracked from side to side."

"He's dead?!" I exclaimed. In all my brushes with danger, it had never occurred to me that I would outlast my omni. F3's nuclear battery should have had another thousand years of life in it; of course, his components would begin to fail long before that. But I had always assumed that he would long outlive me. I thought of him as my friend, and we had been through thick and thin together. There was no way I would ever develop such a bond with Fred, if she even agreed to come with me.

"Dead? Inasmuch as he was ever alive, he's dead, yes," Fred said blandly. "But look on the bright side. *I* might help you in your quest to rescue your beloved from Bartlet's foul clutches."

"Will you?"

"You know, I rather think I shall."

Back to the Surface

Getting out of the lab was more difficult than getting in, as you might expect. Getting in had been easily achieved by a series of semi-controlled falls. But to get back out, I had to actually *climb*, using my single good arm and two semi-useless legs. Fred and F3 I stowed together in a polymer fibre bag. I placed them and the paladin's lantern on the bench under the hole in the air duct, and then set about joining them there. I couldn't make it up onto one of the tall stools next to the bench, so I slid across to another bench, pulled a centrifuge down, and positioned that next to the stool as a first step. From there, with much cursing and huffing and puffing, I was able to climb up onto the bench. Getting onto the big beige machine that I had dropped down to when I arrived was easier, thanks to the availability of a small shelf as an intermediate step.

The final part of the ascent – up into the air duct itself – was by far the most challenging. For a start, the designers of the duct work had not considered the possibility that anyone would try to climb into it from below, so that the rim where the grille had been bolted on was sharp enough to lacerate any hand trying to exert any force at all on it. I had to use the cuff of my tunic as a makeshift glove. Even then I was far too weak to haul myself up one-handed.

However, the designers of the ductwork had made another oversight too: in not having planned for anyone to crawl along the inside of the ducts, they had not provided the hangers with sufficient tolerance to take much additional weight. And after my attempts to pull myself into it caused the duct to drop thirty centimetres or so, it was much easier to half-climb, half-flop into it, albeit with daggers of pain as my bad arm was jarred a few times along the way.

Then it was just a matter of crawling back along the duct to where I had begun; the paladin was waiting below to catch me. In all this I of course eschewed the use of the few ergs of magic I'd managed to hoover up in the labs: I was saving everything for my next encounter with Bartlet. Bartlet! Why couldn't he have been called Skeletor or Mumm-Ra or something sensible like that? How could such a blandly named being end up as a Lich King? And who was I trying to kid anyway? I was going to come off worse again the next time I met Bartlet, no matter how much magic I had managed to scrape together by then.

I introduced Fred to the paladin. At her first sight of him when I drew her out of the bag, my new stand-in omni exclaimed: "And who might this be? Conan the Barbarian?"

"This is my friend the paladin," I explained.

47

"That was an *inspired* choice by his mother," Fred said tartly. "When the registrar asked what her son's first name was, Mrs Paladin replied '*The*,' and despite the fact that the name she had selected was on the list of words which it is considered too cruel to call a child and is therefore banned from use in all civilised countries, the name was deemed acceptable by the registrar, who congratulated the boy's mother on a fine choice, and an obvious improvement over Conan."

"Paladin," I said, "this is Fred, who has agreed to help us. F3 cannot be repaired. He's dead."

"F3's dead?" the paladin asked. "I'm sorry, Edison. Your pocket demon was a fount of knowledge, and I know despite your frequent arguments, it respected you a great deal."

"I'm a fount of knowledge too," Fred said, "and apparently unlike F3, I'm not argumentative. And of course it's not dead, it's a broken machine. But it *is* beyond repair, unless technology has greatly improved since I was turned off. Such units are made to be replaced, not repaired."

"F3 was no ordinary omni," I said.

"Pah!" was Fred's response.

"And no, tech has not improved. In fact, tech has regressed. It's probably at about the Medieval level," I told her. "But there *is* magic. Perhaps the magicians at the Golden Tower can fix him."

"Magic?" Fred squawked. "Did you say magic?"

"Yes," I said glumly. "But even that ain't what it used to be. It's mostly gone from the world, but Bartlet has gathered up rather a lot over his two-thousand-year nap."

"Magic. I see. It all makes perfect sense."

I gathered that Fred was being sarcastic.

"And why is *The* not blue, like you?"

"Until today, the only blue people were my mother and me. Now there is Bartlet too. The thing all three of us have in common is that we are survivors from before the Quacker."

"A minute ago, you said that was two thousand years ago," Fred said.

"It was."

"No, it wasn't."

At this point I should have retorted that Fred had claimed not to be argumentative, but I didn't bother. She would find out soon enough what level civilisation had reached once we reached the outside world and met some of the people of Lar.

There was a pause.

"I had a name," the paladin said eventually.

There was another, longer pause as Fred and I waited for him to tell us what it was.

"My mother took it from me," he said sadly. "She was right to do it."

*

To get back to the surface, I carried the box with the sparrow and the beetle in, and the paladin carried me. More mummies were scattered along the way than there had been before, testament to the way that the dead of the bunker had risen up under Bartlet's influence and crawled out from wherever they had died to subsequently die again in one of the major tunnels. We had a few tricky moments navigating narrow ways, such as the part of the corridor that was mostly blocked by a limestone column, but were soon back in the entrance cafeteria. I asked Fred to make a recording of the oversized arachnids to show Taen if we ever made it to the Golden Tower. She reminded me that they were called amblypygids. I couldn't remember what I had told Taen they were called, and hoped that he had forgotten too.

There was still plenty of the day left, but it was growing gloomier at the surface – the sun having already swung around out of view behind the grey mountains to the west. A cold wind – there was no other kind in Lar – blew from the north down the high valley, shifting high bright white clouds through a sky the colour of my hand.

Speckle was waiting docilely for us to emerge, the paladin's larger horse that I had privately christened Goliath standing beside her. Speckle looked from me to the tunnel mouth and back. I had known Speckle first, but her owner – or really I should say her partner – was now Lexi, not me. By this time, I was rolling along on my crude skateboard again, which we had retrieved from the entrance cafeteria; to Speckle, it probably seemed that I was no different now than when I had gone into the bunker. But I was quite, quite different. I had been through the highs of Lexi telling me she loved me, and of gathering enough magic to walk again, and the lows of losing magic, losing F3 and losing her. All in about forty-seven minutes.

Speckle's coat was a flat grey the colour of thick rainless cloud, with three jet black stars on her side showing where arrows had pierced her flesh on the Greyfield – a barren ashy area that had been ground zero for the Quacker twenty-six centuries ago, and at whose heart was the Entity's lair, the Mountain of Flesh. Edison Jr had saved her life then, and turned her grey by mistake, for she had been covered in the dust of the Greyfield. As I rolled up to her, I showed her to Fred, who knew a fine horse when she saw one.

"A fine grey!" she said. "And I presume this lumpen thing next to her is used for pulling a plough?"

"This is Speckle," I said. "She used to be brown."

"You mean chestnut?"

"I don't know. She had a white speckle on her forehead, and the rest of her was... yes, chestnut."

"I think you mean a star, not a speckle. But I get the picture. Her coat changed, you say?"

So I had to explain what had happened that cold night on the Greyfield: that Speckle had been pierced by three arrows shot by the Entity's minions, and Lexi by one. And the lives of both had been saved by the magic of a toddler who was now known as Edison Jr, a name I had picked for him because I had not expected to cause any name confusion by ever rejoining the party. Prior to that he had no name; an orphan adopted by Lexi, we had just called him 'the boy.' Just like we called the paladin 'the paladin.' I kept the explanation brief: Fred knew what the Entity was, but had no knowledge of what had happened in the two thousand years since the

Quacker had gone off. I would fill in what detail I knew of that on our long journey south.

I touched Speckle's leg, still on my board, and without words explained to her through that contact what had happened to Lexi. I asked if she would help me find Lexi, and the answer was an emphatic yes, signalled by both an image in her mind (me on her back; her galloping through an endless grassland towards a far horizon) and a stamping of her hooves.

Then it was time to release Hal-bird and Taen-beetle from their box. One-handed, I could not clap. *What is the sound of one hand clapping?* I asked myself. The answer was obvious. Silence. The paladin did the honours and with three sharp claps released bird and beetle from their trances. For a horrible moment I was sure that the suddenly-awakened sparrow was going to be terribly peckish and was going to make a snack out of the beetle – but the two animals went their separate ways, the bird whizzing off down the valley and the firefly crawling away into the grass.

"I can't detect any satellites," Fred said.

To which I replied: "Fred, they're dead."

*

In the village of Lar below the hanging valley we sought out Lito, scout Jasso's younger brother, who had been delegated to look after Edison Jr in the paladin's absence. Lito's house was built into the hillside, and like all of the houses of Lar, it was a low building of dry stone. A door and a shuttered window faced the south, where the warmth of the sun came from; the roof was of turf.

"How quaint," Fred said. "Edison, I think you meant technology has regressed to the Stone Age, not the Mediaeval period."

Edison Jr knew that something was amiss straight away. "Lexi?" he asked.

The paladin lifted me off Speckle and set me onto the ground so that I was at the same height as the boy. I took both his little hands in my one good hand. "A bad man took her. But we're going to get her back. It's a long way, and first we have to go to the Golden Tower, so I can be –" here I almost said repaired – "healed. OK?"

Edison Jr nodded silently.

"What do you mean, a bad man took her? Took her where? We should be tracking them from here, not wandering off to the Golden Tower. Which direction did they go?" Lito demanded. He had a very similar appearance to his brother Jasso: stocky, with pale brown hair and a permanent serious expression. Lito braided his hair, and wore wooden beads in it. I had to admit it was a cool look, but I preferred to just periodically cut chunks out of mine whenever it got too long. My hair, if you had forgotten, was as blue as the rest of me. The only implement available for shortening it was a pair of shears otherwise used for giving sheep a haircut – remembering this made me briefly wish that I had looked for scissors in the bunker. Lito was younger than me, but a life in the highlands had cultivated a very practical nature in him. He was a good shot with a bow, could easily start a fire, make a horseshoe, build a house. That sort of thing. I would have been better than him at chess, but probably only until I taught him the rules.

I explained what had happened as well as I could. Lito did not doubt me for a moment. "You'll be able to save her though," was his first comment when I had wound up my tale. "You're the greatest magician of the age. You'll be going Lith Tillac way, I guess?"

I didn't know. The paladin did. We were.

"I'll come with you then. I have some cloth to sell. Strength in numbers," Lito said, looking at the paladin and implying that what he actually meant was 'strength in a large guy who's pretty handy with his big magic sword.' "But first I had better take a look at your arm."

And so, in the growing dusk Lito carefully unwrapped my arm and began to gently squeeze it, which elicited a range of yelping sounds from me. He soon decided that it was broken.

"I've never broken a bone before," I said, to take my mind off the pain. "Except when my mother threw me through a wall. And that didn't really count, because I fixed it myself by magic a few minutes later."

"It will grow back stronger than before," Lito assured me, "but it will take time to mend. When do you want to set off?"

"Ten minutes?" I suggested. Other villagers had noticed that something was up, and I didn't feel like explaining myself to them – or anyone. Lexi was popular in the village, where almost everyone considered her to be a princess – a notion I had deliberately not dispelled, seeing no harm and possible benefit in them thinking that one of their guests was a royal. Now that she had vanished while in my company, the fact that Lexi was widely adored and considered royalty by most was probably not to my benefit.

"It will be too dark to move in half an hour," the paladin said.

"Great. We'll be twenty minutes down the road."

But neither Lito nor the paladin would have it. The former had stock to pack for one thing. And so, in the gathering gloom, there was an awkward moment when several villagers all but accused me of doing away with Princess Lexi out of jealousy. I'm not sure what would have happened without the paladin there to a) support my version of events and b) to glare in an intimidating way at my accusers.

In the end, we left not long after dawn, the four of us on three horses – I shared with Edison Jr – with a pack mule behind carrying Lito's stock. As we went, Fred waxed lyrical about how bucolic the scenery around the village of Lar was. I did not trouble to ask her what "bucolic" meant. I only had thoughts for Lexi, and the predicament she now found herself in.

Somewhere Else

For a brief moment, Lexi felt as if she was turning inside out. Everything went black, and then the world somehow seemed to twist, and although she could see nothing, she knew that in some impossible but true way close things had become far apart and distant things had been drawn together.

She could not speak, nor even breathe; nor could she break the monster's grip on her arm.

Then came a second lurch that was if anything more disorientating than the first; to Lexi it felt as if she had been turned to liquid and was being poured through a funnel. After a few moments of roaring blackness, light banished the darkness, or else her vision returned. Blue fire roared away from her in all directions, haloing everything in cold light. She found that she was standing in the centre of a large circular room with high walls of stone whose main furniture was a curved row of six empty thrones. The thrones had been arranged to face the centre of the room, where Lexi stood; the centre of the floor was marked by a large snarling wolf's head design, which was surrounded by a many-pointed star.

And nearby, four curious figures stood side by side; like the thrones, they were all facing her.

Although her next thought was not to wonder who or what the watchers were, but to realise: *I'm somewhere else. This is not the bunker.*

And then she realised that the monster that had somehow transported her to this new place was still standing right next to her, still gripping tightly onto her arm.

And *then* she realised that she was still holding her dagger. It was the work of a moment to raise it, twist her body, and punch it into the heart of the undead thing beside her.

It grabbed her knife hand with its free one, too late to stay the lethal blow. Lexi and the undead danced a few steps, face to face. The undead was naked, and scrawny, and floated six inches above the stone floor. This close, its appearance was utterly repellent. Its blue face was an irregular patchwork of scars, as if it had been burnt, its blank eyes shone with a blue light much paler than its skin, and its mouth was decorated with monstrously long canine teeth.

"Why did you do that?" it hissed at her, its breath this close almost enough to make her pass out.

Blood – blue – was running over her hand. "I'm sure you took my meaning!" she snarled, and tried to twist the knife to speed the monster's death, or second death. But it was still far stronger than she was, and pushed her hand away, the knife going with it and then falling to the floor with a clatter.

And then she saw that her blow was not a mortal one after all; before her very eyes the wound over the monster's heart closed up, just like that; in moments only a fine scar line remained. Soon even that was lost amid the myriad other marks of ancient damage. The undead thing was unharmed.

The brief flood of blue fire washing around them died away, seeming to sink into the flagstones of the circular room, so that it was all but dark again, the glowing dead thing the only source of illumination, for there was otherwise no light in this place. Wherever they were, it had been until a moment ago as dark as the bunker, but it was *definitely* not the bunker, for it had a completely different style, a completely different feeling. This place and the bunker had been built by different peoples at different times – both were ancient, but which of them was older, she could not tell.

Then came the sound of bony fingers clicking. As if in answer, orange flame appeared at numerous lamps around the walls. And as the level of light waxed, the four curious characters that Lexi had seen earlier became visible once more. The largest of the four was a giant twice her height, clad in plate armour, resting a war hammer as large as he was on the ground between his feet. The smallest was a woman bent almost double by age, her hunched body hardly half Lexi's height. In between those two stood two men, one of whom appeared to have four arms. As disparate as the four appeared, they all had one important thing in common – they were all undead, their empty eye sockets emitting a dim orange glow just like the crawling undead in the bunker. All were white haired, as if they had become undead only after attaining a great age in their real lives.

The four-armed undead was the one whose click had set the fires to life, for he still held one of his hands up in an ostentatious pose.

"Welcome, welcome, one and both!" he exclaimed. If he had seen what had just transpired between Lexi and her captor, he didn't show it. His dried lips did not seem to move as he spoke, but his voice was clear and bright. "You must be our new Lich King and his Queen! Welcome, welcome. I am your tailor."

The tailor wore a black jacket in a soft suede type material. As he introduced himself, he pointed to the centre of his chest with one of his four arms. With a second, he pointed to the other medium-sized undead, who wore a smart long double-breasted suit and white gloves. He carried a single glass of a translucent red drink on a silver tray.

"This gentleman is your butler," the tailor explained. Next, with a third arm, he pointed to the small undead woman, who wore a black dress and hobnail boots and clutched a black feather duster. "Your handmaiden." Lastly, he used his final arm to point at the giant. "This is your guard."

"Do you have names?" the thing standing over Lexi demanded.

Again, the tailor went through the routine of pointing to each of them. "Tailor, Butler, Handmaiden, Guard." At this point the three male undead gave a shallow bow, and the female undead attempted a curtsy that was accompanied by much creaking of ancient joints. "Guard and Butler have lost the use of their voices, but will obey orders. Handmaiden speaks, don't you Handmaiden?"

"I am Your Majesty's loyal servant," croaked Handmaiden, and attempted a second curtsy, in the course of which she almost fell over.

"May we enquire as to your name, Your Majesty?" Tailor asked.

"I am Bartlet," the blue undead said.

"And you, My Lady?" Tailor asked, directing his question at Lexi.

"Stop pretending this is normal!" Lexi snapped. "You people are all dead!"

"There's no need to be rude," Tailor said mildly.

Butler shrugged bonily.

"Perhaps you will furnish us with her name, Your Majesty?" Tailor asked Bartlet.

"I don't know it," Bartlet said. "We only just met."

"We haven't met!" Lexi yelled. "You kidnapped me! Where is this place?"

"Welcome to the Black Tower of the Citadel of Malafert, My Lady, home of the six Lich Kings of yore, and now the new Lich King, Lord, er, Bartlet, the seventh and eternal undying."

The Citadel of Malafert, in the Blessed Vale

Lexi had heard of Malafert, and had heard wild tales of it. So had everyone in the Westfold, south or north of the wall. It was a haunted place, a realm where there were no living things, only dead things not at rest. Malafert was named for its greatest king, the first of the Liches. It was located on the western shore of a narrow valley called the Cursed Vale, which extended deep into the mountains, and was separated from the province of Achi Lomm by a narrow pass called Highstand.

Some thought that the magic of the Cursed Vale was key to eternal life – so that the old and sick often embarked on immense journeys, hoping that if they succeeded in gaining the Vale, or if possible even Malafert, its heart, then they would outlive their own deaths. Most thought them insane. But the moribund travellers were joined by young people too, who journeyed over the high passes into the Cursed Vale swearing their intention to not just *die* there, but to *kill themselves* upon arrival at Malafert. They convinced themselves that in so doing they would obtain a new form of life, one free of all the troubles of their present one. Most thought this group even more insane than the first. But as far as Lexi knew, no-one tried to stop them, at least from making the trip. Once travellers were beyond the high passes, whether the Highstand crossing into the east of the Cursed Vale or The Miser crossing from Erras, a land immediately to the Cursed Vale's north, no-one knew what became of them. It was widely assumed that they either wandered and died, or were killed by the restless dead, becoming like those who killed them. But there were scoundrels aplenty who would take pilgrims' coin to transport them there, and either deliver them to one of the high passes or even abandon them with nothing in the wilderness, telling them they had arrived at their goal.

Malafert was the poisoned heart of the Cursed Vale, the seat of dead kings. But there were no Lich Kings any more, had not been for hundreds of years. Lich Kings gave the dead purpose; when left to themselves they were just restless and spiteful.

So went Lexi's thoughts. But before she had properly gathered them, the four-armed tailor clapped both pairs of hands twice. That was the cue for the butler to venture forwards, stiff-legged, to offer the drink on his silver tray to the blue undead calling himself Bartlet, who was now seemingly recognised by these four walking corpses as their king.

"Our finest," said Tailor, "bottled in the time of Malafert himself."

As Bartlet turned to accept the glass, Lexi scrambled to her feet and away a few paces. There were two exits on opposite sides of the throne room, both large iron-bound doors. But Lexi knew that she had no chance of reaching either of them if Bartlet decided to cut her off. So instead of making a break for it, she merely stood there and glowered at Bartlet as he drained the offered blood.

"The product of murder!" Lexi snarled.

Tailor looked surprised. "The donation of a volunteer, My Lady. King Malafert was well loved by his people, including the living. None of the undead kings since Malafert have ever had such a rapport with the living of the Blessed Vale!"

"You mean the Cursed Vale."

"Cursed by some, and blessed by others." The tailor turned to the butler and said, "Butler, please find refreshment suitable for a living human." He turned to the handmaiden and said, "Handmaiden, please find our new queen suitable attire." Then he turned to the fourth member of the staff, the hulking guard, and said, "Guard, please take up station by the royal staterooms."

The three of them left the throne room through the same door. They all showed little grace in their gaits: the butler stalked like a crane, the handmaiden staggered like a drunk, and the guard plodded like someone up to his knees in mud.

"My Lord," Tailor said to Bartlet, "you may wish to adopt a more informal appearance. You are among friends here. Presently I shall locate you some more appropriate clothing; I do not need my tape measure, I can judge your size by eye. I always keep newly-made clothes on standby, just in case! But we have never had a queen before, so I am afraid that My Lady's clothes might be a little moth-eaten! Please do not judge my ability by my own dress; I have been unable to wear a jacket well ever since I had my second pair of arms grafted on..."

Lexi thought that listening to the dead tailor prattle on would drive her out of her mind in half a day, and that the two silent undead among his colleagues were not mute, merely unable to get a word in edgewise. But his words were having a soothing effect on Bartlet, who first floated down to the ground and then stopped glowing, first from the exposed bits of his body and after a few seconds even from his blue-lantern eyes. Previously hidden by the glow, his eyes, like Edison's, were revealed to be three different shades of blue: the "whites" were sky blue, the irises royal blue, and the pupils midnight blue. Bartlet's dry lips relaxed and widened, hiding his pointy teeth; his face gradually took on the appearance of a living human, not a long-dead one. His transformation made him look altogether less monstrous, but he was still a scrawny blue thing clad in rags, his straggly hair giving him the look of a bald swimmer who had just surfaced through a mat of blue seaweed.

"What is this place, Malafert?" Bartlet asked the tailor. His voice was transformed too – it was now far less harsh, and almost human-seeming.

"It is the city at the heart of the Blessed Vale, named for its first dead king," the tailor said with a bow. "Within the city there is a citadel, and within the citadel there are nine towers, of which this – the Black Tower – is the tallest and most important, and stands at the focus of the other eight."

"I felt a compulsion to come here. Why? Was this your doing?"

"When Lich Kings rise, they are drawn to this place, which is a beacon of darkness to them. The citadel multiplies a lich's strength, and allows him to control more undead servants than he would be able to elsewhere."

"Or she," Lexi muttered.

"You will be our first Lich Queen, My Lady," Tailor told her. "I only speak from experience."

"I am not going to be your Lich Queen. I want you to return me to from whence I was taken."

"She is a feisty one, this betrothed of yours," Tailor commented to Bartlet.

"I am not betrothed to this creature! I was kidnapped by it. My actual betrothed was harmed by it in the process, and may need my help, so I need to return at once."

"You would do well to address your remarks to your king, My Lady," Tailor told her.

"Your king if you want. Not mine."

Tailor stooped to pick up Lexi's dagger. "Do you mind, My Lord? This looks like a perfect item for our gallery. We keep a record of all our masters there. I think it will bear the legend, 'The Dagger King Bartlet's Betrothed Thrust into His Heart in a Lovers' Quarrel.'"

"How is it that you are able to talk, indeed babble on incessantly?" Bartlet demanded harshly. "The others I raised had no voices, no life of their own."

"A sage question, My Lord! The original permanent staff numbered over a thousand. At that time, all of us could speak as fluently as when we were alive. But over the centuries, our numbers have dwindled. Now there are only four of us left, and only two who still remember how to speak."

"Permanent staff?"

"The permanent staff are active always, in contrast to your temporary staff, who have risen only in the presence of an undead powerful enough to be proclaimed their king. All such are voiceless, and have no motives of their own, other than an enmity to the living, which is the other thing that can awaken them – an intruder of that nature. Were our new queen to wander about the lower reaches of the citadel unaccompanied by one of us or yourself, she would be in grave danger."

"I see. And how many are the temporary staff?"

"I do not know, My Lord. When we take census, we may find that they number ten thousand already! More will rise! Smiths will already be sharpening blades dulled by the passage of centuries. In hours the Army of the Blessed will begin to assemble. Already the Clockwork casts a pall over the nearer parts of the Vale, so that the dead need not fear the sunlight! But what am I thinking? I must show you. If it please your majesties, please accompany me. First we will visit the Moon Lab, and from there, the Eyrie!"

Moon Lab and Eyrie

Tailor began to walk, stiff-legged, towards the heavy iron-bound door set in the wall behind the six thrones, hoping that Bartlet and Lexi would follow him.

Bartlet did begin to follow, walking easily now, feet flat to the ground, not drifting an inch above the floor as he had done before. Lexi did not move. She looked the other way, the way the other three undead had left through a similar-looking door on the opposite side of the throne room, and pondered making a break for it.

"Please, My Lady, do not try to leave here unaccompanied," Tailor told her, divining her intentions. "If you did manage to get past Guard, you would find that the temporary staff in the citadel below and the Vale beyond are drawn to the living, and like to drink their blood."

Lexi hesitated.

"It's a hundred miles from here to the Highstand pass. Escape is impossible," Tailor went on.

Still Lexi hesitated.

But Bartlet had grown tired of waiting for her. He raised one of his hands and in an instant she found herself whirling through the air towards him, long silver hair trailing behind. A moment later her right hand was clamped in his left, and he was dragging her along with him like a disobedient child. "Please, proceed," he said to Tailor.

"I will kill you," Lexi hissed at him.

"You won't," Bartlet said, not angry, and hardly even amused by her empty threat.

"Then I'll escape!"

"You won't, My Lady," Tailor said. "And you would be advised not to try to." He opened the door, which was of thick old wood darkened by age and reinforced by black ironwork that was probably scarcely any harder than the ancient timber. Beyond lay a gently curving staircase, which followed the wall up to their left. The ancient carpet beneath their feet bloomed with dust as they trod on it. For a moment it was very dark on the enclosed staircase, but a click of the tailor's fingers produced

61

firelight from wall-mounted torches as before. "There are two sets of stairs in this part of the tower," he explained, "which proceed in a double spiral, each never meeting the other. Hence the doors on opposite sides of each floor."

After climbing through a half circle they reached another door. The room on the other side was gloomy, but not completely dark. Lexi saw that they were above ground, because unlike the throne room, this floor had windows, narrow arched empty slots with no glass nor shutters. The sky outside was heavily overcast, as if a thunderstorm was about to break. In the distance she could see a thin strip of blue daylight marking the edge of the cloudbank.

The room itself was of similar shape and dimensions to the throne room, wide and circular. This time there was a curious machine at its centre rather than a wolf's head/star design. The machine was a large and complicated arrangement of wheels and gears, which were moving almost silently despite being formed of what looked like black stone. A wide column of stone wreathed in writhing tendrils of black smoke rose from the middle of the machine to the high ceiling above. This curious flow emanated from the machine and clung to the column, creeping up it, twining like a diabolical version of the woodbine plant that Lexi was familiar with. Instead of green stems ascending a tree, here living ropes of darkness ascended a stone column.

"Here in the Moon Lab was where Malafert and his successors performed their dark experiments. And it was here that Malafert created the masterwork of Lich magic! Behold the Clockwork!" the tailor proclaimed, bowing stiffly while tucking all four of his arms in close to his body. "This machine was built by King Malafert himself from adamant plucked, it is said, from the very heart of the Earth. We permanent staff knew a new king had arisen today – because whenever one does, the Clockwork begins to turn again, resuming its holy duties even after a pause of centuries! That is why we joyfully assembled in the throne room to await your arrival, Your Majesty!"

The Clockwork was large – as large as the stone house in the village of Lar that Lexi lived in. It dominated the Moon Lab. Around it, along the walls, there were several benches and shelves covered with bottles and jars and lesser machines, apparently the results of other, failed, experiments by Malafert or his successors.

Lexi looked for a weapon amid the chaos – but her dagger, now in Tailor's hands, was easily the best weapon in the room. Conical flasks and bottles with ancient residue dried in their bottoms, tripods, tomes, racks or gadgets would not enable her to fight Bartlet.

"It will run, and run, and will not stop until your reign is at an end, My Lord!"

"Then it will not stop," Bartlet said, with no trace of emotion, as if there was no possibility it would.

"I pray you are right, My Lord, but even King Malafert only reigned over us for two hundred and thirty-six years! Sooner or later a paladin will come along and ruin everything."

Lexi knew a paladin. As far as human fighters went, he was top tier. So for a moment she felt a warm glow of optimism – but only for a moment. In a fair fight, no human could beat Bartlet, who moved faster than thought. Even Edison had stood no chance. If a magician could not win, how could a paladin – even one armed with a magic sword? She remembered Edison flying through the air beside her as if in a moment frozen in time. She hoped and prayed that he would be all right, and surmised that he was. In fact, she thought he might be on his way to rescue her from Bartlet's clutches already – and resolved to escape by herself before he got to Malafert, in case his stupid male pride forced him to face the undead again. But whatever happened, she was never going to wed the creature that was presently dragging her around the Moon Lab.

"And now, with your permission, My Lord: the Eyrie!" Tailor said.

And so saying, he led them up a set of spiral stairs that twined around the outside of the Clockwork. After a complete circle, the stairs passed through the Moon Lab's roof and opened onto what turned out to be the very pinnacle of an immense tower.

A flat roof opened out in front of them, and from its heart rose a fountain of black lightlessness, rising to an incredible height before flaring out in all directions. Now Lexi realised that the glimpse of sky she had seen through the Moon Lab's windows marked the edge, not of a natural cloud, but of the foul emanations of the Clockwork. And now she saw that the glimpses of sky that she had seen, and could see now more clearly, were entirely over the sea; on the landward side of the tower, the black cloud sealed to the Cursed Vale's mountainsides without leaving a gap.

Against the flat horizon of the sea, the blackness could be seen to be a vast disc, its rim a perfect curve. The sun was sinking in the west, but it was hidden from direct view, its existence only shown by light flickering on the swell.

From where they stood, Lexi could not see the ground. Perspective and the strength of the wind gave her the sense that they were very high up. This was soon confirmed when Bartlet marched her forwards on the seaward side of the tower; both peered down from the brink of the precipice. The drop was a long one and ended on a field of black jagged rocks pounded by heavy grey waves, exploding on contact with the shore into white foam like shattered bones.

Lexi had no fear that Bartlet would toss her over the edge. She had never seen the sea before, and was at first stunned by the view. Then she began to grow increasingly angry that this was how she must first see it, that her view of the sea, and the sea itself, should be so sullied by the Clockwork's foul pollution.

"Behold the Eyrie!" the tailor exclaimed, and bowed again. He had moved close to the middle of the tower, in touching distance of the fountain of night, perhaps familiar with the dangers posed by the gusting wind on a roof with no parapet. "The twelve towers you see around you are how it gained its name."

The towers he spoke of were narrow stone structures projecting from the tower top like the points of a crown. Each had a curious niche cut into it at two thirds of its height.

"The tower was once home to twelve eagle pairs, one nesting in each niche," Tailor explained. "They were King Malafert's pride, and the commoners in the citadel below would look up at the sound of their cries and see their great wings block out the sun, and marvel."

"Where are they now?" Bartlet asked.

"Alas, they left the tower when the machine was done, when it became dark, never to return."

The Low Road to Lith Tillac

Now, I may be green – as well as blue – but I have a vague idea which way south is, especially on a sunny day. So, as we rode out of Lar not long after sunrise, I was slightly discombobulated to find that Lito was leading us not south, but east. It turned out that it was better to go east first and then south, because the going would be easier once we had cleared the worst of the easternmost spurs of the complex of mountains in which Lar was nestled. To go south – the direct way to Lith Tillac – would have involved crossing a series of hills and valleys, whereas the main north-south road was further east, and began after the mountains had mostly petered out.

The complex of mountains around Lar and neighbouring villages called the Hundred Hills was but a small part of a vast north-south range reaching to the Greyfield in the north and beyond the Cursed Vale in the south. According to accounts I had heard, in the south it really only became impossible to trace in the riven lands around Syanabyan, the desert city founded on the Westfold's chief electrum deposits. People had various names for the range as a whole – of which the most sensible that I had heard was the Barrier. Everything in the Westfold – all of civilisation, in other words – was east of the Barrier. The only land on the westward side of the mountains consisted of a few relatively small valleys which descended to meet the Shivering Sea, many of them hard to reach from the eastern side. Lar was in the northern half of the Barrier, about a hundred miles south of where the Wall, built long ago to protect civilised lands from the Entity, joined it. So much had I picked up from conversations with locals, although some of their opinions were contradictory. There were no maps in Lar, only shrugs and assertions from folk who had picked up the information fifth hand from their own limited travels or the word of passers-by. What was clear though was that at some stage we would have to cross one of the few east-west passes through the Barrier to reach the Cursed Vale. But first, we had to complete our long trip south to the Golden Tower.

Descending the valley below Lar to reach the north-south road took all morning. I looked out for the warbirds we had encountered the day before, and I know the paladin did too. But there was no sign of them. The pathetic creature they had found next to the mountain stream in Lar had not been worth taking revenge on; it seemed they had finally settled their grudge with me.

When we eventually reached it, the much-vaunted north-south road turned out to be little more than a cart track. It was buried in the thick woodland that had built up by degrees as we had descended, rising from head-high scrubby birch and willow to what I considered to be proper trees – many of them giants with hand-shaped leaves that, if challenged, I would have identified as sycamores.

In the middle of the afternoon we passed an artificial pond, which I could surmise for myself had once been associated with a water mill. The weir that had once created a head of water for the water wheel was cracked and broken; the mill itself was a tree-choked ruin. With Fred's help, I explained to the rest of the party how the mill had worked. Lito thought that this – so far away from any cornfields – was a strange place to grind corn. I did not bother to suggest that back then, instead of the drab late summer green of the woodland trees, a traveller might have seen the warm yellow of ripe wheat and more than a glimpse of the blue sky, that the woodland was the product of the abandonment of the mill, not evidence that it had been misplaced.

We passed other travellers on the road. The teeth-grindingly slow etiquette when this happened seemed to be for approaching parties to signal their friendliness from a distance, then advance cautiously, before having a lengthy conversation about the time of day, the weather, and any news that either party had gathered along their way. So far, the news from the south seemed to be inconsequential – mostly about a royal wedding due to happen in a month or two in Lith Tillac, between Princess Maralla from the capital Toryl Noth and the Duke of Lith Tillac's son, Oxil Denarion. I could care less about royal weddings. The thing I focussed in on was that the wedding was not imminent, and that we would be long past Lith Tillac before it had the chance to slow us down. I didn't know how, but I knew it would impede our journey somehow if it was going on at the same time as when we passed through.

I asked the people we passed how far it was to Lith Tillac. The first lot said eight days, the second lot nine days, and then some bright spark came back with "It depends how fast you go."

At this I could only smile and grind my teeth in fury as we rode on. The distance to Lith Tillac was not affected by the speed of those wishing to get there.

But, out of earshot of that comedian, Lito and the paladin assured me that it would take us four days, not eight or nine, to reach our first waypoint. Most of those going the other way were on foot, and were burdened with goods; some pulled handcarts. I estimated that Lith Tillac was a hundred miles away, and that it would indeed take us four days to get there, notwithstanding interminable chitchat and peace formalities every time we passed someone on the road. Of course, passers-by wanted to stare at me, never having seen anyone blue before. They wanted to try to rub the blue off, ask about my "defeat" of the Entity, that sort of thing. No-one was yet blaming me for the arrival of a new Lich King in the world, so that was a bonus.

The practicalities of travelling by horseback – even on a horse as compliant as Speckle – with one good limb of four, were as unpleasant as you can imagine. Going to the loo was hard to do while retaining any dignity. Changing clothes was impossible without aid, so I didn't bother. I could not get on Speckle by myself, and if I wanted to get off by myself, my only route to do so was to fall off. My legs were not completely useless, but had no strength; my bad arm banged away mercilessly, a constant pain that I tried to bear stoically, telling myself not to be a baby and to think of Lexi's situation. Still, stoical or not, it was tough to sleep. By night there was not even a hint of a glow from Hal's ring: this road and its stopping places had long since been cleared out of any magic they had once held.

Lito and the paladin were sure that there was no danger of brons or raptors in these woods. "Not this far south; not south of the wall," they said, "they were hunted out centuries ago."

This made me feel sad somehow, as well as slightly safer.

"There aren't any tree centipedes in the western mountains either," Lito added, perhaps unnecessarily. Why bring up a threat that no-one's heard of, and then claim it doesn't exist? When asked to explain what tree centipedes were, he described them as giant insects that disguised themselves as dead trees and waited upright in the woods, ambushing their prey by falling on them and skewering them with numerous unpleasant spines. And of course, I knew that the story was bogus, but perhaps homed in on the wrong hole in it.

"Insects have six legs," I said, "centipedes are quite different, and have a hundred."

"Not a hundred," Fred corrected me. "Generally far fewer. They are misnamed. And arthropods are strongly size-limited because of the diffusion rate of oxygen, so tree-sized species are impossible. It sounds like a variety of the 'drop bear' hoax, designed to keep tourists out of Australian woods."

And so I had to explain to the others what a 'drop bear' was – "A harmless tree-dwelling vegetarian bear the size of Edison Junior, a variety of which locals claim are monsters that drop on the unwary and eat them," was my stab at it.

"The most dangerous things in these woods," the paladin said humourlessly, "are other people. No-one should relax just because we're not going to be ambushed by a raptor."

In the evenings we set up camp with other travellers, there being safety in numbers – despite the paladin's warning, you can't go through life trusting no-one, especially on the road. When the other campers had children in their party, they were of course openly fascinated by me. The adults meanwhile largely pretended not to be, but I caught them staring all the time, at which point both parties politely dropped their eyes.

Because I was useless at anything practical, I told the children stories while the adults got on with camping-related tasks. The children asked for a demonstration of magic, but, bending the facts only slightly, I told them I had used it all up in fighting the Entity. So that was the first tale I told each evening: of my own adventure in the Entity's lair, and how Edison Jr (who had mostly zoned out or fallen asleep by then) had saved the day. I retold local legends that Hal had earlier told me, such as the tale of Durthin and Belathin, the two warring brothers after whom a bridge north of the wall had been named, and of the Golden Tower and the magicians Callan and his sister Somel. The latter story was well known, but the children seemed to like my retelling of it. Children like stories.

I reminisced about the old days, my school, the city, my mother, how we were able to speak over long distances, how we travelled, flushing toilets. To my audience the world I described seemed as magical as actual magic. I told fairy stories (Hansel and Gretel) and parables (The Good Samaritan), and, with heavy reliance on Fred's perfect memory, I retold the story of Beowulf. And, just because a happy ending is just a story that hasn't finished yet, I included Beowulf's ultimate fate. In my telling he was an aged hero forced out of retirement one last time to fight a dragon, even knowing that he could not win. His men – all except one, whose name Fred reminded me was Wiglaf – were too cowardly to go into battle (Fred disputing various aspects of the ending, albeit silently by flashing up messages on her screen). Beowulf and the dragon both perished in the fight, and only Wiglaf lived to tell the tale – which, I reflected, was probably the only reason he was put in the story in the first place.

The children were in awe of this tale, and went away to their beds debating among themselves whether it was right that a warrior should die in battle. To them the existence and motives of the dragon needed no explanation: it was simply a force of nature. Nor did any of them mourn its death. Dragons, like brons, like raptors, were there to be hunted out mercilessly until the land was safe.

Until the land was safe from every monster except the human kind, anyway.

In the morning the children were all running around hitting each other with sticks and playing at Beowulf. Strangely they all wanted to be Beowulf and to die heroically with much writhing about on the ground and yelling. No-one wanted to be Wiglaf, even though he was the only character to survive the tale.

Later Fred explained to me what had got the dragon all riled up in the first place: someone had stolen a golden cup from his hoard.

The paladin watched the children running up and down and said wistfully: "There are no dragons any more."

"No," I replied, "but there are Lich Kings."

The Province of Lith Tillac

On the fourth day of our journey the woodland began to thin out. For a time, the largest trees were no smaller than before, but they were more widely spread, the ground under them full of head-high shrubs. These seemed to be a haven for ticks, and every branch seemed to shed a rain of miniature horrors like a parachute regiment of pint-sized drop bears. The track was mostly only wide enough for one cart, with passing places at intervals. So there was no way to avoid passing under the overhanging vegetation, providing good hunting for the ticks which fell on weary travellers like rain. We had to stop in a clearing and groom one another like a family of chimps. The horses needed attention too, as did the nameless mule.

How I was tempted to use magic! I could have dispensed with the entire army of ticks in no time at all, with hardly any drain on the little magic I had in stock. But I kept my discipline, even when there was a tick I could not reach with my good hand. Like a miser, I would not spend even a penny unless I really had to.

In this more open area, it was noticeably warmer than under the dense canopy of the woodland. The roadside was dotted with occasional farmhouses, some in use, some abandoned. Here too we were now able to see on our right the foothills of the Barrier, always with clouds hanging over them, although there was precious little respite from the hot sun ten miles east on the north-south road.

As we proceeded south, the shrubs grew patchy where wildfires had torn through them in a previous warm season; soon the taller types were replaced by knee-high dwarfs, which eventually gave way to a seemingly endless vista of dry yellow grass. We camped in an abandoned village that night, and Fred was finally able to get the view of the night sky that F3 had demanded minutes after he and I had been dug up by Lexi. Like F3 before her, Fred matched her starmap with what she could see and the stars' known proper velocities. Like F3, she came up with an elapsed time of two thousand six hundred years.

"Two thousand six hundred and one," I almost said – stopping myself just in time. Instead I said, "See? I told you?"

"I understand that your omni told *you*," Fred said haughtily.

"Yes, he did. But *I* told you."

That evening, I told a small audience of travellers' children what I called the Tale of Sir Lancelot. I did not merely want to entertain the little ones while the big ones got on with the essential jobs of an overnight stop in the wilderness. I was also interested to see how the children reacted to being placed in a moral dilemma. I gave some background on King Arthur and the Round Table – not mentioning the Quest for the Holy Grail, which had uncomfortable echoes of the real-life quest that had seen all the paladins of the Westfold but one vanish in the search for something that had been in my mother's pocket the whole time.

I tried to give a good account of what I called the Knights' Code, which required a knight to accept an opponent's surrender and spare their life when they were defeated. Then I portrayed Sir Lancelot as the strongest knight of the Round Table, and the most moral (no, I didn't mention anything about Queen Guinevere).

In the tale, Sir Lancelot was riding through the woods one day on his way to complete an important Quest when he came upon a knight and his lady. The knight was furious with his wife about something, and took to beating her. Naturally upon seeing this, Sir Lancelot galloped up and separated them, making the knight swear not to raise a hand against his wife again. Then Sir Lancelot rode on, only for the miscreant knight to pull his sword out and kill his wife (at this point there was a gasp in the audience). So Sir Lancelot turned around and challenged the murderer, who, knowing he was outmatched by the great knight, promptly surrendered, fell to his knees, and asked for mercy. Because of the Knights' Code, Sir Lancelot was forced to accept the murderer's surrender and spare his life. He could do nothing but get back on his horse and continue pursuing his Quest.

The children's opinion was unanimous that Sir Lancelot should have killed the murderer, Knights' Code or not. If he had killed the other knight at their first meeting, the victim would have been saved, I pointed out: would he have been right to kill the man then? This time the answer was no, because Sir Lancelot could not foresee the future.

The Knights' Code was stupid, an older girl said. This was because villains could "play" it. The only way to prevent crime was to punish criminals severely. And the only suitable punishment for murderers was death.

Unfortunately, the paladin had chosen that moment to join us by the fireside. He almost flinched at the girl's words, and I knew he was both thinking of himself and that he agreed with her. So I had to rapidly invent a postscript. In it, the murderer returned to his castle – for all knights had castles – only to find that word of his fell deed had preceded him. The gates were barred to him, and the people of the castle threw stones on him from the battlements until he was driven away. Then he wandered far and wide, cursing his own temper and wishing that Sir Lancelot had not shown him mercy, for he had become an outcast. He was searching and searching for a way to redeem himself – and finally, one day three years later, he found it. In a clearing in the wood, he found Sir Lancelot fighting a giant, but the giant was winning. Sir Lancelot had been knocked off his feet and his armour was broken. The murderer charged in, drove the giant away, and saved Sir Lancelot, who thanked him and bade him return with him to his castle, an outcast no more. But the murderer refused and rode on. He was killed a year later by a gang of brigands.

Unfortunately for me, but perhaps luckily in general, children are not stupid, and my audience realised that I had made up this part of the tale. *But it's all made up*, I thought to myself; it was just that my bit was not quite as well made up as the Medieval part. The paladin said nothing. I hope he didn't think I was trying to patronise him.

We reached the province of Lith Tillac the next day. There was a sort of no-man's land between it and the province of Nymeth. This came in the form of a slightly wider and better-kept section of cart track about twenty paces long, on opposite sides of which stood two stone columns, tall enough to be visible from miles away. Atop these columns the two provinces' symbols faced one another: Nymeth's avatar was a ram, Lith Tillac's a boar.

There were no border staff on the Nymeth side, but a troop of about twenty cavalry were waiting on the Lith Tillac side. They stood beside their mounts in plumed steel helmets and dark leather armour decorated with strips of orange fabric at their joints; their tabards, in fabric of the same colour, were decorated with a large black boar's head emblem. They seemed out of place, as if this was not their usual station; horses and men alike were wilting in the heat of the day. It looked like they were waiting for us. Sure enough, on spotting our approach they began to stir, causing a few jitters in our camp and among a small group of cloth merchants who had latched onto us for safety and were now second-guessing the wisdom of that move.

I though was unconcerned. Perhaps this was naivety on my part. Perhaps it was because where I had grown up, officials, cops and soldiers were almost always trustworthy. Perhaps our companions had different experiences of officialdom – such as being shaken down for bribes before they could get on with their business. Either way I was fairly sure that the soldiers were there to escort us, not to attack us, and rode forwards without slackening Speckle's pace.

By the time we reached the Lith Tillac side, the soldiers were all mounted and were lined up along the roadside as if awaiting inspection. Only their captain remained on foot. He was a young man with facial hair in three generous, well-groomed clumps. As we drew near the Lith Tillac post, he doffed his helmet, bowed, and said, "Lord Hawthorne, welcome to Lith Tillac."

My first thought was to retort "I am no lord," in reply to the captain's welcome. But you should never look a gift welcome askance. Nor did I wish to embarrass the captain in front of his troops. Thus, I struck what I hoped was a suitably dignified tone when I replied, "Please, call me Edison. Your welcome is well received, Captain…?"

"Dissus, my lord, of the Lith Tillac Heraldic Guard. I have been ordered to escort you to the city."

"You didn't tell me you'd been ennobled!" Fred blurted, from her position in my pocket. "I might have been more respectful, if I had known." This rather ruined the formalities.

I explained to Fred that Captain Dissus was merely being polite. He didn't gainsay me, but looked at me curiously, giving me the impression that he thought I really *was* a lord. I wondered if maybe someone *had* made me a lord at some point. It was certainly possible. A series of dignitaries had visited me in Lar after my "defeat" of the Entity. I had been swimming in a deep dark sea of depression at that time, and had not really paid attention to the platitudes of my visitors. One of them might have mentioned something about it, and been disappointed at my indifferent reaction. After Fred's intervention, I had to introduce her, Edison Jr, the paladin and Lito, and vaguely gesture towards introducing our fellow travellers, whose names I did not know.

And so we fell in behind a dozen or so mounted soldiers riding in double file, with a similar number following behind. We moved downhill through open land that began as a sea of dead yellow grass and eventually became a wasteland of bare stones and sand with little vegetation at all.

"It is said," Lito explained as we went, "that a giant boar laid waste to the land around Lith Tillac a thousand years ago, angry that it could not break down the walls of the city. Nothing has grown here since; it resists all attempts to cultivate it."

Fred was having none of that. "The mythological boar is people," she snorted. "People cut the trees down, either to burn them, build houses, or to grow crops. It's what they always do. Clearing the forest reduced the rain and increased evaporation, so the trees never grew back; if enough damage is done, increasing aridity is inevitable."

"Fred, I think you'd like F3," I said.

"Some say it was a dragon," Lito said defensively.

On the face of it, a dragon seemed more likely to cause widespread destruction than a wild boar, even one of colossal size.

Captain Dissus chimed in, telling us that the prevailing theory of the Lith Tillac historians was that the wasteland had indeed been created by a dragon, but that the third Duke Egrom had caused the confusion by adopting not a dragon, but a boar, as Lith Tillac's emblem. The reason for this according to the historians was that many provinces and cities in the Westfold already had dragons as their emblems; as powerful as these symbols were, they were just too common. And so Egrom had opted for the boar, which no other state in the Westfold used, which in turn eventually gave rise to the idea that the dragon had in fact been a boar.

At some stage that afternoon the path started drifting back westwards, and it occurred to me that we might be going out of our way. Then in a large village we reached a four-way junction, and instead of going due south, we began to follow a route that took us nearly south west.

"Should we be taking the south road?" I asked Dissus. "Our destination is the Golden Tower."

"Your accommodation is set for tonight," Dissus said. "After a refreshing night's sleep, your onward journey will be easier."

"You mean you've been ordered to take us to Lith Tillac, whether we want to call in there or not."

For a moment Dissus said nothing, but as we emerged from the built-up area of the village, Lith Tillac itself could be seen in the distance below us. Then he spoke, but only to say: "It isn't far out of your way."

I didn't see the point in arguing. In any case, Lith Tillac was Lito's destination, and we should see him safely there before parting ways. So I just laughed at the captain's evasion and rode on next to him.

Lith Tillac probably counted as an enormous city in these post-apocalyptic times, but as impressive as it was from our viewpoint, I thought it would have been considered to be no more than a small town in the days before the Quacker. Naturally it had large buildings that were better looking than the cities of my day; Lith Tillac had a consistent design theme, all its buildings being formed in a similar style, of the same pinkish stone, while the pre-Quacker conurbations were composed of seemingly random buildings dropped in seemingly random arrangements.

Lith Tillac sat between two arms of a mountain, which rose up to the west behind it and disappeared into shrouding clouds. Its outer limit was what looked from here to be a low wall of great thickness joining the two arms of the mountain, a mile or more out from the city proper. This very practical-looking feature was studded every one hundred metres or so by what looked like very non-practical features: finger-thin towers with crenelated tops, several of which had suffered minor or major collapses over the years, proving just how non-practical they were. That no rebuilding had been undertaken seemed to confirm that point.

A river ran straight from the city, across its hinterland and through a broad grate in the outer wall, running right to left below us to the east. Enterprising folk had dug irrigation ditches into its banksides to permit the growing of crops, but from the mere smattering of green that I could see from here, they weren't having much luck.

A taller wall bounded the city itself, and there were other defensive structures within, including an old castle that Dissus pointed to and named as the Kirlo. Furthest away from us, and at the city's highest point as it rose up the mountain's lower slopes, was the Duke's palace, complete with a collection of towers as delicate-seeming from here as those of the outer wall. Dissus called it Clearview Palace, and noted that cynical locals called it "Clearwater Palace" because in times of drought the trickle of mountain water that arrived in the palace was already undrinkable by the time the lower reaches of the city had the chance to collect some of it.

I had probably known the Duke's name at some point, or at least someone in Lar had told me it once, at which point I had promptly filed the information in the round metal filing cabinet in the corner. But without having to ask directly, I managed to get Dissus to say his name, and his wife the Duchess's: Kosken and Parmellia.

We went down the slope along a dusty road, reaching the river at the point where a bridge crossed it, and rather than crossing over to the south, began to follow it upstream towards the city. The river was lifeless and grey, the stink rising from it ranging from unpleasant to nauseating moment by moment on the whim of the gentle breeze. No plants choked the river's banks and margins, and there was no sign of bird life there, or any kind of life at all for that matter. It was, in effect, an open sewer.

The outer wall was punctured by a gateway that was larger than it had seemed when I had first seen it. My far-off estimate of the wall's height was soon proven to be far off indeed. From the village on the ridge, I had imagined the wall to be ten metres high; it now seemed more like thirty. The gateway itself rose to half that height, which seemed unnecessarily high to me, for no visitors of that size would ever need to pass through it. And if a giant boar ever came knocking, the people of Lith Tillac would not be grateful that some ancient architect had given them a pair of doors big enough for them to let it in.

Soon we rode through the gateway, which turned out to be more of a tunnel, thanks to the wall's thickness – and found ourselves in Lith Tillac proper.

The City of Lith Tillac

Once through the broad outer wall of Lith Tillac, we found ourselves in a wide area of abandoned fields full of knee-high, dry dead weeds covered in burs. The weeds had not much in the way of a root, and the breeze here was strong enough to uproot them and send them rolling across the road like tumbleweeds. When they brushed against fur or cloth, the burs broke free from the parent plant and hitched a lift. The abandoned fields in its hinterland gave Lith Tillac a decadent feel. I presumed the weeds had resisted all attempts to eradicate, or even significantly reduce them, until the farmers had simply given up.

I had not been in a city since my two thousand years plus in suspended animation, but to me Lith Tillac seemed quiet, half empty. Yes, sparse crowds lined our way, curious to see me. Some of the children had even painted their faces blue in my honour. But the streets were not as busy as I thought they should be. The children waved at us and cheered. But there were not that many of them. And I noticed that most of them had no shoes. Lito and the paladin sat up straighter in response to our welcome, something that I was hardly capable of. Edison Jr waved back at them. I was a little uncomfortable – feeling a little hemmed in, a little under the spotlight, and a little bit of an imposter. If the children lining our way knew what I had unleashed upon the world, their cheers might quickly turn to jeers.

As it was, I was grateful when we reached our destination. We had been given an entire floor of a hostelry overlooking a wide plaza. Again I got the sense of semi-abandonment. The centrepiece of the plaza was a dried-up fountain showing a goddess raising her hand to the heavens. I found out later that this was a representation of Suilla, goddess of rain, corn and gemstones. It looked as if the people of Lith Tillac had already run out of the first two of the goddess's provisions; I didn't know about the third. Water had once streamed into the air from Suilla's stone hand, symbolising the way she was supposed to bestow rain on the city folk.

There was no need for money, which was fortunate, because I didn't have any. The accommodations of Lith Tillac had apparently engaged in a bidding war, the largest donator to the palace's coffers winning the prize of putting us up at their own expense. This seemed rather odd to me, but the owner of our hotel soon explained that he was planning to make my visit a central selling point of his establishment: the hotel would be renamed the Edison Blue, and have décor inspired by what was known of my adventures, most of it hearsay and incorrect.

Our suite of rooms was on the first floor; the paladin carried me up the stairs, while Lito carried Edison Jr. It was still only early afternoon, and hot in the plaza, so I was disconcerted on looking out of the window to see a small crowd, including several with blue faces, hanging around outside.

"They must be hot," I said to the owner, who had accompanied us upstairs.

"Yes," he said, "excellent point, Lord Hawthorne." He clapped his hands, and when a servant rapidly attended him, he ordered him to go down and try to sell some penny drinks to the crowd. This was not quite what I had intended, but having no money, I was unable to offer to pay for them myself.

About half an hour later I was sitting with Edison Jr on a heap of cushions and wondering how easily we could slip away and get on with our journey without offending the good folk of Lith Tillac, when we had a visitor. A servant entered and told me that Eyya Lile was there to see me, and spoke as if I was expected to know who that was. Needless to say, I didn't. Eyya sounded like a feminine name, but just in case, I adopted a neutral pronoun.

"Send them in." It felt weird to give an order. It felt uncomfortable. I immediately felt sorry for the servant, a thin young man with very short and tidy hair. There were servants of both sexes in what was soon to be the Edison Blue Hotel, and they all wore the same uniform: off-white baggy clothes, with the baggy bits mostly bunched together by thin black ropes. I hurriedly appended the word "please," to my instruction as a tiny gesture towards making the servant feel slightly more human.

My visitor Eyya turned out to be female, just as I had thought. My room was large, and the cushions I was sitting on were right under the window on the side furthest from the door. Eyya stopped just inside the door – what seemed like half a mile away – and waited in silence until the servant had closed the door behind him on his way out before doing anything else. Edison Jr, suddenly shy, moved to hide behind me.

Eyya was a small woman, older than me but still of an age I would grudgingly call young. Her smile was sunny and mischievous and her hair was too orange to be a natural colour. Her full-length, long-sleeved dress was a floral patchwork of orange, purple, red and pink, and the embroidered design seemed to be based on the tendrils and burrs of the weed that covered the city fields.

"Eyya Lile," she said, still standing on the far side of the room. "Always in the sun." She crossed both her arms and then showed me both her palms in a gesture that I remembered Hal using when I had first met him. Both Eyya's palms showed what looked at this range to be small black dots.

"Edison Hawthorne," I said. I didn't bother with the magicians' salute. For obvious reasons, I didn't get up, either.

"Well! You are unorthodox, not to mention as blue as they say you are!" Eyya said with a grin, hurrying over. "And this little chap is a magician too? It's all right, I won't bite."

"Edison Jr," I said, trying to extricate him from behind me. He was clinging to my shoulders, and pulling him into view jarred my bad arm, making me wince.

"How was your journey?"

"Nothing tried to eat us," I replied, still waiting for Eyya Lile to tell us Who the Hell she was, besides someone who was "always in the sun."

"Do you have any better clothes?" Eyya asked.

"No, he doesn't!" Fred squawked, before I could say anything.

"Hello, is that the demon in a box?"

79

I didn't sense a threat from Eyya; nor did I sense much magic in her. What I hoped was a surreptitious glance at Hal's ring confirmed that its light was not bright enough to be seen against the daylight. But I thought it wise to find out who she was, not just what her name was. "Your name is Eyya and you like sunbathing. But who are you working for, and why are you here?"

"Sorry! So sorry! I work for the Duke, or at least, I work for the King, although I've never met him. I'm a King's Magician, like Hal." Here she folded back the lapel of her dress to show me a silver pin badge representing a fist clutching what was either a bunch of flowers or a bunch of feathers. "You might not know, but some magicians serve with the army, like Hal; others work as advisers to regional governments, like me."

"No, I didn't know." I pulled out Fred, who was still surgically attached to F3's battery. "This is Fred. F3 is broken at the moment. I'm hoping they will be able to fix him at the Golden Tower, when we eventually get there."

"They will! Or they might. Try the demonologists on floor seventy. But where did you happen upon a second demon-in-a-box so soon after your other one was broken? Are they so easy to come by?"

I didn't answer that. I was experiencing the slow sinking feeling of someone who thinks they might have made yet another mistake. The first thing I thought of was that Lito was already out trying to sell, as well as his cloth, the drill bits I had salvaged from the bunker. Then I thought of Fred, who was worth a King's ransom.

I had really not thought this through. I should have kept Fred secret, and I should have never given Lito those drill bits to sell.

I felt like someone staggering into a frontier town after a year in the wilderness clutching a single gold nugget the size of a walnut, suddenly aware of human vultures circling, all of them either after my gold or the location of where I had found it.

So I didn't answer. But I didn't have to. After a few seconds, Eyya jabbed a finger at me and said quietly, with a grin: "You got it in the same place you woke the Lich King."

"You know about that?"

"Of course. Hal told me. In any case, the beacons have been lit, and word has come of a black pall rising over Malafert for the first time in oh, five centuries. No doubt people are already fleeing the Cursed Vale out over the high passes back into civilisation."

"Why does anybody live there, if it's cursed?"

Eyya smiled. "It's peaceful there. The grazing is good. As long as you don't go too far down into the valley, the dead don't mind sharing with the living. But it's best not to die there."

"Why not?"

Here Eyya did her best impression of a zombie, causing Edison Jr to dart into hiding again. "Grrrgh. Mind you, plenty of people do venture down the valley, especially if they haven't got long left. It's eternal life of a sort. How's your arm?"

"It's all right," I said.

"Can I look?"

I held my arm out, and Eyya took both it and my hand. "Hold my hand," she commanded. "Squeeze! It's broken, isn't it? I can't do anything for it, I'm afraid. You'll have to wait until you reach the Golden Tower, they'll fix it for you there."

"Well, in that case," I said, "we had better be on our way."

"Ha! Good one. You can't rush off. You're being presented to the Duke tonight."

The Palace

I didn't want to be presented to the Duke. I wanted to be on my way south. I wanted to be rescuing Lexi. And anyway, I hate hereditary titles. I'm a republican. I said as much to Fred.

"Pah," was her reply. "From what I have seen of this place, it will not be ready for democracy for another thousand years."

"I am against inherited privilege," I insisted, although I hadn't really thought about such things at all until being required to meet the Duke.

"You are in a hurry to get going," Fred said, "but you are dependent on the Duke's goodwill until we reach the southern border of Lith Tillac. Therefore, you should not antagonise him, nor should the word 'republican' pass your lips again while we are here. Don't mention anything about 'inherited privilege.' Just be polite and accept that you are of an inferior class to him. I'll be pleased to teach you all the etiquette you will need to get through your ordeal." Fred seemed delighted at the prospect of teaching me some manners.

"I don't need any etiquette," I muttered. "And I bow to no man, alive or undead."

I was sent to be bathed in the rear courtyard of the hotel. The soaping and rinsing was inflicted upon me by a large bald man with the facial hair of a walrus, who probably had a second job as a torturer. I was unceremoniously dumped into the sudsy water. At one point I was completely submerged in the large round bath, and probably would have drowned were it not for the torturer relenting after a few seconds and yanking me out.

My old tunic was cut off by this gentleman and tossed on the fire before the bathing began, leaving me as naked as the day I was born, save for the strapping on my arm. New clothes duly arrived, although as you know, I had no means of paying for them. These were white, or almost white, as if trying to prove to everyone how clean they were – which they were, for the time being at least. There were little bits of red check on collars and cuffs; the outfit had the feeling of a chef's uniform, as if I was going to be working in the Duke's kitchen. I was unable to dress myself fast enough for the attendant's liking, so he took over that job too. Then he slicked my wayward hair back with a dollop of fragrant grease and released me back into the paladin's care, who carried me back upstairs.

Then, not long after sunset, the paladin and I set out for the palace. I went some of the way on my skateboard, but we faced so many steps on our way up to the palace that my companion ended up carrying both me and my skateboard for most of the journey. The paladin halted at the palace gates and watched as I rolled on alone – well, not quite alone, because of course I had Fred for company.

Eyya was waiting just inside the gate. "That's miles better," she said, "but I don't know why they went with white. It just shows up the dirt."

"They could have given me dirt-coloured clothes instead," I suggested.

"Exactly! Now, here's what's going to happen. We'll advance across the Great Hall, and I'll present you to the Duke. You'll bow – well, have a go. Do what you can. Only speak if spoken to. Address the Duke as 'Your Grace' –"

"He knows," Fred snapped. "I've told him."

"Never, ever turn your back on the Duke, even when departing," Eyya said, unflapped by Fred's interruption. "Don't ramble in your responses. Anything else? Yes. From left to right, you will see the Earl Oxil Denarion, the Duke, Duchess Parmellia, and Princess Maralla. Other advisors and hangers-on you don't need to know."

"Great," I said, in a tone of voice that made it plain I didn't mean it.

"Good! Ready? Let's go!"

Eyya strode off across the palace courtyard; I rolled along slowly in her wake. I was quite slow by nature on my board, but I think it would be fair to say that I did not make my best speed. She annoyed me, so I decided to make her slow down – which she soon was forced to do. With that small victory in my pocket, guards opened ornate doors in front of us, and we entered the main hall side by side.

There was a long distance between us and the four thrones at the other end of the hall. But I could already hear a little *tink-tink-tink* sound and see that Duke Wotsisname was tapping something thin and metallic against the arm of his throne.

It was one of the drill bits I had given Lito.

I winced inwardly while fixing a bland expression on my face, feeling outwitted already in an interrogation that hadn't even begun yet. Rolling forwards beside Eyya, I racked my brains for suitable rhetorical tactics, but came up blank.

As I might have mentioned, the hall was long. This gave me a few seconds to think about things as we advanced between the two lines of fat columns that held up the distant ceiling. Fred would probably describe the ceiling as "vaulted," although it was far too high for anyone to ever jump over it. Sideways glances told me that the walls of the place were lined with guards, statues, coats-of-arms, shields, plaques with writing on that would probably resolve into unintelligible squiggles like something generated by primitive AI when you got close enough, weapons and pedestals with a variety of urns sitting on them.

The far wall, behind the thrones, looked to have three mounted dragons' heads on it. Well, they were definitely dragons' heads, but I was not sure whether they had ever been alive. Taxidermy, or sculpture? It was hard to tell, but they had certainly been painted blue at some point, because the paint was flaking off leaving darker ground colour beneath. The effect, a little like dry brushing on a D&D figurine, did make the heads look quite imposing, real or ersatz.

The floor, meanwhile, was a skateboarder's dream. Smooth, and polished, I felt as if one good punt would send me from one end of the hall to the other. It wouldn't, because my wheels were rubbish; but it was far better terrain than I was used to. Lighting was in the form of giant chandeliers, high overhead, each glowing with the flames of sixty or seventy fat candles. These Medieval light fixtures were suspended from chains attached to the columns, meaning that some mug had to lower them down at dusk, light the army of candles, and hoist them up again.

Naturally I had already forgotten who I was about to be presented to. *Think, Edison!* I told myself. The two most important people were probably the ones on the bigger thrones in the middle of the row of four. Duke Kosken and Duchess Parmesan. Parmellia. On the left, the Duke's son, Earl Oxo – Oxil Denarion, whose second name sounded to my historically-challenged mind like a form of currency in the Roman Empire, and on the right, his bride-to-be, Princess Maralla. They were the Lith Tillac royal family. Like I cared. I was a republican.

The Duke's red outfit reminded me of the style of dress uniform favoured by dictators the world over, coming complete with shiny buttons and pointless adornments. He had a grey wraparound moustache and a chinless beard, a distribution of facial hair that mirrored what he had on top, a band of hair on the back and sides and a bald pate. A glance over to the Earl told me that he was his father's son, with incipient hair loss already visible. The Duchess had an austere look,

84

with long silver hair and a flowing, floor-length, grey-green dress. The Princess looked to be about my age – she had to be ten years the Earl's junior. The deep blue velvety creation she had been forced into wearing had a narrow waist and puffed-up long sleeves. She stared hard at me as if I had somehow wronged her – which I hadn't. Not at that point, at any rate.

Eyya presented me as "Lord Hawthorne," and retired, leaving me sitting alone on the smooth floor about ten metres from the row of thrones and two steps below them.

The interview did not begin brilliantly, and got worse rather than better. The Duke knew about the Lich King, but seemed unconcerned about him. He was more interested by far in the drill bit. Lito had sold this to the owner of a market stall, who had rushed to sell it on to a wealthy merchant, who had bought it and immediately sent it to the Duke with his best wishes. The Duke wanted to know whether the drill bit was obtained in the same place that the Lich King had been entombed? How many more of them were there, what other treasures, other examples of the famous demon-in-a-box perhaps?

It was with something of a sinking feeling that I imagined a post-apocalyptic gold rush with everyone and his dog descending on Lar, or ascending to it, because it was after all mostly uphill, and then ransacking the bunker like seagulls at an abandoned whelk stall. I wanted the people of Lar to benefit from the bunker salvage, not Duke Kosken, even if his city's economy was obviously in serious need of a boost. So I spun a tale that kept as close to the facts as possible. The bunker was a creation of the Old Ones, true, but it was very small by their standards (I justified this lie internally by telling myself the comparison I was making was not with other bunkers, but with other settlements in general). I had not seen any other drill bits there (what I didn't say was that I hadn't looked for any). But (and here I put on my most enthusiastic tone) I had found large quantities of soft paper that the Old Ones had used to wipe their nether regions with.

In the midst of this distraction operation, I began to find Maralla's stare more powerful and unnerving than ever. She was small and dark-haired, and much paler than the rest of the Lith Tillac royals. Her staring eyes were huge and dark.

Help me, O mighty mage.

I suddenly realised that I was hearing Maralla's thoughts.

Inverse Medusa

I am a prisoner here, Princess Maralla thought at me.

What was I supposed to say – or think – to that? I went back with: *I am in no state to help anyone, as you can see, but instead rely on others to help me.*

Evidently she heard me, because a moment later: *You plan to regain your powers.*

Some, I admitted. *Enough to face the Lich King, and save Lexi from him.*

She saw Lexi in my mind's eye. *She's beautiful. I wish I was beautiful.*

I didn't know what to say, or think, in reply to that.

They keep me locked in the tower. They only let me come out on occasions such as this, in case my absence is noticed. Their poverty drove them into this marriage, because the royal family of Toryl Noth are rich, and they knew I would bring money with me. Denarion is a rat. He already has a mistress. He has no interest in me.

This was all very fascinating, but what was *I* supposed to do about it? I was finding it difficult enough just juggling listening to Maralla's telepathic complaints at the same time as discussing the merits of two-thousand-year-old toilet paper with the other three royals.

Listen to me!

I am listening!

Don't ignore me! You're just like them, they ignore me! They can't bear the sight of me!

It occurred to me that perhaps Maralla was not picking up my thoughts very well, or perhaps I wasn't beaming them her way properly.

I'm trying! I thought at her.

But the next time Maralla spoke, she spoke aloud. "I think we should speak about my situation, not the soft paper of the Old Ones."

The Duke tried to ignore her, but–

"You see? All they do is ignore me."

The Duchess, seated beside Maralla, began, "I don't think we should bother our esteemed guest–"

"The fact is, I'm kept locked in my tower room–"

"Maralla, that is enough!" the Duke said sternly.

She didn't think so. Instead of piping down, she leapt out of her throne and moved towards me. "Look at me!" she yelled at the hall at large, spinning around like a top.

But none of the other three did. They all kept facing forwards, so that only when Maralla danced into a position directly in front of them did they see her. "You can't stand the sight of me! Well, I can't stand the sight of you, either!"

"Lord Hawthorne, thank you for coming tonight," the Duke said to me, as if his soon-to-be daughter-in-law really did not exist.

I took the Duke's words as marking the interview's end, and began to roll backwards towards the exit. But I hadn't gone very far when Maralla, dancing and jumping in between me and the Lith Tillac royals, suddenly keeled over. As she went down like a marionette with its strings cut, my first thought was that she was having a seizure. But once on the floor she regained motor control, and grabbed her head in both hands, and writhed and screamed in agony.

None of the royal family moved. The guards around the periphery of the room were as statuesque as the actual statues. The assorted servants and hangers-on behind the thrones did not move either. Perhaps this sort of thing happened all the time. Perhaps this was why Maralla was kept out of sight. Nevertheless, at the risk of causing a diplomatic incident, I stopped trundling backwards, and began trundling towards the stricken Princess.

I did not reach Maralla. After ten seconds, the long-drawn out scream of a Scanners-severity headache came to a halt. And the slightly-dishevelled Princess clambered to her feet. Her hair was awry and she had lost one expensive-looking slipper. Her shoulders were slumped, and her gaze was at her feet.

Then she looked up, and all hell broke loose. Albeit in a quiet way.

First, the Earl slumped in his throne. Then the Duke folded up silently and slid forwards out of his. The Duchess fell sideways. Behind the thrones, the various servants and court staff went down like dominos, falling in sequence as...

...Maralla's gaze swept across them from left to right.

My gentle forwards trundling, which had more or less dwindled to nothing as Maralla regained her feet, suddenly became a vigorous backpedalling, or backhanding.

Movement by the walls made the Princess look that way, and the guards there went down with a clatter of armour and dropped weapons. In less time than she had spent on the ground in agony, Maralla had laid waste to everyone else in the throne room – except me.

The target of my frantic skateboard-pushing was the nearest column. I had no hope that I could reach the entrance door before I suffered the same fate as the others in the throne room. In the absence of any other sounds, the noise of my rolling wheels must inevitably draw this Medusa's gaze.

But Maralla faced front and did nothing long enough for me to get behind the pillar of pink stone.

"What happened?" Fred asked.

"I don't know," I whispered. "Maralla just looked at them, and they keeled over. I don't know if they're dead, or–"

But I realised that one of the nearby guards was snoring, implying that he was probably still alive. Presumably the others were no worse than asleep either. So that was a great relief.

"They said I was cursed," Maralla said. The quietness of her voice told me she was still facing away. "Are you hiding from me, Lord Hawthorne?"

I couldn't tell what tone of voice her question came with: was she making sure I was safe from her gaze, or was she tormenting me?

"Call me Edison," I said.

"My mother couldn't bond with me," Maralla went on, ignoring me. "She was a hideous thing, although she began beautiful, when she had me, she was still beautiful. They gave her this medicine... it came from the Electrum mines at Syanabyan... turned her blue, like you. No, not like you. Not a nice sky blue, like you. My mother went a ghastly silver blue, as if she was turning into metal... and it ruined her. They said it was her illness, but it wasn't. The medicine was worse. But what can a child do, or say?"

The Princess had lost her mind, and with her madness had come the ability to strike people down from afar. I had thought of her as a Medusa, but at least in one way she was less frightening: her victims only ended up taking a nap, not turning to stone. But in another way, she was *more* frightening. She only had to look at you to make the magic work, whereas you actually had to look at Medusa for her magic to petrify you.

"They're still alive, aren't they?"

"I can hear snoring," I said.

"Pity."

"You can't go around hexing people like that," I told her, ready at any glimpse of a midnight blue dress to inch around the column in what would inevitably be a hopeless attempt to stay out of Maralla's sight.

"Hexing? Is that what I did?"

"I don't know what you did. Fred, diplomacy mode on," I said, and slid her (still bundled to F3, of course) out from behind the pillar in a vaguely forwards direction. The two omnis made quite a good hockey puck, sliding easily across the polished floor.

"Hello, your highness," Fred said, before she had even stopped spinning, "I wonder whether I could be of assistance to you."

"The demon in a box. I had not heard that you were female."

"My predecessor adopted an androgynous voice, which was the preference of his owner, Edison."

89

At this point Maralla was probably looking at Fred. If so, her magic did not work on omnis. That was something. But beyond feeling slightly relieved about it, all I could do for the moment was listen.

"You do not interest me, demon."

"I may be able to think of a solution to the current situation, one that benefits all parties."

"Explain."

"Well, if you would be kind enough to tell me what outcome to today's events you would prefer to see, I may be able to devise a way to make it happen. For example, do you wish to return home to Toryl Noth, and your family there?"

"Toryl Noth? No, how could I? It would mean betraying my family's trust. They sent me here to join our House with that of Lith Tillac, and I must fulfil their wishes."

I supposed that the diplomats of the Houses of Lith Tillac and Toryl Noth had quite different futures in mind when they came up with the idea of arranging a marriage for young Princess Maralla, but neither had envisaged her sending the entire court to sleep – literally.

"I wonder," Fred asked. "Do you think that if you were at home, you could be around people, and look at them, without knocking them out? Do you have control over your power?"

"I don't know the answer, demon," Maralla said, "but it is an interesting question." Then: "Guards!" Louder: "GUARDS!"

A few seconds later came the sound of running booted feet. This was closely followed by the sound of several guards falling over, immediately struck unconscious.

That was a no, then. I hoped none of them had fallen on their swords.

"Oh dear," Fred said.

"You'll have to wear a blindfold," I called out.

"I will not!"

"Perhaps you could retire to your bedroom, and never look out of the window..." Fred suggested.

"Make myself a prisoner? Don't be ridiculous."

"Perhaps you could find a remote place, far from any other people, and live there by yourself?"

I could have told Fred that suggesting this to a princess was not going to go down well. Diplomacy mode indeed. Well, if diplomacy fails, what happens next? I wished idly for F3, who would be able to solve the problem instantly if he could only induce Maralla to pick him up. A quick zap and I could scoot over, and somehow blindfold her and tie her up with my one good hand. As plans went, it was pretty thin, but it was more than I had in the real world.

"Demon, you are forgetting that I am a princess," Maralla said. As I had predicted, the answer was no.

As you know, my magic levels were in the gutter. Still, I had a few joules in the battery for an emergency such as this. Could I strike Maralla blind? I could make her pupils opaque, or fill the room with fog... the former I could not stomach the thought of, and the latter was too magically costly. Then I had the idea to blow out the great hall's candles, which cost me almost nothing; it was just a brief swirl of wind. And immediately darkness reigned – although it was not *absolute* darkness. Some light still crept in through the door at the far end of the hall, and the high windows glowed with fading post-sunset grey.

"You don't trust me, Hawthorne?" Maralla asked accusingly.

"Of course," I yelled. "I'm just worried that you'll glance at me by accident, er, before we solve things."

(Before I find a sneaky way to knock you out.)

The entranceway to the throne room was quite a long hallway, and a number of large mirrors with ornate gilt frames were arranged along its length. I had rolled past these on the way in unthinkingly – well, if I had a thought, it was that they must have been put there so that party-goers in centuries past could admire themselves and their splendid costumes on their way to the festivities in the throne room. Now a sneaky plan began to form.

"Please turn around, Princess," I called. "I'm coming out."

"It's safe," Maralla said.

Fred said nothing, which I took to mean I was good to go. Emerging, I saw that Maralla was indeed still facing the other way. Of course, she could turn around at any moment...

What's the time, Princess Wolf?

"How are you feeling after all that? Are you tired?"

"Tired?"

"Whenever I do magic, it drains my energy. I just wondered if it is like that for you."

"I don't think so."

This either meant that Maralla's battery was full to brimming, or that her magic was of a kind entirely different to mine. That Hal's ring wasn't glowing argued for the latter. "Can you do other kinds of magic?" A side-plan occurred to me, that of getting her to pour herself into one of the urns decorating the palace, and then stopping it up. An oldie but a goodie.

"No. I did not know until just now that I could do... *that.*"

"Perhaps we should go for a walk to discuss this," I hazarded. "Well, you could walk and I could roll."

"Let me guess. You would like for us to wander down the entrance hall, where all the mirrors are, in the hope that I might catch a glimpse of my own image and accidentally use this power on myself?"

Plan A was a bit too obvious, then.

"It's disappointing that you would try such a crude ploy. And if I saw myself in the mirror, I would probably see you, too, beside me. Had you thought of that?"

I hadn't. What I had done though was trundle to within ten feet of where Maralla was standing over Fred. My stand-in omni was drawing the Princess's gaze by displaying a series of kaleidoscopic patterns like a twentieth-century screensaver. Fred's screen was by now quite the brightest source of illumination in the throne room.

Maralla knelt to pick Fred up, who said: "Time for a social media profile pic," and showed the view from one of her front-facing cameras: Maralla's face.

The Princess shrieked, and let go of Fred as if burnt. She did not, alas, faint at the sight of herself.

"It's not that bad. We can always use a filter on it," Fred said, clattering to the floor.

It was time for Plan Z. I lunged for Maralla. Most of the impetus for this move came from my one good arm, so it was less than impressive. When I hit the Princess, both of us screamed: she at the indignity of being grabbed, me by the pain that shot up my broken arm.

Of course, as soon as the shock of being manhandled by a blue commoner had worn off, she tried to look at me. Fred had the presence of mind to turn her screen off, so it was suddenly rather dark in the throne room. And I managed to get the elbow of my left arm over Maralla's eyes. My flesh was only separated from the hex stare by a thin layer of material, but it seemed to be keeping me safe for now. The Princess screamed a second time, and tried to throw me off. But my good arm was quite wiry, and she was built like an aristocrat. I held on.

The sound of running feet. Guards responding to the sound of a scream. They brought lit oil lamps. I can only imagine what they made of the scene that met their eyes: everyone in the throne room seemingly dead, and me apparently throttling their Princess on the floor.

"Unhand the Princess!" one of them bellowed as they neared.

I obliged, just for a moment, taking care to stay out of the line of Maralla's sight.

Four guards went down like skittles.

"PA-LA-DIN!" I yelled.

"GUARDS!" Maralla yelled.

The paladin, it seemed, had already begun to move our way at the sound of the screams, for he was the next to appear.

"Edison?" he asked, equally bewildered by what he saw.

"Help me to hold her down! Cover her eyes!"

"What?"

"She's got hex vision!"

The paladin had no idea what I meant, and he had no time to do anything before the next batch of guards piled into the throne room – six of them this time.

Maralla heard them, of course, and shouted: "Get these ruffians off me!"

"Get out of the way!" I yelled at the paladin, who eventually moved to an angle that I deemed relatively safe. I removed my temporary blindfold, hoping to repeat the trick on the new set of guards... but this time Maralla kept her eyes firmly shut tight. Before I could think of anything to do, the paladin moved back into her line of sight, so I had to shift my elbow down again.

"Don't hurt anybody!" I told him, as he barged into the guards, sending several of them flying. But the paladin found himself surrounded by armed men a few moments later, and it seemed as if he was going to be the one to end up hurt.

"STOP!" came a new voice from behind me. "Put your weapons away." I belatedly recognised the voice: the Duke's.

I realised that, all around the room, the first tranche of knocked-out people were waking up.

"Find something to cover Princess Maralla's eyes and bind her hands," the Duke ordered. "Escort her to her rooms."

Dinner for Two

After a moment of silence in due deference to the departed eagles, Tailor led Lexi and Bartlet back down the steps to the Moon Lab.

"Were you here in those days?" Lexi asked Tailor.

"Yes, My Lady, although I was not the tailor then. I was a lowly footman. As the permanent staff has shrunk over the centuries, the remainder have had to take on more responsibilities."

"It's sad about the eagles. Such beautiful birds."

"Pah!" Bartlet snorted. "Malafert could not have known that the spreading darkness would upset his pets so. And he had no choice anyway; if he wanted permanent darkness, he would have had to choose it over the eagles."

They had reached the Moon Lab. Tailor and Lexi both glanced at one another to gauge the other's reaction to Bartlet's dismissive tone. Lexi saw, more by Tailor's glance than any expression on his mostly inscrutably-withered face, that Bartlet's disrespect of the first days of the first Lich King's reign, of the days before that day, did not sit right with him.

"You died as a very old man," Lexi surmised. She deliberately spoke to the tailor, not Bartlet.

"Yes," Tailor said. "Then I rose and began my work anew."

They passed through the Moon Lab and descended the stairs to the throne room. "But you don't hate the living?"

"Of course he does," Bartlet snapped, before Tailor could answer. "How could he not hate a group of people who are always trying to destroy him?"

This time, because they were filing down the stairs, Lexi could not gauge Tailor's reaction. But she resolved to keep asking awkward questions in hope of driving a wedge between Malafert's staff and their new king.

Once in the throne room, Tailor hurried to stand on the wolf's head in the central star. From there he indicated the six thrones with a broad sweep of all four arms. "Each Undying King created his own throne, and placed it on the right-hand side of his predecessor's." He pointed to each throne in turn, going anticlockwise. The first, and largest, was Malafert's. This was made of dark oak held together by rusted iron bolts. The second, square and of black stone, belonged to Omenerat. The third, of skulls and limb bones warped and melted together, was Tursul's. Craxellar's was of forged iron, Arenerod's of pale grey stone slabs that had formerly been gravestones, and the sixth, Hartemon's, was of half-melted green glass bottles.

There was room for another thirty such thrones before the circle would be complete. But Tailor lamented that the tower itself would not last long enough for another thirty Lich Kings to rise. Nothing was forever.

"I am," Bartlet said, and went to sit in Malafert's throne. "I shall have this one."

Lexi watched intently for Tailor's reaction to this sacrilege. As she had hoped, he stiffened noticeably. "My Lord," he said, "that is within your rights. I should though note that the traditional norm is for no new Lich King to use the seat of one of his predecessors, but to build their own thrones anew. That way, each throne serves as a monument to its owner's reign."

Bartlet leapt off the throne so quickly it seemed almost as if he had been burnt. He bore down on Tailor, who did not flinch from his new master. "Is that so? Then find me coffins. I will make a throne of them. The dead will need them no more, for my reign will be eternal."

*

Shortly afterwards, Tailor showed Lexi to her room, which was two floors below the throne room. In between was the dining room, which Lexi merely glimpsed as they passed; it was dominated by a single long table, with display cases along the walls.

"You are no monster, for all that you are an undead," Lexi said to Tailor.

"I am a loyal servant to the rightful master of Malafert and the Blessed Vale, as I always have been and always will be," he replied. "Handmaiden will be along shortly with your clean attire. Please don't try to escape in the meanwhile."

Lexi's stateroom was large, filling a full quarter of the tower's floor area. It was draughty, with mullioned windows without glass; one of the mullions had collapsed, leaving a gap easily large enough to climb out. She poked her head through and saw, a dizzying distance below, the same black rocks and grey waves smashing to white that she had seen from the tower top. Moth-eaten rags of curtains flanked the windows, flapping in the breeze. Malafert did not have visitors very often.

The bed was a worm-eaten four-poster whose curtains were in little better condition than those by the windows. The mattress had probably once been comfortable, but there seemed little left of its structure.

The other furniture was a dressing table with a jug and bowl – an unidentifiable crust was visible in the bottom of the latter – a toilet behind yet another ragged curtain with an open drop below it, a cupboard and some drawers. The cupboard contained bedding that fell to pieces when Lexi tried to remove it; the drawers were empty. Altogether it took her only a minute to search the room; she was leaning out of the window into the cold sea breeze staring up at the Clockwork's black cloud five minutes later when there was a quiet knock on the door.

After much fumbling with the lock, the handmaiden rocked her way into the room. She was carrying a green dress over one arm. Lexi saw that her hands were twisted into claws and had apparently lost most of their dexterity.

"I will kill him," was Lexi's greeting. She was thinking about Edison, and how he was probably on his way to try to rescue her. Edison could not beat Bartlet, so it was going to be up to her to find some way to do that before Edison arrived.

"You cannot," Handmaiden said. "His death is not your gift to give. And the King can never die; he can only unlive."

"Then I'll unkill him."

The handmaiden cackled at that.

The dress was of green velvet, of which several patches were missing. It was full length, with quarter sleeves, and trim that had once probably been off-white, but was now brown. Handmaiden fished a string of large blue pearls from her pocket and made Lexi stoop so that she could hang them around her neck.

The moment drew her closer to an undead than Lexi could ever want to get. She looked down at Handmaiden's white hair and withered skin as the old undead tried to fasten the string of pearls with her claw-like hands and suddenly felt sorry for her.

"How long have you been working here, Handmaiden?" she asked.

"I don't know, My Lady. A long, long time, that is for sure."

"What do you do when there is no Lich King to serve?"

"Keep things tidy. Sweep the floors. Mend things." At last Handmaiden managed to cinch the fastener, for she let go and stepped back. Then she began to rock towards the door, which was still open. "Dinner will be announced shortly."

About half an hour later, Butler knocked and entered the room. He bowed silently and gestured upwards: dinner was served. He led Lexi back up to the floor above and held the door to the dining room open for her.

Tailor and Bartlet were already in the dining room; Tailor was showing Bartlet an exhibit in one of the display cases. Lexi could read the label on the display case from across the room; it was written in large letters of gold leaf and stood out against the dark wood of the cabinet.

THE SHARDS OF THE SWORD OF AN UNNAMED PALADIN, WHO BRAVELY TRIED TO SABOTAGE THE CLOCKWORK IN THE REIGN OF CRAXELLAR

Approaching, Lexi could see several large steel shards in the display case, as well as the sword's hilt with a jagged stub of blade still attached to it.

"The Clockwork is made of adamant, and therefore cannot be harmed by steel," the tailor was explaining.

"What became of the paladin?"

"He had a change of heart. He is now Your Majesty's guard."

The tailor seated Lexi and Bartlet at opposite ends of a table that could have seated twenty-four diners. Bartlet's dinner was a glass of blood; for the living there was meat that had probably been dried two hundred years before, some unidentifiable and unpleasant pickle probably jarred at a similar date, and some freshly-baked flatbread. This was served with wine that looked as red as the blood Bartlet was drinking. A few candles on the table added to the lighting from the wall lamps.

Bartlet drained his dinner in a few gulps. "Were any of my predecessors married?"

"No, Your Majesty," Tailor replied.

"Then there are no protocols – no traditional norms – for our wedding."

"Other senior royals have married the still-living, that is, during their second lives," Tailor explained. "The weddings take place on the winter solstice – and the victim – I mean bride – has her blood drained by her groom as part of the ceremony. A cannula is used to collect the blood into a cup, and all the guests partake of it, symbolising the bride becoming part of the royal family."

Bartlet stared at Lexi down the length of the table. He spoke to Tailor like a landowner discussing one of a tenant farmer's livestock. "We can't wait until winter."

"It may be arranged sooner than that if My Lord wishes. First your new Queen must confide her name in you, that we might write it on the marriage contract between you, for it to be valid for time immemorial."

The room seemed to darken. "You are my servant, are you not?" Bartlet asked quietly, his voice full of menace.

"I am, Your Majesty."

"Then why are you taking her side? Why did you divulge this information in her presence, not when we were alone? Why would she tell me her name now?" Bartlet looked as if he was resisting the temptation to crush his goblet. "We will have to proceed anyway. I will give her a name… Willow. We will call her Willow, after the undying tree."

The tailor bowed awkwardly. "My apologies, My Lord. I did not think that she would withhold her name, or that you would try to wed her against her will. That would not be possible."

"Why not?" Bartlet demanded. "Am I not King? Can I not decide what happens?"

"This is a solemn contract between you, sealed by unbreakable vows, that both must make earnestly and willingly."

"And if I marry her anyway?"

"She will be undead, and your slave. But she will be a pale shadow of what she is now."

"Woman, will you be my bride?" Bartlet barked at Lexi.

Lexi roundly ignored him.

"I said will you marry me!"

"Who me?"

"Who else do you think I'm talking to? Him?"

"The answer is no."

Bartlet banged the table. "Why not? That other? That weakling who could not protect you from me? Your former husband was blue like me, so you cannot hold my colour against me."

"He wasn't my husband, but I would have said yes if he had asked."

"The feelings were one-sided then."

"No. He loves me, but he would never ask that question."

"Why not?"

"Because he does not consider himself worthy."

"Well, that is because he was not worthy. I am going to ask for your hand, and I won't take no for an answer."

"The answer is no. I already told you that."

"My dear, you can either be my undying bride, or my undying slave. It will be for you to decide which."

"You are dead. Vile. Violent. Rude. Aggressive. Disgusting. I would prefer to marry the tailor."

The dried-up old undead tailor stiffened in shock at this suggestion.

Bartlet seemed about to snap back at Lexi, but composed himself. "I will win your affection, dear Willow," he said gently.

"My name is not Willow."

"What would you like me to call you?"

"Prisoner."

"Would you like to know how I died, Prisoner?" Bartlet asked. Without awaiting Lexi's reply, he went on: "I was outside when the Quantum Zero Counterfactual Decoherence Device was used. We had expected it for days, but after a series of false alarms, life at Foxburrow was quite normal. I was outside with a colleague when the alert came in; he panicked and drove back to the bunker, abandoning me three miles down the mountain at the hydroelectric plant.

"By the time I had run back up the mountain, Foxburrow was sealed up tight. The cowards would not dare to open the door to let me in, in case the weapon went off when the door was open. So I argued with them and they stood firm and after ten minutes – during which time the door could have been opened and closed five times – the weapon was actually used.

"The first sign of it was a gleam of pink light spilling over the edges of the hills. Then a flash! Looking down, I could see the bones of my hands as if in an X-Ray. I remember a sensation of inversion, as if I was upside down, back to front, and inside out. Some strange force lifted me into the air and dropped me again. The plants around – tiny things, mosses – grew to enormous size, the size of houses. But as fast as they grew, they withered again at once and died back, changing from vivid green to oily purplish colours, slime, sludge... by that time I could not move at all. I don't think I even had physical form. I felt like a watching, passive pair of eyes just staring out at that insane, rainbow outburst of impossible life.

"Then the shockwave reached me, and I was picked up, flung along, thrown into rocks, my bones smashed... then I was dragged back again along the ground, banging into things, half-drowning in a tide of slime.

"Then pale fire stormed out of the sky, tiny flames landing and burning in the dead grass like a million candles. The fire spread and I found myself burning, but I could not do anything about it, I could only let myself burn. Then oblivion took me. But I was not dead, for an unknown time later I came to. All around me strange life forms were growing up to vast size and just being blown away in the storm.

"I crawled back to Foxburrow, and then, eventually, they took pity on me, on my wrecked body, and took me inside. Then I died. Then, an unknown time later, I lived again, athirst for human blood and bent on revenge. Ha! How they ran from me. How they hid!"

"You murdered all the people in the bunker?" Lexi asked coldly.

"They deserved it," Bartlet said dismissively, "for not letting me in. And anyway, I was doing them a favour. They would have died anyway. Instead of wasting away in the dark, they died with their blood on my lips."

"Only a few kept the door. The others were innocent," Lexi argued.

"Those who weren't running from me were trying to kill me. And then – when I could sense no more of them alive – I rested... I slept... I dreamed... and it was not until when you, my bride to be, came to Foxburrow that finally I awoke."

There was a short pause, and Tailor took advantage of it to make an announcement. "Your Majesty, I have news. The Army of the Blessed has arrived."

101

The Army of the Blessed's Orders

Lexi, Bartlet and the tailor climbed all the way back up to the top of the Black Tower. By now it was fully dark, the black disk emanating from the Clockwork all but invisible against the night sky.

"They are below," Tailor said.

Bartlet strode fearlessly to the tower's edge to look, heedless of the dark, the gusting wind and the sheer drop that awaited a misstep. Lexi followed, keeping her distance from him, using one of the Eyrie's columns for security as she too peered down. At first she could see nothing, because it was too dark; then with a snap of his fingers Bartlet caused a miniature blue star to appear. The star fell slowly, illuminating the scene below as it descended.

And Lexi saw dead people. She could not count them, for there were too many for that. She guessed their numbers to total ten thousand, although many others might have been out of sight around the other sides of the tower. What she saw was not really an army, but a rabble. Some were plainly armed, often with spears; some were armoured. Others appeared to have no weapons at all and no armour and might well have been dead civilians, not warriors. From this height it was too difficult to tell.

"They await your instructions, My Lord," Tailor said.

"Regarding what?" Bartlet demanded.

"Should they drive the living from the Blessed Vale? How should they deal with those they overtake, if so?"

Bartlet turned to Lexi. "Your name?"

"Prisoner."

"Will you marry me?"

"Never."

Bartlet sneered and said, "So be it." He turned his attention to those below, and shouted in a resonant voice reinforced by magic, "Reclaim what is yours! Drive the arrogant living out of your territory! Kill them where you find them, and make them join your ranks!"

The Army of the Blessed didn't cheer those orders. They could not. But a drumming sound rose up from below, the noise of thousands of spears banging against the citadel's stonework.

After that, Tailor began to lead the way back to the stairs. Bartlet followed, but Lexi lingered on the precipice, still clinging to the eagle's column.

"Go ahead! Jump!" Bartlet told her. "I won't try to save you. But I *will* have Tailor sew you back together."

"Don't flatter yourself," Lexi said. "If you want to drive me to suicide, you'll have to try harder." And with that, she detached herself from the column and followed the other two back inside the tower. She knew that she really did have to find a way to kill Bartlet, and soon.

South!

We left Lith Tillac at dawn on the morning after the pandemonium at the palace. I half-expected to get tossed in a dungeon, being blamed for triggering whatever had happened to Princess Maralla. But luckily that didn't happen. Instead, the Duke thanked me for my help, and even seemed to forget about the drill bit and the bunker hoard altogether. Maralla meanwhile was locked in her tower rooms, with strict instructions not to so much as try to peep through her keyhole. Carpenters were summoned to board up her windows, lest her gaze stray down to city folk passing on the streets below.

"Is there a cure?" the Duke asked me in the aftermath, as if I was some sort of expert in the laws of magic.

I didn't have an answer for him, but I promised to ask at the Golden Tower.

Before we left, I asked Eyya to look out for Maralla – without actually looking *at* her or vice versa.

"You are a strange one!" Eyya said. "My job here is to support the Duke's family."

"Who else will look out for her, if not you? And she's about to marry into the family."

"Edison, I rather think the wedding's off, don't you?"

"Please."

"All right! I'll do what I can. It's not as if they're going to poison her food or something."

Which was a rather odd thing to say.

On arriving back at the hotel that evening, I urged Lito to drop everything and rush back to Lar as fast as he could, gather together as many people as he could find, and strip the bunker from top to bottom.

"Are you sure it's safe?"

"Yes," I said. "Absolutely."

A pause.

"Probably."

We were followed by a hundred supporters as we left the city, some of the smaller ones wearing blue facepaint as before. The crowd dwindled as we went, so that by the time we reached the bridge and parted ways with Lito (who had latched onto a small group of merchants heading north) we were down to the twenty most enthusiastic followers. A mile further along the road, we were on our own again.

The day warmed as we headed south. Actually, for quite a bit of the first day we headed a long way east of south, following a track that became increasingly less well used as we went. We passed nobody coming the other way, which at least saved on all the useless rituals and chitchat. It was soon too hot, and none of us were happy, including Speckle and Goliath; around midday we found a little copse of scrubby trees to shelter in from the worst of the sun.

A curious waymarker of two colours of rock, dark and pale, stood on the track opposite the copse. The pale stones made up the top half of the column, and the dark stones the rest. This apparently told a traveller unfamiliar with the road how far it was to the next water: half a day, according to the paladin.

"How does it know which way we're going?" I asked.

"It's on the right, so we're going the right way to find the water," the paladin said, as if this was fairly obvious.

Sure enough, we came across water that evening – or at least a fully dark-rock column indicating that some was nearby. "It's like a sort of Stone Age fire hydrant sign," I said.

The water turned out to be in a storm-cut channel running under a primitive bridge. This had been deepened by successive travellers taking their spades to it, and appeared at least damp. The paladin dug some sediment out, hitting water after only six inches; but he had to dig on for a while to make a puddle big enough for Speckle and Goliath to drink from.

On each day after the first we travelled in two stints – once from before the dawn until it became too hot and then in the cool of the evening and after dark. In the heat of the day, we were usually able to find shelter in one of the dry channels that dissected the landscape, some of which were deep enough for their flat bottoms to be well shaded; other, shallower channels had been improved by earlier travellers by the excavation of overhangs to help the weary to hide from the full force of the sun.

We met our first travellers going the other way not long after dawn on the third day. These two men on horseback were visible from a mile away, and by the time the distance between us had halved I knew who they were and wanted to send Speckle galloping up to meet them. But I knew I should conserve her energy. Water was hard to find, and the forage along the roadside was sorely limited.

"Hawthorne," said one of the men, as our two parties drew near to one another. "Edison Hawthorne." He was wearing a long blue gown covered from top to bottom by iridescent butterflies. His companion was dressed in leather armour, and wore a hooded black cape around his shoulders.

"Hal! Jasso!" I yelled.

I hugged them both one-armed from the saddle, Hal first and then Jasso, trying not to squash Edison Jr in the process. "It's been a while," Jasso said. "You're still alive, I see." This he addressed to me while I hugged him. Then he rode on a step or two to shake the paladin's hand.

"Any news of Lexi?" I asked Hal.

"No," he said. "We have no eyes in Malafert. All we know is that the black pall is spreading, and people are fleeing over the high passes out of the Cursed Vale into Achi Lomm and Erras. Erras is our destination. There is a chance that the dead will try to come through a mountain pass called the Miser, and the garrison there is small."

"Small!" Jasso snorted. "According to the paymaster, there are a hundred soldiers there. But I wouldn't be surprised if we find the fort abandoned altogether when we get there."

"We turn west towards the Barrier this morning," Hal said. "Meanwhile, you should reach the Golden Tower in three days."

At this point I tried to give Hal his magic ring back, but he refused it with a laugh. "You are going to dark places, Edison, and in those places you might find traces of magic. Where I am going to tread, all magic was depleted long ago."

"I might find light traces in dark places. Gottit."

We had hardly had five minutes together when Hal announced that it was time for them to move on. I saw the sense in this, for the sun was inexorably rising in the sky. But I delayed Hal and Jasso long enough to mention our encounter with Maralla.

The ever-practical Jasso opined that there was too much risk in leaving the Princess alive. I was reminded of an encounter in Crickne – probably about four hundred miles north of here – and how ruthlessly he had killed the magician Klim who had been trying to steal my power. Jasso was not someone who left things to chance. Hal though was of quite different character: he thought that keeping Maralla locked up was safe enough for both the palace residents and the Princess, at least for the time being.

"Things change," Jasso said dourly, "except when they're dead."

Lost in the Haze

We rode on south through a parched yellow landscape of dust, sand and bare rock. At times the road was completely buried under drifts of sand, and only the periodic waymarkers assured us that we were on the right track. The days were cloudless, the sun hot in a brilliant blue sky; the nights were cold, the sky an incredible vista of thousands of stars. Most of the desert was barren of even dead plants, but the next morning we reached a stretch where there was a fossilised forest of burnt black trees. It seemed that a great fire had swept this place once, a fire that had consumed all but the larger branches of the trees and from which the land had never recovered.

As we moved through the dead forest, a curious mist began to close in around us. The temperature dropped, which was a welcome change at first. Soon our vision was reduced to a hemisphere about ten metres in radius. It was a hemisphere at whose centre stood Goliath and Speckle, and the only things we could see around us were two or three of the petrified trees, looming out of the haze in front of us and disappearing back into it in our wake.

The drifts of sand around us took on a curious appearance in the diffuse light, seeming more to resemble grey ash than beige sand.

"Do you hear that?" the paladin hissed, pulling Goliath up short.

"Hear what?" I asked.

Speckle did not need to be encouraged to stop walking. She stopped by herself.

"Listen!"

I listened.

Somewhere, far away out in the mist, a very large bell was ringing. The sound was muffled after travelling a vast distance through the cloying fog, but to judge from its deep pitch, the bell was clearly one of immense size.

And the bell spoke alone. This was no joyful set of change ringing after a church wedding. It was just that single, low and mournful toll, repeated every six seconds or so.

Bong.

"So this place is not completely dead after all," I said. Although bearing in mind that the tolling bell seemed as if it was marking a funeral, that was perhaps the wrong thing to say. I pointed Speckle in the direction I thought the sound was coming from.

"Don't leave the path," the paladin hissed, and grabbed Speckle's reins. "It isn't safe. I've heard of this place."

"Well, you used to live around these parts, so…"

Bong.

"It comes and goes throughout the Westfold, this mist. Only rarely is it seen. And with it always comes the trees, and with it the bell. Those who follow the sound… are never seen again."

Bong.

"Magicians have been trying to calculate where and when the mist would come for centuries. The Legion used to publish its predictions in an almanac each year…"

Bong.

"…They thought it showed a place and time where the old world and the world remade were connected. When my father's summons came, they were planning to go to just such a predicted conjunction. But it was far north of here. North of the wall."

I knew the story. None of the paladins who answered the summons were ever seen again. The paladin's father fell into indolence with the help of narcotics. When he wanted to sell his golden armour to feed his habit, son and father fought until the latter was dead, and the former was afterwards disowned by his mother.

Fred had a possible explanation. "Most likely they are junctions—"

Bong.

"—to an alternate version of the universe," Fred said. "There is no reason that the rifts caused by the Quantum Zero Counterfactual Decoherence Device should have all healed up completely."

"Has anyone tried looking for the paladins?" I asked, still facing the sound. "This bell does not seem too far away. If that's where they are, they can't be hard to find, even in this fog."

Bong.

"This bell is not a call for help from the Legion," the paladin insisted. "It is an invitation to our doom. Six hundred paladins thought the bell would lead them to the Holy Grail. They have not been heard of since."

I felt a little guilty about that. I knew exactly where the Holy Grail – er, my No-Spill-Em cup – was. It was at the heart of the Mountain of Flesh, the Entity's lair at the heart of the Greyfield. "Someone ought to tell them it has been found," I murmured.

But I had no inclination to strike off the path into this strange mist and the ghostlike trees that filled it like...

...like stones in a graveyard.

Bong.

It was a peaceful sound, and almost hypnotic in its repetition. As the echoes of each stroke died away, I found myself listening out for the next one.

"That's a big bell," Fred said dreamily. "It has to weigh twenty tonnes."

"How do you ring a twenty-tonne bell?" I wondered.

"Keep moving," the paladin said. "Keep on the path."

Bong.

"You're right, we shouldn't get distracted," I said distractedly.

The paladin was ten metres ahead of us by now. "Come on!" he said, calling over his shoulder. "Follow!"

Speckle's ears twitched. Something other than the great bell was out there in the mist.

Before I had time to panic, a reassuringly quavery old man's voice called out.

"Are you real? Can you hear me?"

"Yes, I think so!" I called back.

The paladin halted and turned Goliath around. He looked like he was tensing to gallop forwards and grab Speckle's reins in case I steered her into the fog towards the voice.

Bong.

"I mean, yes I can hear you and I think I'm real!"

The next call was rather chilling.

"Are you in hell?"

"No!" I shouted. What did he mean, hell? "Do you need help?"

"Don't – don't come any closer! Stay where you are! If you leave the path, you'll never find your way out again!" A pause. Then: "I'll come to you. Wait for me, please, I beg of you in the name of Lord Kerr."

At the invocation of Lord Kerr, whoever he was, the paladin sent Goliath trotting back to join me, Edison Junior, Fred and Speckle.

"Bider," Ed Junior said. He pointed down at a white arachnid the size of a mouse, which was scuttling across the path as if it had somewhere it needed to get to urgently. Speckle reversed several steps away from it.

"Not a spider," Fred said. "It looks like a solifugid."

"Bless you," I said.

"Bider," Edison Junior said firmly.

The old man's voice called out again. "Don't – don't worry about me. Keep going, my friends. Just keep going. Stay out of the fog."

"It's okay. We'll wait for you," I said, trying to sound calmer than I felt.

"I can't reach you. As far as I crawl, you never get any closer. Leave, I say; this old man will soon believe you were a mirage."

I thought about it. There was no way that re-finding a path should be at all difficult, even in dense fog. Therefore, the old man was trapped by some form of magic. If we joined him, we would be trapped too. And I had no juice to break into or out of such a trap. "Don't go anywhere, because we're not leaving you," was my holding statement while I tried to think of some way of reaching the old man without getting lost.

"Remember Ariadne," Fred said, in a tone of voice that said I didn't need any further clues to decide what she was on about.

"Ariadne..." the name rang a vague bell. Rather vaguer than the vast yet clothy bell that was still ringing out every six seconds.

"Theseus...?"

110

Something was coming through, but it was coming through too slowly for Fred.

"The Minotaur...?"

"Yes! That's it! We need a spool of magical thread."

"Will normal thread do?" the paladin asked, rummaging in his pack.

Paracord it was not, but the paladin's thread seemed sturdy enough. He tied it to a tree on the opposite side of the road to where the voice and the sound of the bell emanated from. Then we abandoned the safety of the path and moved towards the voice, the paladin and Goliath leading. Speckle and the rest of us followed, tied to Goliath's saddle just in case we wandered off track.

The path soon disappeared. The only reassurance we had that it was still there at all was the slender line of thread that faded and disappeared in mid-air a little way behind us. The quantity of thread on the paladin's spool was small. There was another in my pack that we could tie on, but together the two lengths of thread would only take us thirty metres into the fog –

– which turned out to be plenty, because we caught sight of the man who needed rescuing before we reached the end of the first string. The man lost in the fog was very old, with long white hair and a long white beard, and he was clad in nothing more than bloodstained and grimy rags. In places on his thin limbs the rags were tied like bandages, making him look half-mummified. He was crawling mechanically forwards on his bony knees, head down, exuding the melancholy air of someone with no hope of ever getting to his destination.

Strange shapes loomed out of the mist around him. No longer were they the blackened and dead trees that lined the path. The first thing I recognised, stuck butt-first in sand that looked more like ash, was a lance. The weapon's ancient pennant hung dead in the motionless air. The next thing that drew my eye was the bright white skeleton of a horse, eroding out of the dusty grey ground like a fossil. There were kite shields, and helmets...

...golden helmets.

Goliath gave a nervous whinny. The sound struck me as incongruous. Like his owner the paladin, Goliath never got nervous about anything.

At the limit of vision, row after row of greatswords were stuck into the ground, in the unmistakeable pattern of a graveyard. Bits of armour were scattered all around, and every piece was...

...golden.

It felt as if we were looking at a very old battlefield that in the aftermath of the fighting had become a cemetery. The reduced range of vision that I had gave me the feeling that the battlefield went on for ever in the mist. It was obvious that we were looking at what had become of the six hundred missing paladins. But they had only gone missing two decades ago, and this desolate place had a sense of permanence, as if it had been here forever. And what could this old man have to do with the lost knights?

The paladin leapt down from Goliath, landing on booted feet with a crunch. He took care to ensure that all of us, human and equine, were still connected to his string. He offered a strong hand to the bewildered old man, who eventually noticed it and clasped it weakly. "Let's get you out of here," the paladin told him. He was not interested in his surroundings. Or rather, he looked to me as if he was actively trying to *ignore* his surroundings. He did not want to see the destruction that had been wrought in this place.

"Is anyone else around?" I asked. "Are there survivors among the paladins?"

Six hundred paladins had been defeated here by a force that might still be nearby. So it was probably best to skedaddle rather than engage in idle chit-chat.

The great bell tolled far off in the fog as if to suggest where that victorious force might be.

"I am a survivor, blue man," the old man mumbled. "The last. She took back the citadel..."

He was too old, surely. He must have already been ancient even when the paladins went missing.

"Sen is my name," he said. "I was only a squire when this happened. They called me a paladin, the others did, but I was never a paladin, not really..."

"The paladins only went missing twenty years ago," I said.

"Either there is no time here, or all time is here," Sen muttered, his head bowed, still on his knees in the dust. "This is a place of pain, a place of torture. She lets me live, just to torture me. She took back the citadel, you see. In vain did we battle until that time when the dead-eyed youth with the warbird on his shoulder came out of the mist. Then we took her place from her. We won! But the boy moved on, and she bided her time... and eventually... she took it back..." Abruptly he pulled his hand away from the paladin's. "Nay, I should stay here, with my friends. But they are not at rest, and I am afraid... afraid of what will become of me, too... six hundred of them there were, all in gold, and me a humble squire... or one less than six hundred, for one did not answer the summons. Gresphi!"

The paladin stiffened at the name. It was one I vaguely remembered, too. "Let's get out of here and discuss this..."

"Curse the man! A thousand times I have cursed him!"

"I am Gresphi's son," the paladin disclosed, with the air of someone admitting to liking pineapple on pizza.

Aha, yes. That was where I had heard the name.

"Do you speak true?" Sen asked, looking at the paladin with one eye, its twin in a squint so tight it appeared closed. "Then you have fulfilled his promise, and I will curse him no more, I will wait for him no more. Bless you and bless him."

"My father is dead," the paladin said. "I killed him."

At this, Sen searched the paladin's expression for a sign of his motivation in the killing. Seeing only a calm sadness, he reached up and clasped the paladin's still outstretched hand as if to forgive him for his fell deed, bowing his head. "You had better make haste, my friends, back to the land of the living. If you stay here any longer, you must stay forever. Go!"

"You're coming with us," I said.

"Blue man, only death can end my quest..."

"The Grail has been found," I told him. I omitted the detail that it had been found in my mother's work coat pocket. I made eyes at the paladin. *Get him on Goliath now, whether he wants to come or not*, the eyes said, or tried to.

"Then the Enemy is slain?" Sen asked dreamily.

The paladin divined my meaning, and effortlessly hoisted the old man onto Goliath's saddle.

"Can evil ever be vanquished?" I asked, trying to talk his language. "It has been defeated, and will not return for a hundred years." I silently caveated my bold assertion with the words *I hope*.

"Defeated..." Sen muttered. "Defeated..."

The paladin began to walk Goliath back along the thread, taking care neither to allow it to become slack, nor to put too much tension in it in case it snapped. The old man grasped the reins tightly, his body soon slumping forwards, folding up until it was doubled like a jockey's, his head resting against Goliath's strong neck.

Ten seconds later, the path we had rashly abandoned reappeared in front of us. But I did not relax until both Speckle and Goliath had all four hooves resting on it. Even then I was a bit twitchy about letting the paladin untie the thread from the burnt black tree. But he did it, and we moved on along the track in what we hoped was the real world.

After about another five minutes of plodding steadily onwards, the mist began to thin and the sound of the bell began to fade. The sun grew stronger, and the temperature warmed.

Soon the mist was completely gone ahead of us; looking back, I saw it was completely gone behind us, too. The bell was silent, and there was no sign of the spectral trees. There was just the usual pale sandy desert and its half-effaced road.

"*Bong*," Edison Jr said.

Half an hour later, we came across a ruined building with a partially-surviving roof. It seemed like a good place to get out of the sun for five minutes; Sen could probably do with a rest, too, although he was so quiet that he seemed to have passed out. I said as much to the paladin, who agreed. When we reached the ruins, he stopped and turned to lift the old man down. But rather than do so, he leapt back in sudden shock.

114

What fell off Goliath's saddle a moment later was a mummy. It had the dried-out look of something that had been dead for a hundred years.

"Oh, how peculiar!" Fred said.

Once he had regathered his composure, the paladin just stood there with his head bowed, staring at his feet, not the corpse nearby. I sat there with my head bowed too, but I was looking at the top of Edison Jr's head.

"Happened?" Edison Jr asked, after a while.

"I don't know, Ed," I told him.

The paladin dug Sen a grave, while I carved his name into a piece of roof timber. Then I racked my brains to think of a suitable epitaph.

SEN

The Last Paladin, Even If He Was Too Modest To Say So

"So now you really are the last," I said, once the paladin had laid Sen to rest.

"I am no paladin," he replied.

"Yes," I said. "Yes, you are."

After a respectful pause, we moved on south.

The Village of Callan

Narrow flood-cut channels continued to criss-cross the way, offering shade and moisture. Some had been bridged in bygone days. Others had undermined the road, creating gaps that had not been bridged since, so that we had to descend into them and ascend on the other side. Such places often had a ramp or steps cut into them, as well as disturbed sand at the bottom showing where travellers had dug for water.

I think we were a little more than one day away from the Golden Tower, all of us except my stand-in omni sick of being thirsty, when I came up with my Theory of Lemonade. "Lemonade," I told Fred, "symbolises civilisation. Back when, it was everywhere, easily accessible, and cost little – but no-one wanted it or valued it. They took it for granted, and only drank it now and then, grabbing a bottle from a shop fridge and paying next-to-nothing for it. Now, in the ashes of civilisation, lemonade is gone, and a single can would be priceless. Your average cheap and nasty pre-apocalypse corner shop would easily be the best shop in the entire Westfold. Just think! People today have never tasted lemonade. They've never tasted chocolate. Well, Lexi has. But it was probably the last piece of chocolate in the Universe."

"You can't just magic up a corner shop like that," Fred said. "And if you could, it could not exist here without the supply chain to produce and deliver everything it sells. If you wanted to sell lemonade, you couldn't charge a fortune for it, because most people here have no money. And just for the lemonade you need lemon groves, a juicing and bottling plant, energy to run it, another plant to make the bottles, another plant to refine oil to make the monomer to make into the plastic to make the bottles, an oil extraction industry including drilling rigs and pipes, plus a steel industry and a mining industry."

"So it's like I said. Lemonade symbolises civilisation."

I went a bit quiet after that, and concentrated on wishing the miles could pass more quickly.

We saw the Golden Tower on the horizon early the next morning. Appropriately enough, it was obviously golden even from far off. The tower rose from a sandy, drab yellow-brown land into a pinkish dawn sky. Improbably thin for most of its length, the tower had a slightly flared top, and there seemed to be a shimmer of light up there at the very pinnacle, almost like the shimmer of air over hot ground that we were well used to by then. By mid-morning, as the sun grew stronger, the tower looked like it was within striking distance. But as if it was a mirage made to torment us, the tower did not seem to get any closer after that, and at times it disappeared altogether in the haze. Eventually we were forced to accept that it would be better to hide from the midday sun as usual and continue our journey when the temperature had dropped a little. We got back on the road in the late afternoon, and only an hour after that, all five flesh and bone members of the party dusty and weary, we finally reached our destination.

*

The Golden Tower was enclosed by a massive wall forming a circle a mile wide. As we approached, a slightly darker smudge at the foot of the wall slowly resolved itself into two collections of small buildings, one either side of the road. The diminutive size of these buildings emphasized the height of the wall above them, and the even greater height of the tower above that, which looked as if it would have reached into the clouds, if there had been any clouds to reach into.

We were a mile or so away when Fred concluded that the tower was about four hundred and fifty metres tall, which was "quite an achievement with such primitive materials."

"Raised in a single day, according to legend," the paladin said. "Callan wanted it to be visible from miles around as a beacon of safety for magicians."

"Strange place to put it," I said.

"It was not quite so dry here then, or so they say." The paladin lapsed into silence for a time. Then he said, "The village to the wall's north grew up centuries after Callan's time, long after the tower and the wall had been constructed. It was inhabited, and mostly built, by non-magical folk, who named their home Callan in his honour. As the light of magic grew dim, the magicians of the Golden Tower in those days began to rely on normal people for some services. When the relationship with the Crown was formalised over a thousand years ago, an embassy was built in Callan for the Court's representatives, but I don't think it's in use now."

The buildings of Callan cast long shadows to the east as the sun lowered in the west. The village's buildings were low, and kept their distance from the road, so that we could see right to the base of the wall from a mile or more away. The wall itself had an arched entryway cut into it. From a distance, the entryway looked to have no door or gate, or if it did, the portal stood open. It was backlit by warm glowing sunlight, and stood out brightly against the surrounding wall, still in shade at that point.

The Golden Tower was, as mentioned, golden. It rose high into the painfully bright blue sky. As I had noticed earlier from a much greater distance, it had a slightly flared top, and there was an obvious shimmer in the air above it, so that I was reminded of a giant Bunsen burner on the hot clear flame setting.

Nearing the village, we discovered the reason that Callan seemed so low: it was because most of it was below ground level. Its builders had dug blocks out of the sandstone and piled them up to make buildings, each block removed serving a dual purpose, enlarging the built space below as well as above. Soon we were close enough to the village to look down into it, and could see that the streets were all below ground level. The buildings went down in terraces, so that the village had the look of two inverted ziggurats, one east and one west of the road. The lowest points of both halves of Callan were small square plazas, whose centrepieces were large metal trees standing in wide circular pools of what looked like water, the trees' tips reaching up almost to ground level.

"The famed Dew Trees of Callan," the paladin said. "They long post-date the Archmage's era, and were raised by the Golden Tower's magicians to supply the grown village with water."

The two vast trees were untarnished by the passage of uncounted centuries. I supposed that their metal leaves must grow cool in the desert night, collecting any water in the air, which dripped down to fill the pools below. They looked impressive, but I guessed that natural condensation alone would not be enough to fill the pools with water. A little bit of magic probably tipped the scales on that.

A road passed between the plazas, connecting the two halves of the village through a tunnel under the main north-south road, the gateway to the Golden Tower. At a glance I estimated that there were a hundred stone-built structures on either side of us, some of them quite large. But Callan seemed empty. There was no movement in the village, and for a minute I thought there was no sound, either. Then I spotted a wisp of smoke rising through a chimney, and before I could even complete the thought *it's a little warm for a fire*, the sound of a hammer on an anvil rang out. So, Callan had not yet been abandoned; some souls still made it their home, the most noticeable from up here a smith.

"I'll find somewhere to lodge the horses," the paladin said.

We were level with the start of the village, at a point where ramps descended on either side of the road to the terraces below. Here, a hundred yards from the wall, the Golden Tower was already hidden from view. It seemed extraordinary to think that the residents of Callan could not see even the tip of the Golden Tower from where they lived.

"You're not coming in?"

"They don't want the likes of me going in. That's why it says 'magicians only'," the paladin said.

"Where does it say that?"

"Right there." He pointed ahead of us to the semi-circular entryway. "You can't read it?"

"There's nothing to read," I said, which was true. There *was* a shimmer about the gateway, like the shimmer above the tower; but if there was anything more than that there it was hardly more substantial than the strange forms we had grown used to seeing in the desert's heat haze.

"I guess you can't see the skull, either," the paladin said.

We carried on approaching the entry way. By the time we had halved the distance to it, I could definitely see a form in the shimmering light, but I wasn't quite sure what it was. There was no writing there, and no skull, I would have sworn to that. If I had to hazard a guess at what I was seeing, it would have been a dragon.

"Beekle," Edison Jr said.

"Maybe. Fred?"

Fred couldn't see anything, or rather she could see the base of the Golden Tower half a mile away through an entry way that looked completely empty.

"We each see what we are supposed to see," the paladin surmised. "Non-magical folk are not welcome here, so that rules me out. You three are on your own from here onwards." He helped Edison Jr down, and then did the same for me, setting me on my skateboard facing roughly the right direction. "Good luck."

119

And without waiting for us to go through the entry way, the paladin turned and began to lead Speckle and Goliath towards the nearest slope down into the village of Callan.

The Golden Tower

The sound of hooves on baked-dry dirt died away as the paladin descended into the village below us. I sat on my skateboard and stared at the shimmering doorway in the Golden Tower's great curtain wall. Edison Jr stood next to me and waited for me to tell him what to do next.

The entry way had no gate, no door, no guard: it was just a shimmering light in a giant archway that told the person looking at it what they needed to know. I thought I saw a dragon, but whatever I really saw, it was made out of constantly shifting blotches and spots that reminded me of a living Rorschach test. Edison Jr saw a beetle. The paladin saw a warning and a skull. Fred saw nothing.

The surface of the wall around the magical gateway appeared to be completely smooth, devoid of the joints in the stonework that the village's buildings had, although it was made of the same sandy stone. This close to, the wall's top was in the sky.

There seemed no reason to procrastinate. If some curse, or guardian, was ready to be unleashed at the entry of any non-magician, Edison Jr and I should be safe enough. "Let's go, Ed," I said, and began to punt myself forwards.

Edison Jr toddled along beside me.

We passed through the shimmer in the air as if it wasn't there, and a moment later found ourselves within the Golden Tower's precincts. The wide area between the circular outer wall and the tower itself did not look quite the way I had expected it to. I was not quite sure just what I *had* expected – some sort of Star Trek universe perhaps, a Garden of Eden filled with the sound of delicately-plucked harps, populated by erudite people in robes strolling around a beautiful garden having conversations about weighty philosophical matters, only pausing occasionally to sniff a rose or something – but whatever I might have expected, the reality wasn't it. The Golden Tower's mile-wide forecourt, rather than a Garden of Eden populated by strolling philosophers debating the merits of one form of magic over another, was a barren wasteland empty of people altogether. Avenues of trees radiated out from the Golden Tower like the spokes of a wheel, but the trees were all dead, every single one of them. Not so much as a single withered leaf adhered to a single branch anywhere, indicating that the trees had been dead for years, if not decades. The only living plants were knee-high greyish shrubs with fleshy leaves whose seeds had probably blown over the thirty-metre-tall wall in a violent sandstorm centuries before. Loose sand had blown in too, and was now heaped around the wall in drifts as tall as bungalows. Only the main path had been kept clear of sand and vegetation, and then not by diligent gardeners, but by the passage of feet.

Or in my case, the passage of wheels. The going was difficult, with a soft layer of loose sand above the road proper that my wheels bit into, bogging me down. Edison Jr could have outpaced me easily. I even considered giving up on the board and crawling or inverting the board to try to glide over the sandy surface, but in the end just carried on pushing myself along as usual.

Even though we were now within its precincts, the tower still seemed a long way away. Golden from top to toe, it reached far into the sky above us. But I could now see that the gold was only skin thick, for at its base the gold had rubbed off in places revealing the ordinary sand-coloured stone beneath. There were plenty of windows, going up floor by floor, making the tower look from this range like a fencepost full of woodworm holes. If I could have been bothered, I could have counted the number of floors – but I couldn't be bothered. There were a lot of floors. The exact number didn't matter.

"A hundred floors," Fred said, "if you were wondering."

"I wasn't."

The day was still hot, even as the sun sank in the west. Dragging myself along on my board was hard work. But I consoled myself that the sun was not far above the wall now, so that in half an hour I would be rolling through shade. *That's the spirit*, I said to myself, *you've got four hundred metres to go, and you're already planning on taking half an hour to cover it.*

"It looks abandoned," said Fred. "Are you sure anyone's here?"

"Yes," I said, rolling along grimly. "Hal would not have sent us this far on a wild goose chase, so there *must* be someone here."

Eventually we reached the foot of the Golden Tower. The entryway had no door, but this time there was no shimmer in the air indicating a magic portal. There was just a wide, arched gap in the tower's base that seemed to lead to a large foyer. At this stage I had to abandon the board, for we had to clamber up ten steps to get to the doorway. This was as difficult for Edison Jr as it was for me, because the stairs were half the poor mite's height. We helped each other up this minor mountain, or at least, we gave each other moral support as we climbed it.

At the top, I dragged myself through the threshold, Edison Jr close beside me. As soon as we were definitely in the Golden Tower itself, I said, to an echoingly empty foyer:

"Hello. Our name is Edison."

I sat there, waiting for something to happen – a magical receptionist to materialise perhaps – but after ten seconds had elapsed, it became obvious that we were waiting in vain.

The reception room of the tower was cavernous, occupying an entire sector of the ground floor, about a sixth of the tower's circumference. Grand staircases swept up in great curves following the outside walls to our left and right; the individual separate stone steps stuck out of the wall with little in the way of obvious support to stop them from falling off. The wedge-shaped foyer's narrow end terminated in a circular room which seemed empty and featureless from here save for the two large open doorways that punctured its wall. Further doorways, complete with doors this time, were set in the walls on either side of the foyer. These obviously led to further rooms, probably sectors of the circular tower just like this one. I thought I could hear a quiet murmur from behind one of the doors. "Let's try knocking at that one," I said

122

to Edison Jr; as the only sign that the Golden Tower was inhabited at all, it seemed like our best chance.

The foyer had a smooth shiny stone floor that appeared to be a single slab of the sandstone that was the universal building material around here. The perfect glaze that topped it looked to me like a thin layer of glass made by melting underlying stone. Callan had probably melted it with a snap of his fingers, just to make it nice looking and harder-wearing. How else could you polish sandstone? *Those were the days*, I thought, and mentally clicked my fingers. *Snap.* And whatever you wanted to be, was. It was at once cool and at the same time a recipe for global chaos. But however the smoothing had been carried out, it made the going easier for me; I was able to slide along on my Lith Tillac clothing almost as easily as if I was still on my wheels.

I knocked at the door with the knuckles of my left hand, and Edison Jr banged on it with the soft part of his right fist, and presently it swung open, revealing a young woman with dark curly hair and an enormous smile. Her bright orange top and green trousers put me in mind of a 1980s Doctor Who assistant.

"I thought I heard a knock!" were her first words. Then she looked from me to Edison Jr and back, and decided to talk to Jr. "Hello!" she said, kneeling down to reach our level. "I'm Merra. What's your name?"

"Ed'son," Edison Jr said.

"And is this your father?"

Edison Jr nodded.

I felt a surge of pride. *He thinks of me, not just as a blue annoyance who stops him from eating bugs and dirt,* I thought, *but as his father!*

"Have you come to have some fun?"

Shrug.

"Come on! Give your father a hug and we can go and meet the other children."

Edison Jr hugged me, and then with only a trace of reluctance allowed Merra to lead him through the doorway. "It's okay," she said to him. "We'll have some fun, and then when your father has finished doing grown-up things, he will come back

123

and see what you've been up to." To me, she said, with a wink: "Kappa's probably on the top floor."

With that, the door closed behind them, leaving me sitting alone in the foyer, wondering whether I had just left Edison Jr in the care of the nursery teacher or a dangerous lunatic.

"I notice she didn't ask who I was," Fred said.

Okay, I was not quite alone. "You were in my pocket. Who do you think *she* is?"

"She introduced herself as Merra," Fred said. "I could hear six other voices from within, all of them small children. The available data point to her being the nursery teacher."

On the Stairs

I picked the right-hand set of steps at random and slid over to it. For a moment I sat at the bottom and wondered whether I should knock at the nursery door again and ask Merra to summon Kappa down to the foyer rather than try to reach him myself. But I was too proud to go back. And so, after a few moments I began to drag myself up. I bent my good left arm, placing it on the second step, then straightened it to raise my body onto the first.

The first step was easy. But by about fifteen of them it was getting difficult. Ten minutes, thirty steps and an enormous amount of effort later, I reached the first floor.

I did not need a calculator to work out that if each floor had thirty steps, then I would have to climb three thousand of them to reach the top. I imagined myself reaching the hundredth floor several decades later, having developed the look of a grizzled blue humanoid fiddler crab, with one arm as thick as a telegraph pole and the broken one having wasted away to nothing.

A young man in scarlet robes spotted me on the first-floor landing and hurried out of what looked like an empty classroom to help me.

Excellent, I thought.

"Visiting Kappa?" he asked. "Would you require assistance in climbing the stairs?"

Looking at a kid operating on one good arm while grimacing in pain at every step gained, this might have seemed like an odd question to ask.

"How many steps is it?" I asked.

"One thousand, two hundred and seventy-three."

"I should be fine," I heard myself say. Partly this was sarcasm. Partly it was my usual stubborn way of sticking two fingers up at nature.

"Very good," the young man said, detecting none of the undercurrents of my words and taking them at face value. Before I could change my mind, he retreated into his classroom and closed the door behind him.

The second floor was only fifteen steps above the first. If this pattern kept on, I thought, the hundredth floor would only be an atom thick or something.

Two more people – magicians, no doubt, but I sneeringly told myself they were not such magicians as me, being capable of little more than parlour tricks – emerged on the second floor. They said hello and overtook, disappearing into a room on the floor above. I slowly followed them up the curving stair.

Moments later one of the two magicians came back past me. She was a middle-aged willowy woman whose outfit was completed by headgear that was somewhat like an old-fashioned hospital matron's or a nun's wimple, except that, like her gown, it was bright turquoise with white detailing and let her silver-grey hair spill out around the edges. "Everything all right?" she asked.

"Yes," I said, although my grimace and trembling good arm said the opposite. I had probably faded several shades by now as well. But damned if I was going to ask anyone for help.

"Good good," the woman said, and passed by.

"That was pretty dumb," Fred said, once she was out of earshot. "I don't see why you can't accept help. If I wasn't carried, I wouldn't get anywhere."

"What step is this?" I asked.

"Fifty-six," she said primly.

"Good. Only one thousand, two hundred and thirty-six to go."

"One thousand, two hundred and twenty-seven."

"Even better than I thought." I had by now climbed enough steps to have completed three-quarters of a circuit of the tower, reaching the side that faced east, which was now in deep shade. There was a window at this step, and peering out, I could see that we were already quite high up. This late in the afternoon, the finger-like shadow of the tower reached all the way to the outer wall, half a mile away.

"Would you like to know what proportion of steps you have climbed?"

"No," I said stoutly.

"Are you sure?"

"Absolutely."

"Why aren't you moving?"

"I'm just admiring the view."

"It's better the higher you go," Fred said, winning the argument.

"I really hope someone here can fix F3," I said, unfairly.

Moments later, the matron passed us again...

...going *down* again, just like the last time she had passed us.

"Hello," she said. Moments later she was gone again.

"Did you see that?" I asked Fred.

"Yes. She is tormenting you, by rushing across to the other set of steps, running up to the next floor, and then descending past you again. Either that, or she has a twin."

Five minutes later, I had gained another five steps, and the thin matron passed us again, again going down.

"I'm going to say something next time," I told Fred.

"Ask her if she is one of triplets," Fred suggested. "Or see if she has developed a sweat by running back up the stairs on the other side of the tower."

When the matron inevitably passed us again, I didn't ask how many sisters she had; nor was she remotely out of breath. I said: "You seem to be making a point about how easy it is to climb steps when you can walk."

126

The matron stopped abruptly and sat down next to me on the steps. "Not exactly. Ponder this: it is quite tiring to climb from the ground floor up a hundred flights of steps, even if your legs are pretty good."

She got up and made to carry on, but I said quickly: "Wait! Are you saying there's a lift?"

The matron turned, and offered her right hand, which I shook awkwardly with my left. "I'm Kappa. Hal has told me all about you, Edison!"

"I thought you were a guy," I said, "although my reference for that idea is two thousand years out of date."

"Sometimes Kappa is male, sometimes female," Kappa said, unperturbed, and naturally having no idea what I was on about.

This close to, I could see that Kappa's gown was heavily embroidered with what I first thought were snakes but eventually realised were actually extremely long lizards with stumpy legs. But the idea of snakes had set my mind on a magical school wild goose chase. Or a wild serpent chase. "Do you have houses here?" I blurted, wondering if Edison Jr was even at that moment on the cusp of being inducted into the Golden Tower's equivalent of Slytherin thanks to some sort of mischievous sentient hat or something.

"Houses?" Kappa was surprised at the randomness of my question. "We have sleeping quarters. There are houses in Callan."

"I mean, do the students get divided into competing factions, each with their own dormitory, uniforms, psychological characteristics...?"

"Edison, we only have sixteen students, and that number includes Edison Jr. The only dividing we do is between young ones and older ones."

"I see," I said, relieved.

"Come and see me later. Your first port of call should be the healer on floor twenty-two."

I glanced up at the stairs above me leading to effectively infinity, and Kappa said: "Use the lift. In the centre of the tower. I won't insult your intelligence by explaining how to use it."

"Ya," I said. "Just press the button and wait."

"Hal said you were a strange one," Kappa said with a smile, got up, and carried on descending.

I followed, at a more sedate pace, reasoning that it would be easier to descend to the previous floor and access the lift there than to go through the hard work of completing my climb to the next one.

Floor 22

Arriving back on the second floor, I managed to open the nearest door and slide inside a large room that turned out to be a classroom. I was relieved to find it empty, and slid towards the centre of the tower, and the circular room that turned out to be a lift.

It must be dangerous, I thought, *not to have doors that close when the lift is not present*. But the magical lift of the Golden Tower had no doors at all, just open doorways that led...

...to a metre-wide stone balcony with no safety railing. Half of the balcony was natural sandstone; the other half had a metallic blue hue. Vertically-oriented handles were built into the wall at shoulder height, almost as if they were there to cling to when the balcony shot up and down. But the balcony was solidly built and solidly attached to the wall. I inched forwards and looked down; two floors below me, I saw a similar balcony at the level of the foyer, and below that that, signs of several underground floors. Looking up, I saw the cylindrical lift shaft rising up floor after floor into the distance, presumably all the way to floor one hundred. A light gleamed there at the very top, its warm luminance pouring down the lift shaft in a very unnatural way, syrupy magical rain falling down a drainpipe that was ten metres wide.

The floor we were on was marked with a squiggle that probably meant 'two.' I said as much to Fred, and added that to find floor twenty-two, all we had to do was to find two such squiggles side by side.

"Presuming that they work in base ten," Fred said.

"Don't start," I told her.

"I haven't. I'm just covering all the bases."

I silently ground my teeth and searched for a comeback. "All your base are belong to us," was the only retort I could come up with.

"Aha! A meme. I know all about memes," Fred said. "Would you like to know the provenance of that phrase?"

"No."

"All right, be like that."

The next question was how to summon the lift. There were no buttons. Of course not. This was magic, not machinery. You probably had to clap or something like that. "Fred, could you make the sound of a clap?"

"Yes, easily."

I ground my teeth some more but did not rise to the bait. "Please do it now."

Fred clapped.

Nothing happened.

"Try twice."

Nothing happened.

"Three times?"

Nothing happened.

At this point we were saved from further experimentation when a magician drifted up past us. It was the young man in the scarlet robes we had seen on floor one. "Decided to use the lift?" he asked cheerfully. "Just don't look down, that's what we always tell the children."

With that he was gone.

"I think you're supposed to just step, or in your case slide, into space," Fred said.

Of course, I had just reached the same conclusion myself. Nevertheless, it was with great trepidation that I crept forwards, hoping the more I was over the lip of the balcony the more buoyant I would feel. The parts of me overhanging the edge felt decidedly lighter, but definitely not lighter than air. Before I could nerve myself to trust the magic of the lift shaft, I let too much hang out, slipped, and fell off the balcony...

...and found myself drifting downwards.

"You have to go on the other side of it to rise," Fred surmised. "It's to stop people from banging into each other."

But I was already out of reach of the second-floor balcony, albeit still falling at a sedate pace. I could not claw my way through the air towards the other half of the lift shaft. The only option was to grab onto the next floor balcony's handles (so *that* was what they were for) and shuffle around to the other side. I missed the nearest handle as I slipped past, and had to grab the balcony itself instead. This was difficult to achieve even in slow motion, but thanks to my near weightlessness, latching onto the stonework with my good hand did not cost me a dislocated shoulder. Safely on the first-floor balcony, I had a little rest, before shuffling around from its sandy half to its blue half (blue represented the sky and therefore up; obvious really). Bits of me that I let dangle over the blue side of the balcony were obviously positively buoyant, so it was with not *too* much trepidation that I launched myself into space once more.

I was pleased to find that I did not plunge screaming to my death, but slowly floated upwards.

I tried to keep count of the floors as I rose, but rather than passing by too fast to count, they passed too *slowly* to count, so that my thoughts were distracted by other things, leading me to forget what number I was on. At first the doorways were all empty, opening into classrooms of which there seemed enough for every student to have their own; then came a mixture of store rooms, laboratories, and levels with actual doors closing off the lift entrance. We saw no-one as we drifted up twenty floors. It seemed that the Golden Tower was long past its heyday.

At length we reached a floor designated by a double squiggle, and I was pleased to grab hold of the balcony to drag myself out of the upward flow.

"You were correct," Fred said grudgingly, "a squiggle is a two."

I found myself surrounded by six open doorways. One of the six portals had light spilling out of it, mostly the reddish light from the setting sun. But there were other signs that the room behind it was occupied – other sources of light, quiet sounds as of whispered conversations, the smell of incense. I crawled that way.

Crossing the room's threshold, I was momentarily dazzled by the light from the west-facing window, so it was a few seconds before I could take in my surroundings.

The room I found myself in was, as usual, wedge shaped. A low couch surrounded by smoky candles on head-high stands was the centrepiece of the room. A large woman in an iridescent green dress with long skirts and powerful shoulder pads watched me from one side of the couch. A cluster of six older children, three boys and three girls, watched me from its other side.

The whispered conversation among the children stopped dead as I dragged myself into view. It was replaced at once by a collective gasp, which soon became a deep shocked silence. Seven pairs of eyes watched me intently. The Saviour of Humanity had arrived. Blue, he really was. Crawling. His once nearly white clothes were stained by nearly a week's worth of wear. So the gasp and subsequent silence in the room were not unexpected, even though the adults I had met so far had politely managed to hide their shock at my appearance.

"Please get on the couch and lie on your back," the woman in green – presumably the Healer – said to me.

I gritted my teeth. I said it was a low couch, didn't I? Well, it was. But it was not *that* low. It was not so low that following this order would be *easy*. And so I slid along to the couch and, reaching it thirty seconds later, tried to haul myself onto it.

No-one offered to help. No-one said anything. There was utter silence from my audience. The only sounds were my straining noises, frustrated grunts and the gasps of pain that slipped out whenever I jarred my right arm. Nobody else moved. I deduced that they were all staring at me, gape-mouthed. It was the horrified gaze of the pupils watching the headmaster try to dance the floss at the school disco.

After about a minute of mostly aimless pawing, I finally managed to gain purchase on the far side of the couch and heave myself onto it. After that I rolled onto my back, gasping for breath.

The whispers started up again. I soon found myself able to tune into them and make out what the children were saying to each other.

Wow.

I know.

I didn't know anyone could go so far into the dark!

I wondered what was meant by that, but before anyone could reply and provide any clues, the adult in the room called a halt to proceedings.

"Silence!" she yelled, clap-clap-clapping. Then, more quietly: "Naman, please set up the deflector. The rest of you, space yourselves out around the patient."

Staring up at the smoke-stained ceiling, I heard rather than saw someone – presumably the boy or girl called Naman – hurry from the room. Moments later there was a change in the quality of illumination in the room; the reddish light of the setting sun was suddenly met by an equal quantity of golden light flooding the other way, out of the lift shaft. The latter still had a curious gloopy raindrop-like quality, only now the magical rain was travelling horizontally, having been steered through ninety degrees by the mysterious "deflector" – which, I told myself, was probably a glorified mirror. I heard more footsteps as Naman regained his or her station. Then the Healer spoke again.

"Children, I want you to begin with his broken arm."

"Are we being tested on this?" a boy asked.

"No, Kerell," was the weary reply, "we are healing a fellow magician, one who defeated humanity's greatest enemy. You may commence when ready."

At that point a low hum developed, and a golden mist grew in the air above my head, seemingly derived from the collision of the low rays of the sun and the horizontal raindrops shining from the lift shaft. The mist gathered itself around my right arm like a swarm of miniature bees. I expected it to provide a gently warming sensation – but instead it was an agonising attack of pins and needles.

I tried to maintain whatever dignity I had left, but after ten seconds I could stand it no more and howled like an ignored baby. I writhed. I twitched. I yelled. The pain grew to a crescendo, along with the humming, which now sounded like the swarm of bees were setting up home in my ears. Then it began to fade, little by little, until after a minute or so I could see again. The golden swarm had retreated into place above my head again, and its hum had diminished, as if the bees were a room away.

"Now, children: restore his legs."

I clenched my teeth and knotted every muscle as the golden cloud descended upon me once more. But this time there was no pain. No pain at all. This time, the sensation was one of gentle warmth. And this time, it was all over in ten seconds. The golden cloud rose above me again, thinned, and vanished.

The Healer clapped her hands twice, and said: "Dismissed! Put the deflector away on your way back down to floor three!"

Stunned, still staring at the mesmerising conflict between the two light sources mingling above my head, I could only lie there as the children ran out of the room, whispering and giggling. Then a few seconds later the horizontal raindrops faded away. Moments after that the sunlight winked out too, as the sun finally dropped below the level of the outer wall. A little diffuse light from the sky still flowed in from the outside, an echo of the direct light of the sun, but now the strongest light in the room came from the murky candles.

"Please," said the Healer, "sit up."

I *felt* mended. But I was gripped by the fear that if I tried to move, I would find out that I was not mended. Gingerly I used my good arm to propel myself into a sitting position, and swung my legs off the couch. How easily they went where I wanted them to go!

"Wait," I said groggily to the departing children, "I haven't said thanks yet."

But the children were gone.

"No thanks are owed," said the Healer.

I flexed my right arm. There was no pain. I clenched my fist. No pain. "They really are," I said.

The Healer came close to me and began to remove the strapping from my right arm. The flesh beneath had the cold blue colour of mint toothpaste. "How did you

133

do that?" she asked. "Go so far into the Dark Place? I've never seen anyone as hollow as you were."

"Dark Place?"

"I'm sorry. I am forgetting that you have no formal training. The Dark Place..." she thought about how best to describe it. "The Dark Place is like a bank you can draw on to spend money you don't have – it's magic at the cost of your own flesh and bone. Barbarian magicians and shamen are said to have used it when the wellspring of natural magic ran dry."

"Lexi was dying," I said quietly. "I tried to reach her, but..."

"True love has that power," the Healer said sagely. "It is the power to reach the only selfless magic there is, the power to give of yourself to save another."

I was going to argue, but held my stupid blue tongue.

The Healer was suddenly businesslike. "If you ever go to the Dark Place again you will lose feeling below the knees again and, until your arm has had time to heal naturally, the break will return. You should show great caution."

I almost laughed at that. "Thanks for the advice. But I don't think I'll be able to beat the Lich King by holding back."

The Healer took both my hands and, stepping backwards, encouraged me to stand up. And I could stand. My magic bank account was empty, but at least the overdraft had been filled in.

"Please," the Healer said, "visit the Seamstress on floor fifty-six. She will outfit you for your journey."

Floor 56

"So there *is* such a thing as magic, after all," Fred said, as we floated up to floor fifty-six.

"I told you there was. And besides that, you had a vampire roaming around Foxburrow, and what is a vampire if not magic?"

"There are vampire bats, and they aren't magic. They just have sharp teeth, and drink blood."

"The Quacker destroyed reality and stuck it back together any-old-how with whatever it found to hand in all the other possible versions of the Universe that shared the same multidimensional space. It also seems to have made memes flesh. Like vampires. You know that."

"Your other omni told you this."

"F3 preferred to think of magic as altered physics."

The floors we were passing all had closed wooden doors, six to a floor. Occasionally we passed magicians going the other way, but the sense was definitely one of an establishment at below ten percent of its capacity.

"Whatever it is," I added, "it has mostly gone now. This place should be buzzing, but it's empty."

At floor fifty-six I grabbed the nearest handle and stepped onto the circular ledge. Stepped! Then I was confronted by six open doorways… but only one was showing a light, so that was the way I went. The room beyond was dominated by a long, high bench, behind which was a wall of square drawers. On the other wall I could see some mannequins dressed in robes and mad hats, as well as a full-length mirror and a couple of zig-zag changing screens. Light – three bright discs on the carpeted floor – appeared to come from invisible spotlights.

The Seamstress, if this was she, was asleep. She was seated at the long bench, and was resting her head on both fists, her elbows on the bench. She had long silver hair, so although I could not see her face from where I was, I thought that she must be older even than my mother.

"Hello?" I asked quietly. "Are you the Seamstress?"

I had hardly expected my voice to reach the sleeping woman, let alone wake her up. But she leapt to her feet in an instant. The curious hats on the mannequins along the wall had made me slightly concerned about the kind of clothes I would be issued with, but the seamstress was dressed sensibly enough to allay such concerns. Her dress was simple in form, wine-red, and a close fit to her bony frame.

"Sigil?" she barked at me.

"Edison," I said.

"What is your sigil, Edison, your sign, your mark, what is your emblem, what symbol gives you your power, which as we all know is of such magnificence to have saved the world, et cetera?"

I think I stared back at the Seamstress with a blank expression on my face.

"Your *sym-bol*." She said the word in two emphasized syllables, like a tourist talking to a baffled local.

I still did not quite know what she wanted me to say. My first thought was of a blue smiley, the logo that I had decorated the paladin's armour with back in the Entity's lair. But before I dug that particular hole, I asked, "What do you need it for?"

"For the pattern of your coat," the Seamstress said, as if this ought to have been perfectly obvious.

I was glad I hadn't mentioned the blue smiley. My mind immediately latched onto the image of a dragon. It was either a dragon or Totoro, and I would have to explain what Totoro looked like. So it would have to be–

"A peacock!" Fred said loudly.

I looked at my pocket, as did the Seamstress.

"A peacock it is!" the Seamstress said, jumping on the idea like a trap closing.

"Now wait just a minute–"

"Your imp has answered. Now stand forwards, I need to measure you."

I imagined that this would be done by magic, but I was mistaken. An old-fashioned tape measure appeared; the Seamstress lifted a flap in the bench, passed through, and took the measurements. First, leg and waist. Then chest, arm and neck.

"I wonder if perhaps..."

"Return in half an hour," the Seamstress said brusquely. "Please visit the demonologists on floor seventy next."

*

"A peacock!" I said to Fred as we ascended towards floor seventy. "What sort of emblem is that? It's not exactly going to strike terror into the Lich King, is it? You

136

could have gone with an eagle or something like that if you wanted a bird. All peacocks do is strut about and hoot."

"A perfect description of you. They are also blue."

"You have never seen me strut," I snapped. "I couldn't even walk when I rescued you."

"You have been able to walk again for about twelve minutes, and you have spent most of that time strutting and hooting."

"I've what! Most of those twelve minutes were spent floating up the lift shaft!"

"Quite a rescue, it was," Fred reminisced. "There was I, sitting in my dead owner's pocket for two thousand six hundred years, when along came Mr. Peacock and saved me from... what, exactly?"

"I have a feeling," I said, "that you weren't so snarky with your previous owner."

"I have no previous owner. You are not my owner."

"This is all because F3 is about to be fixed, isn't it? You're worried that you'll be disconnected from F3's battery."

"No," Fred said sulkily.

"What about a secretary bird?" I asked. "That would have been a cool sigil."

"Yes, but it isn't blue, and it isn't you."

*

The demonologists on floor seventy could not, as it turned out, fix F3. There were three of them, all smoking roll-ups filled with a noxious-smelling weed, and all wearing similar faded, badly-singed red robes. They were very taken by the umbilicus connecting Fred to F3, and spent some time pondering its significance. Then they popped F3 under what one called the "cryptoscope" and muttered some mumbo-jumbo. All three of them sucked in through their teeth like proper tradespeople, before pronouncing: "There's no demon in there."

"No, he *is* the mechanism. It's a very complex mechanism, not a trapped demon."

The demonologists tried another couple of occult gadgets, but they were still looking for a demon that wasn't there. Eventually they began to debate who else in the Golden Tower might be in with a chance of repairing the damage, but came up with shrugs in the end.

*

So Fred and I descended back to floor fifty-six. Although most of the allotted half an hour had passed, I didn't think that the Seamstress would have my things ready. But it turned out that making clothes was fast when it was done with magic.

"Disrobe!" ordered the Seamstress, as I stepped out of the lift shaft.

"Huh?" I asked.

The Seamstress clicked her fingers, and my clothes fell to pieces – all of them. The threads holding the pieces of material together crawled out of their stitches as if they were very thin worms and helpfully wound themselves around a bobbin for future re-use. I hurried behind a screen, leaving F3 and Fred and a trail of remnants in my wake. By the time I got there, all I had on was Hal's ring.

"Blue all the way down!" the Seamstress called.

"Thank you!" I called back from behind the screen, thinking: *she is a sadist*.

Items of clothing were tossed over to me: underwear, a shirt (baby blue, buttons, no collar), trousers (royal blue, in a corduroy-ish material that was probably a magnet for dust and hair). A pair of boots followed, one at a time, although I had already stepped out from behind the screen by then, so they did not hit me in the head when the Seamstress tossed them my way.

"And now, for the crowning glory!" the Seamstress said. "Arms out!"

I obeyed. The Seamstress went behind me and slipped my jacket onto one arm, then the other, then yanked it up to seat it on my shoulders properly. It was close-fitting from the forearms upwards, but baggy around the wrists. Twelve green buttons ran up the front to close the jacket. It gently flared out as it went down, stopping at about knee length. The fit around the shoulders gave it a posture-enhancing, spine-straightening feeling. The jacket felt comfortable and safe, like a security blanket, or a suit of armour that weighed as little as a hoodie. And there *was* a hood, too; the Seamstress pulled it up for me.

I liked the jacket so much I felt an urge to stand an inch taller, to adopt a regal poise, in short... to strut like a peacock.

"Mirror!" said the Seamstress, and a mirror stand dutifully rolled over from its place by the wall until it was right in front of me.

The jacket was mostly blue like my trousers. It had a tessellating pattern of peacocks embroidered on it, with a fan of green-eyed tail feathers radiating out from each. I suddenly decided that I liked peacocks after all. And with the hood up, I could pretend to be badass, like Raistlin or someone. "Fred, you're forgiven. It looks great."

"I wish *I* could see it," Fred called back from the floor. Evidently none of her cameras' fields of view included me.

"There is a pocket over your heart, with a hole so your imp can see out," the Seamstress said.

I collected F3 and Fred, gave the latter a quick view of the coat, and then slid them into the pocket. Fred confirmed that the hole was in the perfect place for her to see out through one of her cameras.

"Have you ever *seen* a peacock?" I asked the Seamstress, suddenly wondering how she knew what one was. They were probably quite rare these days, if they existed at all.

"You made a mental image of one when your imp said its name. I must admit, it is an improbable beast."

"You read my mind?" I wasn't annoyed by this intrusion. All I could think was that I could have had Totoro after all.

"Yes or no?" asked the Seamstress, ignoring the question and posing one of her own.

"It's awesome," I said.

She sighed, and patted one of the peacocks. "The coat will turn most blades, but don't get cocky. It will resist light fire, some elemental magic, and will make you irresistible to the opposite sex."

"Huh?"

"The same sex?"

"No – it isn't that – I mean, I only want to rescue Lexi."

The Seamstress wandered behind her bench and began searching through some of her drawers. A moment later she produced a pair of small daggers, which she tapped on the bench, beckoning me over. "Arms out towards me!"

I complied. Soon she had slipped the daggers up my sleeves. I discovered that there were purpose-built sheaths sewn in there.

"Throwing daggers for self defence! Reach for them, go on!"

I fished about in my left sleeve for one of the daggers.

"Both at once!" the Seamstress mimed drawing two daggers from her own sleeves and throwing them both, back-handed, at me.

A moment later I got it. The blades were of metal that was as blue as the coat, narrow, and not counting the stubby handles, as long as my hands.

"Being a novice, you'll need a catalyst," the Seamstress went on.

"Like a wand, you mean?" I asked, trying to re-sheathe the daggers without tearing my coat.

"A wand?" the Seamstress asked, in the tone of voice my mother might have used if I had asked for a pony for my birthday.

Bless my soul, I thought, *it's Harry Potter.*

"Don't be absurd." The Seamstress rooted about in another drawer, quickly finding what she wanted. "Try these bracelets on."

The bracelets were thick bands of black leather, that with a wave of her hand became blue leather. She embossed them both with the peacock sigil just by staring at them hard. A loop of leather went over the thumb, and I soon saw that they belonged on particular hands, because they were not rotationally symmetrical. With the bracelets in the correct position, a small transparent crystal was touching the life line of each palm.

"What are these for?" I asked.

The Seamstress clicked her fingers and made the crystals blue too. "For channelling your magic."

"Hal doesn't have these," I said. "I would have noticed them. You don't have them either."

"Edison, for all your undoubted talents, you are a complete novice at this. These are given to new graduates who have not made something better for themselves in charms. With these you will be able to achieve very minor magics without using any of your energy. You know. You can show off. Do parlour tricks."

"Perfect," Fred muttered.

"I don't want to do parlour tricks," I said.

"Yes, you do. You definitely do. You can use them to summon objects to you, or send them away. We spend a lot of time teaching our students how to control situations by using just a smattering of magic. By simply making a tiny demonstration hinting at what you *might* be capable of, you will be able to make most threatening people back down without a fight, and therefore avoid wasting any real magic." The Seamstress used a curled forefinger to summon a bobbin to her from the workbench, then sent it back from whence it came by straightening the digit. "With practice, you will be able to deflect an arrow heading your way."

"Seriously?"

The Seamstress looked at me quizzically.

"I mean, that sounds great! I take it all back!"

"Good. Please go to see Kappa now."

"Floor one hundred."

"Ninety-nine."

"Okay, well, thanks for everything." I made my way over towards the lift.

"Oh, Edison?"

"Yes?"

"Wash it in water only. No powerful cleaning agents."

"Roger. I mean, water only. Right."

Floor 99

Kappa was waiting for me on floor ninety-nine, sitting in one of several large comfortable-looking armchairs arranged around a circular rug and a low table. She had removed her headgear, revealing wavy silver hair falling below her shoulders. There was a collection of interesting objects on the table in front of her, but my eyes were drawn immediately to the left-hand wall, where there was a life-sized painting of a young woman. She stood in the dappled shade of a flowery woodland glade, and with her shoulders thrown back and her dark hair trailing in the wind she had a bold, dignified look. The painting was old, and very worn; it looked as if it might even date back to the time of Callan himself...

"Beautiful, isn't she?" Kappa asked with a smile. "Visitors are always taken by her. I could stare at her all day. She never existed; she represents the woman he thought his sister might one day have become."

I twigged. It was a painting of Callan's sister Somel, who had been expelled from her village as a child when she discovered her magic, and disappeared into the wilderness, never to be seen again.

"He never got over her loss," I said.

"No," Kappa said sadly. "He never did. But had he not lost Somel, Callan would never have come here, would never have built the Golden Tower, and would never have taken in banished magical children, and protected them, and trained them to control their powers, to use them for good." After a pause, she added, "Come on then. Let's have a look at you."

And so I wandered forwards towards her, only now taking in the rest of our surroundings: bookcases with enormous tomes, a narrow metal spiral staircase leading up to floor one hundred, open rectangular windows with an almost night-black sky beyond.

I stood for a moment by the ring of armchairs so that Kappa could admire my new jacket. Then she indicated that I should sit down. "So. Now you look the part. Congratulations. Edison Hawthorne, you are now an official magician of the Royal Court, military division. Normally the training lasts seven to twelve years, with a one-

142

year probationary period, but I've decided to compress all that into the next ten minutes."

"I only want—"

"To fight the Lich King, yes."

"No! To rescue Lexi."

"Can you do that without fighting the Lich King?"

"Er, no."

"It would be unseemly for you to not address me as Madam, now you're a King's Magician."

"Er, sorry, Madam."

"Joke!"

I was confused. Kappa explained.

"Only call me Madam if anyone else is present."

"Er, right!"

"Joke! As the greatest magician of the age, you can call me whatever you like, and I expect you to disobey any orders I give you, or any orders that any ranking member of the Royal Family give you, or senior military officers, for that matter."

"Joke?"

"No joke."

"Anyway, I'm not the greatest magician of the age."

Kappa picked up what looked like a china tea cup and sipped from it before replying.

I waited and watched, wondering what she was drinking. Probably not Earl Grey, I thought. As I had noticed from the doorway, the low round table had an interesting collection of bric-a-brac scattered across it. There was another drink, in the form of a metallic blue bottle accompanied by two tumblers on a silver tray. There was mood lighting in the form of what looked like a glowing crystal ball. I noticed a small silver badge, in the shape of a fist clenching some flowers, a duplicate of one I had recently seen Eyya wearing in Lith Tillac. A black wooden box with two fine leather straps holding it shut might have been a cigarette case. Two curiously-shaped metal pieces flanked the silver badge. I couldn't work out what they were for; they appeared to have moving parts, and made me think of spurs, or can openers, or unbaited mousetraps.

"You were," Kappa said, and as if for emphasis, cracked her cup back down on its saucer. "For those few glorious moments, you were. Your power may have been lost forever in that moment, but your achievement will never be forgotten. You have done more for the people of the Westfold than any magician alive, more than *all* the magicians in this building put together, more than any of our generals or their armies, more than any king or queen. Long after the sandstorms have worn the Golden Tower down to a stump, worn it down into desert dunes with a slight metallic sparkle – your legend will live on."

"But that power–"

"Is gone. Yes. And no-one can give it back to you. It's gone forever." She leaned forwards to pick up the black cigarette case and unfastened the two straps. Within, sitting snugly on a bed of crushed red velvet, were six tiny pearls. "They come from far to the west, or some say, far to the east. They are grown in oysters in a special place where a magical spring wells out of the ground, and the people there use oysters to concentrate the magic in the form of these pearls."

I could see from a few feet away that the pearls were magical. But they were not *dazzlingly* magical. I glanced at Hal's ring; it was barely glowing.

"These six belong to the Golden Tower. They were set aside hundreds of years ago for the Defender to use in the last resort should this place be imperilled. There are very few pearls in the Westfold any more, and only a tiny number appear each year. They are a commodity of great worth, and as you might imagine, magicians would kill for them, and have. The agents of the Golden Tower come across perhaps a dozen pearls a year. Half are found in dusty attics or treasure hoards. Our magicians – and others – are always on the lookout for them. The rest arrive by sea, usually on pirate ships rather than the traders they started out on."

"You're saying they're as rare as hens' teeth."

"Hens don't have teeth, so they're not quite that rare, no. Each of these will give you a sufficient boost to perform one important magic. Consume all six, and you will be able to perform one *great* magic. Just crack them with your teeth. The rest will come naturally." Kappa closed the box and tied its straps and then offered it to me. When I reached out to take it, Kappa pulled the box away. "Don't fritter this power away. My advice is to take them immediately before you face the Lich King and not before. You have a plan to face him, I take it?"

"I will have by the time I get there," I said, with a shrug.

"Edison, not many would face this being on their own."

"I'll have the paladin with me."

"Yes, but *you* will have to defeat the Lich King."

"Well, that's fair, since I'm the fool who woke him up in the first place."

Kappa finally let me have the box. I stowed it in an inside pocket. Then with a gesture from her forefinger she magically flicked the silver badge across the table to me. "This is your seal. Don't lose it. Show it if challenged by officious types. It gives you authority to act in the King's name."

I didn't even know the King's name. Nevertheless, I pinned the badge to the inside of my jacket's lapel.

"Good. Now, take this." Kappa poked one of the metal devices across the table towards me.

I picked it up. "What is it?"

"And this." She pushed the other device across.

I picked it up in my other hand.

Kappa snapped her fingers. The little metal devices kicked and squirmed in my hands. There was a sudden burning sensation on both of my palms. I yelped and tried to let go, but the little swines clung on for a few seconds before I could shake them off. But instead of a burn on each palm, I found a small circular tattoo.

"The tattoo knows if you've been good or bad," Kappa said.

"Right. So it's like Father Christmas." Kappa, of course, had no idea who Father Christmas was. So I followed up with, "I just show these to other magicians in case they're worried I'm a psychopath."

"If you want to. Now, what else? What have I forgotten?" Kappa mused. "Nothing, I think. Oh, well, you are supposed to take an oath. I've got the text around here somewhere. But as the greatest magician of the age, perhaps you should invent your own oath, and I should just witness it."

"My own oath?"

"Yes. Swear to do whatever it is you think you ought to do."

I thought about it for a moment. "I, Edison Hawthorne, swear to serve the public, protect the innocent, and uphold the law."

"Sounds good to me." Kappa beamed. "Now, let's go upstairs."

Floor 100

Kappa led the way over to the spiral staircase and stood aside for me. "You first," she said. "Mind your step up there – it's a little dark."

Fred switched her light on without being bidden, and I carefully climbed the metal stairs. My legs felt weak, and grew tired before I was a third of the way up. But I was overjoyed to be able to use them again; pain and weakness seemed a small price to pay for the restoration of my mobility. Reaching the top felt like poking my head into someone's attic. As Kappa had warned, it was dark, and Fred's light was by far the strongest source of illumination.

The top floor of the Golden Tower was completely open. On level one hundred the solid walls holding the roof up and dividing the floor into sectors had been replaced by spokes of sturdy columns radiating out from the hub. The hub itself was filled from floor to ceiling by a mysterious black cup-shaped structure the size of a bungalow. The low hum in the room seemed to be coming from there.

I reached the top of the staircase and made room for Kappa to join me. As the rattle of her footsteps on the metal died away, the hum in the room became more obvious; it was definitely centred on the cup-shaped structure. But, staring at it, I finally realised that the structure only appeared tea-cup shaped because I could not see all of it. I was looking at part of a much larger sphere. A quarter of it must protrude through the floor down into the very top of the lift shaft on floor ninety-nine. The second quarter of the sphere was on this floor, floor one hundred; and the rest, the top half of the sphere, unseen through floor one hundred's ceiling, was out in the open on the roof of the Golden Tower.

"Callan's Sphere," Kappa explained briskly. "This is what powers the Golden Tower. Without this, the lift would not work and the little bits of magic we do day-to-day here would not be free. It is not the magic you are used to – the magic of the earth that you used to defeat the Entity, or the magic of the air that you have managed to draw to yourself whenever you have found some since then. This is sunlight magic. There is water magic too; you hold some in your pocket. And there is another kind of magic, the dark magic of blood and death. When a person dies, their spirit cries out at the moment of its severance from flesh. That magic can be concentrated in blood, or harvested in the manner you harvest air magic. Over this way."

Kappa led me to the right, through one of the rows of columns, and closer to Callan's Sphere. "All kinds of magic can be used for any purpose," she went on. "The difference is how they arise, how they become concentrated. All are part of the energy that binds the universe together. It is the energy that you will be able to use with your catalysts to achieve what to ordinary people will seem like miracles."

"Right, so that makes me like a Jedi," I said. "Cool."

"I beg your pardon?"

"Oh, sorry. I didn't mean to say that out loud. A Jedi is, er, it's a type of person from a story set a long time ago in a galaxy far, far away."

We had reached an area where some large cushions had been scattered on the floor, as if the students held pyjama parties there. In the air directly above them was a black cone, whose likeness to a shower head was only enhanced by the horizontal pipe running from it to Callan's Sphere. Here, it appeared, the Golden Tower's magicians sat in a circle, linked hands, and had a spiritual shower or something. A single small item occupied the open space inside the ring of cushions: an hourglass. Close by there were some free-standing shelves covered by hundreds of small items that looked in the gloom like model castles.

"Be seated," Kappa said. "Do you have anything of Lexi's with you?"

I did not. "No," I said. Then I thought of Hal's ring. "She gave me this, although it belongs to Hal."

"Great. Perfect. Place it on the ground in front of you. That's it. Now, I just have to find something else, won't be a moment." Kappa wandered over to the shelves and, after pacing up and down for a few moments, selected one of the many items there. She returned to the cushions, sat down opposite me, and placed the item on the floor between us, next to Hal's ring. It was indeed a model castle, or at least, a model citadel. Its centrepiece was a tower that seemed to rise straight out of a rocky shoreline. On its landward side the great tower was surrounded by a semi-circle of eight smaller towers, connected to the main tower and one another by covered walkways. All eight towers rose from a city whose outer wall was also a half ring. "We have several versions of this one."

"It's...?"

"Malafert, in the Cursed Vale. What you need to do, is to concentrate on this object, to cast out the net of your thoughts like a fisher on a dark lake, until you find another set of eyes that can see the real citadel. Then, push the owner of those eyes into a black cupboard at the back of its mind, lock it there, and navigate its body to the citadel. Probably best to pick something with wings, we usually do. The connection between you – the ring – should enable you to find her easily."

"Lexi!"

"Remember, your time with her will be brief. See that she is all right. Reassure her that you are on your way. Find out anything you can about the Lich King's abilities that might help you to defeat him. Remember to tell her how to release your puppet from its trance."

"Three claps."

148

"Yes."

"Sounds like magic," I said.

"It is." Kappa slid open a shutter on the base of the shower head above us. Slow raindrops of golden light began to descend onto the model and Hal's ring. Kappa turned the hourglass, and sand began to fall through its neck.

I stared hard at the model of Malafert, which rose off the floor up to my eyeline in the lazy golden rain, and slowly began to rotate.

Edison, I said to myself, *you've got this.*

Long Distance Call

Reaching out towards the Lich King's citadel was nothing like my usual method of magically sensing my surroundings, which was like the way a spider sitting at the centre of a web sensed vibrations all around it. The method made possible by the Golden Tower's magical showerhead and the model of Malafert felt like whizzing through a greyish hyperspace with no features at all other than occasional shadowy glimpses of castles, towers and mountain crags.

Suddenly, as if six blurred images merged into a single sharp one, another version of Malafert superimposed itself over the model. There was a wrench as the model spun away, breaking the crisp composite image again and making my stomach lurch — but a moment later the model was gone, the showerhead was gone, and I was looking at the real Lich King's citadel.

I was looking at the real Lich King's citadel with a pair of eyes that were not my own.

And the owner of those eyes did not like the intrusion. Not one little bit. It rebelled, without words, by blind instinct, trying to push me out.

Relax, I said, and held the panicked flutter down for a few seconds. The mind I had invaded was tiny and could not resist me — so I could have done as Kappa had said, and locked it into a black cupboard for the duration of my stay. But that seemed unnecessarily cruel. Instead, I put out what I hoped was the aura of a supreme yet benevolent being in need of a helping hand.

Or wing.

I took my host's eyes away from the distant main tower of the Lich King's abode for a second, and saw enough in the quite deep darkness to tell me that I was the temporary co-owner of the body of a large gull.

Gosh.

The Lich King's citadel, and the tower at its heart, was shrouded in darkness. The great tower itself was an utterly black finger rising high into the sky, visible only because of dim backlighting from a strip of night sky between the shore and the utterly black cloud flaring out at its tip. Hal had named the black umbrella thing, but I had forgotten what he had called it. The Mushroom of Fear seemed a good name for it. The Mushroom of Fear was probably more impressive in daylight, when the contrast between the remaining sky and the blacked-out disc would have been striking. Hellish red-orange firelight suffused the lower parts of the citadel, revealing the lesser towers and connecting spans. It was a grim place, a frightening place, a place that was probably alive with undead. Or dead with unliving. Or something. Either way, it was not somewhere that anyone would want to visit – unless they had a very good reason.

Looking up and around I saw that the blackness reached far beyond where the gull and I were. I sensed that the gull was worried about the way its home was changing. The Mushroom of Fear rising over the tower was already wide enough to make daytime twilight and nighttime almost impenetrably black, and it was spreading.

I'll fix it, I told my host, trying to exude supreme-being level confidence. *It may take a while, but I'll fix it.* We were sitting on the top of a sea cliff some miles south of the citadel, and I gradually became aware that a dozen other gulls were sharing the ledge with us. These were now eyeballing us with beadily suspicious stares, having somehow divined that something about their companion had radically changed.

I foresaw some unpleasant beak on feather action incoming, and said:

Let's fly.

And we did. My host just leapt off the cliff into a pool of darkness as if it was the most normal thing in the world. The sudden sensation of falling almost severed my connection with the gull, but I clung on. The vertiginous plunge was just to gain speed, for the gull pulled out of its dive and soared up, above the height of the cliff top and above the top of the tallest tower. A moment later everything disappeared, because we had passed into the black. We both felt the sudden grip of cold, and a wooziness that threatened to grow into a complete mental blackout. With a cry of terror, the gull dived out of the black disc again, levelling out only when the world reappeared around us.

I just need to visit someone in the tower and I'll be out of your way, I explained to my host. The gull seemed content to help for now, and headed towards the citadel. Its flight was effortless, with not so much as a flap needed: long shallow glides were punctuated by steep climbs, seemingly achieved by a small change in its wing angle. The gull's eyes were good, but everything was dim – as you might expect from an unlit night with most of the sky blacked out by the Mushroom of Fear. It was a pity that the Lich King had not installed some spooky green lighting like whatsisname did at Minas Morgul, which would have made navigation a lot easier.

Now, where would you keep a princess captive? There was only one answer to that: it had to be the highest room in the tallest tower. I thought as much to the gull, who spiralled down that way, keeping a good distance from the black disc above us. The tower's top was decorated with twelve miniature towers like the points on a crown; it was on one of these that the gull settled for a moment's rest.

The blackness, we saw, emanated through a hole in the centre of the tower's flat roof. At its source, the black was thick, oozing upwards like liquid, not smoke. This close to the wellspring of darkness, I felt nauseous and light-headed. The Golden Tower made magic from absorbed light; the tallest tower of Malafert exuded antilight. The battle was an unequal one. The little bit of me that was projected out here was no more potent in the face of the black ooze than a snowflake trying to cool a griddle.

The gull needed no compulsion to leap off the tower top and make a swooping recce around the top floor. The interior was pitchy dark; a series of unglazed windows did little to allow us a view. I explained to the gull that we should land on a windowsill and stick our beak in to see what we could see.

Which turned out to be approximately nothing. It was far too dim to see a thing.

Should have commandeered a bat, I thought. But I suddenly realised that I could borrow a few ergs of juice from the Golden Tower and reveal the interior by magical means. So I made everything in the top room slightly luminous. The sudden light startled the gull, which gave a hoarse cry and rose an inch off the windowsill. It was not, I hoped, an unfamiliar sound to the denizens of Malafert.

The top floor was empty. Well, it was not empty, but there was no-one in it. It was dominated by the giant infernal machine that was generating the black disc, which began life as a series of ropy tendrils of living night creeping up a central column before it disappeared through the roof and fanned out in all directions in the sky above. The machine itself was a vast clockwork thing composed of colossal stone gears. These should have made a serious racket, but they moved against one another in almost complete silence. The rim of the room was full of benches and shelves covered by half-built machines and ancient glassware, giving the place the feel of a diabolical laboratory. I wondered whether there was anything in the chaos that the gull could casually drop into the giant clockwork to jam the thing up. This seemed unlikely. To me it looked as if anything softer than a diamond would be ground to dust by the massive stone wheels.

Next floor down, I thought to the gull, which hopped around on the windowsill and leapt into space again. I stifled the light behind us.

But the windows on the next floor down had all been walled up a long time ago. This floor was the perfect prison. Or, more likely, the daytime sleeping place of a Lich King; no sunlight could ever disturb him there. Maybe the walled-up windows pre-dated the construction of the infernal machine – they were a sort of heavy curtain used as a stop gap while some mad necromancer worked out the kinks in a machine that would make curtains of any kind permanently surplus to requirements for folk who were terminally allergic to daylight.

Luckily for us, if the Lich King was indeed on the walled-up floor of the tower, he would not be able to glance up from whatever he was doing to see a suspiciously-inquisitive gull swooping past.

We spiralled down another floor and quickly spied a window through which a dim yellow glow crept.

Same procedure, I thought at the gull: we'll gauge things from the windowsill.

And the first thing we saw on alighting on the lichen-specked stonework was –

– *Lexi*.

Still alive.

Unharmed, at least physically.

As beautiful, graceful and resolute-seeming as always.

Lexi wore a rather ancient-looking but elegant dress made of bottle-green velvet. She was seated at what had once been a dressing table (the large compound mirror was a dead giveaway) that appeared to have been repurposed as a study desk. Several stacks of thick old books covered the table; Lexi was reading one particularly weighty tome by the light of a small lamp.

"Lexi!" I said.

Although it came out as,

"Kaah!"

Strange. Hal had managed to make his finch talk. Maybe finches were more versatile in that respect, or maybe it took a bit of practice.

Lexi heard the sound, and turned to see a large gull sitting on her windowsill. Her initial surprise clouded into confusion.

"It's me, Edison," I tried.

"Kaah kaah haah haah," was what the gull said.

"Edison?" she asked.

I nodded my beak vigorously. Then, I thought: *use magic, you idiot!* "Yes, it's me," I said, and the gull did a serviceable job of rendering the words this time. "How did you know?"

"I've never seen a blue seagull before, so it's either you, or I've gone mad…"

"No, it's me. How are you? Has he hurt you? I'm sorry it's taking so long to rescue you, but I'll be there soon."

Lexi put her book down, picked up her lamp and approached the window. She knelt down and inspected the gull by the lamp's warm light. "It's really you?"

"Yes. It's really me. Well, not really. I just borrowed a gull for a bit. I'm in the Golden Tower. They have this thing like a showerhead that lets a magician borrow an animal for a few minutes. I'm sorry, you don't know what a showerhead is. Ignore me. Hal used it to visit me in the bunker. I'm not real, but the gull is. I mean, I am real, but I'm not really here. Does that make any sense?" I was babbling.

"No. But it's you."

"And you're okay."

Lexi set her jaw in the way she did when she wanted to prove that she was unshaken and unshakeable. "Yes. His name's Bartlet. He was around when the Quacker went off, like you. He killed everyone in the bunker. He's been accepted as the new Lich King and has raised an army of undead warriors. He says if I marry him, he won't send them to wipe out the living."

"What did you say?" This was bravado on his part, I thought. Surely Bartlet would not send his forces out beyond the reach of his Doom Umbrella or whatever it was called.

"I said no, of course. What did you think?"

"No, that's good, but if–"

"You want me to marry him?" Lexi demanded.

"No!"

"Good! Anyway, I might have considered it, if I believed that he would keep his part of the bargain. But he won't. And he can't force me to marry him without knowing my name. So don't say it in case anyone hears it, right?"

I had already called Lexi's name, of course, although it had come out as the harsh call of a gull, hopefully leaving any eavesdroppers none the wiser. "I'll call you Rumpelstiltskin," I said. "Or maybe Rapunzel. Listen, there isn't much time. It already feels as if the elastic connecting me to the Golden Tower is tightening. Is there anything that you can tell me about the Lich King? What sort of character is he? Anything that could help me defeat him."

"He's arrogant," Lexi said. "He wouldn't dodge if you threw a knife at him."

The gull must have looked a little surprised, because Lexi elucidated. "Once at dinner I threw a knife at him. He didn't even blink. It was poorly balanced, and bounced off his chest. Not that it would have hurt him anyway. Nothing does. I stabbed him in the heart when we first arrived. It didn't hurt him."

"Rumpelstiltskin!" the gull cried. I wished I had chosen a shorter name. "Rumpy! Be careful. Don't annoy him."

"I'm going to kill him before you get here," Lexi said. "I don't know how yet, but I will."

"Just stay alive. I'll deal with him."

"How exactly?"

The gull shrugged. "I'll figure something out by the time I get here."

"Can I pick you up?"

"Fine by me. I'll tell the gull not to panic."

Lexi picked us up and carried us to the dressing table. Here, I could see several images of a surprised-looking large blue gull reflected in the compound mirror. It was definitely an odd colour for a gull. As well as a human. "They let me read these books. They are histories of the earlier Lich Kings, like Malafert. They think I'm just interested in the history, but the most important thing I want to do is to find out how the other six died. The answers are somewhere in these dusty old tomes."

"You could be right. But promise me you won't try anything."

"Why not? I already tried to kill him. He doesn't care. Like I said, he's arrogant."

I suddenly felt woozy. My vision blurred for a few moments. The elastic pulling me back to the Golden Tower was stronger than ever. It was the magic shower's way of telling me I was running out of charge. I only had moments left. "I won't be able to speak to you again until I get here in person," I said. "I'm on my way. Stay strong. I'll be as quick as I can. When I go, the gull will go into a trance. Put it on the windowsill and clap three times to release it from the spell, okay?"

"Okay."

"Don't marry him."

"I won't."

"Rumpy, I–"

In the Archives

"–love you!"

"Edison," Kappa said with a smile, "I'm too old for you, and we've only just met."

I turned a deeper shade of blue. "Did you hear everything I said?"

"No."

"I didn't even say sorry for taking her into the bunker in the first place. And I didn't tell her how Edison Jr or the paladin were."

"Did you get anything on the Lich King?"

"Yes. He's arrogant. And there's a machine there blocking out the light."

"Yes. They call it the Clockwork."

"You don't happen to have any diamonds the size of hens' eggs do you?" I asked, a sudden idea forming. Or at least a half-idea half-forming.

"No, I don't think so," Kappa said with a smile. She rose to her feet. "But I'll ask around. There's a room made up for you on floor thirty."

I got up too. I got the feeling that our meeting was over; I was being dismissed. But there was no time to waste asleep. The night was the best time for travelling. "Thanks, but I can't stop. I just need to say goodbye to Edison Jr, if you don't mind looking after him while I'm gone, and I'll be on my way."

"He'll be safe here."

"I don't know how I'm going to explain this to the poor kid. Lexi is the only good thing that has ever happened to him. Now *I'm* abandoning him too."

"You're not abandoning him. You're coming back. And he already knows you're leaving, and he knows you're coming back, with his mother, soon."

"Is Lexi allowed in here?"

"No," Kappa said. Then, after a pause, she added: "But she can live in Callan, and Edison Jr can live with you there, and attend day classes here. He does not have to board."

"Great. Well, thanks for everything."

We walked back to the top of the stairs. "Call in on the archivist before you go," Kappa suggested. "Floor minus three." She waited for me to descend ahead of her.

"Right," I said. At the bottom, I said: "This is a bit cheeky, but can I borrow some money? People keep buying me things, and I feel bad about it."

"You can have your salary," Kappa said. "Any expenses you incur can be repaid. See the Bursar on floor seventy-three. He'll give you a month's pay up front."

"Right," I said, heading back to the magic lift.

"And Edison?"

"Yes?"

"Remember to practice with the catalysts."

"I will."

*

The archives were at the bottom of the Golden Tower. The floor there was the only one to have a middle bit you could walk on – all the others had hollow centres like Polo mints because of the lift shaft. The golden light suffusing the lift had diminished somewhat now that the sun had set, but it seemed that Callan's sphere was able to store enough sunlight to keep the magic working by night. And the raining sunlight magic seemed to *puddle* at the bottom of the tower. As I floated down, I saw that the floor of the archives was aglow with what – when I softly landed – turned out to be an inch-deep layer of light. Some ancient magician – maybe Callan himself – had taken advantage of this feature by covering the ceiling with mirrors, which reflected the rising golden light back downwards. The flat ambient light of the archives cast no shadows; together with the hazy ground-level mist, it gave the place an otherworldly feel.

Stone bookshelves heaving with thick grimoires radiated outwards from the central open space like tick marks on a clock face, and set within them was a ring of benches where scholars could presumably consult the ancient wisdom. But tonight, only a single scholar was at work. He was a young black-haired man in a plain grey shirt. All the magicians I had seen so far had been dressed like guests at the Tsar's wedding, so this scholar's plain attire made me wonder whether he was actually a non-magician, a cleaner or something self-teaching on his time off. But non-magicians were not allowed in the tower at all, so perhaps he was a magician with an ascetic philosophy. The only decorative item he wore was a bead necklace, which looked as if it was made, quite crudely, of wood.

"Just leave it over there," the scholar said, without looking up.

"Leave what where?" I asked.

Now the scholar glanced up. Then he jumped a foot in the air. "Oh, I'm sorry! I thought you were Ebbi. Master Edison! Excuse my dishevelled appearance. I wasn't expecting you. Nobody tells me anything." He bowed, and bowed again.

"It's just Edison... and don't worry about not expecting me. I didn't know I was coming." I suddenly realised that I was talking to Taen the Archivist, who in the form of a firefly had accompanied Hal-finch on his visit to me in the bunker. "We seem to be standing in a pool of magic. Is that normal?"

"Yes," Taen said. "The unused dregs of the magic that emanates from Callan's sphere eventually find their way down here. It never seems to get any thicker, so I presume it either evaporates or seeps into the ground. It's handy. Makes it easy to keep Lumi going."

"Lumi?"

"Yes. I used to call him Stripy but he was a wasp then. Since I had a go as a firefly I decided to turn him into a firefly instead of a wasp." He snapped his fingers. A humming noise commenced, and grew closer. Soon a flying beetle the size of a dachshund, with green-glowing hindquarters, droned out from between two bookshelves and approached us. It thumped down on Taen's desk as if hardly able to lift its own weight, which was hardly surprising given its size. I pretended that such creatures were utterly normal in Edison world, when in fact I had hardly managed to stifle a yelp of surprise.

"I've been reading about the previous six Lich Kings, as promised," Taen said.

Naturally I had forgotten that Taen had been doing that, but pretended that I had visited just to hear his report. "What did you find out? So far all I know about the latest one is that he's fast, but doesn't bother to dodge, because he's also arrogant."

"You know more than that," piped up Fred.

At that I had to pull her and F3 out and place them on the table. I let Fred relay the two-thousand-year-old tale of the Vampire of the Bunker.

"So in a sense, he was the first Lich King, as well as the last, we hope," Taen commented, when Fred had told him all she knew.

"If he knew we were calling him the First and Last, his ego would probably explode," I said.

"Perhaps you are right. Though perhaps his overconfidence could be to your advantage, when you finally have to face him."

I thought about that for a bit, and couldn't see quite how. But I agreed with Taen anyway. "True. So what can you tell me about Bartlet's predecessors?"

"Not a great deal on the Lich Kings is to be found in the archives," Taen said apologetically. "I suspect this is for two reasons: first, it has been the obsession of the Legion of Paladins, not magicians, to fight the undead. Second, most of the Lich Kings' affairs have been conducted in the Cursed Vale, out of range of normal spies. Lumi, could you fetch me the History of Araz?"

The giant firefly spread its matt black wing cases and extended the membranous wings beneath, which began to vibrate until they were blurs. Then it lifted heavily into the air and hummed off towards one of the bookshelves.

"As you know, there have been six Lich Kings before now. The first and most well-known, albeit mostly in folklore, is of course Malafert himself, after whom the citadel of the Cursed Vale is named. He reigned more than a thousand years ago, which no doubt means that his tale has become corrupted and embellished in the telling. Let me read to you from Araz, because this is quite interesting." Taen stood and drummed his fingers on the desk, awaiting his familiar's return.

"I imagined that the archivist would be a tad older," I said tentatively.

Taen shrugged. "Someone had to do it. No-one's interested in the archives any more. I mean, who wants to come and read about spells no-one can do any more, or about the histories of magicians who were a thousand times more powerful than them?" He swept his arm around in a circle, indicating the dozens of shelves and the tens of thousands of books on them. "The history of magic is easy to summarise. There was a massive party where everyone got very drunk and had a great time and got into pointless fights. Then they all left and woke up with massive hangovers. Then rats came and slurped up the dregs of the ale from the spills on the table, tipping over abandoned tankards to get at what was within, gnawing through empty barrels to get at the wet bitter wood. Now, a hundred generations of rats later, we are *still* going back to where that party was held two thousand years ago, sniffing about for a wet patch, knocking over dusty tankards to search for a drop of liquid at the bottom, and endlessly scraping the same empty barrels for even the merest hint of a beery aroma."

"Things aren't that bad, surely?"

"Of course they are! That's why I came down here when I graduated. Outside, hardly anyone is able to do magic and hardly anyone who can dares to, because it would be like spending the last few coins you will ever own. Most of the training is how to use minor magic to project the impression of power–" here Taen took note of my catalysts– "to pretend to be a wasp, when we are all flies dressed as wasps, pretending to carry a threat in order to deter an attack we could not defeat."

I thought rather guiltily of the pearls Kappa had given me. You could say I almost clutched them.

"That's what the training does," Taen went on. "It shows you how to puff yourself up, to make yourself look impressive, when behind it all... there's nothing."

160

It seemed as if the peacock pattern had been a perfect choice to adorn my coat after all.

At that point Lumi buzzed back into view. It was flying heavily with a large tome clutched in all six of its legs.

The History of Araz

Taen cracked open the book Lumi had brought him and began to read. Some of the tale he quoted verbatim; for other parts he simply reported the gist.

"Araz was around about five hundred years ago, and his history contains mentions of the first five Lich Kings. It majors on other things, mostly the Enemy you are all too familiar with, for that was the main peril at that time – in fact it has been the main peril for civilisation ever since histories were written, until what you did last year. It also talks about the Sundering, which was naturally a part of the war on the Enemy..."

Taen must have caught my bemused expression, for he hurriedly explained. "You might know that there is a wall between the Westfold and the Eastfold. That came about from the Sundering. Basically, the way we in the West like to describe it, the Easterners were willing to sacrifice us to the Enemy. Not only did they not help us fight, but they would not allow refugees to enter the Eastfold when the North Wall was breached. However. They probably tell a different tale."

Taen now flicked through the book to find the passage he wanted. "He we are. Malafert was the good dead king, and all four of his successors were evil incarnate. Malafert found a way to cheat death, and those close to him survived their deaths too. Living citizens of the Blessed Vale – he means here the Cursed Vale – donated their own blood to King Malafert, and then... something about how they were more reluctant to donate blood to Malafert's relatives and others at Court as more and more people, er, stayed alive after they were dead. Then the wider population began to survive death too, so that much of their lives were spent planning what would happen after their deaths. Weird. But... some allusion here to locusts and wheat...

the number of undead rose and rose, soon equalling the number of the living who had to give up their own life, I mean life force, blood in other words, to keep them alive – I mean undead."

"I can't imagine there was universal agreement to that," I said. "Sure, I can imagine drumming up some donations for Good King Mal, or Great Aunt Petunia, but as soon as it becomes a general tax for complete strangers..."

"Yes. Indeed. Exactly. Araz goes on: After a century or two, the people of Malafert did not know the undead who were demanding their blood. Some refused the request. Others fled the citadel, and the Vale. With blood in short supply, Malafert and the elite began to hoard it. Something... aimless? Confused? Undead scratched at their doors. Others pursued the living, taking by force the blood that had been refused them."

"Wow," I said. "Vampires."

"Thus, the system poisoned itself. The paladins, I think that was in the time of Lord Kerr, declared Malafert's existence a blasphemy, and embarked on a campaign to throw him down. Of course, in those days magic was still rife in the land, and the battles between the paladins and Malafert's undead armies were fought with spells as well as swords." Taen said this as a parenthetical, before beginning to read again. "In the fourth year of the war, the paladins penetrated Malafert's fastness and killed for the second time the King who had first died two hundred and thirty-six years before. But the paladins did not linger in the citadel, instead departing as fast as they could; for their slain comrades were rising up and siding with the defenders against them. But outside, the sun was shining again, and the undead of the citadel remained in hiding."

"Does it say how they did it?" I asked. "How they killed Malafert?" This seemed to be the crux of the matter. Would the paladin and little old me be able to achieve the same results as a legion had a millennium and a half before?

"It doesn't say," Taen admitted. "But it does give the lineage, and some vague information on what happened to the next four. The second dead King was

Omenerat, who apparently got deposed by the third, Tursul. Tursul was himself deposed by Craxelor, who reigned for one hundred and eleven years..."

"Unlucky number," Fred put in.

Both Taen and I looked at her and waited for an explanation. The number was apparently Nelson, which was unlucky because Nelson had only one eye, one arm, and one leg. Except that Nelson in fact had two legs.

"What became of Craxelor?" I asked, moving swiftly on.

"He died in battle."

"How?"

"Or, he was killed by sunlight. Or maybe betrayed by one of his generals. Araz isn't really sure. What he is sure about is that there was a gap of over a hundred years before the fifth Lich King, Arenord, rose."

"And what happened to him?"

"According to this, his second death came about by suicide."

I rubbed my forehead, hard. So far we had absolutely nothing to go on in terms of ideas for defeating Lich Kings.

I think Taen noticed my reaction, because he hurriedly said, "But we do know – not from Araz, because he post-dates Araz – what happened to the sixth Lich King, Hartemon. He was killed by a paladin."

"Yes!" This was more like it. "How?"

"With a magic sword."

The paladin, of course, had a magic sword that I had made for him. Such a creation was far beyond my power now. And I had not exactly had Lich Kings in mind when I conjured it into being. I had modelled it on my conception of what a paladin's sword would look like (Excalibur) and had made its blade glow and perfectly, eternally sharp. "And where is that?" I asked, my heart sinking.

"Alas, it was lost to history hundreds of years ago..."

"Don't worry," I said to myself as much as Taen, "I'll think of something. I usually do. I just wish I had F3 with me."

"Charming!" Fred said.

"I'm sorry, Fred," I told her. "You have been very helpful on the journey here." Partly true. She had also been rather snarky at times. Which was not unlike F3, to be fair to her. "But I'm sure you would not want…" I screwed up my brain to try to wring Fred's first owner out of it, but failed. "You would not want your first owner to quickly develop the same rapport with a new omni as she had with you."

"The name you were looking for was Katya," Fred sniffed. "But your ham-fisted attempt at an apology is noted."

"You have two demons-in-boxes, and one is silent?" Taen asked.

"Kinda-sorta. Well, no, not really."

"They are stuck together?"

I separated F3 and Fred. They were still joined by the cable routing power from F3's nuclear battery to Fred.

"Lumi, have a look at this, would you?" Taen asked of his bizarre insect pet. The giant firefly walked ponderously across the bench in a staccato rattle of claws and began to wave its antennae over F3.

"The demonologists already had a look at him," I explained. "There was nothing they could do."

"They don't know which end of a reefer to light," Taen said, in a tone of voice that said he had a low opinion of his colleagues on floor seventy. "Always borrowing books, never returning them; if they do come back, they are usually singed and smelling of sulphur. The demon boxes are similar, but not exactly alike," he noted, staring at the two omnis on the desk.

"Omni design rather coalesced around a common archetype," Fred explained. "But there was minor variation. F3 was built by the F3Thing corporation, and I was made by Grrl."

"Fascinating. So in the time before, people were able to build boxes like this – I get that – but how did they trap demons in the boxes?"

I thought I'd let Fred answer that one.

"Well, just as you are not a body with a soul trapped within, omnis are not boxes with demons trapped within. Your brain allows you to think. Our processor chip allows us to think."

"I'm not a soul trapped in a fleshy body? Is this not the basis of blood magic?"

"There is no soul. Once your brain ceases to function, you cease to exist as an entity."

"Fred," I put in, "even if that was the way it was, we don't know whether that is the case any longer. In fact, it seems very likely that body and soul have been at least partially separated ever since the Quacker went off. How else do you explain Bartlet?"

"Your theory is that, because a lot of people believed in the human soul, that at the point when reality was torn apart by the device you so creatively call the Quacker, their beliefs became concrete?"

"Put it that way, it does sound a bit mad."

"What were they for, these... omnis?" Taen asked. "As magician's familiars?"

"There was no magic before the Quacker," I said.

"Perhaps the Quacker was magic, as were the Predators before it, albeit of a lesser kind. How else would you describe a device that can shatter reality?" Fred countered. "Perhaps the Entity's mind control was also magic." To Taen, she explained: "Grrls were personal assistants aimed at young professional women. They handled communication, social media – their cameras were world-renowned, they stored contacts, memories, appointments, made bookings and payments, and came with a built-in offline curated knowledge base. Their AIs were equivalent to certificated counsellors, they could navigate, control vehicles, organise gifts for loved ones, advise on style issues, and chat. Grrls were great listeners. WarGrrl was equipped with a taser for self defence, although without the cumbersome harpoons that F3 has. MediaGrrl was capable of editing audio-visual presentations on the fly and had better cameras. All Grrls were excellent personal tutors."

"I see..." Taen said. It was clear to me that he was more confident in translating Araz's five-hundred-year-old History than he was in translating whatever it was Fred had just told him.

Lumi finished waving his antennae above F3, opened his wing cases, and buzzed off towards the bookshelves again.

"He longs to go outside. Of course, he would vanish the moment he left the Golden Tower. But he can dream," Taen said.

"Did he, er, say anything about F3?" I asked.

"Oh. Yes. Lumi found a crack in the mechanism. He fixed it. Was something supposed to happen?"

I pressed the start button.

For a long moment there was nothing. Then F3's screen lit up.

/ F3 /

/Thing/

YOUR WORLD IN AN OMNI

Then the screen went blank again.

"F3!" I said. "F3!"

"No need to shout, Edison," F3 said. "I'm just performing an internal diagnostic."

"Heaven help us," Fred said.

"I see you wasted no time cashing me in for a pink camo model..."

It was so good to hear Androgynous Voice #6 again. "F3, for all I knew you were gone. Kaput. Dead. I thought Fred could help me repair you."

"... I *was* dead," F3 said, confused.

"Your primary wafer was cracked from side to side," Fred explained. "I told him it was hopeless."

"And yet... somehow... here I am. How so?"

"You were just fixed by a giant firefly called Lumi," I told him.

"Perhaps this is a nowhere zone, a strange twilight between life and death, where it seems like reality but your subconscious bombards you with absurdities until you finally realise that everything you perceive is taking place in an entirely internal landscape, but…"

"No," Fred said dryly. "You really were fixed by a giant firefly."

The Silent Garden

Before I left, I told Taen about Maralla's condition, and asked about her prospects. Taen sent Lumi off to the shelves to find a tome called the Annals of Chrysofex, which contained the only data on a similar case that he knew of.

"Chrysofex travelled far and wide, gathering folklore," Taen explained. "He categorised stories and listed as many of their variations as he could find. His annals include fifty-seven versions of the Tale of Callan and Somel, for instance."

This, of course, was the first F3 had heard of our little adventure in Lith Tillac, so I had to give him a thumbnail sketch of what had happened. I had more or less finished when Lumi returned, droning along with a book that was, if anything, even more of a doorstop than the History of Araz. Taen began to flick through the contents pages, which were themselves probably in need of a contents page, such was their length. "Can't remember what it's called… I'll know it when I see it, I'm sure I will. Yes. Here we are. It's called 'The Silent Garden.'"

That didn't sound anything like Maralla's case, but I didn't leap in with both feet just then. I waited while the archivist scanned the dense text. Having skimmed it, he summarised the story. "There's a powerful magician who lives in a big house. He has a daughter and he tries to make her powerful using various magics, feeding her strange foods, et cetera. And the daughter does indeed become powerful. But she cannot look at people or animals without harming them. Thus, all the birds are driven from the garden…"

"Hence The Silent Garden."

"Indeed. After the birds, the staff go too, and when the father dies, the daughter is left alone within four high walls, with only the flowers of the garden for company. Then a young man comes, and begins to talk to her through the gate. Their relationship develops... it's love... then she accidentally glimpses him one day, and he drops dead. Filed under 'Forbidden Love' and 'Divine Justice.'"

"That's it?" I asked. "No happy ending? Who tells stories that don't have happy endings?" (Which was a bit rich coming from someone who had told the tale of Beowulf and the Dragon around several camp fires recently.)

"Sounds rather like a post-apocalyptic version of Rapaccini's Daughter by Nathaniel Hawthorne," Fred said.

"My thoughts exactly," F3 replied.

"I wonder if I'm related," I said.

"No!" both omnis chorused.

"Of course, the tale has origins in earlier folklore," Fred said.

"I am aware of that," F3 replied.

"Guys, break it up!" I said. "It may have its origins in folklore, but it could well be real here."

Taen was scrambling for a quill and paper. "I need a record of this Tale," he said.

It turned out that Rapaccini's Daughter did, in fact, have some similarities to The Silent Garden. Rapaccini's daughter was brought up in a garden full of poisonous plants, which made her completely resistant to poison. But she also became toxic herself. Her boyfriend became poison-resistant and toxic too. When she took a cure for her condition provided by his boss, she keeled over and died. And no-one lived happily ever after (again).

"It's probably best if the Lith Tillacs poison her food," Taen said glumly. "I don't suppose Maralla's condition will improve. If anything, it might get worse."

"They're not going to do that," I replied. Eyya had been confident that Maralla was safe. Thinking about it, the Lith Tillac royals needed the goodwill of Maralla's family in Toryl Noth, so they were not likely to jeopardise that by poisoning the Princess.

"Well," Taen said with a laugh, "you're probably right. But if they do... they had better not make any mistakes about it."

"The injury therefore that we do to a man must be such that we need not fear his vengeance," F3 said.

"Machiavelli," Fred replied. "When you strike at a king, you must kill him."

"Emerson," F3 said.

"Allegedly," Fred agreed. "We'll never know now, will we? It's always men though, isn't it?"

"When you poison a princess, you must get it right first time," I said hurriedly. "Taen the Archivist."

Stepping Out

I left Fred with Taen. I felt bad about abandoning her as soon as F3 was back online, but she seemed happy enough. Taen had a purple-pink crystal that he could set spinning above Fred to recharge her battery, so she should be able to remain online indefinitely. Her "offline curated knowledge base" would be used by Taen to write the first history of the time before the Quacker went bang that was not idle speculation cooked up by imagination or hallucination. There was an entire shelf in the archives about the creation of the world; most believed that the world had been entirely barren until two rival entities, Chaos and Order, had been mysteriously born. The terrible twins had been warring ever since, and the Entity was the child of one of them. (Most thought that the Entity was the child of Order, but others held that it was Chaos's attempt to *mimic* Order.)

After the archives there was one more visit to make before I left.

Edison Jr.

The smaller children were already settling down for the night. The nursery teacher Merra fetched Edison Jr and came out with him. He was in some new pyjamas, and had made a drawing he wanted to show me.

The picture showed a blue person, a greyish person with long hair, a box on a table, what looked like a bear with a giant sword... and a small person standing between the blue person and the long-haired person, holding both their hands.

"Is this for me?" I asked.

Edison Jr. shook his head.

"It's for Lexi! I'm sure she'll love it. I'm going to go and find her, and I'll give it to her then, OK?"

Nod.

"I'll be gone for a couple of days, so I want you to have fun while I'm gone, OK?"

With a nod, Edison Jr turned back towards his new teacher. But I fell to my knees and grabbed him for a big hug. Such a warm soft bundle! Then I watched as he walked back with Merra. Edison Jr. glanced back, just once, and I waved at him.

Then he was gone, and the door was quietly closed behind him, and I was left alone to dry my eyes on the sleeve of my new magician's tunic.

*

It was with a little trepidation that I passed the threshold of the Golden Tower. There was a nagging fear at the back of my mind warning me that, like Lumi, once I was outside the Golden Tower, the magic holding me together and upright would vanish. But nothing happened. I winced all the way to the foot of the steps, treading carefully like a marionette waiting for its strings to be cut. Only after I had stepped onto the sandy path did I relax a little.

The first thing I saw was my long-serving skateboard, which I kicked aside somewhat ungratefully. Looking back as I walked away, I saw that the Golden Tower was slightly glowing in the night. Above, in a deep black sky, a million stars shone in mostly-familiar constellations. It was cool in the night, and the dried weeds lining the path filled the air with a slightly spicy aroma. Something – a cricket or a cicada or maybe a gecko – chirped away in the undergrowth. There was no sign of anyone outside.

I took F3 out of my pocket to give him a good view of the Golden Tower and its garden. Then as I trudged back to the gate, I summarised what had happened in the ten or twelve days between him hitting the wall in the bunker and half an hour earlier when he had been repaired. Passing through the gate, I looked back; a dimly-shining dragon, far more concrete than before thanks to the lack of competing light, filled the gateway. F3, like Fred before him, saw an empty archway.

"It's good to have you back," I said, finishing my tale rather lamely.

"It's good to be alive," F3 replied.

"Damn right," I said, staring up at the beautiful velvet-black sky. "I could have done with your help back in Lith Tillac."

"The old 'pick up the demon-in-a-box and get zapped' ploy?"

"Fred tried something similar by taking a selfie for her."

"We'll get her back," F3 told me. "We'll get Lexi back."

The road over Callan was empty, and looking over its parapet on both sides I saw that most of the buildings were in darkness. F3 was interested to see the two great Dew Trees, one on either side of the bridge. The only sign of life below us still seemed to be the insistent banging of a smith's hammer coming from somewhere deep in the western side of the town. So I descended a ramp on that side and headed towards the sound. It was obvious where the smithy was with the bird's eye view from up on the bridge, but once I was down among the network of alleyways at the bottom of the town navigation became more difficult. The echoing sound of the hammer seemed to come from all directions, and the alleys themselves were a chaos of organic, piecemeal and unplanned construction. They turned corners at irregular angles, and even made U-turns in places. They split and sometimes rejoined, descended or ascended on slopes or steps, crossed under or over each other, and some ended in a blank wall. Their commonalities were that they were all empty, and they were all lined by sandstone buildings that, rather than being built by blocks, had been carved out of the ground.

For five minutes I didn't try too hard to find the smithy. I merely strolled, enjoying the cool night air, enjoying simply being able to walk again. I thought of the last time I had regained my mobility, in the bunker's surface cafeteria, and how happy I had been then, and how reckless. I thought of Lexi, and realised that since visiting her in Malafert I felt a little more relaxed about her situation than before. Her imprisonment was more Disney princess than Clash of the Titans. Rather than

171

worrying about arriving there in time to save her, the thing that began to nag at me as I slowly descended through the alleys of Callan was What The Hell I would do when I eventually *did* arrive. But, much as had been my attitude to school deadlines, I found it hard to be too worried about facing the Lich King again just yet. I had the distinct feeling that all I could do was head in his direction, and hope that something came up before I got there. If form was anything to go by, it would not be until the morning of the exam that terror would begin to grip me and I would wish that I had been motivated enough to do more homework.

Then I turned a corner and the alley I was following suddenly opened up into a square a hundred metres on a side, at whose centre rose a great silver tree set in a walled pool. I had reached the heart of West Callan.

Water steadily dripped from the Dew Tree's metal leaves into the pool below.

"Occult precipitation," F3 said.

"You can say that again," I said.

"Occult precipitation," F3 said.

I leaned against the low wall for a time, dipping my hands into the tepid water. I hadn't seen this much H_2O since the noxious river flowing out of Lith Tillac.

"It's too early for this place to be asleep," F3 said. "Callan must be all but abandoned."

"It's like a gold rush town when everyone has rushed to the next great strike," I said. "Except in this case, there was no next great strike, at least where magic is concerned."

*

The smithy was a single-level building about three ramps up from the Dew Tree. One of its several chimneys was sending orange smoke into the sky. The place had a doorway wide enough to drive a cart through; the interior was hot, and smoky, and lit by a combination of the reddish glow from an iron furnace and several oil lamps on the walls. The smith, wet with sweat, banged away at a horseshoe. So he was probably as much a farrier as a smith. He was also surprisingly young and slender. I rather expected someone who spent his days banging metal with a large hammer to

172

have arms as thick as his legs, but this guy was almost as skinny as me. Tools were laid out on a bench; sacks of charcoal and stacks of scrap metal lined the walls.

Three children stood by and watched the craftsman (their father?) at work. The paladin watched too, leaning against a barrel in the corner. The rest of the audience comprised a tan cat which had encroached as closely as it dared to the furnace, and two horses which peered over a half gate from a gloomy recess at the back of the room: Speckle and Goliath.

As I appeared in the doorway, all eight pairs of eyes clocked me. The paladin spoke, although it was not to say hello, or to remark at how well I was looking, or to scoff at my new peacock-embroidered coat. He had instead been telling the smith and his children the Tale of Beowulf, and had figured something out in the telling.

"You don't think that Beowulf should have had to face the dragon, do you?" He demanded.

"Beowulf...?" as you might imagine, the question did rather come as a surprise.

The smith stopped banging the hot shoe; its angry red colour rapidly faded to dull black. "We've heard about nothing else for the last hour," he said.

"And the Knight of the Lance," the middle-sized one of the three children said. The two older siblings were girls; the youngest was a boy. I put their ages at twelve, ten and six. All three were clad in drab and threadbare clothes, and lacked shoes.

"The Knight of the Lance...?" I asked.

"She means Sir Lancelot," F3 said.

I knew that, of course. But the sight of the three children had swept me into a daydream about returning to Callan after the Lich King had been defeated and setting up a free school. I think it was brought on by the sight of three pairs of bare grubby feet.

The children had been unfazed by my appearance in the smithy, apparently used to regular visits by magicians, even if not blue ones. But the sound of F3's disembodied androgynous voice made them all jump.

"Welcome back, F3," the paladin said. "What was it like, being dead?"

"Quiet," F3 replied.

I went over to Speckle and rubbed her neck, giving her a silent thank you for carrying me all the way from the mountains to the desert. "Beowulf had done enough," I said to the room. "Others should have faced the dragon in his stead." Clearly, the way I had spun the Tale of Beowulf had made his end seem like the death of someone trapped by a code of honour into a hopeless battle. Which was probably what the tale had meant it to seem like.

"He had to set the example," the paladin argued. "And he would have relished the chance to die with honour rather than wither away and die of nothing a decade later."

"Edison," F3 asked, "have you been regaling people with Saxon legends?"

"I had some help from Fred," I admitted.

"What happened to Wigless?" asked the youngest of the siblings.

"Wiglaf?" I asked. "He passed out of history at the end of Beowulf's story." It was a wild stab in the dark. I had no idea whether Wiglaf featured in his own spin-off series. I waited for F3 to contradict me.

"No-one knows what became of him," F3 said. "So his story can be whatever you imagine it to be."

In a Flap

"Rumpy, I—" the gull began, but its voice cut off suddenly and whatever it had been trying to say next became a strangled cry. Its blue colour faded to regulation gull white almost at once, proving that Edison's connection to the bird had been severed.

But it did not lapse into quiescence as he had promised. Instead its mind seemed to snap, and it went berserk. It leapt from Lexi's hands with a harsh indignant yell, fell to the floor, flapped its wings madly, took off, and flew across the room, colliding with a bedpost.

"Kaah! Kaah! Haah!" the gull squawked, and flew back across the room. This time its feet and wings knocked two stacks of books off the dressing table. Then it hovered for a moment and turned again, flying through the four-poster bed, shredding one of the perished net curtains as it went.

Lexi ran to get a cover, thinking to throw it over the bird. It seemed unable to recognise that the window offered it the only way out of the room.

That was when the stateroom door crashed open. The tiny handmaiden was there, staring at the scene. Her expression was unreadable with her glowing but otherwise empty eye sockets and her withered face.

"This crazy bird just flew in the window," Lexi said hurriedly.

Handmaiden closed the door behind her and took the other end of the blanket Lexi had gathered up. After a couple of misses, together they managed to snaffle the gull. Lexi took it to the window and tipped it out. She saw its ghostly white shape fall away in an uncontrolled descent at first, but then its wings opened, caught the air, and it glided away, seemingly unharmed. In moments it had vanished into the darkness.

"What are you scheming, My Lady?" Handmaiden asked.

Lexi thought she must be referring to the presence of the bird, but when she turned away from the window she saw that the undead servant was picking up some of the scattered books.

"I'm going to kill him if I can." Lexi had no intention of making a secret of that.

"You cannot. That gift is not yours to give," Handmaiden replied. Her voice betrayed no anger or reproach. She was just stating the facts as she saw them.

"I won't do what he wants."

"You will, My Lady. Eventually, one way or another, you will."

"Help me!" Lexi implored.

"I am helping you," Handmaiden said. So saying, she picked up one of the fallen books, straightened very slowly, and placed it on the dressing table.

"He is a monster. Why do you support him?"

"My allegiance is to the ruler of Malafert, always and forever," Handmaiden told her, and bent to pick up another book.

Training

We headed west in the cold heart of the night, alternately riding and walking to spare Speckle and Goliath. When the sun rose behind us and began to warm the new day we continued on, but by mid-morning we started to look out for shelter. As usual this came in the form of a water-cut gulley by the side of the road; we passed several that we deemed too small, but eventually came upon one that was ten feet deep and as wide in parts. Access to the bottom was by a dried-up channel that had once carried rainwater from the ancient road surface into the gulley.

The paladin dug for water as usual, although now he was using a new shovel I had purchased at the smith's with my advanced pay. I wondered whether the shovel counted as an expense I could reclaim later. Probably ought to have asked for a receipt. Water soon began to seep into the hole the paladin had made, and he rested his shovel against the gulley wall and took up a sitting position opposite me. Half an hour later a decent puddle had developed, which Speckle and Goliath slurped up.

"Throw something at me," I said to the paladin.

"Eh?"

"I have to learn to deflect projectiles with my catalysts," I explained, showing him my wrists.

The paladin tossed a sandstone pebble at me, which struck me on the forehead before I could even blink. "Ow!"

"You said to throw something at you," the paladin said.

"I wasn't ready."

There was a pause. The paladin sat there and watched the water slowly refill the puddle.

"I'm ready now, obviously."

The paladin tossed another pebble my way. This time I saw it coming, focussed my attention on it, and moved both hands in a gesture that was little more than a flinch.

The pebble disappeared.

"That was impressive," the paladin said. "You made it vanish."

"No. I don't think so. But I definitely did *something*."

At that moment the pebble re-entered our sphere of perception: it plopped down into some loose dry sand in the gulley bottom between us.

"Interesting," F3 said. "It seems you sent it at least thirty metres vertically, to judge by how long it took to land."

This was not an ideal outcome, because it was only by chance that the pebble had landed between us. What if it had been an incoming arrow? I could have deflected it upwards and ended up getting King Harolded.

After half an hour of practice and experimentation I could send the paladin's incoming pebbles in various directions, including right back at him. If both of my hands pushed forwards – then the pebble did a one eighty. A backhand left or right could send them to the sides. An instinctive flinch sent them almost vertically, and both palms down made them crash to the ground. And all without using any actual magic.

But I had to be aware of the incoming pebble; I had to *see* it to be able to deflect it. So if I turned my back on the paladin, he could hit me with ease; even though I knew a pebble was coming my way at some point, I had to sense its flight to be able to do anything about it.

At our next stop I began experimenting with shifting stationary objects. Again, these were small water-rounded pebbles from the bottom of a gulley. I could move the pebbles as if I had an invisible tennis racket; the hardest thing to do was to summon them to me, a feat the seamstress had demonstrated with ease using a bobbin. And when I did manage to summon the target pebble, it invariably shot towards me like a rocket, far too fast for me to correct its flight and steer it to a comfortable catch. Nevertheless, I thought I was making excellent progress.

"Don't go thinking you're a Jedi," F3 warned darkly, observing my efforts.

"I can move objects with my mind, so what else would you call it?"

"You can move very small objects, not X-wings," F3 said. "And I would be very cautious about relying on your telekinetic ability except as a parlour trick."

177

"Why not?" *Telekinetic*. That was a good word, one that I stored away for deployment later.

"Well, it's likely that you apply a hard-to-control but small amount of force against an incoming object, which suggests that your attempt to control said object could easily be thwarted by one of two important factors."

"Which are?"

"One. Mass. Two. Velocity. The two, multiplied together, give momentum. The change in momentum of an object is given by the amount of force applied to it. Which suggests..."

"That I couldn't stop a train if someone tossed one at me. Yeah, I get it."

"A massive slow object, or a rapid small object."

"Killjoy."

"Edison, I do not want to witness your attempt to cut an incoming arrow, I really don't."

"Well," I said with a shrug, "let's hope I never have to."

The Road to Kotmoor Dry

For three days we travelled west through the dry and dusty land, going up long shallow inclines and down relatively sharp declines, gradually gaining elevation with each sloping step. The familiar gulleys followed the valley bottoms, occasionally breaking through to the next valley down. The going was often hard, the road undercut and collapsed in places.

The days were noticeably cooler three days' travel west than they had been at Callan, and the nights were not as cold. There began to be more signs of life, in the form of scrubby bushes in the valley bottoms and strange far-off barking sounds in the night.

We had not long set off one evening, the lowering sun right in our faces, when we passed a fork in the road. The two forks ran almost parallel to one another for some distance, although the right-hand one rose up onto a higher piece of land. A signpost showed me that the destination along each path was an unintelligible scribble. The paladin silently led us down the left-hand fork, and as usual I simply followed him; but F3 had other ideas.

"That's the road to Kotmoor Dry," he said.

The name meant nothing to me. We rode on.

"We ought to go that way, if it doesn't take us too far from the Lomm road," F3 added.

The paladin and I rode on in silence.

"F3 to Earth, we need to take the other fork," F3 squawked.

I sighed. "Why? This looks like the main road."

"It is," said the paladin.

"Because, a long time ago, you promised to go with the paladin to visit his mother."

Now that F3 said that, the name Kotmoor Dry did begin to ring a few faint bells. "Paladin, does your mother live in Kotmoor Dry?"

"It would be a mistake to go that way," he muttered, avoiding answering the question but saying yes at the same time. "I will not be welcome there. They may try to arrest me for what I did."

"How far off the west road does it take us?" I asked.

The paladin stopped moving. He could see which way the wind was blowing. "About twenty miles."

"F3's right. We can afford an extra day to go this way."

"This will bring us only trouble," the paladin insisted.

"We'll just drop in, check your ma's OK, stay for a cup of tea, and ride on," I said. "She'll be pleased to see you. Trust me."

"Trust me," the paladin replied, "she won't be pleased to see me. Only trouble lies ahead if we take this road."

*

The paladin's prophecy of trouble ahead was proven right sooner than he could have anticipated.

The road to Kotmoor Dry began to rise more steeply; for a time, in the gathering gloom, we could see the main west road fall away below us, putting a scale on how far we had climbed. Then dusk began to slide towards night, and the low ground to our south became an inky well of nothingness.

But there was still light ahead of us above the horizon; the usual beautiful high pink desert clouds that I had shamefully long since ceased to marvel at bloomed high in the western sky. The clouds were lit by a sun that had sunk out of view, and seemed to have a magical, ethereal glow. We passed an abandoned waypost – little more than a weed-choked square of mud-brick walls and a couple of small buildings with no roofs. Soon we began to notice more signs that humans had modified the environment once upon a century: low crumbling walls and even places where drains, now full of scrub, had been cut along the roadside.

Then, silhouetted on the horizon maybe a mile ahead of us, we saw four people on horseback, line abreast. We had seen no other travellers since leaving Callan, and the realisation that there might be other humans in this desolate landscape came as a shock to me. For a time it was hard to tell which way the four riders were travelling, as flat black figures at extreme distance; but eventually it became clear that they were coming our way.

Our meeting five minutes later followed the usual "we're friendly" niceties at first: halting at a respectful distance and waving to acknowledge the other party before approaching slowly. The four riders reminded me of a gang of outlaws from a Western movie. The only things they were missing were the Colt 45s on their hips. They had wide-brimmed felt hats and neckerchiefs that could be pulled up to cover their mouths and noses in times of sandstorm... or highway robbery.

I grew increasing edgy as we drew closer. As a city kid, the idea of stopping to talk to strangers was one I had an inherent allergy to. It was just not what you did when passing four strangers in a city. In a city, you avoided eye contact and hoped that the strangers didn't take an interest in you.

When both groups eventually stopped there was ten feet between us. The leader of the four riders spoke first; at the same moment, one of his companions let out a laugh that sounded half-human, half horse. I almost expected to see the glint of gold on his exposed dentition. But there was no gold to be seen – just a couple of gaps large enough to be visible in the deepening gloom. Not for the first time I wished the post-apocalyptic world had heard of toothpaste.

"Nice night," were the leader's first words.

"Well, it's cooler than the day," I replied.

"Where you headed, if you don't mind my asking?"

"Highstand. Official business, you know."

"This the Kotmoor road. Seems like you missed your turn."

The spokesperson had missed a verb, too. But I didn't mention that. "We decided to take the scenic route. Well, it's been nice to chat–"

"Are my eyes deceiving me, or are you blue?"

One of the spokesman's companions snickered at this. The spokesman nudged his horse forwards a pace or two, peering at me curiously.

I stared back at him, saying nothing.

"You *are* blue. Well! So far as I know, there's only one blue kid in the whole of the Westfold. You must be the one they say was supposed to have defeated the Enemy and lost his magic in the defeating."

"No, you must be mistaking me for some other blue kid," I muttered.

"Tell me, are you two carrying anything interesting?"

"Are you?" I asked. There could be no doubt at all now that the four intended to rob us. Why couldn't they just be normal travellers? Not that I was afraid of them. Far from it. The paladin could have uprooted a roadside shrub and bludgeoned all four of them into submission by himself, unless they kept him at range and peppered him with arrows. I could understand them trying to rob *me*. I looked like the robbable type. But had they somehow not noticed that I was accompanied by someone the size (and the appearance, according to Edison Jr.) of a bear? It was probably my duty to arrest them or something as soon as they proved beyond all doubt that they were robbers. But I had no way to do that. And if we just faced them down and rode on...

181

we would only be condemning other travellers to be robbed later. These thoughts passed through my mind in the blink of an eye, before the leader's next question.

"Everyone knows that the blue kid carries a demon in a box that is worth a king's ransom. That true?"

F3 again. People always seemed to want to steal F3. "If you knew how much trouble he is, you wouldn't want to steal him," I said.

"Steal? I just wanted to have a look at it, that's all."

I had reached the limit of my patience. "Move aside. This conversation is getting boring."

There was a sudden glint of light on a blade as the gang's leader pulled out a knife.

I flinched, thinking it was already speeding through the air towards me.

The blade flew out of the robber's hand all right...

...and high into the evening sky. This happened without me intending it to; now, worried that the blade would come back down vertically, just like my first deflected pebble, I quickly picked it out, focussed on it, and was able to backhand-flip it so that it came down on the shadowy slope ten metres below us, where it clattered to a halt amid the stones.

"Put your knife away," I said to the gang's leader, and pushed Speckle forwards. None of the four – all seeming stunned by this display – tried to stop me or the paladin, who followed in my wake. As we rode on, I pulled F3 out of my coat pocket and held him in a position where he could see behind us, so that I could affect an air of confidence when in reality I was feeling a distinct itch between my shoulder blades from the potential sudden arrival of an arrow in my back.

"They have stopped to look for the knife," F3 said quietly when we were fifty yards away. "Nice work, by the way."

"Yes, well, I can't honestly say that you two were a great help."

"Thank you, Edison," the paladin said. "I was fearful that I would have to kill them all."

And that was the point. If we ever got into a real fight, I was going to be useless. The catalysts were tuppenny tricks, and I couldn't waste any real magic because I needed it for when I eventually faced the Lich King. I said as much.

F3 reminded me that I had faced a bron with no magic, no fear, and no plan, winging it and somehow winning. Or at least, scaring it off. That bron had run off into the woods with the paladin's old sword sticking out of it. I wondered where they were now.

"I hope that bron managed to get that sword out, and found somewhere to lick its wounds, and is even now terrorising the forest," I said.

"I hope so too," the paladin admitted.

"But you had gone there to kill it."

"No. I had gone anywhere, looking for anything that would try to kill *me*. I was a fool."

I realised that in all my dealings with aggressive humans I had never done worse than use F3 to stun them. I remembered the time in Crickne when Jasso killed the magician who wanted to drain my magic. He had done the dirty work I could not. The *wet* work. I shuddered at the memory. "You do know they're only going to go and rob the next defenceless people they meet, don't you?" I said.

"Yes, Edison," F3 replied. "Just as the bron will kill a defenceless young deer. You did the right thing. We have bigger fish to fry."

"And they have smaller fish to rob, and maybe fillet," I retorted.

Kotmoor Dry

The Kotmoor road levelled out not long after our encounter with the would-be highway robbers, but the terrain was still too uneven to proceed safely when it was fully dark, even with F3's light to guide us. So we travelled on for an hour and stopped for the night in a roofless stone-built shack just off the road. F3 kept watch in case the highwaymen came looking for us.

They didn't.

Kotmoor Dry sat on a wide dusty plateau a couple of hundred metres higher in elevation than where the road had forked. We rode into the town in the middle of the afternoon of the following day, its precincts marked by a ruined sign that had fallen to lie face down in the sandy soil. Little else at first hinted at any sort of civilisation. The fields along the roadside were apparently abandoned and full of thistly weeds that released a not-unpleasant spicy aroma in the warmth of the day. The paladin noted the fields around us and could not stop scowling and chuntering about them. I thought he was cursing the indolence of Kotmoor Dry's farmers... but he had other reasons to be upset by what he saw, as I discovered later.

We saw no people until a mile out of town, when we came across a dead man hanging in an iron-bound gibbet by the side of the road.

"If they try to arrest me..." the paladin began.

I interrupted. "I'm not going to allow that. As the King's representative in these parts, I am the law."

"The King's Law does not reach this far," the paladin muttered grimly. The presence of the dead guy in the gibbet did not augur well for the level of civilisation we should expect in Kotmoor Dry, that was for sure.

"You really don't want to be here, do you?"

"No," the paladin said. "We need to be out of here quickly, before I kill someone else."

Not far past the beginning of the town proper, marked by an unintelligible scribble cut into a large boulder by the roadside – the road split. The paladin indicated that we should take the northern path, which he called the back lane, or the Old East Road. The other way – the southern fork – led to the town square along the New East Road.

Kotmoor Dry was quiet, but not as quiet as Callan had been. We passed a couple of shifty-looking men pulling a handcart, a small group of children clad in beige rags and without shoes, and a couple of tan dogs, which fell into file behind us. The track we were on followed the course of a dried-up river bed, which ran along its northern side; almost all the mud-brick houses lining the road were on the opposite side. The dried-up river bed was choked with fleshy grey-green shrubs, which to judge by the twittering coming out of them seemed to be full of little finchy birds.

Unpleasant-smelling refuse heaps soon began to mingle with the fleshy shrubs, eventually displacing them altogether. In places, the rubbish piles all but filled the empty watercourse, seemingly waiting for a rainstorm to flush them downstream. Another group of children scattered at our approach, disappearing out of sight down an alley between two houses. The walls of mud-brick on our left were mostly high enough to hide the buildings beyond; breaks and open gates revealed glimpses of single-storey houses, some white-washed, all with tiny shuttered windows.

The paladin said nothing, but I could sense that he wanted to turn back to me and raise his eyebrows to say: "See?"

I struggled to think of a comment as chirpy as the finches by the roadside, coming up blank.

The further along the back lane we went, the less mean the place became. Soon we could glimpse the tops of the houses over the high walls, since most were now two-storied. Now their gates were usually double, the openings they sealed wide enough to drive a cart through.

Eventually the paladin pulled Goliath to a halt in front of the gates of one such house and swung out of the saddle. He walked up to the gates and tried to open them, finding that they were barred from within. Thus thwarted, he banged loudly on the dry wood. Our stray dog companions fled a little way at the sudden noise, and other dogs in the neighbourhood started barking.

We waited. "Someone's coming," F3 reported after a while.

Whoever they were, they didn't open the gate.

"What do you want?" called the voice of an unseen man.

"Olena Korland," the paladin said.

There was a long pause. Then: "No-one here by that name."

"Are you sure? She used to live here."

"No-one here by that name," the man insisted.

"Do you know where she is?"

This time the man on the other side of the gate did not reply.

"She was well known around here," the paladin said, his words softening and almost trailing into silence, just like the barking of one of neighbourhood watchdogs.

"Do you know where we can find her?" I asked loudly.

"No-one here by that name," the man said for the umpteenth name.

The paladin had given up; he began to walk back the way we had come, leading Goliath by his reins. I dismounted and followed. "We're getting somewhere," I said.

"Are we?"

"We know your name is Korland, for one thing."

"Is it?" the paladin asked emptily. "Maybe it was once, but not any more." He did not turn around to look at me. Instead he led us down an alley that led to the south. Again some children scattered out of our path, this time down side alleys running between the backs of the rows of houses. The cut-through was a short one; a minute later we emerged into the dusty square that called itself Kotmoor Dry's town centre.

Most of the buildings facing the square were boarded up. The only person in sight was a hurrying woman with a babe in arms who was making a curious bleating sound, almost as if she was carrying a swaddled lamb, not a child. Seeing us, her pace did not slacken, and if anything it redoubled; she disappeared into one of the shops, the door slamming shut behind her.

A well sat in the centre of the square, surrounded by a circular wall. A large evergreen tree stood over the well, casting a deep pool of shade in which a gang of small sandy-coloured cats were lazing like a pride of miniature lions. Several of them sat up to look, either at us, or the two similarly-coloured dogs that were still following us.

We advanced a little way into the square and stopped to survey our surroundings. F3 asked to be given a virtual tour, so I spun him around in a circle, giving his cameras a view of each building in turn. These were all made of the mud bricks that seemed to be a ubiquitous building material in Kotmoor Dry. The roofs were mostly thatched with a local grass, but they were also mostly in poor condition and in need of a do-over before the next time it rained.

There was a strange scent in the air, not unlike the spicy aroma of the fields, but with an added sweetness that was bordering on sickly.

"Try Old Rap's," the paladin said. "Someone in there will know where to find her. I'll water the horses."

"Old Rap's?"

"The tavern." The paladin gestured back the way we had come; ten metres to our north, with one of its walls forming the side of the alley, was a ramshackle two-storey building whose windows were hidden behind closed shutters. Like all good saloons, it had a hitching rail and a water trough in front of it – although the rail was empty of horses and the trough was empty of water.

"Right." I handed Speckle's reins to the paladin – not that she needed reins to be led, they were more there to prevent me from falling off – and sauntered towards the tavern.

Old Rap's sturdy and rustic door stood wide open, but the interior was too shady to see with eyes set for the brightness of the town square. The only way to find out what was inside, was to *go* inside; so I tugged down the waist of my coat, Jean-Luc Picard style, and strode purposefully into the bar.

It took a moment for my pupils to adjust to the relative gloom within.

I eventually made out five pairs of eyes staring at me. They belonged to a man standing behind the bar, two old men sitting close to the doorway, another man sitting in the corner by the window, and a kid of about ten, who stood in the middle of the room frozen in mid-stride as if it was one of those sudden silences in a game of musical statues.

The kid was dressed in the kind of garb I had seen children wearing throughout my travels in the Westfold. He had no shoes. His top was threadbare, and his coarse trousers were too long, so that his bare feet were mostly walking on their well-worn hems. He had a grimy face and the wayward hair of an anime hero, gathered in several tufts, not in his case for ease of drawing but stuck together by grime. His cheeks had a healthy-looking ruddy glow amid the dirt that mostly covered them.

The kid was the first of the bar's customers and staff to react. He glanced at the man in the corner and hurried out of the back of the bar, as if at a secret signal from him.

I walked up to the bar, trying to model the look of a confident law-enforcement official from the big city entering a backwater drinking hole. The barman, or bar owner, whichever he was, was larger around the middle than the other three men. He had a deliberate moustache and an accidental beard, one resulting from a few days' neglect of his shaving routine. He was pretending to polish an earthenware jug with a rag far too filthy to ever serve the purpose. I half expected a shotgun to be mounted behind the bar, and for there to be a whiskey bottle and two shot glasses waiting on it for a customer. But there was no gun, and the jugs and cups all around were earthenware, not glass. There was no piano in the corner with three missing keys. So Old Rap's was not quite frontier town saloon bar – but almost.

"I'm looking for Olena Korland," I said.

"Do you want a drink?" asked the barman.

There was a quiet snicker from the guy in the corner. I glanced his way, and noticed that he was positioned to watch the square through the slats in the window shutters. But for the sword lying on the table in front of him, he could have been Kotmoor Dry's resident gunslinger: blonde-haired, and blue-eyed, he was dressed in what looked like a leather waistcoat and a shirt far finer than the other three men's. A cigarette even smouldered between his lips.

For the first time since becoming a Royal Court Magician, I showed my badge, peeling back my coat to show the barman the silver flower-clutching gauntlet pinned to the inside of the lapel. "King's business," I said.

"Do you want a drink?" the barman repeated.

I sighed. Kotmoor Dry was not the place to come for conversation. "Lemonade?" I asked.

The barman had never heard of it. "Beer or spirit."

"Two beers," I said.

"Four coppers."

I produced a coin that I guessed was more than adequate payment – it was silver – and left it floating at eye level between us. The barman glanced at me suspiciously, glanced at the money suspiciously, and then grabbed the cash like a praying mantis seizing a butterfly. When the coin had disappeared, he set about pouring beer into two cups. I didn't taste it. Instead, I picked the cups up and sauntered over to the table where the two old men were sitting. A glance their way when I entered had told me that they were only pretending to drink beer from cups that had been empty for an hour. Standing over them confirmed my theory that they were both nursing empties, so without asking permission I sat down to join them.

"Thirsty?" I asked, and pushed the beers across the table towards them. I didn't use the catalysts for fear of knocking the cups over. "No strings attached. Sociable is my middle name."

"Who are yer, Mr. Sociable?" one of the old men asked.

"Edison Sociable Hawthorne, Royal Court Magician. My friend–"

"We know who your friend is," Blondie said from the corner.

The atmosphere in the bar suddenly changed. I felt like a fly who had just realised that its feet were stuck to a spider's web and needed to remain very cool lest the trap spring.

My brain whirred. Of course, that the paladin was recognisable was not surprising. Perhaps announcing his mother's name had been a bad move: but how else would we find out where she lived?

There was a brief silence as all five present in Old Rap's pondered their next move. Then the second old man spoke up.

"How long are yer staying, Magician?" he asked. "Will ye be gone by dark?"

"As soon as we've spoken to Olena, we're out of here," I told him with a fake smile. With the greatest possible care, I edged the beers towards him using the catalysts. Both he and his companion watched them go with fixed gazes. "Everyone knows where she lives, right? So there's no harm in you shortening our visit by telling me where to find her."

It was a bit of a non-sequitur, but for some reason, it worked. The second old man grabbed both of the beers, but his companion grabbed one of the two from him, suddenly afraid of missing out. It was the second old man who told me what I wanted to know.

Olena Korland

The paladin's mother lived in a tiny place down an alleyway not far from the town square. Her house was single-floored; its roof was thatched with the rough grass that was the most common roofing material in Kotmoor Dry. A small yard separated the house from the alleyway, with a trampled-dirt path leading to the front door. A half-dead tree leaned over the crumbling front wall; the garden gate, wedged open against a tussock of dry grass, looked as if it would fall off its hinges if anyone tried to close it.

We brought Speckle and Goliath into the garden, where they began to nibble at the vegetation in a half-hearted way that said it was not the choicest fodder. The paladin made the mistake of closing the gate, and it did half collapse in his hands. He ended up propping it up, mostly blocking the entrance but not quite.

I stood by politely and waited for him to knock, which, after a pause of a few seconds, he did. It did not take long for the knock to be answered.

Olena Korland opened the door. She was slim to the point of thinness. A leather tie cinched her long straight grey hair. She wore an old faded gown. The linen top she wore beneath it was embroidered with ears of wheat; once white, time had yellowed it to a buttery shade of yellow. A large white gold ring on her right forefinger caught the fading sunlight. "So. You're back," she said coldly. "You don't belong here. Go, before they string you up."

"You are right," the paladin agreed. "I should not have come."

He turned to go, but I stood in his way. "Let's not be too hasty." To the paladin's mother, I said: "We've come a long way, Lady Korland. Can we talk inside? We promise not to outstay our welcome."

"You already have," she replied. But as she retreated back into the shadows within her house, she left the door standing open, which I took as an invitation to follow her.

The front room was small. A curtain separated it from the rest of the house, which I estimated to consist of another room of about the same size.

The furniture was a single armchair, a footstool and a crude sideboard with a tarnished mirror. Like the garden, a single narrow diagonal way was clear of obstructions. The rest of the floor was covered by wicker boxes, books and papers, dust, grass, flakes of wood and spilled ash. Two statuettes of horses – one black, one white, and easily the most valuable items present – stood on the mantel over the fireplace, which was deep enough to allow cooking in a small cast-iron pot hanging on a chain.

Olena had already descended into the armchair. The paladin perched awkwardly on the footstool. I stood by the cold fireplace and looked at the horse statuettes. They were indeed fine pieces; like Lady Korland, they were out of place in their poor surroundings. Like the gold ring and linen tunic, they were relics of her former privileged life. "I like the horses," I said, by way of small talk.

"Are you a magician?" Olena snapped at me.

No small talk then. My usual conceited style of conversation seemed inappropriate for the situation, so I just said: "Yes. My name is Edison."

"Show me your palms, Edison."

I did so. They were blue, of course; the little black dot inflicted upon them by Kappa's tattoo machines was clearly visible on both.

"Why are you blue?"

Again this was not the time for a quip. "I come from the time before."

"Why, was everyone blue then?"

"No, but I was buried for two thousand years – and in that time... this happened."

"How do you know Lord Korland's murderer?"

I told a very brief version of the tale of how I had come upon Olena's son fighting a bron in the wilderness.

She immediately fixated on the word *wilderness*. "In the wilderness? Were there many people around?" Olena laughed, a laugh that was almost an insane cackle. "No? Then he was not helping anyone, was he? He was trying to find an honourable way to die, in vain hope of expunging his guilt. Pathetic."

Her words made me think of the Tale of Sir Lancelot that I had relayed in camp on our way south from Lar. Here, the paladin was not Sir Lancelot, but the knight he had spared, who had been rejected by his people and had wandered the land in search of redemption, a true knight errant. I decided to change the subject. "How long have you lived here, Lady Korland?"

"Don't call me that. I am Lady Korland no more. I am Olena for a little while longer. But in answer to your question, I have been here for ten years. I was lucky they didn't run me out of town or string me up after what happened, lucky they let me have this place."

"You had done nothing wrong," the paladin muttered.

"Hah!"

"Who drove you out of our house?" he asked.

"Why?" Olena asked sharply. "Are you going to go and murder them like you murdered Lord Korland?"

The paladin said nothing to this; he dropped his gaze.

"Well? Are you?"

"No, Mother."

"Don't you dare call me that."

"Your—" I began, but Olena cut me short.

"I have nothing to offer you, I'm afraid," she said.

"We have dried fruit and biscuits," I said. I had to go into the yard to get them from Speckle's saddlebags. Three teenaged boys had taken up station in the alleyway opposite Olena Korland's house. All three were lounging against the wall smoking; the lowering sun half-lit their faces. The youths avoided my gaze while I was in the yard. I resisted the temptation to ask them whether they had finished their homework. Returning, I found that a small folding table had been placed down for me to put my offering on. No-one touched the food, although Olena stared at it fixedly.

Conversation had stilled while I was out of the room, so I decided to try to start it again. "Olena, your son is a good man. Whatever happened here—"

I could tell by the way she was glowering at me that I had phrased this poorly.

"He has dedicated his life since that day to helping others. I would not be sitting here without him."

"Helping others? Like with the bron? No. He has dedicated his life to trying to salve his conscience."

The paladin had had enough. "Please excuse me, Mother," he said. "I must take care of the horses."

Olena and I sat in silence, listening as the paladin first shifted the ruined gate, and then led Speckle and Goliath away. When we could hear hooves no longer, Olena asked: "What brings you to Kotmoor Dry, magician?"

"We are just passing through on our way west," I said.

"This place is not on the way to anywhere."

"I insisted we take a short detour to find you."

"So he could ask for forgiveness?"

"No. So that he could see that you were all right. He still wears your locket, you know."

"He has no right to it!" Olena hissed. "It belongs to Lord Korland. Just like the armour he stole."

"The armour is lost," I admitted.

"Typical of him! Steal something, then lose it!"

"Actually, it was mostly my fault."

"Will you be staying long in Kotmoor Dry?"

"Everyone keeps asking me that," I said mildly.

"And the answer?"

"We have no business here, other than to speak with you."

"Well, you've spoken to me, so I expect you'll be wanting to keep moving."

"We'll leave in the morning. Our horses could do with a rest."

Olena looked at me sharply. "I think you'd be better to leave before dusk."

"Why? What has happened here?"

"Nothing has happened here since the day my husband was slain. Magician, you travel with a murderer, and everyone here knows him for what he is."

"May we call again in the morning?" I asked, moving to the open doorway.

"In the morning!" Olena gave a cackling laugh that was a sudden departure from her haughty bearing. She found my question intensely amusing. "In the morning! Yes. Why not?"

I left the food.

Outside, the three youths were still leaning against the opposite wall. Their conversation suddenly stilled, they watched as I tried to prop the gate up in its place, but made no move to help. I noticed that all three had short knives in their belts. Seeing the blades, I immediately tensed, ready to deflect a sudden attack with my catalysts or run like an antelope, whichever option seemed more promising at the time. But the youths did not attack me; they merely sauntered after me down the alley with the air of a bunch of hyenas following a bleeding wildebeest.

"F3," I muttered, too quietly for my followers to hear, "thanks for all your help."

"I did not wish to complicate matters," he replied. "I thought you were handling a difficult situation rather well."

"What's your diagnosis?"

"She's frightened. Everyone in Kotmoor Dry seems frightened. The question is, what of?"

Dusk

The fiery heat of the day was fading, and shadows covered most of Kotmoor Dry's town square by the time I reached it. The square was empty. There was no sign of the paladin or the horses.

"On your left, in the shadows," F3 said.

194

It was the kid from the bar. He was holding—

– he was holding a *crossbow*.

Click.

I flinched, and the bolt streaking towards me suddenly veered away into the sky on my right. I didn't have time to control its flight; a few seconds later the bolt hit the packed dirt of the town square point first and went in a couple of inches.

The kid ran off down the alley. "Hey!" I called after him. "Come back! I won't hurt you."

After that incident, the three youths following me hung back; they entered the square but lurked at its far side, watching as I approached Old Rap's Tavern. The door to the bar was closed. It was also locked.

"Rap! Open up!" I called, and knocked on the door. Rapped on the door, in fact.

"I'm not Old Rap," a voice I recognised as the barman's called back. "Old Rap's dead."

"Well open up, whoever you are."

"We're closed."

It was far too early to be closing time. "We need a room," I said.

"We're full tonight."

I couldn't help but laugh at that. But I had heard enough. It was quite difficult to grip the bolts holding the door closed with the aid of my catalysts, because they were on the inside. But I could sense them well enough to slide them open after a couple of false starts, and I immediately shoved the door open before the barman could reinstate them. But he was not trying to re-seat the bolts: he was fleeing. First he ran behind the bar, then he crashed through a door behind it, and then he crashed through a second door that ended up banging shut in his wake. The barman was gone.

"I just want a room," I said mildly. "I'm not going to hurt you."

But no-one could hear me. I was alone in the tavern. I meandered over to the bar to wait for the paladin to return, sniffing the contents of a few of the earthenware bottles, none of which smelled very appealing. After that I went to sit by the window.

My view of the square was limited by the slats of the shutters, but I could see that the three youths had gone. The trickle of men visiting one particular establishment on the eastern side of the square had dried up completely too, leaving the square entirely empty of people. It was too dark to make out the crossbow bolt, or to see whether any of the cats by the well were still there.

"Thanks for spotting that kid," I told F3.

"Based on the bolt's trajectory, I think it would have missed you anyway. There was no time to explain that."

"Do you think he was aiming to miss?"

"Unknown."

It was almost dark by the time the paladin returned. He had not lodged the horses somewhere as I had imagined he would; he led them behind him and hitched them to the rail outside Old Rap's. "There's a hosteler," he said, "but I didn't trust the owner. I'm not leaving them there," he said.

"Bring them in here," I suggested, "I'll clear a space. The barman won't mind. Well, he won't know about it until he has to clear up tomorrow. He wouldn't let me in – and when I let myself in, he just legged it."

In fact, I did not have to move many of the tables after all to accommodate our horses: there was a small yard out the back which was fairly secure and actually had small amounts of grass for them to nibble on. We led them through the bar by F3's light.

"By the way, a kid tried to put a crossbow bolt through me," I told the paladin.

He looked me up and down, noting that I was uninjured. "You used the catalysts?"

I shrugged. "F3 said it was going to miss anyway."

"This place never used to be as bad as this," the paladin said. "Something is terribly, terribly wrong."

"Something is wrong, and no-one will say what, including your ma. She said we could call in the morning if we like. I left the food."

"Thank you."

"Well, I guess this means we get the pick of the rooms," I said. "I can't remember the last time I slept in a bed."

Midnight Visitors

I awoke to the sound of F3 beeping. At first I thought I was late for school – but after a few befuddled moments I realised that it couldn't be that, because F3 liked to use my mother's voice to get me up for school in the morning. This beeping of his was a far more subtle alarm. It was an alarm that was not meant for widespread broadcast. Then as I shook sleep off, the dream of school vanished as real memories crowded it out. Kotmoor Dry. Old Rap's. Weird stuff.

F3 was propped up on the window sill looking out over the square through a compound window.

I sat up in the dark, and asked: "How long have you been beeping?"

"Twenty seconds. Mark."

"What's happening? Kevin."

"People are coming this way, and there's something a little odd about them."

I scrambled over to the window to take a look. There were indeed people moving in the town square, but they were almost invisible in the dark. All I could see was a curious slowly-bobbing diffuse golden glow that seemed to come from a set of poor-quality lamps. Turning to F3's screen gave me a better view: the glow belonged to a loose gang of people slowly walking our way. Their eyes gleamed brightly, as eyes tend to do when illuminated by infrared in the dark.

I ran next door to wake the paladin. F3 showed him a short video of the approaching gang. "What do we do? Run out the back?" I asked.

The gang, the more I looked at the three-second clip F3 kept showing, had a certain shuffliness about their gaits. Some had swords, but most seemed to be armed with agricultural tools, including a scythe and a couple of sickles.

The paladin seemed to sag a little. "It's me they are after," he said dreamily. "I must face them alone. You go. I'll catch up with you on the road."

"No way," I said. "Whatever we do, we stick together." I puffed out my chest. The effect was probably ruined a second later when the gang started banging on the tavern door and I jumped a foot in the air.

The paladin hurried to the stairs.

"Don't kill anyone," I said.

"It's too late for that," he replied, "far too late."

Downstairs, I placed F3 on the bar where he could both light the scene and use his harpoons to cut one or two of the mob to size. Then I lined up a row of earthenware jars and cups, ready to use my catalysts to launch them through the air at the first person to come through the door, more in hopes of causing a distraction than a deterrent.

"Can you shift those things?" F3 asked.

"If I'm scared enough, probably," I replied.

"You could use magic," he said. "I mean actual magic."

"F3, you know I can't spare a drop. I have to save everything for when we get to Malafert. And anyway, at a push, I could just throw them manually."

"Your throwing arm has always been terrible."

"That was until I had to haul myself around on a rubbish skateboard for months on end."

"Point taken."

There was something weird about the way the gang were banging on the door: they were chopping at it with their axes and swords, not trying to break it down. I supposed that it didn't really matter: whether they broke it down or chopped it to pieces, the barman was not going to be happy about the state of his door when he saw it in the morning.

But the paladin, seemingly tired of waiting, decided to let the mob in. He pushed a table behind the door so that it would only open wide enough to let one assailant through at a time, then he slid the heavy bolts open.

The foremost of the mob immediately burst in – and I, standing behind the bar waiting to serve them their drinks, suddenly *fell* in.

I needn't have worried about the paladin killing any of the mob.

The mob were past killing.

The mob were *already dead*.

They had a look I had seen before, with leathery skin and shrunken lips revealing a permanently gleeful expression. What I had taken to be F3's infrared light reflecting from within living eyeballs was in fact the dim glow that I knew from the Lich King's minions in the bunker. But unlike the first dead people I had encountered, these guys could walk, and hold a sword, and swing it.

My first thought was that the Lich King had caught wind of our mission and had sent a squad after us from the local graveyard. But I instinctively knew that wasn't what was happening. This was something else. What was it the paladin had said?

The first dead guy through the door was wearing leather armour over tattered shreds of clothes. He introduced himself by swinging his short sword at the paladin. I was able to use the catalysts to send the blow wild, and after that was pleased to discover that I could steer the undead's hands tolerably well, not just send a blow off target. Twisting my arms together made the confused undead follow my lead, almost as if I was controlling a marionette. Thus entangled, the foremost attacker was helpless to do anything about a swift blow from the paladin's far weightier sword, which knocked his head clean off like a golf ball off a tee.

But that was not the end of the matter. Both the head — now having rolled away under a table — and the body were still just as alive as they had been a moment before. Whatever magic it was that was animating them had not been dispelled by severing head from body.

"What do we do?" I yelled.

The paladin, now grappling with the headless undead, said: "They will perish in sunlight!"

"F3, how long until dawn?"

"Four hours, give or take," F3 replied.

The paladin had now dropped his own sword. He tripped the headless undead, wrested its weapon from its grasp, and skewered it to the wooden floor like an insect in an entomological cabinet. But even then it kept on wriggling and trying to free itself from its impalement. The head, meanwhile, had grown some stumpy little legs and was walking slowly but determinedly back to reunite itself with its body.

By now a second undead had shouldered its way through the half-open doorway. In the cone of light from F3's torch, he had the air of an actor entering the stage. This one was smaller than the first, and swung a sickle at the paladin in a manner that said: *I really don't like you.*

This time I couldn't intervene easily, because from where I was standing I couldn't tell whether the swing was going to hit the paladin or not; if I tried to steer it off course, I could have ended up making things worse. But the swing was a wild one, leaving the undead off balance and its sickle stuck in the floorboards; a shove from the paladin sent it sprawling to the floor.

"It's me they want!" the paladin yelled.

Yes. That was what the paladin had said. "So you keep saying!" I yelled back. He might have been right — on the other hand, it might just be that he was the only target within melee range so far, so he was the only one they were trying to hit.

The third undead through the door met the full force of the paladin's blade and went flying into the sickle-wielder. This duo was for a moment clumsily entangled with each other. Then they managed to separate themselves and lurch back to their feet...

...just as a fourth undead entered the bar. I threw a jug at it — the old-fashioned way. It caught the newcomer a glancing blow; the jug smashed to pieces on the wall.

The decapitated head was now in the process of reuniting itself with its body.

A zombie walks into a bar, I thought wildly, *and the barman says...*

I couldn't think of a punchline.

...and the barman says...

...and the barman says...

...I'm sorry for the slow service, we only have a skeleton staff on tonight.

I'll get my coat, I thought, and shouted: "We need to go!"

And by some miracle, the paladin looked around at me… and nodded. He knocked a couple of tables over to slow down the pursuit and vaulted over to my side of the bar.

F3's light showing the way, we fled out of the back of Old Rap's, running with Speckle and Goliath for a bit until we thought it safe enough to tie their saddles. Then we rode north up the alley to Back Lane; F3 reported that we were easily outdistancing our pursuers.

Half-way along Back Lane the paladin stopped Goliath and said: "I have to go to Kotmoor Hall."

"What is going on here?" I asked. "Those dead guys were not sent by the Lich King."

"No. No they weren't." The paladin stared at his feet. "At first I thought they had come to punish me for what I had done. But then I had a darker thought still, and I – I'm worried that I'm right."

"Right about what?"

"Edison, it might be dangerous at Kotmoor Hall – I can't ask you to risk your mission–"

"I already said, we stick together whatever happens," I told him. "In any case, we have to face a Lich King in about twenty minutes. Whatever this is, it can't be that scary. Which way?"

The Dark Secrets of Kotmoor Hall

Kotmoor Hall was a couple of miles south of Kotmoor Dry on the Lomm Road. The undead-infested tavern was now between us and it, so to make sure that we didn't encounter our bony friends again we had to ride in a wide loop that took us west out of the town entirely before turning south and eventually east and joining the Lomm road.

"If they're following us, they're going to be getting dizzy," I said.

"I don't think they are," the paladin said. Then he thought about it a bit, and added: "They probably *are* following us, quite by accident. They'll be coming back down the Lomm Road to reach the place they shelter during the day. If sunrise catches them in the open..."

The night was quite chilly. As usual, there were no clouds; a brilliant starscape of a million distant suns arched over us. There was no sign yet of dawn; F3 confirmed that it was still over three hours away. The empty Lomm Road we were following was lined with shallow ditches and half-ruined dry-stone walls. Beyond the walls lay endless fields of the ubiquitous spicy weed, a ghastly thicket of silver spiny bushes in F3's light.

"You're going to have to fill me in," I told the paladin, after waiting interminably for him to tell me what was going on. "I'm flying blind here. What do you know about all this?"

"They came to punish me," the paladin said emptily. "All those men who came... were men that I killed ten years ago. I told you what happened that day..."

"You put on your father's golden armour and rode out to kill the magician who made the drug he was addicted to," I remembered.

"I told you also that I killed his servants. I could have escaped from them. But I chose to fight, and they... they chose to fight, too."

"You won twelve against one, with a magician as well?"

"A paladin's armour has strong magical protection," the paladin explained. "And of course, physical protection too. And you saw what manner of men they were like when they were alive. Only half were guards. The other half were house-servants and labourers..."

"Right, I'm with you so far. You killed the magician and all his servants. Then, after they were dead, you fled the town and wandered the land trying to do penance for your sins. Meanwhile, somebody raised the servants from the dead and used them as servants who worked twice as hard for less pay than the old servants. Or less pay than the old version of the same servants." A thought occurred to me. "Are you *absolutely sure* you killed their boss...?"

"His name was Melur. Yes. I killed him all right. I separated his head from his body. Another magician must have heard of Melur's demise and come to Kotmoor Dry to take over his evil trade."

"Exploiting a sudden gap in the market. I get that only a necromancer could have dead servants, but that isn't usually essential for the drug-selling game."

"Only a magician can create the drug. By itself, in its raw form, tentacula is mild and harmless. Only when infused with magic does it have the capability to destroy the lives of those who take it. They need take it only once to become slaves to it forever. They live for nothing else and are good for nothing else. They take the drug and find peace for a time. Then when the effect wears off, their only thought is how they can quickly return to that peace."

"It must have been hard living with someone–"

"Hard or not, there can be no excuse for what I did. Only penance."

"Tentacula...?" F3 prompted.

The paladin laughed bitterly. "These fields are full of it. You thought this was food? Weeds that have overtaken abandoned farms? Luckily for the indolent folk of Kotmoor, the plant more or less grows itself. You would indeed call it a weed if you were trying to grow food here. The leaves are stripped and pulverised. What is left is cured under the sky until it is ready to roll. It's sold and used all over the Westfold – you've seen many people smoking it on your travels. But what Melur did was something else. His product had no name. My father called it 'stuff.' It produces a far more potent effect on its user, but it can only be created with an infusion of magic."

Magic, as you know, was in short supply in the Westfold. If Melur had to use his magic to infuse every batch of "stuff" then he would soon run out. I said as much to the paladin, who laughed bitterly.

"No. He would not run out. His magic was not your magic. It did not come from the ground, or the air, or the sun. His magic came from blood. The dealers brought him three things: the tentacula they wanted to be infused, money and an animal. Usually it was a chicken, but sometimes a larger animal was used for a bigger batch. For wealthy users like my father, money was all that was required. Of course, the money ran out in the end, and our possessions had to be sold to keep the addiction going. Dealers know how to drive a hard bargain, to buy things for a fraction of their worth."

Two whitewashed gateposts loomed out of the night on our right. Their twin gates were fixed wide open, their feet stuck fast in tussocks of dead grass. The paladin drew Goliath to a halt and climbed down; I followed suit. "There were two guards constantly on duty here," he said, laughing bitterly. "The idiots waved me through. They would probably be standing here now, but instead they are walking back from town."

F3 decided this was a good time to quench his light, and neither I nor the paladin objected. I knew he would monitor for danger using the infrared wavelengths of his cameras. We went through the gate and began to walk up the long drive to Kotmoor Hall leading our horses, treading carefully as our eyes adjusted to the darkness.

"So this was your house once?" I whispered.

"Yes," the paladin replied. He did not whisper back, and in truth the sound of the horses' hooves striking the stone track was louder than his voice. The implication was that whoever was in the big house ahead was already well aware of our approach.

A minute's walking took us to another gate, again wedged open by vegetation. This marked the division between the farmland and the grounds of the house proper. I could already see a small collection of buildings in the dim beyond the gate, faint as ghosts in the night.

Kotmoor Hall was straight in front of us. It was three floors tall, with its top floor built into the slope of the roof as a line of dormer windows. Over to our left was a collection of outbuildings: two cottages, sheds, and a strange tall cylinder that I only recognised as a former dovecote a minute later when F3 put his light back on. No lights were showing anywhere in Kotmoor Hall or the cottages; then again, it *was* about three in the morning. But this was no ordinary darkness, no ordinary quiet. I got the feeling that our approach was being watched by someone within the big house, and I was already wondering whether it was worth maintaining the stealthy approach when F3 gave me a good excuse to abandon it.

"In the ditch, to your left," the omni said quietly.

It was too gloomy to see what he was on about. "Show us," I said, pulling F3 from my pocket.

At once, harsh white light flooded the road and the ditch alongside it.

The ditch was full of dry bones.

Now, I would make a terrible archaeologist, but even I knew that among the mix of bones were plenty that were human. I knew that because some of them were skulls.

"Oh no," the paladin said. He stopped walking and seemed to wilt where he stood, staring at ten years of murder.

It was obvious that the bodies in the ditch had knocked over a domino in the paladin's mind and set off an unstoppable chain reaction. He leapt to the conclusion that his actions a decade before had wrought this hell in Kotmoor Dry, as surely as if he had killed these people...

...these small people...

...these *children*...

...himself.

I thought he was wrong. But there was nothing I could say at that moment that would stand that domino back up. Terrible things – unthinkable things – had happened here, that would not have happened if the paladin had not ridden out that night to kill the magician Melur and his servants. That much could not be disputed. It did not matter that other things, possibly worse things, might have happened if he had just ridden out of Kotmoor Dry without stopping here.

A single glance into the ditch was enough for me. I didn't bother to look too closely. It didn't matter how many dead children there were here. We didn't need to call in a pathologist to tell us how they were killed, or at a pinch ask F3. Whoever or whatever had killed them was up ahead in the big house, waiting for us.

As you know, I have a particular approach to dangerous situations. My modus operandi is to charge forwards, find out what the dangerous thing is, and then run away from it screaming. So before the paladin had regathered his wits, I was already half-way across Kotmoor Hall's forecourt. The exiled son of Kotmoor Dry was still just standing there in the dark behind me, staring down at the bodies in the ditch, bodies he could no longer see because I had taken F3's light with me.

The big house was solidly built of finely-shaped stone blocks, over which there was a generous thickness of once-whitewashed render. Its front door was three steps above the ground level, set behind a wide portico that spanned the entire frontage. Each floor had six windows, each formed of sixteen panes of glass that looked as if they had not been cleaned in a decade. I expected to see faces there looking down at me, but the cone of F3's light picked out no watchers, only grime, broken windows and heavy curtains. The two cottages on the left-hand side of the forecourt had an abandoned feel about them: their doors stood wide open, the storm shutters over their windows closed as if permanently. I imagined that these two outbuildings were where most of the undead servants spent their days, hiding within from the hurtful sun.

A cart with a broken wheel stood to the right side of the forecourt near the low circular wall surrounding a well. Beyond the well and the cart, by F3's light, I glimpsed what looked like a giant heap of ash.

"I can hear something," F3 said quietly. "Go around to the left."

"Wait here," I said to Speckle, and let go of her reins, leaving her standing in the middle of the forecourt. Then, by F3's bright white light, I pushed around to the side of the house through knee-high grasses. Half-way along the side of the house I noticed a pair of cellar doors, almost flush with the ground and buried in a decade's worth of dust and dead vegetation.

"In there," F3 said.

I approached warily. The doors were held together by a great clunky padlock.

"In there?" I asked.

"In there."

I breathed deeply, pretending to try to clear my mind, and knelt down next to the cellar doors. Even shining F3's light straight into the mechanism, it was hard to get a grip on the padlock's levers. By the time I managed to open it with a clockwise spin of my right forefinger, the paladin had caught up with me; looking back I saw that he had left Goliath with Speckle.

The cellar doors were heavy, their hinges rusted almost to immobility. It took all my strength to open first one and then the other. The hinges shrieked in protest as I lifted the doors, and I was none too careful about how I let them fall. There could be absolutely no doubt that our presence was known about now.

I shone F3's light down into the black void at my feet, and saw three children cowering in the corner of the cellar. As the light picked them out, their hands covered their eyes and they screamed in abject terror.

It's not just chickens any more, is it? I thought to myself. But I didn't say that. Instead, I shaped a reassuring smile that the prisoners probably couldn't see and said, "I'm from the government, and I'm here to help." The screams of the children softened to mere whimpering, though it probably had nothing to do with what I had said. Panning the light around their cell, I saw a door into a further part of the cellar; apart from that, and the children, all that there was to see was the packed dirt of the cellar floor. It was too far for the children to climb out my way, but I reasoned that the door presumably led to stairs up to the ground level and a better way in and out. "It's OK. You're safe now. But I'll have to come around the other way to let you out," I told them, trying to remain calm and to exude an air of confidence that I did not feel.

"Don't leave us!" blurted one of the children, a boy whose age I put at ten.

"Melur has taken Wodrin and Tula," said another, a slightly older girl.

I almost spluttered with surprise. What did she mean, *Melur?* Melur was dead…

…wasn't he?

Dancing with the Dead

Melur, the magician who had fed the paladin's father Gresphi's addiction, had been killed ten years before. The paladin had made it quite clear that Melur's death had not been in any doubt: his head had been separated from his body. That was usually enough to kill most people. So the name pronounced by the children in the cellar made no sense. And yet I was uncomfortably reminded of the undead soldier that had survived disassembly at Old Rap's.

Two of the three prisoners had spoken so far. As if sharing their duties out, it was the third, a girl probably of an age with the boy, ten years old, who spoke next. "Don't let him kill them!" she urged.

"I take it that door's locked?" I asked.

"Yes. But we can't go that way anyway because Melur's there," said the older of the two girls.

"Did you say Melur?" I said this half-turned to face the paladin, who shook his head. *Not possible*, the headshake said.

I shrugged at him and leapt down into the hole. I was trying to be cool, but the drop was slightly further than it looked, a combination that meant I regretted my jump for the next ten seconds. Hobbling around in pain, my mobility was not helped by the way the three children immediately pounced on me as a safe haven like a pack of remora on a passing shark. "It's OK guys," I said, trying to prise them off. "You're safe now." After a pause, I added: "Probably."

"I'll go around and let you out," the paladin called down, and began to move away.

"I'll see if I can open it," I replied, but I could tell he was already out of earshot. It was going to be hard to open the door with my catalysts, not just because I couldn't see the bolts holding it shut, but also because I had three children hanging off my arms. "I need free hands for a bit," I said mildly, and the children shifted their grips onto my coat. I was able to shuffle to the door and inspect it by F3's light. This was too bright at first, the glare from the ancient dried wood making it impossible to see anything on the other side of the numerous but tiny gaps between the joints in the door. Once F3 had dialled the brightness down to ten percent of its maximum level it was much easier to see where the bolts were.

Clunk.

Clunk.

The door swung open. I moved forwards, and the three children let go of me like blossom parting from a cherry tree in an April wind. They preferred to wait in the relative safety of their now-open prison to see how I got on with Melur before daring to cross its threshold. Looking back at them, I said: "I'll check if it's safe."

Immediately outside the children's cell, passages ran right and left to other parts of the cellar, while straight ahead of me a set of stairs rose up to the ground floor. That seemed to be the obvious path to take to reach the front door. I climbed cautiously, keeping F3's light on a very low setting. When I was half-way up I heard a great crashing sound, which I guessed was the paladin breaking the front door in.

Before the echo of the crash had died away, it was followed by the most pained and unearthly wail I had ever heard. A bright pulse of eerie green light washed down the stairwell from above as if a bizarre alien bomb had gone off.

Slightly dazzled, I hurried on up the staircase. Three seconds later I reached the top and found myself in a doorway opening into Kotmoor Hall's great hall.

The great hall took up most of the first two floors of the house. It was a large open space dominated by an enormous fireplace at its far end. A large cauldron sat on a tripod there, but it was not presently in use, for the fire had died down to mere embers. A long table ran front to back, with benches lined up alongside for seating. The table was covered in drug-making paraphernalia: ceramic jars, pestles and mortars, knives, combs, baskets of what was presumably blocks of cured tentacula ready for processing, sieves, bottles and funnels, a couple of dim oil lamps and even a cage with four worried-looking hens peering out of it. The place reeked of tentacula – it more than reeked, in fact, because the smell made walking into the hall like being punched in the head, and gave me an instant eye-watering headache.

A large armchair was set by the smouldering fireplace. A dead man was sitting limply in the armchair like an elderly person placed there by a relative to warm their old cold bones. When alive, the dead man had been a giant, as large and as strong as my friend the paladin. Now his stature was the same, but there was precious little meat on his bones, which had dried to sticks. I was relieved to see that his eyes were not glowing: no undead, this.

But the acidic radiance that had dazzled me on the stairs came from elsewhere in the hall. This weird green light was already fading, but it was still bright enough to turn the walls, the mezzanine balcony above and the ceiling above that an unpleasant lime colour.

The light came from Melur.

Melur had been dead for ten years, but was doing a fair job of hiding it. He was a little withered thing hardly any larger than the child whose life-force he had just drained. He had on a shabby black robe cinched in the middle by a gold-decorated belt and wore an abundance of jewellery, including a pendant on a chain and bangles that rattled on forearms that had dried to leather. His long hair was as black as his robe, and he had a moustache and beard from whose centre twin rows of peg-like teeth gleamed.

Smoke rose from Melur's victim, and an acrid stench along with it, enough to almost overwhelm the reek of tentacula. One of Wodrin or Tula had been reduced to a withered husk little more than bones. Released, the corpse fell to the floor, a steaming and smoking shell.

Like I said, the source of the radioactive glow in the hall was Melur himself. Every bit of his exposed flesh – face, forearms and bare feet – was radiating green light, making him look like a Doctor Who monster from the 1970s.

The undead magician stood near the centre of the hall, mostly facing away from me towards his front door, which after all had just been smashed in by a large and imposing intruder. He spared me no more than a glance before returning to stare at the paladin, who made his way slowly but deliberately down the little hallway into the hall.

"So the reports were true. You have returned to cause more mischief," Melur snarled at the paladin. He did not wait for his visitor to reply, but with a gesture threw a wall of force forwards, knocking the paladin flying back out of the hall. Another gesture slammed the door closed behind him.

He'll be fine, I thought. He usually was.

Then the wizened old thing slowly turned to look my way.

With the new angle, silhouetted by the fading green light emanating from the flesh of his neck, I could now make out the stitches that held Melur's head on.

"Nice work," I said. "Did you do the stitching yourself?"

Melur grinned at me. The grin formed as slowly as he had turned my way. It was an unpleasant sight. "Not too old to be drained," he said. His voice, as a dried-out undead person with a crudely-reattached head, was as raspy as you might imagine.

I was waiting for him to send a wall of force my way, as he had done with the paladin. But he didn't do that. Instead, after moving slowly, slowly, slowly to face me... he suddenly moved almost too quickly to see.

He's going to bite my–

My hands moved faster than my thoughts, snapping up to cover my neck.

And, as if his entire move had been executed at lightning speed but entirely pre-programmed, Melur went through with his bite – except that his peg teeth fastened on my left hand instead of the left side of my neck.

A vampire, brilliant, I thought vaguely. Pain shot through my hand and a dizzying sensation swept over me.

"Use magic!" F3 said. I was still holding him in my left hand, which was now clamped to my neck, so there was no way he could usefully deploy his harpoons.

"No!" I yelled. Instead of using magic, I used metal. With my right hand, I reached around behind my head, pulled the throwing dagger from my left sleeve, and stabbed Melur in the back with it. I probably would have thought twice about making this move on a living person, even if they were trying to bite my neck. As it was, I probably went too soft on the blow, partly too squeamish to stab somebody properly and partly worried that I would shove the blade right through my opponent, out the other side and end up killing myself with it.

Melur didn't seem to like it too much. He unfastened his teeth from my hand, shot back to the centre of the hall as fast as he had shot out of it, skipped effortlessly onto the long table and vaulted from there up to the mezzanine balcony above in one smooth movement. Then he balanced on the balcony's railing like an acrobat on a beam and stared back down at me. "I taste magic," he hissed. "You are a magician."

"That's right, bozo," I replied. I noticed with slight nausea that Melur had left a trail of glowing-green blood spatters behind him.

At that point I was somewhat relieved to see the paladin bursting back into the great hall to rejoin the battle.

"Murderer!" the vampire hissed, pointing down at the newcomer with one accusing finger. "Murderer!" he repeated. "Murderer!"

"I heard you the first time," I muttered. But it turned out that he wasn't talking to me. He wasn't even talking to the paladin. He was talking to the *dead man in the armchair*.

And the dead man in the armchair was listening. His empty eye sockets began to glow with warm golden light. He slowly straightened up and began to rise. Only now did I notice that there was a large sword resting across his knees.

"Murderer!" rattled the now-standing undead man, who had turned to face the paladin.

Normally the paladin would be gleefully charging into the fray, undeterred by the size and nature of his foe. But this time he was frozen to the spot, completely immobile. Although he had drawn his sword, he was holding it limply in one hand, its drooping point almost resting on the floor. Something about Melur's lurching monster had dismayed him more than any other foe could have.

It took me another second to twig: Melur's undead guardian was none other than Gresphi, the paladin's father. His sword was as long as he was tall, and far outsized the paladin's. With two skeletal hands Gresphi raised his weapon up. He stalked forwards two staccato steps and brought his weapon down in a mighty blow. And the paladin was still standing there slump-shouldered, stunned, hardly even able to half-heartedly respond to the attack.

It was the kind of blow that the paladin could normally avoid in his sleep. But this time he was not going to avoid it awake, and it was going to cut him in half. At the last possible moment, I realised that he was neither going to dodge nor block, and that it was up to me to save him. Pushing was easier than pulling: so I pushed Gresphi's greatsword away as hard as the catalysts would let me. It was enough –

more than enough. The blow missed the paladin by miles and the giant sword crashed against the wooden floor. Gresphi staggered, looking like a drunken cook trying to kill a scurrying cockroach with a six-foot rolling pin.

I had to snap the paladin out of his daze, fast. The first thing I could think of to shout at him, like a second at a boxing match, was "Get your guard up!"

The paladin glanced my way, and, amazingly, obeyed me.

Then something came hurtling down from the balcony: Melur had picked up an ornamental axe on display there and hurled it telekinetically at the paladin. I steered it out of harm's way, but it was too heavy and too fast for me to do anything as useful as send it back the way it had come, towards Melur. F3 would probably have said something about 'momentum' at this point. Next, Melur made a dramatic gesture, and another axe shook itself free from the wall behind him and flew at the paladin. Then came a set of fluted plate mail, which disintegrated in mid-flight; only a few bits of it hit their target, individually too light to cause much harm.

Melur cast about him for more ammunition, and found a set of antlers from an unknown beast among the items on display on the wall. This time, rather than steer them away, I carefully guided their flight towards Melur's undead slave. Several points disappeared into his back and appeared again from his chest a moment later. Gresphi was staggered slightly by the blow, but he was entirely unharmed by it. The dead father went straight back to swinging wildly at his living son, the horns puncturing his torso looking like a bizarre giant parasitic tick clinging to his back.

Again Melur looked around him for more ammo.

I took the chance of the slight lull to charge up the two flights of stairs to join him at the balcony level. But the instant my head appeared above the level of the balcony floor, I became Melur's next target. This time the missile was a low hardwood table. It was too close already and too heavy to steer away, but I managed to drop down flat on the stairs fast enough that it sailed over my head and smashed into the wall behind me.

"Use magic!" F3 said.

"No!" I argued. I scrambled forwards, staying low and moving to my right so that the heavy balcony railings gave me at least partial protection from Melur's next missile. But he was already back after his old target. Gresphi's armchair flew from the fireplace towards the paladin, and I was too late to intervene. It struck home, knocking the paladin off balance. "Sorry!" I yelled down, hoping that the armchair was softer than it looked. The blow had not harmed the paladin; in fact, it seemed to knock him out of his stupor, because after that he began to defend his father's blows more actively, seeking to counter the undead's haymaker swings.

I crawled along, wincing as a wooden chest smashed into but luckily not through the railings next to me. Then my nose bumped into a pair of grimy feet. Looking up, I saw a girl – Tula? – standing there motionlessly, staring into space. She was probably traumatised at having just witnessed her fellow prisoner go up in green smoke as fuel for Melur's unearthly powers.

"It's OK, you're safe now," I said optimistically.

Tula, if that was her name, just carried on staring into space.

"Run and hide downstairs," I told her.

Nothing. Hypnotised.

Meanwhile, the flow of missiles coming my way had dried up. This was because I was close to Tula, and Melur didn't want to pulverise his organic battery before he had the chance to drain her of energy. Instead, he directed more missiles at the paladin, the first of them a basket of refined tentacula from the hall table. I was able to deflect it easily.

The paladin and his father were each giving as good as they got now. I wondered whether undead ever got tired. Probably not. The paladin's magic sword was glowing – well, it had of course been glowing before, but until now its light had been too dim to see in the eerie green incandescence of Melur. Did this mean that Melur's battery was already running flat?

"Operation F3 saves the day," I whispered.

"Roger," F3 replied. "Where?" He immediately switched his light off, which was not that obvious a move since it was already only at ten percent brightness.

A little way further around the balcony there was a large sideboard made of dark wood. I scrambled past it, setting F3 on its top facing back towards Tula in what I hoped was a not too unsubtle move. This I combined with grabbing a large china plate and tossing it, frisbee style, at the necromancer. It was probably one of the paladin's family heirlooms, I thought with a mental shrug; a moment later, having missed its target, the plate smashed into a thousand pieces on the back wall.

The next thing Melur's telekinesis seized upon to throw was one of the oil lamps on the long table. Like the paladin's sword, their formerly dim light was brightening as the undead magician's luminance faded. From my position I could no longer see the paladin and his father because they were hidden by the balcony floor, so rather than try to steer the lamp into the undead Gresphi, I had no choice but to dash it against the floor instead. The glass cracked and a little pool of burning oil began to spread around it.

Melur's green glow was definitely fading now. It was no longer incandescent; it was dim, more like the light from a glow worm than an LED torch. He went back into slo-mo mode, turning anti-clockwise by degrees, still balanced with withered bare feet on the balcony railing. At some point in his turn the dagger in his back came into view, a trickle of pearlescent verdigris slime trailing from where it entered the dead flesh. Seeing it there, my instinct was to recall the blade; perhaps the leak would grow faster when the little steel plug in it was gone.

Reaching for my dagger with the catalysts was hard, but once I had hold of it, it shot towards me, rotating in mid-flight so that it was going blade first. I thought about trying to catch it, but dropped my hand out of the way just in time; the dagger thudded into the wood-panelling behind me and stuck fast.

And the green flow *was* stronger.

Melur suddenly went into fast-forwards mode again. But he didn't come after me. Instead, he darted into a stairwell on the other side of the hall that was the mirror-image of the one I had climbed up. He disappeared so fast that it took me a moment to decide whether he had gone upstairs or down: up, a splash of green told me. I followed him as far as the stairwell; looking up, I saw only darkness, and a trail of luminous spatters.

Then I realised that rather than pursue the necromancer, this was my chance to intervene decisively in the other battle. For a moment it was two against one; and if I could help the paladin win against Gresphi now, it could be two against one again if and when the undead magician reappeared on the scene. The paladin and his father were back in view now that I had gone half-way around the balcony; they were still trading blow for blow. They were well matched. But one of them, I reflected, was definitely *drier* than the other, and there was a little puddle of fire within easy reach. All I had to do was to push the flame over to the undead paladin, set light to his moth-eaten robes, and let a natural exothermic reaction do the rest. But to my frustration I found that I could not move the flame no matter how hard I pushed it with my catalysts.

Rapid footsteps scampered across the ceiling above me. It sounded as if Melur was again in fast-forwards mode and was hurrying through the top floor towards the opposite stairwell.

Below me, I noticed that the oil flame had snagged onto the wicker basket that Melur had thrown earlier. Its cargo of greenish-greyish bricks was scattered around too, and one or two of them were smouldering. What to pick up? What to throw?

In the end it was obvious: the oil lamp itself. There was still enough oil within it that it would continue to burn if removed from the puddle it sat in. And it was light enough to move with the slightest effort. So I flipped it up and steered it into the undead's side, avoiding the crablike antlers clinging to his back. Tiny droplets of fire exploded in all directions, and Gresphi's clothes caught at once. The Frankenpaladin monster didn't seem to notice. He was focussed entirely on killing his son.

In slo-mo, Melur appeared on the balcony opposite me. In sudden fast-forward mode, he scuttled over to seize Tula. He was hardly glowing at all any more. But I had to act fast to save Tula and stop him from recharging.

I ran forwards, and as I had hoped, Melur turned to face me, keeping his fodder in front of him like a fleshy shield. Poised to bite Tula's neck, he rasped, "Leave my house, magician!"

"Or else what? You'll kill the girl you were going to kill anyway?"

"This is not your house," F3 said from the sideboard.

Melur turned to locate the source of this strange disembodied voice.

There was a little click as F3 released his harpoons. Before they hit home, I had time to wonder whether a high voltage shock would have any effect on an undead necromancer.

It did. All Melur's dry old muscles went into spasm. He let go of Tula.

I ran forwards, not quite knowing what I was going to do when I reached them.

Then F3 flashed his light. For a tenth of a second it was like daylight in the great hall. Melur was blinded.

I ran on.

F3 flashed again.

I reached the withered old monster, grabbed him, and propelled him over the balcony. I half-expected him to just float off into the air, but he fell like a stone and landed heavily. He was no longer glowing at all.

And before he could move, the paladin charged over and chopped his head off.

Second time lucky, I thought.

The burning Gresphi, for a moment still in pursuit of his son, faltered when his master's head was removed. He took one final step before collapsing, his second-time dead corpse quickly enveloped in fire and smoke.

Tula, suddenly released from her spell, shrieked in my ear.

And Melur's reign of terror in Kotmoor Dry was finally at an end.

Dawn

Watching Kotmoor Hall burn rather than trying to save it seemed to be the right thing to do. It would probably have been impossible to douse the fire anyway, because it was already well alight by the time the battle was over. There was a moment of confusion when Tula snapped out of her trance and thought that I was a demon that had been raised by Melur and was therefore a threat.

"It's all right," I said. "It's over. He's dead. Properly dead this time."

Tula looked where I was pointing, through the balcony railings where the headless necromancer lay close to his burning bodyguard. After that Tula let me show her to the stairs down from the balcony, and reaching ground level we met the other three children coming up the cellar stairs. Then all five of us legged it through the burning hall to the front door, zigzagging between flaming patches and ducking under the worst of the smoke.

The paladin was ahead of us, carrying the still-smouldering body of Wodrin in his arms. A panicked clucking from the hens made me go on a diversion to pick up their cage, so I was the last of the six of us out of Kotmoor Hall. I released the birds on the forecourt; they sprinted away a short distance, and then, feathers slightly ruffled, settled down to pecking for seed in the dust.

The paladin had laid the body of Wodrin down by the well. It was too hot to go back inside the hall, so to find a cloth to cover him with I went poking about in one of the cottages. The children, meanwhile, scarpered as far as the other side of the forecourt before turning to watch their prison burn. Returning with a perished curtain I had pulled down from inside a window, I covered Wodrin as completely as I could.

The paladin ignored me: he sat on the low wall around the well and stared at his feet. Fearing that I would end up falling backwards down the well if I joined him there, I sat nearby on the dusty ground instead.

My hand hurt. Looking down, in the waxing light of the flames, I saw that my blood looked a murky grey-green colour. "I'm bleeding," I told F3.

"Fix it with magic," he replied.

"It will probably stop eventually," I said vaguely. Then I remembered something else. "One of my daggers is still in there. I suppose that's had it."

"Your dagger? Summon it. You did it before."

"Yes, but I could see it then."

"What's it made of?" F3 asked.

"I dunno," I said, although there were no consonants the way I said it. Then, I clarified: "Metal."

"Brilliant," F3 said. "Well, depending on the melting point of the metal, you'll be able to retrieve it when the fire is out, or not."

Dawn approached; the stars were fading as the sky lightened. The fire of Kotmoor Hall roared up, sending a vast column of black smoke into the sky. The roof fell in. Windows smashed one by one. The reek of tentacula was powerful, even in the relatively clean air where we were sitting.

I watched the flames. The children huddled together and watched the flames too. The paladin stared at his boots.

By daylight the house was mostly gone; starved of fuel, the fire had died down. The column of smoke was just as thick, and in the cloudless sky and flat landscape it must have been visible for miles around. It rose up, hardly drifting in the still air until it reached an altitude where stronger winds began. Then the top sheared off and began to spread eastwards.

An hour after dawn a group of six slovenly-looking men with a handcart walked up from the direction of Kotmoor Dry and tried to take delivery of that morning's refined product. Seeing them, the children ran to hide in one of the cottages. The paladin was still ignoring the world. So it was up to me to speak to them.

The men already knew – but could not yet comprehend – that no more refined product was coming, ever. The great black column of smoke had told them that much when they first set out for Kotmoor Hall that morning. They knew what the source of the fire had to be in this barren landscape. But they had come to collect the stuff anyway, in vain hope that the conflagration they could see was related to something else. They looked sweaty and pale with fear, almost as if they were already suffering withdrawal symptoms. But that was probably just me reading too much into things. After all, I thought, the golden rule of drug dealers was for them not to get high on their own supply.

"Where's Melur?" one of the men asked me. I couldn't help noticing that all of them were armed with long straight daggers.

"No-one here by that name," I said. "Just me and the chickens."

"You're a magician? Are you taking over?"

It took me a moment to realise that the gang's spokesman was wondering whether I was planning to take over running the supercharged tentacula trade now that I had deposed its former kingpin Melur. The men had spread out in an arc, almost as if they were thinking about attacking me. A heavy tread behind me drew their nervous gazes. I turned to see that the paladin had walked a little way towards us, and that he was pointing back up the track towards the main road. The dealers got the hint and wandered off.

A little later, two different men came to try to deliver a basket of refined tentacula for processing into stuff. Like the others, they must have known from miles away that their trade was ended; again some part of them just could not accept that as of that morning Kotmoor Dry had fundamentally and irrevocably changed. "What will we do?" they asked me, panic etched into their faces.

"Try growing corn," I said helpfully. "Open a stand selling tortillas." The men said nothing. They turned and left, retreating with a slow tread and occasionally glancing over their shoulders, just to check that they weren't dreaming.

I pulled a few buckets of water up from the well to give to Speckle and Goliath to drink. Then I sat down again on the ground near the paladin. For a long time we didn't speak: as before, I watched the fire dying down, and he stared at his feet.

"Ten years ago," he said eventually, "I lit a fire in this town. Then I fled. Only now I have returned does it become clear how much damage that fire wrought."

"Paladin," I said, "you just saved this town."

"Too late," he said. "Too much has been destroyed." Abruptly he launched himself to his feet and strode towards one of the wooden sheds, which turned out to be a tool store. He came back out with a long-handled red-rusty shovel, leapt over the ditch into the weeds beyond, and began to dig.

Hearing the sound of metal on stone, the four children came back out of the cottage. Sizing up the situation, they decided to help the paladin dig Wodrin's grave, and three of them filed over to the shed to see what tools were available. Tula came my way instead: she had found a cleanish piece of cloth to tie around my wounded hand.

"Thank you for saving us," she said to me, bandaging me up.

My usual chirpy style of response seemed out of place, bearing in mind the body close to my feet. So I merely said, "I'm sorry we were late."

Tula went to help dig the grave. I watched her go, thinking: there's no point *me* helping. All five of us can't dig a single grave at the same time. But the paladin soon spread the children out in a line: he was intending to bury the human corpses from the ditch, too. *Dammit*, I thought, and forced myself to go and join in.

By mid-morning, the paladin had dug two decently-sized graves. The children and I were flagging, having barely managed one between us. The soil was stony, parched as hard as concrete, and hell to dig. The movement soon started my hand bleeding again; I watched as a blue stain crept over the off-white material.

"Use magic to dig," F3 advised.

"Stop saying that!" I told him. "You're no help, you know that? Come on everybody, it's break time." The children at least agreed, but the paladin carried on digging as if he was in a life-or-death battle with the ground. I gave out the last of our food, seeing no alternative but to share it with the children we had rescued. Then I wandered over to the charred shell of Kotmoor Hall, half-hoping that I might be able to find my missing dagger.

I stood in the threshold – the lintel was still intact over the doorway, although most of the front wall was gone – and looked down into the cellar, where most of the surviving wood from the roof, the upper floor and the ground floor was heaped up. In the ashes between the thickest beams, I saw a gleam of blue-white metal. This turned out not to be the dagger I was looking for, but was instead a small rectangular ingot.

"Electrum," I said to F3. "I remember now. My dagger's made of electrum, or it was." I took him out of my pocket so that he could see down into the rubble.

"That's not your dagger, and it's not electrum," F3 said.

"No, it's an ingot. But it's the same metal. It's the same colour, anyway."

"Electrum isn't blue."

"Yes it is."

"It would have melted in the heat."

"No it wouldn't." I gingerly clambered down a little way along a charred beam to get a better angle on the ingot so that I could summon it to me. The ingot was small, about the size of a bar of bath soap that was in need of replacing. By poking about and moving bits of rubble I discovered that Melur had amassed quite a hoard over the years. There were probably at least five hundred of the little bars; whatever container they had been in, it had been incinerated by the fire.

"I suppose this is worth something," I said, rubbing soot off the ingot. There was a logo of a dragon stamped on it, and some indecipherable writing arranged in an ellipse around that. "There may be enough here to, I dunno, build an orphanage or something." I was already thinking grimly about what would become of the four children we had rescued.

"It would have been cheaper to not let the place burn down in the first place," F3 pointed out.

"It was too far gone to put it out by manual means without a high-pressure fire hose. And it turns out I can't do anything with flame, at least not with the catalysts alone," I said.

"You're worried about what will become of those four," F3 deduced, referring back to my earlier comment about the orphanage.

"Yes."

"You wonder how they could possibly return to their parents in Kotmoor Dry, when those parents probably gave them up for a few weeks' worth of drug?"

"Yes," I said miserably.

"Things will be different now."

"Yes. But will they be better, or worse?"

I meandered back towards where the gravedigging was going on, thinking that I had no excuse to continue slacking. Even the children had gone back to work.

Then I saw a reason to prevaricate further. A lone figure was walking up the track towards Kotmoor Hall. I went to meet her.

Olena Korland moved in a dignified way. She looked like the chief mourner at a funeral. Reaching me, she asked: "Is he at rest?"

The tumblers whirled. She was referring to Gresphi.

"Yes," I said.

"He was a good man once."

"Your son is a good man now."

"I know." She noticed my hand. "You're injured."

I shrugged, trying to play it cool. "Hopefully I'm not going to become a vampire."

"No," she said solemnly. "Not now the one who bit you has died."

Which was reassuring in a non-reassuring sort of way.

"Thank you for bringing my son back to me, magician," Olena said. We began to walk back to where the paladin and the four children were digging.

"This was not quite the homecoming I had hoped for," I replied.

"Many in Kotmoor are already missing what Melur provided for them. Some will die from its lack before they cease needing it."

"I can recommend herbs that might reduce the symptoms," F3 said. After this intervention from an apparently disembodied voice, I had to introduce him to Olena. "If we head south to Lomm," F3 added after that, "we can send some supplies back to you from there. We have funds now."

I showed Olena the electrum bar. "Is this worth anything? Will we be able to purchase enough herbs with it?"

"Forged in Syanabyan by dragonfire," she read, her thumb further cleaning the design and text I had already had a go at. "I should think so, yes," she added.

"Can you look after the rest? There are quite a lot more in the rubble."

"I will see to it that they are shared out," Olena Korland said with a nod. "They belong to the people of Kotmoor, not me."

"What about these children? I don't want to send them back to their parents..."

"They can stay here with me," Lady Korland said. "We'll move into the cottages until the big house is rebuilt."

We were close now to where the graves were being dug. The children had noticed us, but the paladin had not.

"Ronan," Olena Korland called out. "Ro!"

The paladin froze in the middle of a savage strike with his shovel. Slowly he turned to look our way.

Highstand Pass

"I thought she called you Conan for a minute," I said, for probably the tenth time.

"I think I preferred things the old way," Ronan said with a groan.

"I'll still call you the paladin. Ronan the paladin. *Sir* Ronan the paladin? Doesn't have quite the ring of Conan the Barbarian, but..."

It was three days later, and we were approaching the Highstand Pass. The road was narrow and winding, leading us up the flank of a sheep-grazed valley that was shockingly moist and green compared to the dusty lands we had grown used to. A trickle of refugees from the Cursed Vale passed us going the other way. Naturally I attracted a lot of attention, but it was nothing I wasn't used to. No-one blamed me for their misfortune, and I just felt guilty about it and said nothing.

We left Kotmoor Dry not long after Olena Korland gave her son his name back. I poked around and found my dagger; once electric blue, it was now a hideous green colour with rainbow highlights, seemingly where the heat of the fire had damaged its surface. The handle had entirely burnt off, and only a narrow metal core remained. I thought it was ruined, but F3 demurred. The handle could be replaced easily, he said. He also claimed that it was emanating an excessive quantity of green photons, which were not merely a reflected subset of the incident light. Very faintly, my dagger was glowing. Some of Melur's blood magic seemed to have rubbed off on it. I wondered whether that made it cursed or holy.

"It's cursed if the pointy end is stuck in your flesh," F3 opined. "If you're the one holding the handle, it's holy."

It took us half a day to reach Lomm, where I had a new handle put on my cursed/holy dagger and we bought a cartload of medicinal herbs to send back up the road to Kotmoor Dry. Of course, there was no knowing whether the salesman on the Lomm market would make good on his promise and actually deliver them. I hinted that Lady Korland would probably put in another order once she had taken delivery of the first, but we had no choice other than to take his word on trust and keep on heading west.

The Barrier Mountains had been visible from Kotmoor Dry as a smudge of clouds on the western horizon; as we drew closer, the land rose, and the foothills of the mountains came into view, enveloped entirely by dense grey weather. There was no way of telling what elevation we had reached, or at what elevation Highstand Pass was at; all that we could tell was that the character of the land had changed, and that we were steadily climbing. Every turn in the Highstand Road was marked by a large stone figure that looked like a fish/human hybrid out of a tale by H.P. Lovecraft. A passing refugee told us that the figures were there to protect the roadway from being washed away in a storm. I didn't tell them that was a crazy idea. Maybe it wasn't. The world since the Quacker was a crazy place.

But there were also more practical measures in place to stop the road from washing away. On the upslope side, a ditch had been cut; rainwater from the mountains above us turned these ditches into pleasant little babbling streams, half-choked with mosses and rushes and other plants that the passing herbivores did not find very palatable.

And there were herbivores aplenty needing a bite. The refugees from the Cursed Vale had brought with them their sheep flocks, which were kept from straying too far from the road by assiduous dogs. But the pickings on this side of the pass were thin indeed, leading to strife between the incumbent graziers and the refugees –

which as the representative of a king whose name I could never remember, I was occasionally called in to mediate on. The grazing was poor and there was little enough to eat for their own flocks, said the resident shepherds; the refugees said that their livestock would never survive the journey to reach the hoped-for safe haven if they were prevented from grazing along the way. My proposed compromise was that the refugees' flocks should be allowed to graze as long as they kept moving. If they reached somewhere that grazing rights had not been taken up in, they should be free to stop.

Anyway, I told them, we were on our way to kill the Lich King, so everything would soon be back to normal, and the refugees would be able to return home. They looked from me to the paladin and back, thought about what they were fleeing from... and kept on down the mountainside.

Highstand Fort sat in the middle of the pass like a giant exhausted stone spider. The spider's body was the fort itself; its legs radiated out and up the valley sides in a series of defensive walls tapering in stature the higher they went. At the level of the road, the walls rose to an imposing six metres; they eventually petered out a hundred metres up the valley sides, by which time the terrain was so steep that a wall probably became superfluous. The upper reaches of the pass were shrouded in twisting clouds most of the time, billowing and ripping through from the west. But in the way the rapid clouds came together and tore themselves apart again moments later, the more distant parts of the walls occasionally came into view. Overhead, the clouds were thick and silvery; squally showers of icy rain struck every few minutes. At first the change from the dry hot ground to the east was refreshing; but I had soon had enough of the cold and wet.

Reaching the fort, we found that there were more refugees in it than soldiers. The latter were mostly old men; some of the more enthusiastic among them saluted me. Not knowing the form, I did not salute back, but replied verbally – *good morning, hello, how are things?, good to see you* were a few of my tries.

A ginger-haired sergeant with a shabby red jacket marking him out from his drab-uniformed men was in temporary charge of the fort. Sergeant Pinz seemed to be pleased to see us and asked me what his orders were. Of course, I had no orders for him; we were just passing through. His hopes of being relieved of command dashed, he seemed to brighten when he realised that he had a trump card to play. He was about to close the pass, he said; scouts had reported that the undead army was only a mile away, and any attempt to go down the road into the Cursed Vale would be suicide. He was waiting as long as possible to shut and bar the great doors, because a trickle of refugees was still passing through, and his commanding officer, a captain called Evon, had taken twenty men down the road two days before and not yet returned. Either way it would be suicide for us to proceed, so our only viable option was to help defend the fort from the oncoming onslaught.

"Let's have a look," I said to the paladin, who agreed. I picked out a family of refugees who were camped out on the inside of the fort's rear wall and wandered over to them. They numbered four, and had a pack mule to help them carry their burdens. Three generations were present: a wiry old man, a youngish woman, and her two children, a girl and a boy. All four looked pale, cold, and exhausted.

"Will you be here for the next hour?" I asked them.

"Depends what happens with the dead," said the woman, jerking her head towards the west.

"Would you mind looking after Speckle for a bit? And my friend's horse?" Without waiting for an answer, I pressed Speckle's reins into the hands of the girl. Seemingly numb with shock, she was standing there just staring into space with an expression that reminded me uncomfortably of the way Tula had looked when I found her on Kotmoor Hall's balcony. "I'm Edison," I said. "What's your name?"

"Urna," said the girl, slowly seeing us.

"Urna, this is Speckle. Would you mind holding her for me?"

"She's beautiful," Urna said, suddenly noticing Speckle.

I took that as a yes. "She used to be..." I groped for the right colour, "...chestnut. A powerful magician turned her grey. If you like, I'll tell you the tale of how it happened when we get back." I said this in part to deter the family from fleeing with our horses. Knowing that there was something magical about Speckle might put them off, I hoped. But looking at them I got the feeling they were just normal people in a tough spot and could be probably be trusted. I certainly had more trust in them than in some of the soldiers around, who seemed fidgety and ready to drop their spears and abandon their posts the next time somebody sneezed.

"Men took our horses," Urna said, stroking Speckle's neck.

That meant that those same men had probably ridden past us on their stolen horses in the last day or two without us having any reason to suspect them of malfeasance. We had probably said hello to them assuming that they were humans, not monsters. I couldn't think of a suitable platitude to say to Urna about that, so I just told her that we would be right back, and left Speckle in her care. The paladin wordlessly handed over Goliath's reins to her younger brother, and followed me.

Sergeant Pinz led us through an open portcullis, over a narrow bridge crossing a stone-faced trench, past another open portcullis, through a square courtyard surrounded by tall crenelated walls and out onto the road beyond via a large gatehouse. If the Highstand Fort represented the division between the Cursed Vale and the Westfold, that first step beyond the threshold meant we were officially in the Lich King's Realm.

The road ahead of us was flat for a time, but heavily rutted by cart wheels and riven by transverse ditches built in centuries past to slow forces attacking up the road. Bridges over the ditches had recently been reduced to single planks that could be crossed by foot traffic but would be easy to drag away when the enemy arrived – not that there were any soldiers out there to do the dragging, but I guessed that was the principle. The walls flanking the road were little more than ferny piles of rubble.

A small number of refugees were running our way, the large gaps between them a function of their athletic prowess, how far they had come, and when they had set off. Each moved flat out, but all were flagging. Most had no possessions beyond what they were wearing, any baggage having apparently been abandoned on the road up the valley in the name of haste. Having just ridden up the other side, I could well imagine how exhausting being pursued up it on foot would have been. *Slow down and you die*, I thought. All the refugees I could see looked young and fit. There were no old people and no children. I wondered whether that meant that only the young and fit had survived the climb.

I began to walk down the road, the paladin beside me. Sergeant Pinz lingered near the gatehouse. "How close are they?" I asked a man running towards the fort.

"Get out of my way," was his breathless reply as he reached us.

"They're close," I said to the paladin, stepping aside.

The road ahead of us began to slope downwards, and as it did so it disappeared into the ground-level cloud. By the naked eye, I could now see only four refugees running up the slope below me. "F3?" I asked.

"These four are the last of the refugees nearby," F3 replied. "There are others behind them."

"You mean *undead* others? But it's broad daylight."

"Evidently the clouds here are dense enough that the undead don't care about whatever rules you think they ought to be abiding by vis-à-vis their sensitivity to sunlight."

That was a pity. I had hoped that we could at least travel freely by daylight until we reached the Mushroom of Fear spreading out from the top of Malafert. Even that plan was now looking rather far-fetched, to say nothing of my vague idea of hiding by night along the way too.

The third of the four refugees running towards us tripped and fell. He looked young and fit to me, so I assumed he would be up in a trice. But he did not get up. The woman immediately behind him – the last refugee on the road – ran past him, but skidded to a halt two paces later and turned to help. I was pleased to see that it was not yet everyone for themselves. Or not quite everyone for themselves. Then I noticed that the reason the man had been reluctant to get up was because he had an arrow in his calf.

I looked back. In the mist fifty metres behind me, a dozen grizzled veterans looked down from the gatehouse wall. The great iron-bound door in the stone gatehouse had been swung shut, but enough of a gap had been left to admit one person at a time. "Don't shut that gate!" I yelled and began to run forwards.

It would have been acceptable to stand and gawp, to just watch to see if the last two refugees made it. But that was not my style. As you know, I prefer to run towards danger, find out what it is, and then leg it screaming. Anyway, once I started moving I felt committed to the rescue. Getting half-way to the three-legged refugee pair and then doing a one-eighty would look worse than not helping at all.

"I hope you know what you're doing," F3 said.

"Not really, no. How can I? It's too foggy up here."

Grey figures were emerging from the mist down the slope. They were still quite distant, but were closing fast. One of them stopped to launch an arrow our way; I steered it harmlessly aside with the catalysts.

The woman was half-dragging the man, who seemed to be unable to put any weight on his skewered leg. "Can you stand?" I asked, arriving at their position. On the face of it, it was a dumb question. But the man answered it anyway.

"No – I'm sorry–"

I was about to tell him not to be silly, that he didn't need to apologise for that, but any further conversation was rendered unnecessary by the arrival of Ronan, who simply picked the man up, turned around, and began to lumber back towards the gatehouse with him. The woman ran with them, easily catching up. I remained where I was, and turned to look back down the road.

"Why aren't you running away?" F3 wanted to know.

"Because I'm faster than them, and I can't be seen to overtake them."

"Don't put on a show."

"I'm not," I said, as if this was a ridiculous suggestion. But an observer would have noted that I was standing legs apart, hands on hips, chin up, facing down the track in a defiant pose. Something told me to turn sideways on, in case I didn't pick up the next arrow flying my way; getting turned into a blue kebab at that moment would not have been ideal.

I could now see scores of the Lich King's mob, and more were emerging from the clouds all the time. Most of the undead charging towards me had been dead for some little while. Centuries, perhaps. They rattled along in rusty armour that was now far

230

too loose for them. Many had tarnished helmets with tattered plumes. I wondered whether these happy-looking soldiers had perished fighting earlier iterations of undead armies governed by earlier Lich Kings. But among these near-skeletons were more than a few with plenty of flesh on their bones. People who were undead now, but who had been alive not long ago. Their deaths, and undeaths, were on my conscience. Among them were civilians, men, women and children still in the clothes they had been wearing when Bartlet's minions had killed them. Some had arrows sticking out of them.

Another arrow flew over the heads of the vanguard, and another. Both were off-target, so I just let them sail by. And a dark half-idea came to me then, to let the next one that *was* on target find its mark. But I knew that the time for punishing myself for the deaths of those who now wanted to eat me was not now. My guilt would have to stay bottled up until after I had killed Bartlet, if I didn't die trying. So I turned and legged it. By the time I started moving, the mountain track below me was full of undead.

The pass was, er, impassable. Ronan and I would have to find another way into the Cursed Vale.

A Vision in the Mist

The dark pall had by now spread so far from the Black Tower that Lexi had lost track of whether it was day or night. It hardly mattered either way. She spent her hours reading ancient books, or trying to. They were almost all in unfamiliar languages or even different character sets than she was used to. A few had illustrations in the margin in inks that were still bright even after an immense passage of time. All her hunting was in pursuit of a single quarry: the manner of death of the six previous Lich Kings. Unlock that secret, and she would be left with one or more tactics for killing Bartlet.

At that moment, Lexi was engrossed in a tale apparently written in the time of the fourth Lich King, Arenord. This polemic detailed all the ways in which Tursul, the predecessor he had overthrown, had been a terrible king, thereby justifying the coup. What it had not yet even hinted at was the manner of Tursul's assassination.

There was a curt knock at the door.

Lexi ignored it.

Someone opened the door and entered without waiting for an answer. She heard the tailor's voice say, "My Lady, King Bartlet requests your presence in the throne room."

Lexi barely glanced up at the bowing Tailor before turning back to the book in front of her, although the text was already swimming in front of her eyes.

"I think you will want to see this," the tailor said. He turned and went back out of the room, leaving the door open behind him.

Lexi placed a little bookmark horizontally on the page, indicating the exact line she was trying to decipher. Then she picked up her little lamp and followed the Lich King's servant. They went up the long curving stairs, past the dining room floor, and on up to the throne room above.

Bartlet was sitting in his new-made throne on the extreme left of the row, now of seven. As he had promised, he had made his seat of state of old dark coffin wood, which was bolted together with rusty iron and decorated by representations of large white worms crawling in and out of it. He had not made a throne for Lexi. He had taken to wearing a soft matt black gown with a hood that he could throw up to hide most of his face. His blue stick hands and blue stick feet were often all that could be seen of him; his face was usually hidden in a pool of shadow cast by the hood, so that only its two blue glowing eyes were visible. Today was no exception. "Come and stand by me, my betrothed," Bartlet ordered. "I have caught a glimpse of your loyal lapdog."

"We are not betrothed," Lexi said flatly.

"We are going to be together for eternity," Bartlet told her, "so whether or not we are betrothed yet is not important."

"Not to you. Why are you so obsessed with marrying me? Why don't you marry one of the thousands of people in this city who are already undead?"

"They are but hollow shells," Bartlet said. "I knew you were coming to my tomb hundreds of years before you did. I dreamed in my long sleep, and in my dreams I saw you. And then when you finally came, your presence in that long-quiet place was enough to awaken me at last. The dream told me that I must have you by my side, or lose my sanity over the course of my eternal reign. It said we would disagree at first, about everything, but that disagreeing at first was best, because disagreement is spice, and agreement is boredom. That way, our relationship would develop over time, and last forever."

"I will be a hollow shell when you marry me," Lexi spat.

"Not if the appropriate ceremony is observed at the wedding," Tailor said, bowing her way.

"Hurry, betrothed," Bartlet said, "if you want to see him again while he's still alive."

But Lexi did not hurry. She did not move at all, enjoying the chance to annoy her captor. Bartlet though was characteristically short of patience. He beckoned her with one straight blue forefinger, and she felt herself sliding unstoppably across the flagstones towards him. The sudden journey reached its end when she was beside him, standing on his right at the end of the arc of thrones.

"When you are Queen," Bartlet said, "I think I will make him your personal servant."

Then Lexi looked back the way she had been dragged, and saw Edison.

An image of him was floating in mid-air, in a cloud of mist ten feet in front of Bartlet. Edison was sporting a new three-quarter-length jacket in royal blue, a shade darker than his skin and hair. He was standing in the middle of what looked like a mountain track, hands on hips, staring directly at Bartlet almost as if he could see him. The image of Edison was quite small; if he had actually been in the throne room, he would have been standing all the way over at its far side. But then he began to move closer – or rather, the *viewer* began to move closer to him.

And Lexi realised that she was looking through the eyes of one of Bartlet's undead soldiers.

An arrow streaked past, shot by someone standing behind the undead whose view they shared. It was not on target for Edison, who ignored it. He stared down the track for a long moment as an unknown number of the dead closed in on him. Then he turned and ran away. There was some sort of structure or wall behind him, dimly seen in the mist; Edison reached a door in it and passed through, out of sight.

"That wall marks the end of the lands of the dead," Bartlet said solemnly. "Every yard we have taken so far belongs to us by right. Should we go further? Have you reconsidered your answer?"

"No," Lexi spat.

"Then we go further. If your lapdog lives, if he can find a way to sneak past my soldiers, he should arrive in three to four days. We will see if you reconsider then."

"I won't."

"We shall see. We shall see. Meanwhile, how goes your research? Have you found any answers in your dusty tomes? Have you discovered yet a way to slay me?"

Lexi said nothing.

"Well?" demanded Bartlet.

This vision of Edison meant that time was running out to find the answer she needed in the books she mostly could not read. All she knew was that sunlight was the one sure cure. One book said that if the machine casting the dark pall were to stop, then the Lich King would die. But there was an in-built paradox: only the Lich King's death could stop the Clockwork. One source mentioned an ancient sword called Wolf Star, but didn't know what had become of it. The Wolf Star device featured in many decorations Lexi had seen in the Black Tower, including on the very floor of the throne room. Why the sword's name should be shared by the Black Tower's decorations was a mystery.

"Daylight is the only sure way," Lexi admitted, through gritted teeth.

"What a pity I have a device to create permanent night!" Bartlet crowed. "Have you found out how to stop the machine?"

"It will stop at your death, and you will die at its stop," Lexi said bitterly.

"So what you are telling me, my dear, is that my reign is going to be a very long one."

We'll see, Lexi thought grimly. *We'll see.*

Running Edge

Once we were back inside the fort, the wounded man was carried away to have his arrow removed. The paladin, Sergeant Pinz and I wandered back through the various divisions of the fortifications, ending up on the eastern side where the refugee family were still (I saw gratefully) looking after Speckle and Goliath for us.

"It looks like Captain Evon is not coming back," Pinz said dourly. He pointed at me. "That puts you in charge, Lord Hawthorne."

"Me? I'm leaving," I said. "I need to get to Malafert somehow. You're in charge, Sarge."

"Don't tell me," Pinz muttered bitterly, "your orders are to hold the pass to the last man."

"No!" I yelped. "I don't want you to waste any lives, Sergeant. Protect the refugees. Abandon the fort when you have to. Retreat as slowly as you can, keeping the civilians ahead of you."

The old man in the refugee family looking after the horses barked something unintelligible at me. He punctuated his words with a jabbing motion.

"F3?"

"No idea."

But the girl dutifully holding Speckle was able to translate for him. "They advance by night, and then shelter in daylight, in dense forest or in homes they have captured. He says to burn the forests and homes after you've passed them so that the army of the dead cannot advance as quickly. The darkness is far behind them, but they don't need it if they avoid sunlight. Up here in the clouds they can operate all day and all night."

"Thank you, Urna. Thank you, Urna's, er, grandfather. Pinz, only burn stuff as a last resort. Retreat until you are out of the clouds. Then retreat by night. Sortie forwards by day and find where the dead are hiding, then drag them out or burn them out."

Sergeant Pinz saluted, wished me luck, and hurried off. The sounds of shouting and clashing steel showed that the undead had already begun to assault the first wall.

"Grandfather says he knows another way around," Urna said.

I was all ears. Urna translated as her grandfather gestured and rambled. Five minutes later we had a new route into the Cursed Vale – but it was a way that Speckle and Goliath could not go. I leaned in close to Speckle's neck and silently said to her, "Would you mind looking after this family for a while? I know you are missing Lexi, but the way I have to go to get to her I cannot take you. We will find you wherever you end up, I promise."

I was good at making promises. To Urna, I said: "Speckle is the finest horse in all the Westfold–" at this Speckle gave a snort in protest, so I corrected myself, "in all the world as far as I know. She will look after you and your family until I or her true owner return for her."

"How will I know her true owner, if you aren't with her?"

I smiled at that. "Speckle will tell you, won't you Speckle?"

A snort and a stamp of hooves.

"She understands your words?"

"All horses do. Even Goliath. But most of them pretend not to."

A minute later the paladin and I had grabbed all we needed from the saddlebags. I told the family to help themselves to the food that was left. Then I rambled on about not overworking Speckle, giving her plenty of rest, not overloading her, brushing her down properly, cleaning her hooves, not tying the saddle too tight or keeping it on too long... and I promised to tell the tale of how she came to be a grey with three black stars on her flank when we met up again. I suggested the family headed to Kotmoor Dry and ask for Olena Korland. That way, if any of us did return from the Cursed Vale, we would know where to begin to look for Speckle.

With that, the paladin and I went back through the open portcullis and up onto the second of the fort's four defensive walls. Then we headed south along the ramparts. This part of the fort was sparsely manned; most of the men were concentrated on the gatehouse and the bits of the first wall that were next to it. The wall was flat where we joined it, but as it ran up the valley side, it began to steepen, and proceeded in a series of terraces. At first these single-step rises were ten metres apart, then they were five metres apart, then one; by the time we were half-way up the side of the valley, we were climbing what was effectively a set of narrow stone steps, and the wall on our right was so reduced in size that it would have been possible for an attacker to jump over it. But anyone trying to jump it here would be at risk of falling half-way down the valley if they landed wrong.

Soon the wall was a cross between a staircase and a ladder, and we had to use our hands for balance for fear of being pitched off the eastern side by the gale. Squally rain pecked at our faces, and the stone was numbingly cold under our fingers. My injured hand was soon throbbing horribly. Ahead, we could not yet see the top – but we could see that soon the wall was going to peter out altogether, leaving us with a climb up a vertiginous rocky slope. Behind, the fort was invisible, swallowed up by the billowing clouds. Sounds of battle floated up to us, although the wind gave them a muffled, faraway tone.

Ronan climbed ahead of me, and faster than me too. I was beginning to wish for gloves. My legs were burning and my lungs bursting. And I had the terrifying feeling that my mission was going to come to a squelchy end when a gust of wind knocked me off the side of the cliff. I concentrated for all I was worth on not falling off. But the paladin had kept his wits about him.

"On our right," he called down. He didn't stop climbing. A glance up at his retreating boots gave me the feeling that I was clinging to a sheer rock face, and I had to grab on tightly with both hands as a wave of giddiness swept over me. Then I looked to my right, and saw, two walls away, a posse of undead soldiers mirroring our climb up the valley side. We had somehow attracted a dozen of them from the battle below. Like us, they were concentrating on climbing for now. But they found time to glance menacingly my way with their dim-glowing eye sockets.

A few metres later we reached the end of the wall, and the end of the shaped steps. Urna's grandfather insisted that there was only a short distance to go to the top from this point, although there had been some difficulty translating how he was measuring that. There was quite a bit of shrugging, too, as if he couldn't quite remember.

"If you fall off, you can always use magic and fly," F3 said helpfully.

The thought of trying to use my catalysts to steer my own sudden descent gave me another rush of vertigo, and once again I had to cling on for dear life. "F3," I said through gritted teeth, "the next time you are climbing a sheer rock face, I promise to not to say a word."

"It's not sheer," F3 chirped. "It's barely seventy degrees, and there are plenty of handholds."

The paladin was out of sight in the swirling mist above me. I concentrated on trying to catch him up.

After about another five minutes, which felt like a day or two to my panicked mind, I reached a sudden inflexion in the slope. The steep hard rock, dotted with ferns and tiny flowers, became a less steep but more barren loose scree of shattered grey gravel.

"Angle of rest," F3 said. "Easy going now."

"Thank you," I muttered. I still climbed on all fours, although as F3 had said, the scree was not too steep to walk up.

"I thought I saw an interesting saxifrage back there," he added. "But I thought it best not to mention it."

"Thank you," I muttered again.

Suddenly Ronan's strong arm reached down and pulled me up over a frost-shattered block, and I found myself on the top of the ridge that Urna had told us was called Running Edge. The landscape around us was one of pulverised slatey stone, patches of brown moss, bits of lying snow, and rapidly moving swirling mist.

Occasional large boulders were sprinkled around us in the scree, or perhaps they were bits of rock still attached to the mountain. I didn't know. The narrow ridge we were on rose up to our left, rapidly disappearing in the weather. Somewhere up that way was a snow-capped peak, whose name Urna had translated as The Crab, although there had been a bit of to-ing and fro-ing with her grandfather before she called it that. To our right, the ridge ran down alongside the Highstand Road and eventually petered out among the green pastures of the Cursed Vale. But our path lay forwards, into the next valley along to the south, which according to the old man gave us a good chance of arriving at a part of the Cursed Vale where the undead had not yet bothered to go. Unfortunately, they seemed to be following us there.

I had stood there gasping for breath for no more than a few seconds when F3 said: "Company."

And out of the mist to the west, along the flat top of the ridge, came the Lich King's minions.

"I'll catch you up," the paladin said, and drew his sword.

"Don't wait too long," I said.

"Don't go down too fast," he rejoined.

"I'll wait at the bottom," I said.

"I'll find you," he said.

Which turned out to be a rather optimistic plan.

Descending

Going down from Running Edge was easier than going up it. But it was hard for me to control my descent. The first thing that happened when I began to go down was that the scree began to shift beneath my feet, so that I was more sliding off Running Edge than climbing down it. I managed to steer my first slide into a scrubby bush that had somehow taken root there and was solid enough to bring me to a stop. That seemed like a good method of descending, so I picked another bush and slid towards that. This time though a large raft of material broke free from the surface and I ended up surfing past the target bush in a cloud of icy grit.

Then the scree suddenly ended and I sailed over the edge of a cliff.

Idiot! I thought, *you're going to have to learn to fly this second and squander most of your magic!* But before I could do more than think about it, I realised that the drop was a short one. In sudden panic about landing on my back and smashing the magic pearls in my pack, I managed to twist around to land face-first before the ground hit me. No cat-like landing this; it knocked the wind out of me, so rather than try to get moving again right away, I took a moment to take stock of my surroundings.

The slope below me looked shallower than the one we had just climbed up, which was a relief. The south side of Running Edge was also much greener than the north side. Stunted bushes, their branches all pointing east with the prevailing wind, soon gave way to a patchwork of dwarf and taller conifers in various shades of green, with sections of bare ground showing where recent slides of rock or snow had taken place. Clambering to my feet and beginning to descend again, I found that the boulders here were mostly covered in a thick blanket of moss, giving them the look of tech-startup office furniture. Ferns filled the gaps between them, making my footing insecure and the going tough; but as soon as I was in amongst the conifers, at least the wind and the horizontal rain that it brought with it died away.

The happy gurgle of clear running water drew me to a little stream, which I followed for the next five minutes, reasoning that it showed the most direct way down the mountain. Then I reached a small waterfall and began to pick my way around it.

That was when there was a sudden rattling noise and an undead soldier rolled past the end of my nose, flew into space, and shot straight into the waterfall's ferny plunge pool with a splash hardly any louder than the roaring water. The idyllic scene immediately seemed polluted.

"Hey!" I yelled at the undead, which was struggling upright, waist-deep in water, "get out of there!"

Two glowing eye sockets turned to look my way. They locked onto me. The soldier had lost its helm and spear in the water, but it was undeterred, presumably hoping to chew me to death now it could no longer skewer me. But I was standing six metres up on the lip of the waterfall, and the undead was not immediately able to figure out how to get to me. It wasted quite a bit of time trying to scramble up the sheer sides of the waterfall.

I was safe for a moment or two, but it would not do to linger in case the Lich King's soldier had colleagues nearby. Instead, I carried on with my plan of following the stream. This meant having to pass closer to my undead friend, but a quick spin of my catalysts tipped it over into the water and enabled me to gain a little ground on it. The little stream merged with another a short way below the waterfall. By now the water was rushing along gleefully and many of the boulders in the watercourse had been lodged there long enough to get worn smooth. At some point I saw easier going on the opposite side of the stream, tried to cross, and slipped. The bone-numbingly cold water dragged me along with it for ten metres before I was able to scramble out. Naturally my brief dip left me completely soaked, but the thing I was most concerned about was the possibility that I might crack one or more of my magic pearls.

"I'm not waterproof!" F3 complained loudly.

The undead was closing in behind me, so with a twizzle of the catalysts I knocked it off balance again. It disappeared under the surface of the water and I lost sight of it for a moment; a few metres downstream, it collided with a line of rocks and managed to right itself there.

Then I discovered that the undead soldier did indeed have a couple of colleagues. The sounds of their movements drowned out by the noise of the stream, they were already quite close to me by the time I noticed them. One of the two, an archer, looked like he had been a casualty in the same army as his colleague; he was more lightly armoured, but had the same centuries-old dried leather skin. The other undead was fresh. When recently alive, he had been an oldish guy, a soldier, probably part of Captain Evon's lost squad. He had a sheath for a short sword, but no sword. A broken arrow projected from his chest showing what had killed him.

This guy's death, and his undeath, is on me, I thought. Stunned, I was rooted to the spot for a moment, and the archer took the chance to let an arrow fly my way. It missed, though the arrow whistled by close enough to get me moving again. I went upslope a little way, darting from tree to tree in search of a blob of resin to seal F3's harpoon holes. By the time this rudimentary waterproofing was complete, all three of my undead friends were on my side of the stream, so I had to take a rather roundabout way to get back to the water.

Two more torrents joined my stream twenty metres further along, making a combination fast and wide enough to look a little scary.

"Are you sure about this?" F3 asked, having divined my intentions.

"It beats running," I said, "and the dead guys can't float."

Except perhaps for the fresh one.

"Don't break a leg, or drown!"

"I'll try not to." I reached the water, jumped in, sat down, and took the brakes off. The water carried me a good distance before I had to use both feet to prevent myself from crashing into some rocks. As I clambered around them I looked back; one undead was being swept towards me, one was wading my way, and one was following along the shoreline.

On the other side of the rocks I climbed back into the water again, letting the current take me. I bumped along for a bit, using my boots to avoid crashing into obstacles. The water was getting faster now, and I began to think it might be time to climb out. Fewer boulders now showed themselves above the water's surface: underwater obstructions were hinted at in the way the dark water humped itself up here and there, but they were harder to assess, and harder to avoid. I told myself I would find a suitable spot to halt and look back; if it was safe, I would get back onto dry land.

Unfortunately the current had other ideas. My stream was joined by more tributaries, and was now wider and deeper than ever. When I tried to reach the shore, I found myself inexorably pushed back towards the middle, where the flow was fastest. Then the river suddenly dropped down a couple of metres in a short space. At the foot of this mini-fall I found myself completely submerged for a moment. When I bobbed up again I found that there seemed to be less stream ahead of me than there usually was. It seemed to end abruptly ten metres ahead, as if—

—I was about to shoot over a waterfall.

I had time to yell, "This was a mistake!"

Then I was over the edge.

Regulus

"Another triumphant escape," F3 said. "Can you get this resin off? I feel as if I'm suffocating."

"Yes," I said, but I didn't move.

The lake had no shore as such, or if it did, I hadn't yet been able to reach it. After a terrifying plunge down the waterfall, I spent an even more terrifying length of time whirling around in circles under the water like a rat in a washing machine's spin cycle. Then, gasping for breath, I surfaced in froth-topped but calm water and found myself in what I soon christened Lake Mosquito.

I swam for the water's edge, but as mentioned, there was no edge that I could climb out onto. First there was a thicket of bulrushes growing through the surface of the water. Then a thicket of reeds. Then silty mud rose up amid the reed stems, finally reaching the water's surface. But the mud was soft, hardly any firmer than the water it had replaced. I found a sizeable tussock that had risen above the general level and seemed to be quite dry, and rested against that for a length of time that was planned to be a few moments but ended up becoming several minutes through a combination of inertia and exhaustion.

I was pleased to see that I had descended far enough down the valley to be out of the realm of semi-permanent cloud. Sunlight beat down from an almost unbroken blue sky.

Then the mosquitoes began to find me. With a high-pitched whine, the first of them whizzed into view, vanishing again as I swatted at it, sending a spray of muddy water into the air from my wet cuff. One became two, and two became six; before any of them could latch onto me, I pulled my hood up and slid off my tussock into the warm swamp to immerse my hands. That left my face as the only exposed skin, so I had to keep puffing air at the little swines to keep them off.

"This place is supposed to be deserted, right?" I asked F3. "The only humans in the Cursed Vale have been in the lands below the Highstand Pass. It's been like that for hundreds of years. So how is it that as soon as a human appears – bang – there are hundreds of mosquitoes waiting to suck his blood?"

"There are probably leeches in the water too," F3 pointed out.

"You had to say that, didn't you?"

"The mosquitoes and other miniature horrors around here feed on other animals, like deer, the rest of the time. But when a defenceless morsel like yourself drops in, the dining offer is just too tempting."

Other than the whining of the mosquitoes and an almost constant wheezing that I had put down to bush crickets singing in the reeds, the swamp was quiet. That made the sudden sound of something Very Large slopping about in the water nearby all the more startling.

"Are we far enough south for crocodiles?" I whispered.

"It might be a monkey crab," F3 opined quietly. A monkey crab was something we had met with much further north, near the camp in Crickne where Lexi mined for pre-apocalypse metal. It looked like the skins of two horses crudely stapled together, equipped with giant claws, and imbued with infinitely patient life. It liked nothing better than to eat humans or other animals who went too close to the water's edge. And it probably quite enjoyed finding a defenceless morsel resting against a tussock nowhere near the safety of the shore.

That was when a great terrible voice spoke.

"You're not a water deer."

244

The whatever-it-was slopped closer. It was definitely talking to me, but I kept my eyes closed and my hands clamped onto my tussock, just in case.

"Are you dead?" the voice boomed.

Not yet, I thought.

"Closing your eyes doesn't make you invisible, you know," said the voice.

I risked a peek.

It was *a crocodile!*

A talking crocodile!

A red talking crocodile!

A giant red talking crocodile!

A giant red talking crocodile, with wings that, spread wide, could have powered a tea clipper!

No, not a crocodile, you idiot.

A dragon.

I moved, slowly turning to face the vast reptile, and said: "I was just tired. And where I used to live, if I wanted to be invisible, people would have had to pretend that I *was* invisible."

I could only see one of the dragon's two eyes from where I was. It was as wide as a cartwheel, and as deep as the ocean. The eye narrowed suspiciously.

"In that land," I babbled, "feelings were more important than facts."

Looking back at it now, it had been a mad world. But at least there were no dragons in it. Or at least, the dragons there were only imaginary.

This one was red, and very real. I racked my brains to try to remember what alignment a red dragon had in D&D. The only colour I was sure about was golden, which was Lawful Good. I had the distinct feeling that red dragons were firmly in the Evil camp.

"You're probably thinking you'll be safe from dragonfire in the water," the dragon guessed.

"Am I?"

The dragon pulled one of its forelimbs out of the swamp and flexed a claw like a demolition crane's grab. Its scales were like dinner plates. Its horns could have impaled six people at once, like a human kebab. "You look like a wizard," it said.

"I am a magician of the Royal Court."

"Only a wizard would drop in like that," the dragon mused, as if it hadn't heard me. "Anyone else would walk. Although everyone else around here is dead."

I was still formulating my response to that comment when another disturbance came to the swamp. The first of the undead had arrived. It was the recently-killed one of the three that had been chasing me, the only one with no armour, the only one, in short, with any hope of floating. The undead man's head breached the water surface twenty metres away, and he rose up step by step until his top half was clear of the water. He came my way, the glow in his eyes invisible in the bright daylight.

Then something extraordinary happened. The undead's skin began to blacken and peel, issuing a stream of smoke. In two more paces his hair was on fire. Then his hands caught, and his face; soon he was a staggering column of fire and smoke. Before he was half-way to me, he tumbled forwards and stopped moving, the flames still merrily devouring the bits of him that were clear of the water. The flames quickly spread to nearby dead reed stems, but the fire soon burnt itself out.

I wanted to say something unpleasant about the Lich King. But I suddenly realised that I had no idea how the dragon felt about him. "How do you feel about the Lich King?" I asked.

"How do *you* feel about it?"

"I'm reluctant to say," I said. It would be useful if I got a steer from the dragon before announcing my allegiance or opposition. In hindsight it had been a stupid question on my part.

"Go on. Do." That giant hypnotic eye stared into mine.

I tried to remember what folklore I knew about dragons. The only thing I knew about real dragons in the post-Quacker world was that they were feathered. That meant that everything I knew about dragons was wrong, because this one was

246

definitely scaled, not feathered. Did dragons get along with the undead? It seemed unlikely. Dragons probably didn't get along with anything much, including magicians.

I took a deep breath, and said: "I've come to put him out of his misery."

There was a long and pregnant pause. Then: "Good." The dragon settled down into the swamp. Marsh gas bubbled up around it. Soon only its head was showing above the water.

"So you're not going to eat me?" I asked hopefully.

The dragon's eyes were closed. But it wasn't invisible. "I don't eat talkers," it said. "Never have." Twin ranks of teeth longer than my daggers were revealed every time it opened its mouth.

"I'm glad to hear it," I said. "I'm Edison, by the way. My companion is F3."

The dragon's eye opened wide again. its voice was suddenly very loud. "Companion!"

I hurriedly produced F3, picking the bits of resin off his harpoon ports as I did so. "He's – he's a demon in a box," I explained.

"No I'm not," F3 said.

"I am Regulus," the dragon said, and the eye closed again. It basked in the warm sunlight.

"Well, if you'll excuse us, er – *Mr.?* – Regulus," I said, "we'd better be heading for the Lich King's castle." *Always be polite when talking to a dragon,* my mother would certainly have impressed upon me if there had been dragons around when she had been bringing me up. The dragon did not overtly object to being called Mr. Regulus, so I thought it safe to think of it as a 'he' from that point onwards. I began to wade towards where I hoped the shore was, and then thought of another thing I ought to mention. "My friend the paladin will be along shortly. He doesn't usually say much, but please don't eat him."

"Paladin!" the dragon exclaimed. His eye popped open again.

"Er, yes. He is the last of his kind."

"I know something about a paladin," Regulus mused, talking to himself. "Now, what is it?"

I was now standing waist-deep in the loose mud, and was slowly sinking. I waited patiently. At least the periodic jets of air from Regulus's oversized nostrils seemed to be keeping the bloodsucking flies off.

Eventually: "No, it's gone. Good luck with your quest, Edison and F3."

I waded on.

"Do you have a plan to defeat the Lich King?" the dragon called after us.

"No, not really," I said, turning again. "I'm just going to wing it when I get there."

"That's it! I remember now. I know where there's a sword." With that, the dragon relaxed and settled back down to rest.

I waited. As I hoped, an explanation was eventually forthcoming. Ten seconds later:

"It's imbued with magic. A paladin used it to slay the previous Lich King. Or was it the one before that? Time passes, you know. It must be five hundred years since the last one. It's in the next valley to the south. The Valley of Heroes, they call it, or that's what they used to call it before they all died. Now no-one calls it anything. Only I know the old name, and now so do you. I can show you the way if you like."

"Sure. That sounds great," I heard myself saying.

"Excellent!" Regulus said. "There's just one small favour I'd like to ask of you in exchange for this most important information."

The Valley of Heroes

"Small favour?" I asked, my heart sinking.

"Oh, no need to look so glum," Regulus the dragon said warmly. "I ask only this. If you should happen across any gold, or trinkets, shiny things, you know, in the place where the sword is kept..."

"You'd like them?" I asked. Dragons were renowned for collecting vast treasure hoards. Or at least, they were when they only existed in the collective human imagination.

248

"The fact is, I already have more treasure than I need," Regulus explained. "Not that I need it at all. And anyway, it's a little hard to get at right now, at least, until your deed is done, and then everything can get back to normal."

I looked quizzical at that, so the dragon elaborated. "I live in Rascen's Spring. As a wizard, a magician, you've heard of it, I presume?"

I hadn't.

"Ah. Well, that's not so surprising. It all happened such a long time ago. Rascen was a king, who found a magical spring under a mountain – well, he didn't find it, someone else did, but being a king, he took it, and everyone forgot whoever it was who had *actually* found it, so they called it after King Rascen rather than the nobody. And as magic in the wider world steadily dwindled, the magical spring's value only grew. Rascen built a castle around the entrance to the caverns holding the spring to protect it and moved his court there. Well, others did the work, but he gave the order, you know, that sort of thing. He dug out – well, he ordered some of his minions to dig out – hundreds of exploratory tunnels under the mountain, looking for another spring like the first. Then someone dug a hole in the wrong place, and the water found a different way to flow through the mountain, and the magical spring ran dry. Then they dug all the harder, and plugged every leak they could find. But it was all to no avail, because before they could repair the damage, a Lich King rose in Malafert and killed them all. Well, he had his minions do it, as Lich Kings are wont to do. Then, when everything had quietened down a century or two later and all the undead people had gone back to being dead people, I moved in."

"I see," I said.

"Now my home is infested with things just like the thing that just emerged from the swamp. I am disinclined to remove all of my hoard and place it elsewhere. Nor am I able to winkle every one of the little rats out of the catacombs that surround the main cavern. I like to sleep on my hoard, and that is rarely peaceful if undead things keep pinging arrows at me. You see, they rose up at the minute the new Lich King came into being. I should have cleared them up decades ago, you know, swept them up and put them on the doorstep? It was on my list of things to do. But I was too lazy. And now they've driven me out of my own home."

"So you want to start a new hoard?" To me it seemed more logical for the dragon to just fly to Malafert, incinerate Bartlet, and as soon as all the undead irritants in his home had dropped dead again, reclaim his original hoard. I was beginning to hope that he could be induced to do my dirty work for me. If, that is, he could actually breathe fire. And if he was able to kill Bartlet without flaming Lexi.

"Not that I have an unhealthy obsession with shinies," Regulus said. "And there's no point collecting them any more."

"Nowhere around here to spend it?"

"How much do you know about dragons, Edison Royal Court Magician?"

"Not very much. Someone once told me they were feathered, not scaled."

"Hah! No. Well, not for hundreds of years. The kind to which you refer haunted the frozen lands, but I have not seen one for an age. Most of us are scaled, like me. Or were. I haven't seen another dragon since – well, I don't remember when. Since before the last Lich King, that is for sure, or maybe the one before him. That's why collecting shinies is pointless. Male dragons do it by instinct, to decorate their homes so that they can impress visiting females with their treasure-hunting prowess. As far as I know, I'm the last of my kind, just like your paladin friend is the last of his. Hmm," Regulus mused, "the last paladin, you say? There seemed to be quite a lot of them before. Mind you, I am going back a bit."

"They all went on a quest for the Holy Grail, except one, who was – unable to join them. My friend is his son."

"Well, I'm sure there will be more of them soon enough. Humans come and go so quickly these days."

"Yes, perhaps you're right." I began to wade on again, to where hoped-for dry land awaited me. "Am I going the right way?" I called back.

"Not really, no," Regulus said. "You need to cross to the other side of the lake, climb the ridge to the south, and you'll find the Valley of Heroes on the other side at the foot of the junction of three steep cliffs."

My shoulders slumped. I was more than half inclined to forget the Side Quest for the Sword then and there.

"Don't look so glum, Edison," Regulus said. "I'll give you a lift over."

*

I don't like heights – or should I say drops – at the best of times. Whizzing through the air in the talons of a dragon was as terrifying as you can imagine. At least over the swamp and the lake I was able to tell myself that I would probably survive the fall if Regulus accidentally let go of me. But when we soared up over the ridge, so that I was looking down on a long drop to a jagged expanse of bare rock, the needle on the terror metre pegged out and stayed there for the next twenty minutes.

Regulus did not let me ride on his back. He picked me up like a fluffy toy in a seaside arcade machine. So all he would have to do would be to relax his bunched talons, and I would be plummeting towards the ground at an acceleration of ten metres per second squared.

But as soon as we crested the top of the ridge I could see our destination, and fixed my gaze firmly on that. The Valley of Heroes reminded me very much of the far-distant valley where the bunker entrance was. Like the one above Lar, the Valley of Heroes was a hanging valley, intersecting a larger, broader one at its foot. Its sides and base were the yellow-green of half-starved but hardy mountain grass. A hundred grey stone tombs were scattered across the valley floor in a seemingly random pattern, many of them small, but a dozen or more quite imposing, as large as a detached house.

We swooped down at the edge of the cemetery and Regulus let go of me a few feet above the ground.

"Oh, I'm sorry!" he exclaimed, in response to my yell and the small thud that followed it. "I thought we were closer to the ground than that."

I was only too happy to be back on *terra firma* again. But I was still soaking wet, and could not go further without doing something about it. First I took my pack off. I had an urge to check whether any of my six magical pearls had survived, but didn't want Regulus to know about them in case he felt like using them as the first items in his new hoard. So I left the pack unopened and took my boots off instead, emptying the water from them onto the ground by my feet.

"Wet?"

"Yes."

"Isn't there a spell for that sort of thing?"

"If there is, I don't know it," I said.

"I could blow-dry you if you like," Regulus said.

I could not tell from his tone of voice whether he was joking. Naturally I did not fancy that, so I improvised a little magic instead. One by one I used the catalysts on each item of my clothing, first tossing them into the air and then keeping them there, spinning them as rapidly as I could to exclude as much water as possible by centrifugal force. For a time I was entirely naked, proving, if Regulus was interested in that point, that I was blue everywhere. When I put the clothes back on, they were disappointingly wet – but at least drier than before.

"If this was a film, I'd be bone dry by now," I moaned.

"A film? A thin layer?" Regulus boomed.

"People used to watch stories made of light projected on a screen, and called them films," I explained. "In the stories, people who were wet in one scene were rarely wet in the next."

"Such stories are not meant to be real," the dragon said sagely. "They are there to teach you about life." He curled into a ball the size of a bungalow and seemed to settle down to sleep. "It's the big one in the middle," he said. "I'm staying here, because there's no room to stand over there. The gravestones get between my toes."

"Right," I said.

"It's cursed, so be careful," Regulus added.

"Right," I said. Then: "How do you know it's cursed?"

"I saw them doing it. Laying the curse on it I mean. There was a group of wizards gathered around it, chanting some mumbo-jumbo and jumping from foot to foot playing tambourines. I was watching from the crag, for, er, no particular reason."

I turned to gauge Regulus's expression. But how do you gauge the expression of a dragon? Especially one whose eyes are closed. I shrugged. However cursed it was, the tomb could not be more cursed than the bunker had been.

There was no formal path between the tombs, which I soon found numbered far more than a hundred. Plenty of small tombs were all but hidden in the knee-high grass until I hit them with shin or toe. Many of the tombs were inscribed with words in an unfamiliar language, which F3 tried to pick up as we went. His task was made more difficult by the way many of the words were heavily eroded or effaced by yellow and grey lichen.

The graveyard could not be said to have a middle in any manner other than mathematically, but one tomb was definitely more important-looking than the others. It was formed of finely-jointed, un-mortared stone, and rose in a series of steps like a ziggurat, each of which would have been a good jump and a scramble to climb up. I walked around to its west-facing side, where I found a doorway that looked scarcely big enough for a hobbit. Several lines of writing were carved above the doorway, and F3 was now in a position to translate them.

"*Kal Myridon*. That's his name. *Slayer of the One Who Walked in Darkness*. Referring to the Lich King, no doubt," here F3's voice dropped three notches in volume. "*Lost his life in single combat with the Fell Dragon Regulus. One two one two.* That either refers to the year it happened, or is something to do with marching. *Might through fearlessness. Death awaits all those who enter.*"

I backed up a few paces to the corner of the tomb to look at Regulus, who was insouciantly resting his head on his great red claws, eyes closed. I went back to the doorway and said, "There's more to this than meets the eye."

"Or the on-chip optical sensor," F3 agreed.

The little doorway was barred by an iron gate. An enormous padlock held it shut; both padlock and gate were rusted almost to oblivion. Certainly any working parts in the lock had long-since fused together, making the catalysts useless. "This doesn't look like enough security to deter graverobbers," I said.

"According to Regulus," F3 said, "everyone in this land is dead, so there *are* no graverobbers."

"If there really *is* a death curse, this is going to be a pretty dumb way for this rescue mission to fail," I said, by way of delaying trying to open the tomb's gate, or rather, delaying the moment I would have to ask F3 for an idea about how to open it.

"People always write that sort of thing on mausoleums," F3 scoffed. "They don't mean anything by it. Well, they mean to deter graverobbers, but they are lying about the death curse."

"They were lying before the Quacker went off. Now that the world is Quacked wide open, they might be lying, and they might not."

"Point taken."

"I need to smash this somehow."

"Use magic."

"Nope." I cast about the neighbourhood for a loose piece of stone, and eventually found a piece that had probably cracked off a nearby tomb twenty winters before and looked a good size for smashing things. "Apologies, whoever's tomb this is a bit of," I said aloud. The rusted padlock disintegrated after three strikes.

But the gate was still impossible to open. The hinges themselves were thoroughly fused. I sat on a nearby tombstone to ponder the problem.

"Use magic," F3 suggested.

"Nope. Look, it can't be that solid. If only we had a rope."

"A rope wouldn't help, because we don't have a block and tackle, and if we did have a block and tackle, it *still* wouldn't help, because the gate opens inwards anyway."

"If only we had someone with a bit of muscle." Saying that of course made me think about the paladin. I hoped that he was all right, and that he was still descending the mountain. Because if he reached the bottom and found no sign of me there, he would probably think I was dead... and set off for Malafert on his own. And if he did that, it would probably be the last anyone would ever see of him – alive, at least.

The Tomb of Kal Myridon – 1

I sat on an unknown minor hero's gravestone and pondered the iron gate separating me from the tomb of Kal Myridon. A chill wind blew up the valley from the west, making me wish my clothes were dry. The half-dead grasses filling up every gap in the cemetery danced in the breeze, but they were the only thing moving in the landscape. There were no trees in sight, no birds, no flowing water, no clouds. A hundred metres to the north, a sheer cliff rose up to the ridge Regulus had just carried me over. That too was lifeless, a wall of barren grey rock whose base was buried in a thick heap of scree. I looked for something to rest my eyes on, and settled on the unfamiliar script above the doorway into the tomb's interior. Then for some reason I had a sudden craving for a digestive biscuit, or twelve. It seemed like an odd thing to crave in a land that had not known a digestive biscuit for more than two thousand years and never would again.

After a minute's thought, I picked up my trusty lump of stone, and at the risk of ridicule from F3, banged the gate's hinges a few times, hoping that would free them.

It didn't.

Then I picked up the broken padlock and its shackle and sat down again. The red-rusty metal was gritty to the touch. "If only we had oil," I said. "If only there was an olive tree…"

"Yes," F3 said sarcastically. "Then, all we would need would be a hydraulic press, and we could squeeze a few millilitres of oil out of each of a hundred olives, and try to dribble it into a gap between the moving parts of the hinge that aren't there."

"If only we had acetone."

"Yes. If only we'd thought of this before you were sealed into your mother's animation suspension ovum, we could have borrowed some of her nail varnish remover just in case we might need it two thousand five hundred years later."

"A crowbar then. Any kind of bar. Anything to get a bit of leverage. A large stick."

"Use magic."

"Never." Thinking about it some more, I realised that we already had a little leverage – the width of the gate. And while I had already tried pushing it… there was

255

a tiny gap between the gate and its jam that would be the perfect place to bang something like a cold chisel in, to widen it from a crack to a centimetre. It was a start. For the cold chisel I had the broken shackle of the padlock. For a lump hammer I had my trusty piece of tombstone. After a few blows the end of the shackle was in the crack, which was now a centimetre wide.

"Stop banging!" F3 said. "I've got a headache."

"You don't have a head," I said mildly.

"Use your caveman tool to apply leverage now, don't keep hitting it."

That was what I did, at least until the shackle fell out. The gate was still open a crack; with a monumental effort, I pulled it hard shut again. Then I heaved against it, trying to open it a crack again. After ten minutes of to-ing and fro-ing like this, I finally made a gap wide enough for me to slip through.

The temperature dropped rapidly in the tunnel beyond the gate. I found myself walking half-crouched down a dingy low corridor sloping into deepening darkness. F3 popped his light on without prompting, to reveal, five metres ahead... another gate. But this one and its padlock were in better condition, and I could open the latter with my catalysts, and the former with a single good hard shove.

A few metres past the second gate the tunnel ended in a ledge, below which there was a six-metre drop down to a large squarish room. I peered down from the edge, playing F3's light around the rather bizarre scene. One side of the room was taken up by a large raised stage or platform, on which hundreds of weapons were arranged in a grid pattern. There were swords, pikes, staves, lucernes, war picks, spears, halberds and other bizarre creations that I had no names for. Each weapon was stuck vertically into a socket in the stage, so that a miniature forest of steel had been created. "Is it like *The Last Crusade*, so you pick the weapon least likely to be a Lich-killer?" I whispered. I don't know why I whispered. There was no-one in Kal Myridon's tomb to hear this blue wannabe Indiana Jones or his demon-in-a-box sidekick Small Square.

"We already know we are looking for a sword," F3 reminded me, lowering his voice to match my whisper. "Only seventy of the weapons on the platform are swords."

"Right, but how do we know which one is Kal whatsisname's?"

"Myridon. Er, because it's magic, and you have a magical detection device?"

"Why didn't I think of that?" I wondered. Then I wondered too how to get down to the floor level – and as importantly, how to get back. But there were easy handholds in the wall, so climbing up and down was easy. It almost looked as if the handholds had been placed in the wall *deliberately*. What then was the purpose of the drop?

I gave this question a mental shrug, and carefully climbed down until I reached the dusty floor. I slowly approached the stage, staring at Hal's ring. It was emitting only the faintest of glows, even when I directed F3 to shut his light off completely for a minute. I walked up and down in front of the array of weapons, and the intensity of the ring's light hardly wavered.

"It seems to be marginally brighter towards the left-hand end," F3 opined.

"OK," I said. I went to that end and pondered my choice there. Among all the other kinds of weapons there were plenty of swords: short swords, long swords and greatswords. I really didn't want the magic sword to be a greatsword, even though I was hoping that I wouldn't be the one eventually wielding it – although I knew the paladin would be strong enough to handle a giant sword, I would be the one having to carry it to him. A short sword did not feel epic enough. A one-handed sword with enough room on the handle for an occasional use as a two-hander – that was the sort of sword that felt right to me. "F3?"

"No idea," the omni admitted. "Nothing seems to stand out."

"No. Of course, it wouldn't. There's no point trying to hide an ostrich in a chicken coop. I'm just going to pick one."

F3 did not object. So I clambered up on the stage, wandered back a few rows, selected a random sword, and gingerly pulled it from its socket. As if in response, there was a distant thud somewhere far below us in the bowels of the tomb, the cranking of some gears, the sounds of chains winding around a sprocket... then nothing. My long sword was not the jackpot. I put it back where I had found it and looked for another. Then, just as I was reaching out for another similar-looking sword–

"Wait!" F3 said.

"What?"

"Listen!"

The cranking of gears came again, more loudly than before. This time, the sound seemed to be coming not from below, but from the far corner of the room. A curious dark slot had appeared there. This rapidly grew until it was wide enough for F3's light to get in. By that stage it was obvious that a section of the floor was actually the roof of a lift, which was now rising up...

...to release its passenger.

Long before the lift rose far enough so that it could step out, it was quite clear what the passenger was. This gave me a few seconds to process the news that I was about to be attacked by a walking skeleton. The guardian of Kal Myridon's tomb did not look very impressive. When alive, it had been an average-sized person. Its little sword was rusted almost to oblivion, and its shield looked terminally worm eaten. What had once been a padded cloth jacket now hung around its shoulders in little more than shreds.

The skeleton's eye sockets, empty of eyes but emitting the usual eerie glow, locked onto me even before it exited the lift. As it stepped forth, the lift began to descend once again.

"Oh well, at least there's only one of them," I said to F3. Then I did something ineffably stupid. I grabbed a nearby short sword, hoping to use it to fend off the skeleton.

At once another distant thud came from below my feet, followed by the cranking of gears and the sound of chains winding around a sprocket.

Naturally, like a thief who has just been spotted putting something in his pocket by an eagle-eyed shopkeeper, I put the sword back into its slot again. But it was obviously too late. The damage was done.

I used the catalysts as the skeleton came after me. First I had to put F3 back in my damp coat pocket to free my hands. Then, with a bit of handwaving, I managed to get the skeleton's bony arms wrapped around one another, his shield and sword temporarily unusable.

"What do I do?" I asked. "Find the right one and leg it...?"

The skeleton carried on coming after me, constantly trying to untwist his arms as he staggered along. I kept twisting them back. My hands probably gave the appearance of someone juggling invisible balls.

"No," F3 said calmly.

There was a bang and a loud cranking of gears. The dark slot appeared in the floor again.

"Well! Any ideas?"

"This is a trap," F3 said, as if he was discussing something as innocuous as a packet of wine gums. "These weapons are bait. None of them are the weapon we are looking for."

"Thanks Obi-Wan," I babbled, dodging between the ranks of weapons to get further from my skeletal pursuer, who had now reached the stage and was trying to clamber onto it. "Do I take it that the sword is—"

"Below, yes."

"Where the skeletons are coming from?"

"Technically, yes."

At that point I seriously considered legging it. But I now realised what the drop down from the entrance corridor was all about. It was there so that a would-be graverobber, whether blue or not, fleeing in panic, would find himself run through by an avenging guardian skeleton before he was half-way up the wall.

The dark slot in the floor that apparently heralded the arrival of another skeleton was now half a metre tall.

"I've an idea!" I yelled. If F3 had anything to say about it, I didn't hear him, because I was screaming and running–

–towards the lift.

I arrived there just as the second skeleton was ready to step out. Behind me, I could hear the staccato steps of the first one, whose arms, now out of my sight, had immediately come unbound. I hoped that he was still too far away to stab me in the back.

The second skeleton lunged out of the lift towards me. I shot my hands up, and his sword and shield shot up too, almost as if he was surrendering. Then I barged past him into the lift, and waited for it to descend.

And waited.

And waited.

What if there was a pressure pad so that the lift would not descend if there was someone in it?

Both skeletons were close. With a flourish like a conductor, I managed to make them collide, setting both off balance.

Then, at last, the lift began to descend.

Both skeletons crouched.

There was not enough room for them to get back into the lift.

But they came anyway.

I yelled for myself and the unfortunate guardians alike. Two slabs of stone passed one another like scissor blades as the lift descended. There was an unpleasant grinding crunch. Bits of the two guardians fell into the lift with me, while most of them was left on the surface level.

"Health and safety, health and safety," I muttered, stamping on the remains of the guardians, which were not taking deadness fairly. One set of remains consisted of a skull, a shoulder and all of one arm, which still gripped its short sword. The other skeleton was reduced to a skull and two mangled forearms. One of its hands held the shattered fragments of a wooden shield, the other its rusty weapon. Only the one-armed skeleton could wield its weapon at all, and even then its attempts to kill me looked like the flapping of a broken windscreen wiper.

"Don't die down here," F3 said. "I don't want to be stuck down here until the next idiot tries to steal this sword, which might not happen for another five hundred and sixty-two years."

"What do you mean, the *next* idiot? And what did you mean by *technically*? How could the skeletons be *technically* down here?"

"You are an idiot, so the usage there was accurate. I used the word 'technically' to soften the blow a little."

"Thank you, it didn't work."

"Noted."

For a few seconds our view of the world was limited to four square walls of cobwebby stonework representing the interior of the lift shaft. Then one of the four squares developed a dark slot at its base, which rapidly grew. Soon F3's light showed that we had reached a corridor.

"Please no skeletons, please no skeletons," I whispered, still stamping on One-Arm's arm.

The lift ground to a halt with a heavy thud.

The corridor beyond was empty.

The Tomb of Kal Myridon – 2

I was reluctant to step into the corridor at first, as if there was some safety to be found by staying in the lift. But if there was any kind of safety in the lift, it was purely psychological: there was no button I could press to retreat to the weapons room if a platoon of skeleton guards came charging out of the darkness. And the longer I stayed in the lift, the longer I would have to keep dancing around One-Arm, who was still not taking deadness fairly and trying to slash my ankles with his rusty sword.

The corridor leading from the lift was square in profile and faced with damp stone. It led away on a straight course for about twenty metres before turning a right angle to the left. But half-way to the corner, a second corridor joined the first in a T junction. Naturally, from where I was, I could not see what was around either corner. F3's bright light cast hard black shadows in both places, and picked up ragged cobwebs and glistening condensation on the corridor walls.

There was nothing for it but to inch forwards.

Finally daring to leave the lift, I was pleased to see that One-Arm was not capable of pursuit. His efforts to chase after me only ended up with him spinning around on the spot. His completely disarticulated companion could only glare sullenly at me with his golden-glowing eye sockets and champ his teeth in frustration.

The branch in the tunnel turned out to be very short. It terminated in a floor-to-ceiling iron turnstile, behind which an undead skeleton waited to be released. Seeing me, it struggled against the bars in a sudden frenzy, but the turnstile was locked – it looked as if the mechanism allowed a single skeleton out each time a weapon was taken from the stage above. Many more skeletons were visible in a kind of holding pen behind the front one, who was now firmly wedged into a quadrant of the turnstile. It was his turn to be released next, but for now he could neither go back, nor – until someone pulled another weapon out of the stage – could he go further.

I backed away from the skeleton pen and followed the other path. Turning the corner, I saw what looked like the gleam of daylight ahead of me, although F3's light was still far brighter. "Light off," I whispered, and F3 obeyed.

The corridor ended twenty metres further along, in a chamber whose centrepiece was a stone-built sarcophagus with a supine carved figure on top of it. A narrow cone of daylight shone on the sarcophagus from directly above.

"Bingo," I breathed.

"Be careful," F3 warned.

"You know me," I said, suddenly feeling optimistic about my chances again.

"That's why I said be careful."

So I was careful. My carefulness even extended to staring at the ground in case there were pressure pads or something to activate traps like poison dart throwers hidden in the walls. Approaching the burial chamber, I saw that a thin scattering of dead leaves and dust covered everything in the cone of daylight, both the sarcophagus and the stone floor beneath it. The carved figure on top of the sarcophagus was a life-sized paladin, complete with gilt finish to represent his golden armour. The golden stone knight gripped a long sword that ran the length of his body... but it was obviously only a stone representation of a sword, not the real thing. That, I reasoned, must be in the box itself.

The stone lid of the sarcophagus was about ten centimetres thick, and was snugly seated on top of the recess beneath. Well, I thought, I didn't have to actually *lift* it. All I had to do was slide it far enough over that I could poke F3's light inside and maybe reach an arm in. So I rubbed my palms together and gave it a shove.

Nothing.

"Use magic," F3 advised.

"Nope," I said.

"Looking for this, demon?" a chilling voice asked.

I leapt a foot in the air, instinct telling me that a magical greatsword was swinging my way. Landing again and getting my bearings, I saw who – or what – had spoken.

A tall stone throne stood in the darkness of the far side of the burial chamber. And in the throne sat a paladin – or rather, a golden-clad mummy who had formerly been a paladin. The mummy's eyes glowed with a diffuse golden light. The large sword resting across the arms of the throne glowed the same colour too.

I took heart from the fact that the mummy hadn't leapt across the room to kill me already, and groped for something appropriate to say. "Hello," I said, "you must be Kal Myridon."

"I was Myridon once. And you are?" the mummy rattled.

"Edison Hawthorne," I replied. "Royal Court Magician." I flashed my badge.

"Which King or Queen do you serve?"

"King Someone," I said. "I can never remember his name. I've never actually met him."

"And King Sum-Wan sent you to steal my sword?" Myridon leaned forwards, as if about to launch himself out of his throne.

"No," I said hurriedly. "I only want to borrow it to kill the Lich King. I'll bring it right back when I've finished."

I had inadvertently hit the jackpot. "A new Lich King!" Kal Myridon marvelled, leaning back in his throne. "I knew it. I could *feel* it. There were whispers. A few weeks ago, a sudden pulse of energy swept through the cemetery. All the dead in their tombs awoke. I sensed their restlessness. I heard their voices. Then it's true."

"Yes."

"I've never seen a *blue* magician before. Why have they sent *you* to obtain Wolf Star? Why not send a paladin?"

"I volunteered," I said. Then I thought I had better say *why* I had volunteered. "The fact is, I started all this, so it is my duty to end it."

"You started it? Explain!" Myridon demanded.

So, still damp from my dip in Mosquito Lake, I sat on Myridon's empty sarcophagus and tried to. The undead paladin remained sitting in his throne three metres away and listened intently to my tale. I told him about exploring the bunker, about the way Bartlet had taken Lexi, and my circuitous route to get this far via Lith Tillac, the Golden Tower and Kotmoor Dry. I introduced him to F3 as my "demon in a box." Something told me not to mention my friend Ronan the paladin, because I did not want to mention that the reason I had not waited for him was Regulus, the dragon who according to the inscription on his tomb, had killed Kal Myridon. The best plan would be to get Myridon to hand over the sword and then escape from the tomb without saying anything about the dragon snoozing above us. Regulus and Myridon were not likely to meet on friendly terms to say the least, and I could do without the resulting complications.

By the time I had finished, I was no longer sitting in a cone of daylight. In the outside world the sun had set, and the light in the tomb was dim, coming only from the undead's glowing eye sockets and his sword.

Myridon was silent for a bit. Then he let out a great sigh, and said: "Thank you for your tale. It sounds like an adventure from the good old days. Back then, all I had to do was fight undead. Now I *am* the undead."

"I remember the good old days too," I said. "All I had to do was remember to do my homework."

"I did your homework," F3 corrected me.

Kal Myridon trembled with effort for a few seconds and eventually managed to stand up. "I will come with you, Edison Hawthorne. It will be my honour to face a Lich King one more time, and smite that villain's head off with my trusty Wolf Star."

Myridon's sword – whose name I had deduced was Wolf Star – hung limply in his right hand, its tip resting on the ground. Quivering with the strain, the undead paladin managed to lift it up a little way.

"Great," I said weakly, not knowing what else to say.

"All that we need," Myridon said, "is for your friend in the chamber above us to activate the lift, and we can be on our way."

"Friend?" I asked, suddenly going cold.

"Yes. Your companion, the one waiting in the weapons chamber for your signal."

I think by the way I began to rub my temples so vigorously, Myridon deduced that I had come alone.

"Oh. So we're stuck here forever. Well, it is nice to have a bit of company for a change."

"I thought there would be another way out," I said, although I was lying. In fact, I hadn't thought about getting *out* of the tomb at all, so focussed had I been on trying to get *into* it.

"The lift can't be activated from below?" F3 asked.

"It wouldn't be much of a trap if it could," Myridon explained with a dry chuckle. "The only other way out is up." With his free hand he pointed to the blank void above the sarcophagus, where diffuse daylight had earlier crept through.

I shone F3 that way.

I saw a narrow chimney set in the vaulted ceiling. It looked wide enough to crawl up, but I'd need the help of a team of acrobats standing in a human pyramid to reach it.

"Use magic," F3 said.

"You always say that," I replied. "It's your answer to everything."

"Well, you are supposed to be a magician."

"I told you. I'm saving every drop for when I have to face Bartlet again."

"No need to worry," Kal Myridon told me, "Wolf Star will do the deed."

"He's fast," I said, looking at the undead paladin tottering near his throne. "Faster than the eye can see."

"Then how were *you* planning to hit him with Wolf Star?" Myridon asked mildly.

I wandered over to have a look at his sword, and saw how it had come by its name. The faint glow coming from the long straight blade smudged its look from afar, but close to seemed more to enhance its detailing. The cross-guard was in the form of a shallow downward arc, and the handle was easily long enough to enable two-handed use. The design on the pommel had given Wolf Star its name: a snarling wolf's head surrounded by a halo of points representing the rays of the Sun.

"Beautiful, isn't it? Here, have a go." Myridon moved the sword my way with a great effort, and I reached out for it. "It's cursed," he said, "but I can give it to you without you coming to harm. I think."

I snatched my hands away.

Myridon gave a rattling laugh. "It's not *really* cursed. Here, go on, try it!"

I gingerly took the sword, and found that holding it while resting its point on the ground was easy. Lifting it up to a guard position was hard. Even harder was swinging it to any great effect. There was no way either of us were going to hit Bartlet with it. Ronan could easily have swung it. But I remembered how fast Bartlet had moved in the bunker, and knew that even Ronan would not be able to tag the Lich King with it. "The Lich King is too fast," I muttered.

"Spiders are not so fast as flies, but they still win against them," Myridon intoned.

Great. So I somehow had to make like Peter Parker and spin a web in which to trap Bartlet, then sting him with Wolf Star.

But first I had to get out of this place. I went back to stand as close to the chimney as possible, craning my neck to look up with F3's light until my neck began to complain. It was too far to jump, and there was no way to climb.

"If only we had a bow and arrow," I said. "I could tie a rope on and…"

"…end up losing an eye when the arrow came back down?" F3 asked.

"We could fill this place with water, and float up the chimney," was my next gambit.

F3 did not even bother to reply to that one. Kal Myridon merely stared at me with his glowing eye sockets.

"The vaulted ceiling," I said. "We pull out the right stone, and…"

"…get buried under a hundred tonnes of rubble and soil?" F3 asked.

"You're not helping!"

"Use magic."

I knew that I could use magic to float myself up the chimney. And I also knew that in the grand scheme of things, it would cost very little magic indeed. F3 would probably tell me something about potential energy if I asked him about it, which I was most emphatically not going to do. But such was my aversion to using any magic now that the thought of floating up the chimney almost made me nauseous. And I knew that if I tried to float up there using the catalysts alone that it would be like trying to win the fairground game where you have to throw a ping-pong ball into a jar.

"Let's try the lift," I said. Anything to put off having to use even a smidgeon of proper magic. So I led the way back to the lift, the undead paladin lurching along behind me. Kal Myridon stopped to say hello to the pack of skeletons behind the turnstile. Then, when we reached the lift, he stabbed both of the hapless animated skulls with the point of Wolf Star. The golden sword burned through their bones at a touch, and their eyes dimmed for a final time.

"Goodbye lads, your shift is done at last," he said sadly.

My first thought was that I might be able to reach above us with my mind and somehow use the catalysts to pull a weapon out of the stage, thus activating the lift again. But because I could not see the weapons, I could not grip them. After five fruitless minutes I gave up that idea, warning F3 to say nothing. Kal Myridon stood by and waited patiently. He was completely silent. He didn't even breathe.

267

"I've an idea," F3 said.

"Don't say it!"

"No, it isn't that. This is different. Let's go back and have a look at the turnstile."

So that was what we did, leaving Kal Myridon staring into space by the lift. We examined the mechanism from a safe distance while the foremost skeleton thrashed away wildly in its attempts to get to me, like a football fan locked out of the stadium on derby day. F3 soon identified that the lock of the turnstile was operated by a pair of rockers, one at the top and one at the bottom, that popped out of the way when a hidden gear turned. The two rockers popped up again when the turnstile had gone through a narrow arc to prevent it from moving through more than a right angle, therefore letting only a single guardian skeleton through each time the device was activated by someone stealing a weapon from above.

I could move both of the latches with the catalysts; the skeleton would be free to push the turnstile through a right angle, in turn triggering the lift-raising mechanism.

It all sounded great apart from the bit about the skeleton being released; it would naturally run forwards and try to stab me with its ancient blade. I would have to disengage both locks and immediately turn my attention to not dying. It seemed doable.

I went back to the undead paladin and got him to stand inside the lift to wait. Then I got as close to the turnstile as I dared and popped both the locks.

The skeleton pushed forwards. The turnstile turned through a right angle.

The rattle of chains came from deep within the tomb machinery. Success!

I temporarily knotted the skeleton's arms together with a quick spin of the catalysts, then legged it for the lift. I hurtled in and stood next to Kal Myridon, saying, "That should do it." Then: "Any second now. Any second..."

The skeleton caught me up just as the lift began to rise, but the undead paladin simply held Wolf Star in his path; the guardian ran onto the glowing blade, and his own light went out instantly. "Your duty," Kal Myridon told the corpse, "and that of your comrades, is done. We have a worthy need for Wolf Star, and must protect it from treasure hunters no more."

A minute later we were back in the weapons room.

A Meeting of Old Foes

Kal Myridon and I made our way out of the cemetery by F3's light.

"Kal Myridon," I said timorously, "there's something I need to tell you about how I found this place…"

But Myridon had already caught a distant gleam of white light on red scales, and his tottering pace speeded up. "Regulus?" he asked in a voice like the sea washing cobbles on the shore.

"Kal Myridon?" Regulus asked, in a voice like tombstones falling over.

I winced, expecting neither of the former foes to let bygones be bygones. I predicted that the renewed battle would last about three seconds and would end with Kal Myridon going up like a human torch. Still, I consoled myself, I could peel his burning fingers from Wolf Star and take it.

"You're looking well, old friend! You don't look a day older than when we last met!" the undead paladin said.

"You're looking – um – better than you did when I last saw you," Regulus allowed.

"Well, you *had* just bitten me in half. They stitched me back together. Of course, I *was* still dead. Just a bit more tidy."

"No hard feelings?" Regulus bellowed.

"Old friend," Kal Myridon said, "I didn't want to fight you. I knew I would end up dead."

"Then why did you?"

"Well, in the end, I couldn't stand the way they kept staring at me. *When are you going to deal with the accursed dragon*, they said, *like you dealt with the Lich King*."

"Ungrateful so-and-sos," said Regulus sympathetically. "You'd already done heroic work. Who could ask for more?"

"I told them I was going to lose. I mean, it's quite obvious that one man cannot beat a dragon. *No, no*, they said, *the great Kal Myridon will throw the fell beast down.* So when I could stand it no more, off I went."

"You didn't go easy on me, did you?"

Myridon laughed. "No! Couldn't get near you with that flaming breath you kept hitting me with. And even if I could, Wolf Star was made to kill *undead*, not dragons. By the way, how did things turn out after you chewed me in half? Thanks for spitting me out again, by the way."

By this point I had settled down on a nearby gravestone, wondering whether I still existed. The parallels between Kal Myridon's final battle and Beowulf's were inescapable. Life imitating art, perhaps.

"I don't eat talkers," Regulus said to the undead paladin. "Like I said to whatsisname – that blue kid that was here a minute ago – I do incinerate them or bite them in half if they try to kill me."

"Too right. It's all they deserve."

Regulus told Kal Myridon about the construction of his old foe's tomb, which he had watched silently from a nearby crag. He waxed lyrical about the parades of mourners at Myridon's funeral and the curse laid about the tomb by the gang of sorcerers.

"That must have been around about the time I woke up," the paladin surmised. "How long ago was that? The seasons fly by with nothing much happening and only centipedes to talk to."

"I know what you mean. It's a long time, that much I know. Half a thousand years, I think."

"I should have been dead ten times over," Kal Myridon lamented. "Instead, I just sit there in the dark for centuries on end doing nothing except listening to the centipedes. And all they ever do is moan about joint pain."

Do centipedes really get joint pain? I wondered. It seemed doubtful. I did know they had expensive cobbler's bills.

"Where is he, that blue kid, anyway?" Regulus muttered. "He promised me shiny things."

Shiny things. Ouch.

"Over here," I called. "There weren't any, I'm afraid. But if you help me to kill the Lich King, you can have your original hoard back."

Regulus narrowed his eyes. "You brought me *nothing?*"

"I have a few bits," Kal Myridon said, hurriedly jumping in to save my bacon. "There are a few gems in the hilt of this dagger they dressed me in, and there are a dozen pieces of gold in this pouch they tied to my belt."

"Put your money away, Kal! I will accept the blue kid's offer."

"Edison," I said.

"But do not be thinking that dragonfire will avail you aught against the Lich King. It will not. I will escort you as close to Malafert as I am able to. After that, you two will be on your own."

"Us three," F3 said.

"Unless you do more than talk, little box, I think two is right."

The Road Down from the Valley of Heroes

After the two old foes had enjoyed a good old chinwag, Kal Myridon and I set off west from the cemetery towards where it joined a larger valley heading north. Regulus meanwhile settled down to sleep, promising to catch us up sometime after sunrise.

The valley we were descending towards would take us west of Mosquito Lake, and join the Cursed Vale itself a day's walk further. I wondered how far down the mountain Ronan had got. My little detour had taken quite a while, so he ought to have reached Mosquito Lake by now, even if he had gone the slow way. But he would find no trace of me there. Where would he go? Looking for my trail in the valley we were heading for too, and eventually following it into the Cursed Vale?

The going was fairly flat at first, but Kal Myridon was still very slow. His armour was heavy and cumbersome, and Wolf Star was not the easiest thing to carry. His ancient boots fell to pieces within a mile so that he was walking on his withered feet almost straight away.

"Shall I carry something?" I offered.

The first thing he gave me to port was his golden helmet. Its beautiful feathered plume had all but disintegrated, and most of what was left crumbled to dust as I put the helmet under my arm.

Next he stopped to unclip his breast and back plate, at which point several large purple centipedes fell out and scurried away into the rocks. As the main part of the armour, this was not light. I hung it over my head and pack and wore it like a bizarre metal tabard, but now it was my turn to be slow: not only was it heavy, but my thighs kept banging into it as I walked, and its weight meant that I was unsteady on my feet. It was cold in the pre-dawn morning, but I began to steam under the extra weight.

The sky began to brighten, making F3's light seem to fade by comparison. Shadowy hills appeared on our flanks, backlit by the approaching day.

Soon we reached the foot of the hanging valley where it began its descent into the larger valley below. Here we found ourselves on the wrong side of a small stream. As I stood in a clump of rushes and nerved myself to cross, I looked back to make sure Kal Myridon was keeping up. He had fallen back a bit, so I took the chance to sit on a rock next to the stream to wait for him.

"Edison," the undead paladin said uncertainly, "I want you to take Wolf Star."

"Eh?" I said, and turned to look his way again. Kal Myridon had stopped ten paces away. In the flat warm light of early morning the glow of neither his eyes nor his sword was visible.

"Don't bother with the armour," he quavered. "You won't be able to carry it. But the sword – you will need the sword. And remember my words. Remember what I said. You do not have to be as fast as he is to catch him."

A thin whitish steam seemed to be emanating from Kal Myridon's hair and beard. He was beginning to burn.

"Take heart brave soul! Nothing bad will happen to you as long as you hold Wolf Star!"

Which was quite a hot take coming from someone holding Wolf Star who was currently on fire.

"Thank you for rescuing me from my tomb," the undead paladin croaked, "it was nice to meet you, and to meet good old Regulus again. But I cannot be the one to kill your new Lich King. You must be the one to do that."

"Kal?"

Kal Myridon was properly on fire. His hair crackled, and acrid smoke rose into the dawn sky.

"It's hot, it's hot," he said, and walked into the stream. There was a sizzle and a cloud of steam as his feet entered the water. "The sun knows me for what I am!" he cried. "Farewell, Edison!"

Standing knee-deep in the fast-flowing water, he reached out to offer Wolf Star to me. Before I could react, his burning hand fell off at the wrist and both sword and hand fell into the icy stream. A moment later Kal Myridon's mummified body lost its animation. It toppled over into the water, which fizzed for a bit, and then went back to its happy gurgling.

"Whoops," F3 said.

I dropped the golden helmet and threw off the plate mail. Then I went upstream a few metres to drink from the cool clear water where there would be no danger of it containing charred bits of the undead paladin. After that I sat miserably on a mossy boulder and watched the day brighten around me.

"The sun was still behind the mountains," I said.

"We should have foreseen this outcome."

F3 was right. In hindsight it was obvious that, as an undead, Kal Myridon would perish in daylight. But the thought had not even occurred to me. Had it occurred to him? As a specialist undead fighter, it must have done.

I sat there for about half an hour just staring at the wind moving in the rushes and at little brown and beige speckled birds that kept hopping about on the streamside. Then the birds suddenly leapt into the air and whirred away. I looked up to see half the sky blotted out by a vast pair of red wings.

Regulus swooped down and landed on the other side of the stream. Before I could explain what had happened, he asked in his deep booming voice: "Was it quick? I would not like to think that he suffered."

"You knew this would happen?" I asked.

"We both knew," Regulus said. "It was what he wanted."

We sat in silence for a while, a smallish blue human and a giant red dragon on opposite sides of a gurgling mountain stream. The scene would probably have made quite the composition if only there was a photographer around to catch it.

"You still have your other paladin," the dragon said at last.

"I'm not going to wait for him," I said, Regulus's comment crystallising a question I had been internally debating.

"You stand a better chance together than apart."

"We stand no chance together or apart," I said. "Please, if you see him, tell him to go back."

"He won't," Regulus said. "If I know anything about paladins, he won't. Nor will he forgive you for not waiting for him."

"That much he will. He will understand my reasons, even if he disagrees with them." But Regulus was right that Ronan would not turn back. Which meant that if I went first alone and died, that he would go second alone, and die too.

Abruptly I launched myself to my feet and waded out to where Wolf Star was. Its location was marked by a golden sparkle on the frothing water's surface. I reached down with both hands to grab it, finding enough room on the handle to avoid Kal Myridon's carbonised fingers.

Returning to shore, and immediately reminded about how heavy the sword was, I gingerly picked away at the remains of the undead hand in what I hoped was a respectful way.

Regulus watched all this in silence, his great eyes narrowed. When the hand was freed, he said, "Throw it in the water. Then he will never stop travelling."

Instead of throwing the burnt hand I waded back out into the icy water, lowered it down into the chuckling foam, and released it. I stood there for a long moment, thinking that a certain solemnity was required. Then when a suitable amount of time had elapsed, and my feet were beginning to go numb with cold, I left the stream and picked up Wolf Star in both hands.

Feeling rather ridiculous with my giant sword, I walked down the valley a hundred metres to where the larger valley cut across it, causing a sudden steepening of the slope. A few miles away on the far side of the valley, the early morning sun gleamed on snowy mountain peaks. Below, I traced the path of my little stream to where it joined a larger watercourse flowing north towards the Cursed Vale. There was a large abandoned settlement down there – a thousand buildings, all of the same grey stone, almost all no longer with roofs. Some of the buildings had become nurseries for scrubby trees to grow in a landscape that was otherwise full of knee-high rushes and low shrubs.

Regulus followed me with crashing footsteps. He sat beside me on the lip of the slope and said, "You do not have to do this. If you know you cannot win, why die trying?"

I looked to my right, down the valley to where it met the Cursed Vale in the middle distance. I fancied I could see a darkness in the haze there. I had said that I had no chance against Bartlet, but I didn't believe it, not really. Call it my usual optimism bias if you like, but something told me that I *could* win. I just hadn't figured out how yet.

"Well," I said, "if I die trying, I'll become an undead, and I'll try again."

"In that case," boomed the dragon, "would you like a lift?"

The Lost City

My second flight by dragon was no less terrifying than my first. But bearing in mind my destination, I found I could not get too worked up about the prospect of plummeting to my doom if Regulus accidentally let me go. The distant city of Malafert with its vast dome of synthetic night had for a time the look of somewhere that had just been obliterated by a strange kind of nuclear weapon. But this was no weapon: it was a shield against the hateful light. Flying closer and eventually under the disc of impenetrable blackness that I called the Mushroom of Fear, the cheerful day soon vanished. The land beneath the Mushroom darkened rapidly, first to the darkness of a thunderstorm, then to the utter blackness of deep night. The verdant green of the Cursed Vale faded, the colour draining from it to a flat deepening grey tone that made me think of night falling – but here, night was falling horizontally, not temporally.

I could see nothing of the heart of the darkness, Malafert itself; ahead of us there was just ever-deepening night. Then, as if a quiet roar was suddenly silenced, Regulus steered up, directly into the blackness, and I could see nothing at all save for the dim golden glow of the sword Wolf Star. He soon dipped back down out of the void, complaining that it felt as if the darkness was gnawing at him. But by then the air beneath the void was hardly any less dark.

"If I can find it in this confounded darkness, there is a place on the very edge of the Citadel," Regulus explained, "at the foot of the wall that separates it from the larger city, where a tunnel once carried water. Here, there is a grate to prevent small things like you from intruding, but it has long since rusted through. Something as tiny as yourself could no doubt creep inside and use the waterway to reach far into the Citadel, perhaps all the way to the base of the great tower itself. For on the walls and in the courtyards, the dead will be swarming, and you will find yourself soon joining their ranks if you try a direct way."

"You know this how?" I asked.

"I saw it when I flew past once, maybe a few decades ago. I don't suppose the grate is in a better state now than it was then. There is water below the wall, where I can drop you for a soft landing. I cannot linger there, because the archers of the dead are quick to find their mark. I wish you luck, and hope we meet again one day, wizard Edison."

"Me too," I said vaguely. But I wasn't really thinking about what I was saying. Instead, thoughts and ideas whirled around my mind about what I would do when I eventually came face to face with Bartlet again. I wondered whether I might be able to use the catalysts to help wield Wolf Star, to make it dance the way Ronan would do if it was in his hands. It was too heavy for me, but a combination of muscle and the catalysts could perhaps do the job.

Other ideas, or half-ideas, or tidbits of data kept popping into my thoughts. The death of Kal Myridon made me think again of somehow putting a stop to that infernal Clockwork in the top floor of the great tower that was the source of the Mushroom of Fear. Also swirling in my thoughts were Lexi's words that Bartlet was arrogant, and would not dodge. Perhaps he might let me take a wild swing with Wolf Star, not knowing its lethal effects on the undead?

"Nearly there," Regulus said suddenly. He was already swooping downwards.

I could see very little. I could tell that the ground was a long way away. On our left, at our height, a vertical structure caught a stray gleam of light from somewhere. I eventually identified it as one of the crumbling lesser towers that were connected by covered walkways to the great tower at their focus. The main tower itself was an utterly black cylinder set in a sky only a shade lighter, so even harder to make out than its satellites. I knew that Lexi was somewhere within the main tower. There was no sign of a light in a window this time, but that meant nothing: her room might be on the other side of the tower.

Down and down we spiralled. I had the sense of the ground rushing up to meet us, but could not see it. I half-expected to be pulverised against one of the city's buildings at any moment. But I told myself that Regulus must have better eyesight than I did to be travelling this fast–

Then the dragon let me go.

There was a moment when I wondered just how far I was going to fall – but it was just a moment, for the next thing I knew I was landing in a miniature explosion of wet mud. As you might imagine, after falling from an unknown height to hit unseen ground, my landing was not a good one. But at least the mud cushioned the blow. I fell to my knees and Wolf Star sank to half its length in the sludge.

"Get to the wall," Regulus boomed. By the sound of his voice and the audible flaps of his great wings he was already climbing back into the sky.

"Thanks—" I began, but stopped speaking with a yelp as something whizzed past my nose in the dark.

An arrow.

It was soon followed by another.

"Get to the wall, get to the wall," I muttered, squelching a few steps in a few different directions. "F3, which way's the wall?"

Before F3 could show me, Regulus did. He flew along the citadel wall's top, breathing fire as he went. Several things up there bloomed into instant incandescence, some of them *moving* things. The sudden fiery illumination showed that the wall was about thirty metres away from me, and about as tall.

With a long-drawn-out yell that I quickly regretted as I ran out of breath, I charged for the wall. Or perhaps a better way to put it would be that I furiously plodded that way through the mud.

What looked like a burning bundle of sticks fell from the wall, landing close by; the mud doused the skeleton's fire, and he righted himself and immediately turned his attention to me. But, trying to nock an arrow, he quickly discovered in an almost comical fashion that his bowstring had burnt through, so he was reduced to trying to flail at me with the bow itself.

Neither of us were very fast through the mud; if anything, my bony pursuer was gaining. But Regulus's incendiary strafe had caused the rain of arrows to become a trickle, so I was able to reach the foot of the wall unharmed. Then I turned to face the skeleton, thinking I didn't have room to start climbing before it got to me. Not that it had anything to easily kill me with. It could have stabbed me in the foot with one of its arrows or nibbled my ankles, but a judicious kick would probably have seen me climb out of range. Nevertheless, the safer option seemed to be to deal with it on the ground and then climb.

And as I turned to face it, the smouldering skeleton stopped advancing and froze in place for a long curious moment, as if deciding whether or not to attack me. The undead soldier eventually gathered its wits and came after me again.

My swing of Wolf Star was clumsy – but the skeleton did not attempt to block or dodge the blow. The golden-glowing blade burned straight through the undead archer's left arm, ribcage and spine and out through the other side, and I thought again of Lexi's words about Bartlet.

He won't dodge.

My foe's eyes went blank and he fell dead in the mud.

"Did you spot the grating?" I panted. "Please say you did."

"Yes," F3 replied. "Ten metres on your left, then start climbing."

"Roger," I said, pacing big squelch-sloshy steps along the base of the citadel wall.

"You had better hurry," F3 said calmly. "Several hundred undead are approaching at speed. There is a possibility they may be unfriendly."

A glance told me that, indeed, hundreds of pairs of shining golden eye sockets were coming my way. They were yet distant, their glowing eyes like a swarm of will-o'-wisps hovering over a haunted marsh. "Light on for a sec."

F3 obeyed. The cone of his light revealed that I was standing on the edge of a wide plaza, which had filled up with mud as a centuries-long lack of maintenance had eventually seen its drainage system fail. Beyond the lake of mud lay the foremost buildings of the city proper; most of the structures I saw in that brief glimpse were in a terrible state of repair. The angry undead issuing from these decrepit ruins were like a swarm of ants spilling out of their nest in response to an intruder. The lack of arms of most of the horde identified them as the former living – and current undead – residents of Malafert. Only a few of the mob had swords or makeshift weapons.

I swung my backpack off for a moment so that I could tie Wolf Star to it. Then I turned my back on the 'possibly unfriendly' horde and began to climb.

A Visitor

For Lexi, trapped in the permanent night of the Black Tower of Malafert, an unknown length of time had passed. She was beginning to go frantic from the lack of daylight. She had no sense of time, no way of knowing how long it was until the time Bartlet had estimated for Edison's arrival at the Citadel. She hoped Edison had a plan for dealing with Bartlet, because she had found no useful hint about how to kill her captor despite what felt like weeks scouring the library for historical records. The books she had found only covered the lives – undeaths? – of the first four Lich Kings. Of these, two had been deposed by other undead and two had been killed in battle. The first to die in battle had been Malafert himself. Malafert had been killed in battle with an army of paladins, although the way Lexi read it the fighting had mostly been magic-based way back then. The fourth Lich King, Craxelor, had died in battle far away from the Black Tower, and no undead scribe had recorded any details about exactly what had happened. The two usurpers (the third and fourth kings) had somehow successfully drained the power of their predecessors. No-one had bothered to write about the undeaths of the fifth and sixth Lich Kings.

All she had found out about the Clockwork and the fake night it poured forth was that nothing but the death of the incumbent Lich King could halt it. It was made of a substance called adamant, which mortal weapons and earthly materials could not harm.

Stopping the Clockwork seemed the best chance, and yet it was hopeless. Edison was not going to arrive with enough power to battle Bartlet directly, so that was hopeless too.

She tossed the book she was trying to read aside and selected another.

That was when there was a quiet knock at the door. Handmaiden entered without being bidden. "My Lady," she croaked, "your presence is requested in the throne room."

Lexi said nothing. She dropped her book back on the dressing table without opening it. She picked up her lamp and stood up. Then she walked past Handmaiden, out of the stateroom and onto the stairs, leaving the undead servant in her wake.

Lexi plodded up the stairs, past the dining room where the butler was pouring blood into a single crystal glass. They looked at each other for a long moment, the butler pausing his pouring, becoming as still as a statue; then Lexi moved on.

She reached the head of the next set of stairs and let herself into the throne room. Here, the lighting, though dim, was enough to see by without her lamp. She did not stifle it, but put it down by the door, not wanting the trouble of relighting it if her visit was going to be a short one, as it hopefully was.

Bartlet was sitting in his coffin-wood throne, staring at her with his glowing blue eyes. Tailor stood nearby, holding what looked like a black coat or a long dress over one of his four arms.

"Welcome, my Queen," Bartlet said. "See what Tailor has made for you. It will be perfect for our wedding night."

So the garment was a dress, rather than a coat. Tailor let the dress fall to its full length. Lexi could not see its detail from where she stood, and she had no intention of going any nearer. She turned and picked up her lamp—

The throne room door slammed shut in her face.

"Stay awhile. I insist," Bartlet said. "Tailor here has worked his fingers to the bone on your wedding dress. Haven't you, Tailor? The least you can do is to show your gratitude by trying it on."

"Perhaps My Lady would prefer to try it later..." Tailor said tremulously.

"Try it *later?*" Bartlet repeated harshly. Then he vanished.

He reappeared a moment later standing right in front of Lexi. Normally he reacted to her slights in good humour. But this time his face was a mask of fury. And Lexi suddenly realised that his anger was aimed at Tailor, not her; nevertheless, she would be the one to suffer the consequences. Bartlet grabbed her neck before she could react. Then he pulled her forwards, and down towards the floor.

Tailor gasped.

"I'll kill you," Lexi muttered, her face pressed against the cold stone floor.

"I'll unkill you," Bartlet grated, pretending to laugh as he spoke in her ear. His breath was foul. "You can either be you afterwords, or nobody, a hollow like those who aimlessly wander the city below. The choice is yours. Now stop your haughtiness, and try on that dress. I want to see you wearing it. Tailor!"

"Yes, My Lord?"

"Bring it!"

The tailor stalked forwards and stood close by, holding the dress in two of his four arms.

Bartlet held Lexi down easily with one hand, and with the other began to systematically shred the bottle green dress she was wearing, tearing it into strips. Lexi struggled with all her might, but the Lich King was too strong. Far too strong.

Tailor turned his back on the scene as more and more bare flesh appeared through the ruined dress.

Bartlet shredded and shredded Lexi's clothes in a fury until she was completely naked. Then he rested his knee on her back to keep her pinned down while he shredded the ragged remnants for good measure. Soon only rags remained. "Now," he said in a voice pretending to be calm but crackling with tension, "let us see how that dress becomes you."

But Bartlet did not release her at once. He kept her pinned down by her neck for another minute as she struggled uselessly against him. Then, his point proven, he let her up.

Lexi stood up, glaring at him, and reached to take the black dress from the tailor's outstretched arm. She pulled it over her head and down to its full length and smoothed it out.

Tailor remained facing away.

Bartlet merely stared at her for another long minute, then he said: "That's better. You may look now, Tailor. Isn't she a picture? I think your efforts deserve a round of applause." The Lich King began a slow hand clap, the sound dull because of his withered hands. Then he made Lexi join in like a human marionette, clapping her hands in time with his.

Eventually Bartlet tired of this game and began to walk back to the throne.

Lexi stared hard at Tailor, who kept his head bowed. Getting no reaction from him, she turned to leave.

"Where are you going?" came Bartlet's sharp voice.

"Anywhere else."

"Stand beside me, my queen-to-be, and tell me how your research progresses. Come on. I won't bite. Not yet. Have you found a way to kill me? Your time is short."

Lexi walked past the guilt-wracked Tailor to stand beside Bartlet's throne. Here, she arranged herself facing the same way as him so that she would not have to see his hideous dried-out visage.

"Well, well," Bartlet mused. He spoke in a tone of voice that said he had just worked something out or noticed something interesting.

Lexi refused to show him any respect by asking him what he referred to.

But there was no need. Bartlet was eager to tell her.

"We have a visitor," he said. "The lapdog has arrived already." So saying, he waved one of his skeletal hands and conjured an image in front of them. Once again, one of the Lich King's minions had its eyes fixed on Edison.

There was very little light on the scene. What there was mostly came from the sword that Edison was holding in both hands, which was as big as he was and glowed the colour of ripe wheat. His new jacket was frayed and caked in mud. He stood with his back to a high wall, from which a little warm light came, and it seemed to flicker like fire.

Edison swung the heavy sword clumsily.

Bartlet's conjured image was instantly dispelled.

Edison had found a sword that could kill undead! For a split second Lexi felt a surge of hope. Then she realised that he didn't have a hope of hitting Bartlet with it. The Lich King was far too fast, the sword far too heavy. Where was the paladin? Surely he would have been better able to use such a heavy weapon? Weapons of any sort were not Edison's style at all.

"Interesting," Bartlet intoned. "He has found a weapon that can sever my connection to my people. Of course, it cannot harm *me*."

It's Wolf Star, Lexi realised. It was the sword mentioned in several of the texts that she had laboured over, the sword that had the power to kill a Lich King, but had been considered lost. Edison had somehow found it.

Bartlet loved the sound of his own voice. "Perhaps," he said, "rather than make him your lackey, I could strike him with his own blade, so that he will have no second chance at life. What do you think of that? I could just cut his thread."

Of course Edison would very much prefer to be properly dead than become one of the walking dead. So would almost anyone. So Lexi immediately considered asking Bartlet for the opposite.

Instead, she said, "You don't care what I think of that. You will do whatever pleases you."

"Oh, but I do care, my dear," Bartlet protested. "Please, tell me what I should do."

"I think you should stand still and let him hit you with it, if you are so sure it cannot harm you."

Bartlet found that idea highly amusing. He threw back his head and laughed heartily. It was an unpleasant, dry, rattling sound. "My dear, you must try harder. The lapdog will be here soon. There is not much time left for you to plead for his life, or death, or undeath."

The Tale of the Last Dragon

Ronan Korland was harried by undead for quite a long way on his journey down the valley. The Lich King's soldiers only gave up the chase when he had descended to an elevation where the fog and rain began to break up. Here the dead were unwilling to follow him, and they hung back in shady spots in the densest patches of trees. On his way down he saw plenty of evidence of Edison's flight, including multiple crossings of the principal stream. Then all traces of his friend disappeared.

Ronan followed the northern side of the waterway until he reached the point where it cascaded over a steep cliff.

Had Edison gone over the edge? Had he drowned?

He picked his way down to the lake below in the lengthening shadows of afternoon. In the shallows a hint of smoke in the air led him to a scorched undead. Around it there were extensive areas where something very large had flattened the reeds and stirred up the water. The flattened vegetation and disturbed mud spoke of some enormous lake monster of a kind he did not know.

How the presence of the monster pieced together with Edison's movements he could only guess. There were no signs that Edison had emerged from the swamp. Putting the evidence together painted a bleak picture.

Ronan searched along the shoreline until dusk, and then he went up into some rocks to think. He sat with his back wedged between two boulders and listened and watched as night fell.

In the morning, he decided to continue his journey alone.

Below the lake, a series of rapids led down to a lower valley. From a vantage point on a crag near where they began their descent, he could see, far to the north, a black smudge on the horizon showing where Malafert was.

Down in the valley, he followed an old road through what had once been a series of farmsteads, heading north towards the Cursed Vale. Here a shoulder of high ground to the west hid the darkness of Malafert. The sky was blue, the air crisp and cool, and the cheerful chirruping of small birds softened the desolation of abandoned homes.

Then his eye caught sight of something large in the sky.

Ronan stopped walking. He stood in the middle of the road, closed his eyes, and breathed deeply for a few moments. A memory stirred in his mind, of sitting on his father's knee and hearing the Tale of the Last Dragon. It told about the last surviving dragon in the Westfold, which had engaged in a reign of terror after his mate was killed. It was a tale of slaughter and destruction in which the avenging dragon had eventually been thrown down by a regiment of paladins.

Even as a small boy, Ronan had not known where his sympathies lay in the story. Humans had killed the dragon's mate to protect their livestock. So natural justice seemed to demand that the surviving one of the pair should take his revenge. But he did not know which humans had killed his mate, and to him all humans were alike, so he killed them indiscriminately. His anger and grief could only by stilled by his own death. Little Ronan could only think of how he wished he could see the dragon. That made him wish that in the story, it had prevailed over the men who fought it. But that would mean the death of brave men. Why could they not go their separate ways in peace? Even little Ronan had known the answer to that. It was because some things could never be forgiven.

Then, as so often when he closed his eyes, Ronan saw an image of himself in his mind's eye, saw himself killing his father, the same man who a decade before had sat him on his knee and told him legends of dragons, elves, sea spiders and eel-men.

Not the same man, he told himself.

A lost man, an unbidden voice replied, *but a man who could have been found. Instead of trying to find him, you murdered him.*

Ronan's eyes snapped open. The dragon, black against the sky, circled him twice and then came in to land. As it descended, he saw that it was red, a rich crimson red the colour of freshly-spilled blood. It had been hard to gauge its size in the sky, but as it thumped down fifty paces ahead of him, he saw that it was the size of a house. The last few beats of its wings as it settled gusted against his face. He did not flinch.

The great red dragon sat in the road blocking Ronan's way and watched him with its great sly eyes and waited to see what he would do. *So*, Ronan thought, *this is what made the mess on the lake shore. This was Edison's fate, and it will be my fate.* He reasoned that trying to go around, through the abandoned farmsteads, would be pointless. If it wanted to, the dragon could easily cut him off. Like a cat with a mouse, it was intent on tormenting him before it killed him. *Well*, Ronan thought to himself, *this mouse is a rat. A rat with a magic sword.*

He approached the dragon, keeping his sword sheathed for now. Surprise was his only chance.

"Who are you, little man?" the dragon boomed, its voice like distant thunder.

"I am the last paladin," Ronan said. He didn't know why he said it. He certainly didn't believe himself worthy of the title. But it seemed the right thing to name himself to a dragon that was about to kill him.

"And I am the last dragon," the dragon said. "So we are well matched."

Again Ronan was reminded of the Tale of the Last Dragon. Perhaps *this* was the last, lingering here alone for centuries in these abandoned valleys, protected from people by their fear of the dead. "Perhaps," he agreed.

"But if you were truly a paladin, you would be clothed from head to foot in golden mail," the dragon pointed out.

"I lost my armour," Ronan said, "twice. But my sword is magic." He had stopped walking ten paces away from the dragon's nose. He didn't know why he was telling the monster these things. Its eyes were deep; locked onto his, they seemed to exert a hypnotic spell over him.

"You are wondering whether perhaps you might be able to leap forwards and, with one mighty swing, lop my fat head from my scaly neck before I even knew what was happening," the dragon predicted. "Now why would you want to do that, when we have only just met?"

"Have you ever killed a person?" Ronan asked.

The dragon seemed to shrug. "Yes," it said.

Ronan tensed. Still he kept his sword hand low, by his side. The situation was hopeless.

"Have *you?*" the dragon asked.

Ronan's reply was instant. "Yes," he said simply, and his chin drooped with shame.

"Then perhaps it is I who should be slaying you, rather than the other way around?"

"I saw marks in the swamp above. I had arranged to meet my friend…"

"I see. So you think that I am still picking bits of his gristle out from between my teeth?"

"I have no evidence of that, other than that he has vanished."

287

"Let me tell you something true, Mr. Paladin, which you can believe, or not believe, as you choose. I do not eat talkers. I never have done, and I never will. I sometimes bite them in half and spit them out if they try to kill me, or incinerate them. But eat them, no."

The monster had no reason to lie. It could admit to killing Edison without fear of reprisal. One snap of its jaws or a puff of its fiery breath, and Ronan's attempt at vengeance would meet a sudden end.

Ronan sighed heavily. "You are not my enemy today," he said. "Now, may I pass?"

"You seem to be heading northwards," the dragon observed.

"I am. My enemy the Lich King is there."

"Your friend Edison is ahead of you. He told me to tell you to turn around and go home."

"Go home!"

"I said you would refuse. Any true paladin would."

"Whatever I am, I am refusing. Now, may I pass?"

"You'll never catch him. I gave him a lift all the way to the foot of the citadel."

"You helped him? Why?"

"Because my home is infested with dead things pretending to be alive things, and I hope that if Edison is successful in his quest, then they will go back to being dead things who accept their station in life. I mean death."

"I have to hurry," Ronan said. But still the dragon would not let him by.

"I wonder whether you might do me a favour," the dragon said.

"I'm listening."

"I have a splinter. It's itchy. Would you mind?" The dragon made a sinuous half-turn, showing him its left flank. There was an arrow sticking out from between two plate-sized scales. "I only end up pushing them in deeper if I try to get them out myself. I'll end up spending all day rubbing against a boulder..."

"I'll do it," Ronan said quickly. Maybe once the arrow was out, the dragon would let him on his way. He advanced slowly, clambered up on the dragon's thigh, and reached up to grab the arrow. "Ready?" he asked. But he did not wait for a reply from the beast. Instead he yanked the arrow out straight away.

The dragon roared in pain, sending small birds scattering into the sky. It half-started to its feet, removing Ronan's footing. The human fell into a dense patch of vegetation. By the time he had staggered to his feet, the dragon had settled back down. "Did you get it all, Mr. Paladin?"

"My name is Ronan, Master Dragon, and the answer is yes," Ronan said. He held up the arrow's point to prove his.

"Well, Ronan, my name is Regulus, and I am indebted to you. Although as I incurred this irritation in the act of helping your friend, perhaps we are even after all. But I do know where there is some armour that might be your size, if that would be of interest?"

"I cannot delay," Ronan said.

"*Golden* armour? Lightly singed. One owner?"

"Thank you, but I had better hurry."

"Never fear, I'll give you a lift. Then I'll take you to Malafert. But if I drop you where I dropped Edison, you'll never catch up with him. I'll have to think of something else. But if you survive, you will probably have to help me with a few more splinters."

Thinking of a Master Plan

By F3's light I climbed up the sheer citadel wall with the recklessness of someone who thought that fate had something far worse in store for him than a long yell and a sudden squelch. There were crevices aplenty for fingers and toes alike, and handholds of ferns and grass, although some of them, dead from lack of sunlight, came away in my hands. At one point a china teapot shattered on the stonework nearby, tossed at me by one of those below; but looking down, I saw that the glow-eyed masses were not following: they were simply crowding together at the foot of the wall, unwilling or unable to continue the pursuit.

The grating was as Regulus had described it, covering a wide circular opening with a stone-faced tunnel beyond. The lower third of several of the grating's vertical bars were rusted to oblivion, leaving a gap easily wide enough for me. Passing through, I found myself in the lower reaches of a gently-inclining and seemingly endless straight tunnel. My walk under the Citadel began in six inches of stagnant water, which in a far-off day would have been far more unpleasant to flounder through. You could almost say that my way led, not so much into the heart of darkness, but into the bowel of darkness. But the Citadel today was full of undead people, who probably didn't use the toilet. The smell in the sewer was not too bad: a thousand years of rainfall had washed away all trace of the foul taint it had no doubt once had.

I walked up the tunnel, F3 lighting my way; but my footsteps became more sluggish as I went. Eventually I sat down in the curve of the wall, my feet just clear of the water, to think.

"Ideas?" I asked hopelessly.

"I'm thinking," F3 said, which wasn't very hopeful.

"You know, if this was a movie, I'd be confronting the supervillain in freshly-laundered clothes." Once, my peacock-embroidered blue jacket had been beautiful. Now it was frayed at the sleeves and covered in twelve layers of mud.

"You can still strut," F3 said.

"That only impresses the peahens," I muttered. "What do you think a tiger would make of a strutting peacock?"

We sat in silence for a time. It was what you might call "delaying the inevitable."

Eventually, F3 said, "I have an idea. It's a terrible idea, but it's all I can think of."

"I've an idea too," I replied, "and mine is terrible as well."

"Are you going to tell me what it is?"

"You go first."

"No, you."

So I somewhat reluctantly gave voice to my idea, which sounded more of a long shot the more I said about it. Then F3 told me his idea. Any hope I might have had that his idea would be viable, or even marginally better than mine, was soon dashed.

"I told you it was terrible," he said, when he was finished outlining the plan.

"So did I," I replied. "I think we go with yours."

"No," F3 said, "as stupid as it is, yours has the greater chance of success. We go with yours, and hold mine in reserve as a fallback."

It made a certain amount of sense trying it that way. But there was a large element of chance in it.

"If this goes pear-shaped, and by some miracle you end up in one piece…"

F3 completed my sentence. "I'll do what I can to look after Lexi, yes. But that won't be necessary. We're going to win."

"You're just saying that to make me feel better."

"Obviously."

"Listen, it's about that time when—"

"You tell me how much you love me?" F3 asked.

"F3, you've been solid. I wish you luck in whatever comes next."

"Edison, you've been my favourite owner."

"You've only had one owner."

"Like I said."

"Honest answer. How do you rate our chances?"

"Honest answer? About 3%."

I thought for a moment. Three in one hundred?

"One in thirty-three and a third," I said, standing up. "I like those odds. Let's rock."

On the Stairs of the Black Tower

The drainage tunnel terminated in a large octagonal chamber that was knee-deep in (thankfully) quite unoffensive water. F3's light revealed banks of vertical chutes in the walls that had once brought waste from the tower above down to this point. In its heyday a sluice had allowed water to be fed through this room, pick up all the unpleasant things that had fallen down the chutes, and carry them down the tunnel to deposit them from a great height onto the adoring people of the city below.

"Good King Malafert must have loved his people as much as they loved him to bestow such gifts on them," F3 said.

"Much as in our day, the process for dealing with waste was quite simple," I said. "Make it someone else's problem by flushing it."

A short set of steps led out of the water on one side, ending their run in an iron gate that no-one had ever bothered to lock, perhaps reasoning that no would-be intruder would be mad enough to try to clamber up through the royal sewer. The corridor beyond the gate was utterly dark. And it suddenly occurred to me that, depending on how populated the Black Tower was, F3's light might already have been visible to the inhabitants for quite some while. So I got F3 to kill the light and stood very still and quiet for a bit to listen. Without F3's light, the only illumination was the spectral blue glow emanating from the blade of Wolf Star.

"This could be the shortest rescue mission in history," I whispered.

"Not really," F3 replied in a low tone. "It's been going on for three weeks already."

"I bet the earlier Lich Kings were a good deal slower than Bartlet, making hitting them with a magical sword rather more achievable," I said wistfully.

"It's all right to be scared," F3 said.

"I'm not scared," I said defensively.

"Now that it's quiet, I can hear that your heart rate has gone up to one hundred and sixty."

"H'mm. I should never have had that second can of Coke," I muttered.

All was quiet except for my pounding heart, so I proceeded, setting F3's light at ten percent of maximum. Beyond the gate lay a short corridor lined with musty store rooms; at its far side, further steps led up through a half circle and ended in a heavy door that was shut fast. An icy draught poured through around its edges.

"Before we go any further," I said, "I don't want to know how many steps there are in the tower."

"I can't tell you how many steps there are, because I don't know myself."

"Good." And with that, I edged the door open. The long-disused hinges gave a shriek of protest, potentially alerting half of the tower to our presence. I didn't bother to close the door behind me.

I found myself in what had once been the grand entrance hall of the Black Tower. Like the waste-disposal room below, the hall was octagonal. Its ceiling was a dizzying height above; some way between it and the floor, an extensive mezzanine level had once given less sociable guests a good view down on whatever public event was ongoing in the hall.

The floor was a polished-smooth stone I told myself was marble, with a large star-shaped design at its centre; tip-toeing forwards, I saw that there was a snarling wolf's head within the star – mimicking exactly the design that featured on the sword I was currently struggling to heft.

"Malafert himself created the means for his own destruction!" I whispered to F3, who had probably figured this out too but had remained silent, having assumed that we were supposed to be operating in stealth mode.

F3 did not reply. I immediately wished I too had remained silent.

To my right, a wide passage led to the hall's main entrance. Along it, several sets of large double doors stood wide open, and at its far end, thirty metres away, I glimpsed a squad of undead guards. These were clearly some sort of elite force; they were larger than the normal soldiers, and F3's light showed that they were clothed from head to foot in plate mail. Their armour reminded me very much of Kal Myridon's, save that rather than plain golden, it was a rough mix of black, silver and golden, as if it had once been golden but the gilt had been sanded off or painted over.

It was almost as if I was looking at undead paladins.

The squad were motionless and facing away when F3's dim light flicked past them. But that little glimmer was enough to wake them up. There was a series of heavy clanking sounds as they began to move.

"They are coming," F3 said, somewhat unnecessarily.

I ran for one of the two sets of stairs that swept up the outside of the hall to the mezzanine floor, and bounded up them two steps at a time. The sound of the pursuing guards was like a mini avalanche, but I was relieved to discover that they were not fast. They had mostly been employed for standing in the way rather than chasing fugitives, and even though they were probably eternally tireless, all they could do was plod along after me. I could easily outpace them, although my own speed was beginning to slacken off long before I reached the first waypoint in my ascent of the Black Tower – the mezzanine balcony.

There was only a single exit from the mezzanine: a pair of double doors in its back wall. Running that way, in my mind's eye I saw myself throwing those doors open, finding only a cupboard, and being forced to descend the stairs opposite the ones my pursuers were climbing to search for another way up. But I was relieved to find that there were indeed further stairs beyond. This next set rose up in a tight spiral rather than a broad curve. I was pleased to find that the double doors could be secured on the inside by a sturdy beam. I had to drop Wolf Star to lift it up into place, and even then I was at the limit of my strength. But my efforts were worth it. I thought it would take the undead paladins quite a while to knock the doors down.

"If I die," I told F3, panting and sweating and leaning against the doors, "or undie, or whatever, the first thing I'm going to do is go down into the old city and find a launderette."

"Not a bath?"

"That too. Remind me to tell you about the bath I had in Lith Tillac sometime."

After catching my breath, I began to pound up the spiral stairs. "Did you see the floor at the bottom of the tower?" I asked F3.

"How could I miss it?"

"What do you think it means?"

"What you said it means. King Malafert made, or probably caused to be made, the very sword you are presently carrying."

"Yes," I panted, "but what I meant was, why create a weapon that is one of the only things you are vulnerable to? It makes no sense."

"It makes perfect sense," F3 said.

"Yes?"

"Early in his undead reign, Malafert foresaw a time when he might cease being Good King Mal and become something else, something evil, perhaps unutterably evil, corrupted by an eternity of clinging to undeath. So he provided that potential future with a means of ending his reign. Wolf Star."

"It's a theory," I admitted, and then concentrated on putting one foot in front of the other. I soon lost count of the number of steps I had climbed, not, of course, that I wanted to know. Various half-thoughts kept spinning around my mind: how ancient tribes had discovered that taking the high ground in a battle was advantageous, and how by the time I had reached the summit of this climb, I would be so tired that a sparrow would probably be able to knock me over with a wingtip. The possibility that there might be guards above me as well as below me was a recurring worry. Then there was the foresight – or recklessness – of Malafert to see to the creation of the very anti-undead sword I was presently carrying. Kal Myridon had used it to kill the last Lich King, or the next to last; where had he obtained it?

Every twenty steps or so, a tiny excuse for a landing appeared in the middle of the staircase, off which a single doorway always opened. I never explored any of these floors of the tower, reasoning that my goal lay higher. But I was eventually forced to stop climbing when the stairwell came to an abrupt halt in front of another such door.

I gave myself ten seconds to regain a semblance of composure before opening the door and stepping over the threshold. I found myself in what was unmistakeably a ballroom. Its high walls were covered in a mixture of drapes and tapestries, both threadbare, the former billowing in a breeze that came through holes in once magnificent many-paned windows. Four doorways led out of the curved outside of the ballroom, which seemed impossible at first until I realised that they were the beginnings of covered walkways leading to the Citadel's lesser towers. Beyond the doorways and the glimpsed windows nothing could be seen but the false night being generated by the infernal machine in the tower's top. The Wolf Star motif again dominated the polished floor. Once upon a day, King Malafert had danced here, danced on the symbol of his own mortality. On one side there was a small raised area where a band had played. Somewhat disturbingly, after their last gig they had left all their now-mouldering instruments behind. The walls were lined with benches and seating of a more imposing sort, including chairs that could only be described as thrones. And as with the great hall now far below, there was a viewing area above, where tired revellers had once leaned against the stone balcony rail and watched the dance below.

Then, from somewhere up on the balcony but out of view from where I was standing, came a heavy tread. I was not alone in the ballroom.

Guard

A figure appeared at the top of the ballroom stairs. This was the sequel to a dozen thunderous footsteps, which had given me some sort of a preview regarding the newcomer's size.

My first thought was a grateful one: *it isn't Bartlet*. My second thought was: *this guy's big*.

But I only realised just *how* big he was when he finally stamped into view. He was both wider and taller than the door I had just passed through, which told me the only way he was ever going to return to the ground floor of the Black Tower was through one of the adjacent towers or via a window. He was clad up to his neck in dark plate, made quite matt by extensive patterned engraving. He had long white hair and a withered face, his dried lips revealing two rows of yellow peg teeth.

His weapon of choice was a war hammer that was as large as I was. The war hammer did not look much like a hammer, but I think that's what a student of Medieval weaponry would have called it. It was vaguely T-shaped, and decorated with an array of lethal-looking spikes; the giant undead carried it easily in one hand in a manner that somewhat reminded me of a priest carrying a cross.

As the giant thundered slowly down the stairs towards me, I had the chance to try to knock him off, to send him crashing to – and maybe even *through* – the ballroom floor with a flick of my catalysts. But I waited, wondering whether the best

296

plan was to wait for him to reach the bottom of the stairs and then use up a bit of real magic to simply fly past him up to the balcony. I could surely outpace him if I could get past him.

But as the armoured monster reached the bottom of the stairs, I held my ground for a moment. I suddenly had the crazy idea that he was not coming after me – that his course would bring him *close* to me, but not close enough to clobber me with his war hammer. I moved further away from his path, and he did not turn my way. He seemed to be heading directly towards the door to the lower parts of the tower.

You're not going to fit through there, I thought.

But he did not intend to try. Instead of opening the door and attempting to squeeze his massive frame down the stairs, he simply turned his back on it, thumped his warhammer on the floor, and stood there, glaring at me with his glowing orange eyes.

"So I can go forwards but not back, huh?" I asked him.

He said nothing. He did not acknowledge the question.

So I shrugged and began to climb the stairs he had lately descended.

"If your heart rate goes any higher, it's going to go pop," F3 said quietly.

"You should have heard it when I was about to face the Entity," I replied. "It was so loud I could hardly hear myself singing *Walking on Sunshine*."

The next floor was the library. A central lounge area with comfy chairs and low tables was surrounded by bookcases covering the entire circumference of the walls, all the way up to the ceiling. F3's light picked out a dead oil lamp on one of the tables. A small pile of books sat next to it. A thick layer of dust covered everything except for the books and lamp. This must be where Lexi had been finding her reading material. If only she had been browsing here at this very moment, we could have–

We could have what? Avoided dealing with Bartlet? Gone back downstairs through the giant guard and his undead paladin chums and whatever else had turned up in the meantime?

On the next floor the landing opened onto a kitchen. I poked my nose in briefly. Empty.

On, up I went.

Handmaiden

On the next floor the landing opened directly onto a short corridor that apparently terminated roughly in the centre of the tower. Here, three doors opened into three different rooms. One of the doors was open, and with F3's illumination I glimpsed a four-poster bed that I thought was quite similar to the one I had seen a week before through a seagull's eyes.

I approached cautiously. An open book, face down on the carpeted floor, drew my eye.

A faint scratching noise came from the room. I could tell that the room had been in darkness before our arrival, even though the feeble light of an oil lamp might be hard to see in the glare of F3's LED beam.

"Rapunzel?" I whispered.

There was no reply. Just the scratching sound, like mice in the wainscot.

I reached the doorway.

Lexi was not there. The only presence in the room was a very small, very wizened female undead who was cleaning Lexi's mirror with a long threadbare duster. She wore a lacy black dress and hobnail boots; it was the sound of the latter scuffing against the carpet that I had heard. Her eye sockets glowed, as was the norm for undead. For some reason she either hadn't noticed me approaching Lexi's room or was pretending that she hadn't. When I appeared in the doorway, she froze in the middle of sweeping her duster over the compound mirror and turned her head – just her head – to look at me.

Then she attempted a curtsy, slow and stiff and almost in slow motion. "Welcome, My Lord. You must be here to see King Bartlet," she said, looking me up and down in a motion that made her head look like an animatronic appendage on a fairground mannequin. "I am the handmaiden."

"Edison," I said. "Is – er – Rapunzel somewhere around here?"

"Master Edison, you'll be wanting the throne room. Two floors up." With that, she leered at me and turned back to her dusting.

I backed away a few steps, spun on my heel, and returned to the staircase.

Butler

Two floors, the handmaiden had said, but I poked my nose into the next floor for form's sake. It was the dining room and was dominated by a long table with enough seating for two cricket teams. The table was devoid of plates and cutlery.

An undead butler stood near my end of the table. He carried a silver tray on which was a crystal glass and a bottle of either claret or blood – the liquid within was strikingly red in F3's light.

With a gesture he offered me the tray.

"No thanks," I said, "I'm driving." I turned to go back to the steps, but with a sharp *ting-ting-ting* the butler attracted my attention again. I saw he had tapped his glass with a tiny spoon, as if about to give a speech. But he said nothing. Instead, he gestured with the spoon at a display case on the wall. Its label read:

THE SHARDS OF THE SWORD OF AN UNNAMED PALADIN, WHO BRAVELY TRIED TO SABOTAGE THE CLOCKWORK IN THE REIGN OF CRAXELLAR

When I had read that, I looked back at the butler, who was staring at me with his dimly-glowing eyes. He said nothing. But he was trying to tell me something.

"Put my sword in the Clockwork?" I hazarded.

No reaction.

"*Don't* put my sword in the Clockwork?"

No reaction.

"Thanks for all your help," I said, and turned away again. I half expected another *ting-ting-ting*, but there was nothing. I had seen what the butler wanted me to see. What I made of it was another matter completely.

299

Tailor

"Better kill the light," I whispered, approaching the foot of the final set of stairs.

"Agreed," F3 said, and flipped the switch.

His light had only been at ten percent of maximum up to that point, but it was far brighter than the feeble baby blue illumination cast by Wolf Star. My sword's point to the fore, its dim light meant that I almost accidentally stabbed the next member of Bartlet's undead staff on the stairs.

On edge already, and startled by the suddenly-looming figure on the stairs, I jumped a foot in the air. Bartlet's fourth servant had four arms, white hair like the other three, and he was clad in a shabby velvet coat. Righting myself, I got ready to run the undead through: although his four hands were empty of weapons, he was definitely blocking my way.

"Greetings, My Lord," the servant said, and bowed. "I am the tailor. I am sorry that we should meet on such terms."

I thought he was making reference to Wolf Star's point being an inch from his nose at the lowest point of his bow, and bemoaning the fact that I was hostile, but he wasn't.

"I should not be standing above you on the stairs like this," the undead went on, as if we had met in a scene from a period drama, he was alive, I wasn't blue and carrying a glowing sword, and I wasn't going to visit a Lich King but Mr. Darcy's Aunt Catherine instead.

"Don't worry about it," I replied tersely.

"You must be the young man we have heard so much about," the undead said.

"All good I hope," I said, and waited for the tailor to get out of my way.

"If you will give me your name, I will be pleased to announce you to His Majesty."

"No thanks," I said, and hefted Wolf Star, trying to look more confident than I felt. "I'll announce myself."

"Very well. Good luck, Sir." The tailor backed up a step or two until he reached the landing of the throne room floor, where he was able to edge to one side to let me pass.

I joined him on the landing. The door to the throne room was large and ornate, and made of dark and ancient polished wood. I looked at it for a long moment.

The tailor watched me.

I leaned Wolf Star against my shoulder long enough to straighten my coat.

Then I grabbed the sword again and opened the door.

Banter with Bartlet

The throne room was not completely dark like the rest of the Black Tower. Warm orange flames bloomed from lamps in many places around the walls, producing a level of light equivalent to about half an hour after twilight. In the dim it took me a few moments to get my bearings, during which time I stood still just inside the door; I heard the tailor closing and locking it behind me, which seemed unnecessary if not downright vindictive.

The throne room was round and took up the entire floor, its single continuous wall following the tower's circumference. Grand windows had once alternated with the lamps along the walls, but the former had long since been bricked up. Such a move must, I guessed, have pre-dated the invention of the Mushroom of Fear that produced a shield of artificial night over Malafert. None of the Lich Kings had ever bothered to restore the windows even though they were now safe from daylight with or without them. The only furniture was a row of seven thrones, arranged in an arc so that they were all facing the room's centre. No two of the thrones were alike; my eyes whizzed along them to see that Bartlet was sitting in the leftmost of the seven, and that Lexi was standing on his right.

Lexi was wearing a long, black, rather Gothic dress with sleeves of gauze and flowery cuffs. Her feet were bare, and her hair was in disarray. Bartlet was holding her left wrist, preventing her from leaving his side. The vampire himself was wearing a full-length black gown, his hood up as if he was trying to imitate Emperor Palpatine. Twin blue spots of light showed where his eyes were; the rest of his face was in darkness.

Both Bartlet and Lexi, of course, were looking my way. I spoke to Lexi.

"Hello Rapunzel!" I said, affecting a cheerful tone.

"Edison, be careful!" she called.

I began to walk casually towards the centre of the room – where the usual Wolf Star motif was to be found.

"Kneel," Bartlet said. His voice was dry. It took him a while to get the single word out, because he elongated its middle quite a bit.

"Hello Neil," I said. "I'm Edison."

"So the lapdog arrives at last," Bartlet said, unperturbed by my crude attempt at humour.

"I see my station in life is rising," I replied. "When we first met, I was nothing. Now I'm a lapdog. I call that progress."

"You took your time getting here, lapdog," the vampire sneered.

"Yeah, well, I had to sniff a lamp post on the way."

I don't know why I was trying to antagonise Bartlet. Well, I wanted to chop his blue head off at some stage, and that was unlikely to be achieved without antagonising him at least a little first. Unless he didn't see it coming at all, which didn't seem likely. But I saw the snark fight as the part of the fight I could actually win; inconsequential as it might be, it seemed worthwhile to get a point on the board.

"You look tired," Bartlet said, his tone not betraying any trace of annoyance so far. "It is so many steps up from the sewer."

He knew I had come through the sewer? How? "I've climbed taller towers," I said with a shrug. It was a lie, of course. I had been to the top of the Golden Tower, but there I had taken advantage of the magical lift.

"Kneel before me, lapdog, and I will consider sparing your life." Bartlet gestured with his free hand: *down*.

"What do I get if I stand on my hind legs and turn in a circle wagging my tail?" I asked.

"If not to kneel, why have you come?"

302

Apparently the long sword I was presently clutching in both hands was not enough of a clue as to my intentions. I played along. "I've come for the prisoner."

"You mean my betrothed? Why not use her name?"

"I already did. Rapunzel."

Bartlet chuckled humourlessly. Rapunzel was a dumb choice of fake name of course. While it might fool those with no memories of the time before the Quacker, it would not be likely to fool any of the few who pre-dated it, a club that Bartlet was of course a member of. "Are you going to take Rapunzel to safety through the same sewer you crawled up to get here? Are you going to cut your way through all my guards with the sword you can hardly lift? Or are you here to try to smite me with it?"

"That depends on you."

"Oh?"

"It depends if you stand still long enough."

At that moment, Bartlet vanished from his throne.

"I don't think I will," a voice whispered in my ear, probably a tenth of a second later. Bartlet's lips were practically brushing my neck. *Note to diary: vampire hunters need high collars, probably infused with garlic,* I thought wildly. I didn't bother to swing Wolf Star at him, knowing that I would be too slow, knowing that the blow would miss.

Bartlet didn't bite: he suddenly moved again, disappearing and reappearing a moment later standing beside Lexi. "*Sit* my dear," he said, "I insist."

And Lexi, moving very slowly and clearly fighting his will every step of the way, shuffled a short distance to her left and sat down in Bartlet's throne, which appeared to be made of old coffin lids assembled into a rustic chair by a hurricane passing over a graveyard.

"I'll kill you," she hissed at him.

"Say nothing for now my dear," he said, drawing a virtual zip to seal her lips. "Just sit back and enjoy the entertainment."

Then Bartlet was gone again – and again, the first thing I knew of *where* he had gone was when I realised he was now standing beside me. This time, instead of whispering in my ear, he gave me a shove that sent me off balance. The Lich King had tired of losing in the game of snark: the physical battle had begun.

Battle with Bartlet

As you know, I had a plan for this moment – or rather two of them, neither with a promising chance of success. I haven't told you what they are yet, but I *can* tell you that both plans involved Bartlet getting overconfident. Unfortunately, overconfidence is no guarantee of failure. So there was a high chance that Bartlet would become overconfident and *still* crush me like a bug.

The initial shove made me stagger a few steps before I regained my balance. Logic told me that I was already winning, or rather, I was losing but in a way that led to a potential future in which my Plan A or F3's Plan B would come off and I would end up winning eventually.

The Lich King vanished again and reappeared standing on the wolf's head design in the centre of the throne room. He hadn't even bothered to lower his hood yet. "I could have killed you several times already," he said.

"I know, I know, Barty, you just want me to suffer a bit first," I rejoined. I was about to add what a disgrace he was to the rather small community of Blue People in the post-apocalypse, but I didn't have time. He vanished again.

At that precise moment I swung Wolf Star, guessing where he was going to reappear. I didn't overdo things, not wanting to lose my balance completely when I missed.

But that's what happened. Wolf Star sliced the air with a satisfying swoosh... and Bartlet appeared from nowhere and shoulder-barged me from the opposite side. I was sent sprawling; the floor was well polished, and I ended up falling and sliding and rolling and regaining my footing in a way that I hoped gave the (true) impression that I had never battled anyone hand to hand before.

"Are you enjoying this, Rapunzel?" Bartlet yelled. To me, he shouted: "Hit me!"

I tried to. I really did. But again Wolf Star only cut the air, and before the arc of the blow was complete, I was flying through the air once more. This time the Lich King had shoved me in the back, hard; I did a complete somersault and would have landed in a heap if I hadn't used a tiny bit of actual magic to ensure that I landed on my feet.

It was a game of cat and mouse, except in this version of the game, the mouse had nowhere to hide and no way to escape, and the cat was so fast it was invisible.

But at least the mouse was carrying an enormous sword.

Once again Bartlet had retreated to stand beside the throne where Lexi had been forced to sit. Her eyes were wild, but she could neither move nor speak. I could tell what she was thinking: "Please tell me you have a plan, Edison!"

I grinned at that. I had a plan all right, or two of them. Both involved Bartlet beating me to a pulp.

"I will get your name from him," the blue vampire was saying to Lexi, "at the end, he will give it to me." Then he disappeared again.

I tensed every muscle. A split second later, something hit me in the ribs, hard, and I was whirling through the air. The wall was coming up fast. I hit it sideways on, again cheating with a little real magic to land feet first with two boot soles flush against the stonework. Then I sprang forwards and landed in a ready stance again. I silently fixed my three broken ribs.

"Bravo!" Bartlet laughed. Now he was standing at the other end of the row of royal seating, next to a throne of dark wood and giant rusty bolts. Of the seven, this one and Bartlet's were the two largest, seeming to bookend the five smaller thrones between them. "How long do you think you can keep this up?"

"Why?" I asked. "Have you got an appointment?"

"Her name? Her real name?" Bartlet demanded.

I didn't bother to reply.

"I have a choice to make," Bartlet mused. "I can take your sword from your hands and end your existence here and now, completely and finally. I can kill you and have you serve as my Queen's footman. Or I can lock you in a dungeon until you die of old age and then become an undead, and bring you forth before my eternally undying bride to remind her of you, and together we will laugh at how pathetic you are, and toast our immortal reign."

To give this insane speech Bartlet stood still for so long I was tempted to throw one of my daggers at him. But the idea that he might stab me with it a moment later was a powerful deterrent. So I did nothing; I merely gripped Wolf Star with both hands and judged my next blow.

"Impress my Queen," Bartlet said. "Try harder."

Again he disappeared. I tensed every muscle against a blow I would not see coming, and swung Wolf Star in a guess at where he might appear.

This time around, he shoulder-charged me and I was knocked over like a skittle. I slid all the way across the room until I bumped into one of the seven thrones quite close to the one Lexi was in. It was a rather tasteful design made of partly-melted green bottles.

Lexi looked down at me. I looked up. She could only move her eyes at that moment, but they were very expressive. "Don't die, you idiot!" was how I interpreted their look.

"I've got this," I said, and slowly got up. I hobbled away, towards the Wolf Star design in the centre of the room. I would have to play my trump on the next round, before Bartlet tired of the game and really hurt me or killed me–

Then he thumped me harder than ever and I found myself flying through the air towards the wall again. I used a tad of magic to take the sting out of the impact – not enough to be obvious – but still ended up crashing into the wall sideways, banging my skull and several limbs on the stonework.

I fell in a heap, accidentally on purpose releasing my grip on Wolf Star, which clattered away a pace or two.

I looked for Bartlet, and there he was in a flash, standing over the sword, looking down on me. Now that I was disarmed, he no longer saw me as a threat.

What happened next depended on him.

Bartlet stood over Wolf Star. He was two paces away from me. I watched him through eyes that were mostly seeing stars.

F3 watched him through a hole in my coat pocket.

Both of us waited to see what Bartlet would do.

It was the longest second of my life.

A Spider Catches a Fly

I lay on the floor in a heap by the wall.

Bartlet, the blue vampire, the Lich King, the vengeful handyman, stood over my sword Wolf Star. He looked down at me with a hideous expression. Finally he had let his hood down so that I could blearily see the mesh of fine scars that covered his entire head. When some idiot in Central Command had fired the Quacker, all those years before, the strange radiation had flayed his skin off. Some of his nose was gone, as was half the cartilage of his ears. He had no hair. His eyes glowed blue.

I wanted to make a quip about him lowering his hood, but couldn't immediately find the words.

Seeing Bartlet's scars made me think that, yes, he had been wronged. But his revenge had been out of all proportion to the wrong that had been done him. In Foxburrow he had killed those who had wronged him and those who were innocent without discrimination. He was now killing folk in the Cursed Vale and beyond who knew nothing of Foxburrow, of the Quacker, or of his grievances. And he had to be stopped.

Lexi watched the drama from across the room, magically bound into one of the seven thrones, unable to move and unable to speak.

F3 watched for Bartlet's next move from his position in my coat pocket.

And then Bartlet *made* his next move.

He stooped to pick up Wolf Star.

He held the long sword with its faint blue glow aloft in his right hand as if it weighed nothing.

307

It was a fittingly triumphant pose, because in a sense, he had won.

But in a real sense, he had also lost.

"So," he said. "This is the sword that was supposed to... supposed to..." Bartlet's voice trailed off into silence. He stared at the hand holding Wolf Star as if it was an alien thing that would not obey his will.

"Gotcha," I said.

"NYAAGGGHHH!" Bartlet yelled, finding his voice again. That was when his sword hand erupted into a ball of blue incandescent flame. A moment later it was too bright to look at directly. And the light brightened still, and the yell became a drawn-out scream of utter agony, drowning out the roar of the flames.

I had to look away completely, so bright was the blue fire. It was as if someone was trying to arc-weld Bartlet's hand to Wolf Star's handle. An acrid smoky stench of burning flesh filled the air.

I used the wall to help me regain my feet.

Bartlet stood a few feet away, looking like a bizarre recreation of the Statue of Liberty.

"Dodge this," I said.

F3 flashed his light, just as he had done with Melur. It was probably unnecessary given the blue fire erupting from Bartlet's hand, but it certainly couldn't hurt.

I threw one of my daggers. With the catalysts I steered it right to where I sensed Bartlet's heart was, if he still had one.

And as Lexi had promised, he did not dodge. The blade slid between the Lich King's ribs until its tiny hilt stopped it. A white flash rimmed with a black corona seemed to halo the vampire for a split second.

Then Wolf Star fell to the ground with a clang, and for a moment I thought that Bartlet had finally been able to let go of it. But he had not relaxed his grip; his arm, completely carbonised by the heat, had broken off at the elbow. The stump was still ablaze, blue flame jetting from it.

But Bartlet was not finished, even with one arm burnt off and his heart transfixed. Still screaming, moving fast, but not at his usual supernatural pace...

...he ran away. He crashed through the locked door of the throne room in an explosion of burning splinters and sprinted up the stairs towards the floor above.

Afterglow

Bartlet carried the furious blue fire with him as he fled, so that the low-lit throne room suddenly seemed as black as night. I was left slumped against the wall, my head spinning, my ears ringing, and an enormous after-image of the monster's supernova hand filling my vision.

"Should have worn my shades," I muttered. Not that I had any. But it would have been cool to slip them on just as Bartlet's hand exploded. "Would have been like Richard Feynman at the Trinity test." I blinked rapidly, but the after-image refused to clear.

"Feynman looked through a windscreen, not sunglasses," F3 said.

"Pedant," I muttered.

"Edison!" It was Lexi's voice. She was shouting. Her voice seemed both muffled by the ringing in my ears and much closer than before.

Running footsteps, already close and getting closer. "Are you all right?" she asked breathlessly, arriving.

"I will be after a nice cup of tea and a biscuit," I said vaguely. I reached out blindly, and was cheered to find that Lexi grabbed both my hands in hers and squeezed them hard.

"Can you move?" Lexi asked. "He's heading for the Moon Lab. We need to get after him."

Get after him? This seemed a peculiar notion. "He's just crawling off... into a dark place... to... die..." I said. But the gaps between my words lengthened as I spoke, and by the time I reached the end of the sentence I realised that I was a screeching U-turn wrong.

Bartlet was crawling off into a dark place to heal.

And I knew just where he was going to do it. What Lexi called the Moon Lab must be the on the floor immediately above us. The oily black stuff coming out of the infernal Clockwork there was probably like a healing fountain or something, and he was probably bathing in it already. There wasn't a moment to lose: we needed to head off his regeneration before it got going to have any chance of winning.

"We need to get after him," I said, repeating what Lexi had said a moment earlier.

She let go of my hands. "Can I touch the sword?" she asked.

"Yes, of course," I replied.

I paused briefly.

Then: "I think."

Then: "Kick it over, just in case."

Lexi kicked Wolf Star over. Its blue glow had faded to the deep yellow that it had shown when Kal Myridon had been holding it in his tomb in the Valley of Heroes. Looking down at it now, the sword hardly seemed to have an unnatural shine at all; what seemed to be a soft glow playing along its edge could easily have been nothing more than a trick of the light. Bartlet's hand and lower arm, blackened and smoking, were still attached to the handle. A few judicious stamps shattered the carbonised flesh into black dust.

Then, with the slow deliberation of a very old man, I picked the magic sword up. "I give Wolf Star to you of my own free will," I said to the empty room, and placed Lexi's hand on the handle. Then I let go of it. Everything was fine, as it had to have been.

"Come on!" Lexi said, and she grabbed my hand and dragged me towards the stairs. "F3, light!" she ordered.

F3 dutifully flooded the stairwell with light, and we began to climb. But I was too slow, and Lexi detached herself from me after only a couple of steps, running on ahead.

"Be careful," I said, and redoubled my efforts to keep up.

Into the Darkness

Regulus flew below the void, explaining that the blood magic flowing through it would sap his strength. Even so Ronan Korland could see nothing anywhere, the false night cast on the land below as deep as any genuine one.

The dragon said he was swinging out over the sea to make it safer to approach the citadel of Malafert. His plan was to drop the paladin on the southernmost tower of the arc of eight that half-encircled the tallest tower on its landward side. A damaged but passable roofed bridge linked the two towers, so the human would be able to reach the Black Tower most of the way up.

Still Ronan could see nothing: there was just the darkness, the rush of the wind, and the powerful beating of Regulus's vast wings.

Suddenly there was a light so bright that it felt invisible in a strange and impossible way. The flash seemed to shine through the very stones of the Black Tower, unseen until that moment but now revealed to be close by. The flash made Ronan think of white light that had a black halo, or of grey light that had somehow been split into black light and white light.

A moment later the gleam was gone, and with it the Black Tower faded back into the night.

"What was that?" the paladin shouted.

"A powerful magic! Too late for the southern tower!" Regulus said. "The battle has begun! I'll have to drop you on top. Get ready to land well, for I cannot linger there. There will be opposition!"

The dragon beat his mighty wings, three times, four times, rising fast. Then the great claws holding Ronan let go. He was hurtling through a void alone, rising, rising, falling, falling – in his mind's eye, falling all the way to the foot of the tower, dashed into a million pieces – then he clatter-thudded onto the roof of the Black Tower, rolling, sliding, and eventually, stopping.

The paladin got his legs under him. He was surrounded by utter darkness. He could equally well be standing on the centre of the roof, or its precipitous lip. There was no way to tell.

His chest plate clanged, and he realised that an arrow had just bounced off it. Quick as a flash he pulled his sword, and just as quickly changed its course to intercept the swinging weapon of an undead that was suddenly revealed by the sword's magical glow.

Another arrow banged into his back, but again it spun away harmlessly. Ronan rapidly turned in a complete circle, hunting for more opposition, using the dim sword light as his lantern. Close by, he saw his first attacker, scrambling back to its feet. The others were too far away to be seen by the light of Edison's magic sword; only their faintly glowing eyes betrayed their presence. The sword tip passed through a void of night, disappearing completely for a moment: it was the fountain of darkness flooding into the sky, and it showed him that he was near the centre of the tower.

Then he saw a roof hatch a few paces away, and steps that led down into darkness.

But a blue light grew in the darkness below.

And a sound grew below too. It was an endless scream of pain, and it was waxing moment by moment. Only one entity here could scream forever without taking a breath. It was the Lich King, and it seemed that Edison had sorely wounded it.

Ronan did not hesitate. He hurried far enough down the roof steps to be able to close the hatch behind him. It could be barred, and so he barred it. Better to only face enemies from one side.

Blue light waxed in the room below.

Descending the steps, he saw a blue man on fire, screaming, running, and for a moment he thought he was looking at Edison. But he remembered that the Lich King was blue, too. His right arm was mostly gone, and what was left was an inferno of blue light.

In the centre of the room a large stone clockwork device spewed thick ropes of night up a central column. It was to this that the Lich King fled, like a man on fire running to water. He plunged what was left of his arm into the black stuff, and the blue light was immediately quenched.

The room grew dark. The only light was now the dim glow of Ronan's magic sword.

It was healing the Lich King. The darkness was healing him.

Ronan did not hesitate. He charged forwards, bright sword to the fore. His enemy saw him, but could not respond, unwilling to tear himself from the black flow that was soothing his injury.

Then the sword struck home, and both paladin and undead went tumbling, smashing into something hard, a tall bench, going over together, carrying with them an array of glassware, much of it shattering on the stone floor.

The next thing Ronan knew was that he was spinning through darkness, pushed away by a violent shove from the Lich King, whose only thought was to get back to that blissful honeyed flow of darkness. The paladin's movement was broken by another bench, again resulting in a shower of bottles and flasks onto the floor.

A moment later he was on his feet and charging back into the fight.

In the Moon Lab

At this point, you're probably wondering how I did it. You're thinking, *when is Edison going to tell me how he cleverly snared the Lich King and burnt his hand off?* Well, it just so happens I've got time to tell you now, while I'm stumbling up the seemingly endless curving staircase leading from the throne room to the Moon Lab.

My initial inspiration came from something that Kal Myridon had said:

Spiders are not so fast as flies, but they still win against them.

To be fair to my own underwhelming brainpower, this comment sent me down a lot of blind alleys. Could I somehow magic up a set of unbreakable Spider-Man threads and truss Bartlet up in them before lopping his head off?

The answer to that was a resounding NO. But something the old undead paladin had said a moment earlier eventually came back into my mind. As a joke, when handing me the sword, he had pretended that Wolf Star was cursed. But what if it was *really* cursed, so that anyone but the rightful owner who touched it would instantly regret it? Laying a curse on it would be easy. I had the six magic pearls to convert into an extremely potent spell.

There was just one very small problem: how to get the Lich King to pick it up? The only answer I had was to drop it at his feet. That was Plan A.

F3's Plan B also involved dropping the sword, but assumed that Bartlet would not touch it. Bartlet, F3 surmised, would step over the discarded weapon and stand over me for a little bit of taunting until he got bored and either pulled my head off or drank my blood. It was during the taunting that F3 planned to flash at his brightest intensity and I would use the catalysts to lift Wolf Star and stab the Lich King in the back with it. It didn't matter how fast Bartlet could dodge if he didn't see the blow coming.

Both plans involved me getting beaten to a pulp, or at least beaten to a point at which dropping the sword seemed like accident, not artifice.

The ruse had worked wonderfully – but it was strictly a one-off deal. Not only would Bartlet never fall for it again, I had used up all six of the magic pearls to construct the curse; they and it were now gone forever. So the time for patting myself on the back was probably after the matter was settled, not while it was still in doubt.

Above, ahead, I heard the sound of a load of glassware being smashed to pieces. This was nothing to do with Lexi, whom I could still see climbing ahead of me. I pictured Bartlet crashing around his lab like a crazed scientist looking for the pills that stopped him from becoming Mr. Hyde and kept him as Dr. Jeckyll. Bartlet, of course, wanted to remain Bartlet, not a husk of Bartlet that had been dead for twenty-five centuries.

But he didn't need to touch the lab equipment: only the night generator, the infernal machine, the great stone Clockwork. Here he would find the salve he sought.

Then there was another great crash from another load of smashed glassware.

Lexi reached the top of the stairs and paused for a moment. Then she hefted Wolf Star and charged forwards out of view.

"Hurry!" F3 said.

"I am hurrying!" I replied. In fact, I was on my last legs. Because I had used all the magic from the six pearls to curse Wolf Star, I had not charged myself up at all. The little magic I had used to keep myself from serious harm in the throne room had wiped my account clean. And I had taken quite a few bumps along the way. Nevertheless, sensing that Lexi was in serious danger ahead of me, I redoubled my efforts.

Five seconds later, heart thudding and breath heaving, I arrived at the Moon Lab's threshold and by F3's light saw a desperate struggle taking place. Three figures danced in the beam of light, surrounded by a chaos of overturned benches and smashed equipment. Bartlet I expected to be there. Lexi I *knew* to be there, because she had entered the room moments before me. But the presence of the third figure I saw made no sense at all.

It took me a few moments to realise that the figure I was looking at, resplendent in a full set of golden plate mail, was not Kal Myridon risen from his second death to do battle one last time, but Ronan Korland, who had somehow got hold of Kal's armour and arrived on top of the Black Tower...

Regulus...

The Lich King stood between Lexi and Ronan, facing the paladin; his stump no longer burned, and now merely smoked... or so I thought for a moment, until I realised that the flow of what I took to be smoke was going in the other direction, *to* the burnt limb rather than away from it. The infernal Clockwork's blood magic was healing Bartlet's wound.

Rockets of black smoke were erupting from Bartlet's torso, almost too fast for the eye to see; but with the magic sword I had made for him Ronan deftly severed all the demonic tentacles one by one as they reached him. But cutting these incoming harpoons had been much harder before F3 had been there to cast light on the battle, and several of them had already struck home – and, I saw with horror, *through* Ronan's chest plate. The stumps of Bartlet's earlier darts hung out of narrow holes there, fuming with dark magic.

Lexi stood behind Bartlet, swinging Wolf Star with both hands. Like Ronan, she was too far away from the Lich King to strike him directly; like Ronan, too, dark lances were flying at her one after another, and she was battling to keep them at bay. I saw with horror that she, too, had already been struck; F3's light gleamed on bright red blood running down her arm.

The barrage of smoky tentacles that Bartlet was sending after Lexi and Ronan reminded me of the old arcade game Missile Command, where the player had to use an impossibly clunky trackball to shoot down incoming nukes. Sooner or later there were too many incoming rockets to possibly defend them all, and it was game over.

"Do something!" F3 said.

I had to do something, F3 was right. But what? New ropes of black smoke were harpooning towards Lexi and Ronan every moment. Bartlet's scream of pain had turned into a roar of anger. The Clockwork was still ticking away. A river of night was still pouring out of it, and a portion of that flow was wrapping itself around Bartlet's ruined arm, healing it.

"Use magic!" F3 implored.

F3 was right for once. But as I had no magic left in my account, I decided to lean on my credit card. The Healer at the Golden Tower had warned me of dire consequences if I went back to the Dark Place again. Well, it was time to test her theory.

My electrum dagger still skewered Bartlet's heart, which didn't seem to have inconvenienced him in the slightest, perhaps because it no longer beat. Annoyingly, he was facing away from me, so it would be difficult to move it the way I wanted to with the catalysts alone.

I summoned the dagger back to me.

With the catalysts.

With real magic.

With extreme prejudice.

The dead heart was in the dagger's way, but nothing was going to stop it from returning to its owner. Not muscle, not sinew, not bone. The flesh gave, and the throwing knife erupted from the Lich King's back, bringing his heart with it.

Something resembling a misshapen blue kebab flew towards me like a rocket, squirting out a mist of royal blue liquid as it came.

Idiot, I thought, dodging out of the missile's way and falling at the same time. With a *crack*, the dagger struck the stonework above me, sticking fast.

As I fell, there was a second *crack*, a pistol shot that seemed to emanate from about half-way down my right forearm. This was accompanied by an explosion of pain that told me that my arm had snapped again, just as the Healer had promised.

Bartlet's heart was still beating after all, and rhythmically squirted blue blood down onto my head from where it was lodged in the wall. And it was a relief to see that he had felt the loss of his heart, for those smoky ropes that he was sending towards Lexi and Ronan instantly went taut and seemed to crisp up and vanish.

Lexi saw her chance. She stepped forwards, swinging Wolf Star in a great arc from right to left. The glowing blade seemed to make no sound as it sliced into one side of the Lich King's neck and out of the other. *Good*, I thought. He must be dead now, or no longer undead.

Bartlet's head fell off his shoulders and rolled, and it rolled my way.

The head's eyes still glowed blue. It was still alive.

So was the rest of him; or at least, it was still standing.

"Let me guess," I quipped at Bartlet's head, when it stopped rolling nearby. "It's only a flesh wound?"

The head could not form words. But it could form legs. A dozen little pseudopods sprouted from where it had lately been joined to its neck. The head righted itself and began to trundle back towards its body on the raft of miniature tentacles, squirting out a cloud of night around it as it went, trying to conceal itself like a disturbed squid.

Not so fast, I thought. With a supreme and agonising effort, I used the catalysts one last time. I flipped Bartlet's head up into the air and flew it over the Clockwork, until it was hanging suspended in mid-air above one particularly large pair of the machine's gears.

It's a win-win scenario, I told myself deliriously. *If his head stops the machine, daylight will return. If it doesn't stop the machine, his head will be turned to paste.*

So saying, I let go.

My aim had been good. It was not exactly a three-pointer, but the head fell right in between the two gears.

I realised that I had been screaming with the pain of using the catalysts with a broken arm, and ordered myself to stop.

The headless undead was still alive, and in fact it had resumed the flow of dark arrows from its torso towards Ronan and Lexi to such an extent that it was almost invisible beneath them, giving it the look of a human sea urchin. The paladin was hit again, and was clearly badly hurt, for he staggered back to the wall and began to slide down it. Lexi was in a fury, her sword blindingly fast, seemingly magnetically attracted to the streamers of darkness, severing several with each blow.

Bartlet's head was drawn into the mechanism of the Clockwork and disappeared.

Why aren't you dead yet? I wondered. *Are you about to become one with the Clockwork and emerge like a terrifying stone-built demonic Transformer? Was throwing your head in there the latest in a long series of wrong choices made by yours truly?*

Then the Clockwork missed a beat.

Actually, scratch that. Because a second later I realised that it had missed *two* beats.

Then the two missed beats became five, and five became ten, and then, with a sound like air escaping from a balloon—

The daylight returned.

Instantly the windows all around the lab turned from the utter black of false night to the dreamy azure blue of a beautiful early autumn day. Sunlight lanced into the room from the southern side, and although it did not reach far across the floor, the Moon Lab was now far too bright for an undead's comfort.

The shadow sea urchin exploded into a tower of fire, its many flexible arms instantly frazzling like your eyebrows when you accidentally lean over a Bunsen burner on invisible flame mode. The Lich King's body remained upright for a while as the merry flames consumed it...

...and then it collapsed in a heap.

Bartlet was dead again.

Probably.

Aftermath

"Paladin!" Lexi yelled, and ran to the fallen hero, avoiding the reeking bonfire that was all that was left of Bartlet's body.

"Ronan," I said weakly. "His name's Ronan."

She didn't hear me.

My elbow was wet. This confused me a moment, until I realised that my own broken bone must have punctured the flesh of my arm, and I was bleeding. I resolved not to pull up my sleeve to see what that looked like.

Lexi pulled Ronan's helmet off and threw it aside. His face was grey and lifeless. He did not see her.

I sat and watched as she pulled off one piece of Ronan's armour after another. Blood – her own – dripped from the fingers of her right arm. Once she had Ronan's chest and back plates off, I was able to see that his shirt beneath was extensively bloodstained. He looked like Boromir in the cartoon version of the Lord of the Rings. Full of holes leaking red. I had nothing left to try to heal him with.

A sudden voice spoke from close by.

"All too brief, the reign of darkness."

With a great effort I turned my head to see the tailor lurking in the shadows at the top of the stairs. I didn't bother to reply.

"I can preserve your friend, if you like," he added. "I am the tailor."

"Preserve" sounded a lot like "pickle" to me. I didn't think Ronan needed stitching up like an old coat, just so he could be buried tidily.

"Do you mean dead?" I asked.

"No, alive."

"Alive as in not undead?"

"Alive."

"Heart still beating? Are we talking about Ronan Korland as Ser Gregor or Ronan Korland as Ronan Korland was ten minutes ago?"

The tailor regarded me blankly with his curious glowing eyes. "As he was, so shall he be again."

"Lexi!" I called, or tried to. My voice failed me. I tried again. "Drag him over here."

Lexi turned then, and saw me propped up against the wall and the undead servant in the shadows two steps down from the threshold. "Give me a hand," she said.

"I can't just yet," I said. In fact I could barely move at all.

"There's too much light for me," the tailor said apologetically.

And so Lexi had to drag Ronan across the stone floor through shards of glass by herself. Passing close by me, she asked: "Edison, are you all right?"

"Absolutely," I said. "Just a bit winded, that's all."

"Are you sure?" she asked, looking down at me suspiciously.

"Yep. Go. I found out his name. It's Ronan. I'll be all right. Go!"

"I'll be back in a minute," she promised. Then there was the slightly awkward job of moving the comatose paladin into range of being picked up by the guard, who had now thumped up the stairs to stand behind the tailor. Then the small procession went down the stairs, I presumed to the darkness of the throne room, where the tailor would be able to use his needle and thread in comfort.

"You overdid it, didn't you?" F3 asked, when they were gone.

"Did you hear my arm go? It was like a gunshot. *Bang.*"

"What about your legs?"

"I don't want to try."

"Try! You'll have to eventually."

So I tried. But I couldn't get up. In fact I could hardly move at all.

"Try!" F3 repeated, unaware that I already had.

"They've gone again," I said.

"You'd better let me have a look at your arm."

"It's fine."

"You said it sounded like a gunshot!"

"It doesn't matter. We won, that's what matters. As long as Ronan is all right. I should have waited for him. I should have waited."

A Greenish-Blueish Seagull Squawks

I must have drifted for a few minutes, because the next thing I knew, the scene had changed slightly. The sun had moved around a little, cutting in deeper through the next window along to the right of the one it had mostly been shining through before. Bartlet's body had been mostly reduced to ash, and only a few wisps of smoke rose from it now, streaming off almost horizontally and out of one of the windows.

Khaah-kah-kah-hah-hah!

It was the laughing cry of a seagull, and it came from somewhere nearby, perhaps on the Black Tower's roof.

"No thanks required," I muttered. "All in a day's work."

A few seconds later the gull swooped in through the window and landed on one of the benches, skidding to a halt in a clatter of equipment. "Khaah-kah-hah!" the gull said emphatically.

No ordinary gull this. It was a greenish-blueish colour, and had a small dab of black on top.

"Khaaak! Edison? Are you all right?" After a few false starts, the gull managed to begin to form words.

"No," I said wearily to Hal-gull, "but Lexi's okay."

"And the paladin?"

321

"He's in the O.R."

"Khaaak?"

"He's with the tailor."

"Khaaak?"

"He's hurt bad, Hal, and I don't have any juice left to save him."

The gull's beak drooped. "I hope he pulls through. You'll be all right though, once you get back to the Golden Tower."

"I'm not coming back, Hal." I said this quite emphatically, although I had only just realised it at that very moment.

"Khaaak?"

"I can't come back. Not after what I've done. People have been killed – I don't know how many people, hundreds maybe."

"Thousands, I should think," the gull said.

Thanks, Hal-gull, I thought.

"But you've put things right," Hal added, perhaps realising that he had said the wrong thing.

"Not really. I just stopped it from getting any worse, that's all."

"The people love you, Edison. You're the most popular magician in the entire Westfold. No-one needs to know how all this started."

"*I'll* know, even if no-one else does. And I'm not going to forget it in a hurry. How am I going to look people in the eye, knowing that my stupidity has cost so many lives?" I changed the subject. "Are you calling from the Golden Tower? I thought you were heading to Erras with Jasso?"

"The pass was overrun, Edison! Whoops, don't think of that as your fault. I would have died, but for Jasso dragging me out of there. That wasn't your fault either, or wouldn't have been if I had died, and the members of the garrison who were killed..."

"Hal, you're not helping."

"Edison, listen. I'm running out of up. I had to fly a long way to get here. I'll call tomorrow, okay? We'll talk about it then."

322

And with that, the gull clammed up. Its feathers reverted to the usual white and grey, and it settled down on the bench amid the bottles and conical flasks. In moments it was so still that someone coming into the Moon Lab would probably assume that it was stuffed.

I tried to release it. With my good hand I slapped the floor three times, which was painful, but didn't free the gull from the spell. "I'm sorry, Mr. Gull," I said vaguely. "You'll have to wait until Lexi comes back."

A Non-Proposal Accepted

The next thing I knew it was dark. Lexi was kneeling close by, shining a lamp in my face. "Edison!" she said, for what I guessed was the umpteenth time.

"Sorry," I said, "I nodded off there for a bit."

"Why didn't you tell me you were hurt?" she demanded.

"How is Ronan?" I noticed that Lexi had changed out of her black lacy wedding dress, and looked to be wearing the same rough work clothes she had been abducted in.

"He is stable for now," said another voice, which turned out to belong to the tailor. "But he needs healing, such as only a magician or a witch can apply."

In the background, the handmaiden and the butler were sweeping up broken glass and Bartlet's ashes. Everything seemed to be going into the same dustpan, which showed a surprising lack of reverence for their former master.

"Sorry about the mess," I muttered in their general direction. Then: "Be careful around the seagull."

Both Butler and Handmaiden looked around at me then, and both quickly located the gull still sitting peaceably on one of the benches.

"You had a visitor?" Lexi asked.

"Hal."

"Why didn't *your* gull sit nicely like that when you left it? Instead, it went crazy."

The answer to that, I thought to myself, was probably because of the way I had mismanaged my takeover of the bird, using persuasion rather than force.

Handmaiden cackled loudly. "It just so happened to fly in your window! How stupid do you think I am, My Lady?"

"Enough, Handmaiden!" Tailor barked at her.

"I liked the black wedding dress," I said to Lexi, "although I'm glad you managed to hold out long enough not to need it."

"Well," Lexi said, "I thought someone else might ask me one day."

I said nothing.

"Today, perhaps."

Again I was mute.

"Edison, are you going to ask me to marry you?"

There was a long and increasingly uncomfortable pause. The handmaiden and the butler stopped sweeping. Four pairs of eyes, three of them glowing, stared at me. I finally blurted, "No." Then I hurriedly had to explain why. "Lexi, I can't go back, and I can't ask you to stay here in this draughty old tower with only the Addams Family for company. Edison Jr needs you back in Callan."

I thought Lexi was going to explode, but she didn't. Instead, she said: "Just as well, because I was going to say no."

"You were going to say no?" I demanded.

"Would it be better if Butler, Handmaiden and I were to leave?" the tailor enquired. All three of them were still standing by listening to the conversation.

"No!" Lexi and I said at the same moment.

Jinx, I almost said.

"We're far too young for that, Edison," Lexi explained.

"I'm twenty-five," I said. *"Centuries."*

"You should try asking me in ten years' time, if we're still alive. But if you *had* asked me now, I would have agreed to take your ring, and to give you mine."

"Really?" I asked, brightening. "But I've already got your ring. And I don't have one to give you."

"There are thousands of corpses in this citadel," F3 put in. "I am sure one of them will furnish a suitable token of Edison's love."

"I'm not giving Lexi a dead woman's ring!" I muttered.

"That would be perfect, F3," Lexi said.

"Anyway, I still can't leave, and you can't stay," I pointed out.

"Actually, begging your pardon, Sir: you can't stay here either," the tailor said apologetically.

"I can't?"

"If you stay here, you will sooner or later perish, and by the natural course of things you will inevitably rise again and become our next Lich King. And while the permanent staff might be grateful to have another lord to serve, I do not think it would be what *you* would want."

For a moment the best future I could think of for myself was a life in one of the abandoned farmsteads below the Valley of Heroes, if I could somehow get myself there, and somehow feed myself there. Perhaps I could make friends with the sparrows or something. But the tailor had not finished speaking.

"Would Sir like a pick-me-up?" the undead servant asked.

"No, I'm fine," I said.

"Yes, he would," Lexi said.

"Butler, please search the cellars for something that might refresh a living mage," Tailor said.

The butler bowed, passed his broom to the handmaiden, and walked stiff-legged to the stairs.

Lexi stood up, fetched the seagull, placed it on the window sill, and clapped three times. With a squawk it took off and flew into the night.

"I've got something for you," I said.

"What is it?" she asked.

"Inside pocket." I nodded down at my once-beautiful peacock-embroidered coat, now scuffed and stained with mud and blue blood. I probably could have reached it myself, but it seemed better and generally more dramatic to get Lexi to do it.

She reached inside my coat, and her fingers closed on... "A rolled-up paper?"

"Yes, that's it."

The paper was wet, frayed, and blue at one end where I had bled on it. "Careful!"

Lexi carefully unrolled the paper. She saw a picture of a greyish person with long hair and a blue person, and standing between them, holding their hands, a very small person. The picture also included a box with a face and a giant bear-like thing holding a sword.

I watched tears spring into her eyes, and felt them springing into mine as if she was a mirror.

"We're going to go back," she said. "All four of us."

I Am Forgiven

About half an hour later, the butler returned with a tarnished silver tray bearing two crystal glasses, a bottle of dubiously red liquid and a small wooden box. The tailor meanwhile set up an occasional table and covered it with a white cloth, whereupon the butler ceremoniously deposited his offering on it and bowed deeply.

"I don't drink blood," I said, wondering what was in the box. What sort of things did Lich Kings have as a snack? Dried eyeballs dipped in chocolate by their optical nerves probably.

"The wine is rather old, but it is not blood," the tailor said.

The butler carefully lifted the lid of the box with his white cotton-gloved fingers.

Within the box, nestling on a bed of crushed blue velvet, were four magic pearls.

*

I have to admit, it was a strange sensation, seeing the magic pearls at that moment. I wanted to dive on them and swallow them all in one gulp, but I also felt disgusted by the sight of them. It felt as if I had gone on an almighty bender and woken up with the world's worst hangover, promising myself never again would I take *that* particular stimulant. Now, here in the little box in front of me, I was presented with the ultimate hair of the dog. I hated the way I found myself staring at those four little pearls the way a wolf looks at a lamb.

In the end, I only took two of the four, one to heal myself and one to heal Ronan. I managed to resist the other two; I told the butler to hide them and to not tell me where he had hidden them. I washed the two I consumed down with a gulped half glass of wine, which was so bitter I would have spat it straight back out if I had been on my own. As it was, with four people watching me, I made myself swallow it.

"Mm," I said, lips puckered. "A little oaky for my taste."

The paladin had been put in Lexi's room. He was grey and still when, by then fully restored, I arrived at his bedside. His torso was covered in fine black stitches where the tailor had closed his many wounds.

I placed both hands an inch above his chest, closed my eyes, and willed him better. "I'm sorry I didn't wait for you," I said, expecting him not to be able to hear me yet, or if he could hear me, not to be able to speak.

But he could hear me, and he could speak. "You wanted to face your nemesis alone. I understand that desire. And again I have you to thank that I'm still alive."

I opened my eyes. Ronan was looking up at me blearily. "That wasn't it," I said, dropping my gaze in shame. "I wanted you with me more than anything else – except for one thing. I wanted you to live. So I went ahead alone. But it was stupid of me to leave you behind, because I knew that when I failed, you would follow the same path anyway, and die too."

"Forgiven," the paladin said. He raised a great bearish paw off the bed, and I grabbed it with both hands.

"You have the tailor to thank for keeping you alive up till now," I said. "Those stitches are his handiwork."

"I should not slay him then."

"No, probably best not to."

"Right."

"By the way, I didn't ask Lexi to marry me, and she said no."

"Er... congratulations?"

"Thank you. Your armour is ruined, I'm sorry to say. By the way, I briefly met the guy who owned it before you."

"I don't deserve it anyway."

"Yes, you do. And I happen to know that there are other sets around here that will probably buff up nicely."

"Where did you find the sword?"

"In the hand of the guy that was wearing your armour. I'll tell you the story some time. But we need to decide what to do with the sword now."

"Place it in the Golden Tower?"

I sighed. "I get the feeling we should leave it around here somewhere. Being guarded by the dead will deter casual treasure hunters. But if a new Lich King should rise—"

"Then a true hero will come for the sword."

"Yes."

"I want to see it properly before you dispose of it."

"Deal."

After Party

Early the next morning I made my way to the Moon Lab, to try to wangle my throwing knife out of the stone block it had stuck fast in the previous day. Bartlet's heart had burnt to a crisp, and crumbled off the blade at the slightest touch. But it proved difficult to extract the dagger without cheating by using magic. The catalysts were no good, and I was back to being miserly with magic. The two (at least!) magic pearls somewhere in the building played on my mind, but I was firmly resolved to leave them be. So I was reduced to trying to wiggle-tug the blade out, and was not seeing much movement.

Then came an enormous thud on the Black Tower's roof.

"Is anyone still alive in there?" boomed Regulus's voice.

"Yes!" I shouted up. Then, not sure the old dragon had heard me, I walked up the curving steps to the roof, leaving the problem of the dagger for later.

"What's your name," the dragon said, seeing me. It was not a question; it was hello. He was taking up half the tower's roof, uncomfortably hemmed in by the stone points that ran around its circumference.

"Edison," I said. "Hello Regulus."

"That's what I said," Regulus said. "I just thought I'd see if you or that other human was still alive. I've got my hoard back, you'll be pleased to know. The dried-up swines who had taken over Rascen's Spring dropped dead like flies when you killed the Lich King. I presume you've killed him? I noticed the weather has cleared up as well."

"Yes," I said, "he's dead all right. Or not undead any more. I hope. And Ronan's all right too."

"Ronan. That's what I said," the dragon said absently.

"Listen, Regulus, er, we're having a soirée later, and you're welcome to come."

"What's a soirée?" the dragon asked.

"Sort of a get together."

"A party, you mean? What's the occasion?"

"Oh, er, no occasion. Just, you know, sometimes it's nice to, you know, socialise a bit… we're having it up here on the roof, but we have to wait until sunset, because four of the guests will go up in smoke if we don't. Can you come back then?"

"I think I'll wait here," Regulus said. "I need a snooze, after all this excitement." And with that, he settled his great red scaly head on one of his forelegs, tucked his vast wings in, closed his eyes, and went to sleep.

*

The attendees of the party on the Black Tower's roof that evening were one dragon, three living humans, four undead humans and one omni. Regulus's long body, coiled around most of the inside of the twelve narrow towers that decorated the rooftop like the points of a crown, made a sort of safety barrier for the seven others with legs. Two avatars made brief guest appearances. One of them was Hal,

329

and the other, incredibly, was Edison Jr. He had been training all day to take over the body of another living thing, and Hal had held his hands until they had reached some gulls they could borrow. Theirs was only a five-minute visit, but it was great to (sort of) see Edison Jr. It was also rather humorous to hear him trying to speak using a gull's beak, when he could say few words at the best of times.

When the gulls flew in, the paladin hurriedly produced a small box, within which was a ring. This had been found, not on a dead person, but in the Black Tower's treasury. Its original owner, of course, was dead. But at least it had not been taken from a mummified finger. The ring was rather too grand for my liking – gold, and encrusted with what looked suspiciously like rubies. My first thought was, "If Lexi wears that in public, someone is going to try to steal it, and she might end up getting hurt, or killed."

"Say what you would like to say to her," the paladin told me.

What felt like a hundred pairs of eyes watched me. I turned a deeper shade of blue. "Lexi, I..." I grabbed one of her hands and placed the ring on her palm, not on one of her fingers. Then I folded her hand around it. Then I began again. "Lexi, I love you. I always seem to fall down when I meet you..."

It seemed the right moment to kneel.

"I will always pick you up again, you know that," she said, smiling at my embarrassment, and hauling me back to my feet.

"I will always go to the ends of the Earth to find you," I said, "but please don't go there if you can help it."

"I'll try not to."

"Quick," I said, sensing an opportunity to curtail things. "F3, we need to capture this moment."

"Roger," F3 said.

I darted away and propped him up against one of the mini towers. "Everyone look at F3," I said, hurrying back to stand next to Lexi.

They did, although I daresay none of them knew why. Regulus was at the back of the group, with his head on the right. Two unusually-coloured gulls were perched on his nose. In front of him stood Ronan. I stood next to Ronan, and Lexi stood next to me. The four undead permanent staff stood on Lexi's left.

"Say fromage," F3 called.

Several people said "fromage," in various degrees of confusion, and in Edison Jr's case, a strangled squawk.

There was a bright flash.

On a Mountain Above Gan Trost, Province of Gomm

To Urna, the winter forest was so still and so watchful that it gave her the feeling of a graveyard. The rasp of her breath and the snap of her axe she saw as an alien presence, creating sounds where there should have been none. She missed her home on the high northern flanks of the Cursed Vale. There, the air was never still; here, every time the quiet was disturbed by snow falling from a drooping conifer branch, she whirled around in fright.

The day was cold, but Urna didn't feel it, because working kept her warm. Only if she stopped for a rest did she begin to cool down. And as she stopped and stretched for a moment, it amazed her as it always did how quickly the sounds of work disappeared as if they had never been. It was as if the forest just swallowed the sounds up. After the stretch, she looked around in all directions. The sound of axe work in her ears meant she would not hear any approaching presence. What she was afraid of, she didn't know. But there was a reason more than the bitter cold that people didn't live in these mountains any more.

Having satisfied herself that nothing was creeping up on her, Urna walked a few steps to talk to Speckle. The grey horse looked as cold and sad as she always did. There was nothing for her here. Urna had to spade out heaps of snow so that Speckle could nibble on last year's dead plants. She hated the bitter and tough conifer needles that were easily available all around her.

331

Seeing her so dejected always made Urna's heart melt. She rubbed Speckle's neck. "I'm sorry, Speckle dear, I wish I could jump on your back and we could just run away, but…"

Speckle snorted and tried to stamp a forehoof. It didn't really work in the snow. Edison had told her that Speckle understood what she was being told, but Urna knew it deep down, really.

"I could take off your harness and let you go, what about that?" It was the twentieth time Urna had made this offer. "I'll get into terrible trouble when I go back, but… I don't know… would you be all right out there, on your own? Could you find your way down the mountain and find your real owner? Maybe the Princess could tell Edison where we are, and he could come and help us one day?"

Before Urna even knew what she was doing, she began to unbuckle Speckle's harness. But Speckle, now free, just stood there in the snow, refusing to abandon her human friend.

Then Urna saw where the harness had cut into Speckle's coat, and burst into tears. She wheeled away and cracked her axe against the tree she was working on. "I'll smash them! I will!"

It had taken a long time to fell the tree, and if anything it took even longer to chop off all its side branches. The main bole would be used for building, while the side branches would be stacked and used to make charcoal. There were plenty of fallen trees, but they were no good for building, being half-rotten. Every sticking out stump of branch snagged on the ground and made Speckle's life harder when the time came to drag the felled tree back to camp. So Urna spent a long time trimming her trees to spare Speckle's legs.

When the time came to return to camp, Urna got behind the tree and leant her weight to it to help the horse get it moving. As they went, Urna told herself she would have to return before it got dark to collect the stacked branches. Left too long, they would get damp.

Rotten, the gang's ringleader, was watching out for Urna's return. His real name was Rodon, but Urna thought Rotten suited him better. She also had secret names

332

for the other three that were close to their real names but better reflected who they were: Ammer, the second in charge, she called Hammer. Luce, the woman, she thought of as Loose. And Sheem, their dogsbody, she called Scheme.

Camp was a small cluster of buildings around a mine that had been abandoned decades earlier. The gang had dragged Urna's family up here after they had captured them, seeing in them free labour in the mine. They didn't even know what the miners who had once lived here had been looking for. Urna picked up that someone in the town at the bottom of the mountain had mentioned the mine, and the gang had seized on the idea of re-opening it. Of course, they were too lazy to do their own work. But Urna's family were not the best slaves. Grandpa was too old, and too obstinate. Urna's brother Milem was too young. That left Urna and her mother to do all the work.

"Is this the best you could find?" Rotten demanded, when Urna was in earshot. He was standing idly with Hammer and Loose, leaning against the side of the best cabin – the only one with a snow-tight roof.

"Look at her, pushing the tree!" Hammer exclaimed, and gave his trademark braying laugh.

"That horse looks on its last legs," Loose put in. It was not the first time Urna had heard her say such a thing. In fact it felt like she said it every day.

"What took you so long?" Rotten asked.

Urna felt obliged to answer, having been far enough away to ignore his first question. "I had to search deeper in the forest…"

But he wasn't listening, and nor were his gang.

"We should take it down to Trost with the next load of charcoal and flog it off," Hammer opined.

"Don't be a fool," Rotten said. "It's too distinctive. We can't sell it. And what do you think we'll be eating up here, come spring? If it dies in harness, it will save us the trouble of cutting its throat."

Hammer and Loose laughed at this.

Urna had by now reached them, and was un-harnessing Speckle, who, as Urna knew, understood every word. Well, Urna was not going to stand for it. "You will not hurt her!" she shouted at Rotten. "You will not hurt Speckle!"

"Or else what?" Rotten snarled. He closed the distance between them with two strides and gave Urna a backhand slap that sent her spinning into a snowdrift.

Speckle surged in between them, protecting her friend.

"What are you going to do about it?" Rotten shouted at her. But he didn't know that she could understand him.

Urna, slowly extricating herself from the snow, caught a glimpse of colour out of the corner of her eye, something out of place in this monochrome world of deep winter.

Blue.

It was Edison, the King's Magician from Highstand. He was blue from head to foot. His trousers were blue. His boots were blue. Fan-tailed birds decorated his blue coat. And most distinctively, his face was blue.

He stood not far away, square on to them, his arms folded as if he had been watching them for some little time.

"I am disappointed, Vight," he said, "very disappointed."

A Few Moments Earlier

It took me a long time to get in touch with Speckle. When I finally did, I still had no idea quite where she was beyond that she was half-way up a snowy mountain somewhere in the Westfold. Sometimes I was able to hear some of the things she heard, and eventually I heard the name Gan Trost. Taen knew where that was.

When we finally got to Gan Trost, we soon found someone who knew the gang we were looking for, and pointed us to the right mountain to climb up.

Six hours later we caught a glimpse of our destination through a bend in the path, and Ronan, Lexi and I halted and got off our horses to discuss how to approach things. I probably vaguely said something about scouting out the lie of the land, but neither

Lexi nor Ronan heard me. They were busy debating how we should keep Edison Junior safe during our visit. So I wandered on up the track on foot on my own.

Five minutes later, I reached the tiny snow-draped hamlet. There were perhaps ten buildings in all, a mixture of cabins and stores. Each was built on stone foundations and had upper parts formed of logs. One or two were in reasonable shape, but the majority were hardly more than snowy humps. Large conical spoil heaps were dotted about the settlement, and to a casual eye they too looked as if they were made of snow. Away to the left was a cave mouth, which looked like a natural feature that had presumably been expanded within by the hopeful miners of yore. The first sign of life I saw was Goliath, who was hitched up to a sled in a central open area, facing my way. It was good to see the big old nag, and seeing him confirmed that we had finally found the right place.

My pace gradually slackened as I stepped into the mine complex. After Goliath, the next living things I saw were a woman and a boy, who emerged from between two buildings on my left struggling under the burden of a heavy sack. The three of us saw one another at the same moment, and I raised a finger to my lips to signal for silence. Not only did they not say anything, mother and son stopped walking, too.

Then, ahead, I heard raised voices. I made my way towards the sounds. As the angle between two buildings changed, a group of four people came into view, and with them was the unmistakeable slate-grey form of the very best horse in the world. Three of the people were the bandits we had encountered on our way up to Kotmoor Dry. The other was Urna, the girl I had entrusted Speckle to.

I was in time to see one of the gang give Urna a backhand slap that knocked her off her feet, and Speckle front up against him to protect her. Good old Speckle.

Urna, getting up, was the first to spot me. The others, one by one, followed her gaze. When they had all seen me, I folded my arms and said coolly, "I am disappointed, Veidt. Very disappointed."

Two of the bandits hurriedly moved to flank their boss, the one who had given Urna a slap. All three of them stared at me as if I had dropped out of a flying saucer. After a bit, the boss looked at the man on his right. Then he looked at the woman on his left (he was an equal-opportunities employer). What he saw in their expressions was that neither of them were called Veidt, nor had any idea who Veidt was.

The leader of the three was older, with a greying beard. His right-hand man was taller than him, his beard darker. His left-hand woman was shorter, with matted dark blond hair. All three wore the same grey clothes and the same grey hats, although the woman had pulled hers down fully over her ears.

"Either of you two called Vight?" the boss asked.

"Veidt," I said.

"Vight," the boss said.

"Have none of you read The Watchmen?"

None of them had. Most of them were probably unable to read, although, I reminded myself, they could have looked at the pictures. If, that was, a copy of The Watchmen existed anywhere on Earth, which seemed unlikely.

All three of the gang were looking for Ronan. They wouldn't know his name, of course, but were pleased to note the absence of the hulking gorilla who had been at my side last time we had crossed paths. A question was probably beginning to nag at their minds: how had I managed to track them down?

As I mentioned, I was disappointed. But not with Veidt. I was disappointed in myself, for passing by the bandits on the Kotmoor road, knowing that they would do something horrible to someone else. It was a form of karmic justice that the people on the receiving end were also people that I had met. But ever since I had caught a glimpse of the gang out of one of Speckle's eyes, I had not been able to find an answer to my paradox. There was no different course that I could have taken, even with the benefit of hindsight. Not all problems had solutions. There was nothing I could do but let the gang go, knowing that they would rob someone else. Here, they seemed to have added slavery to their rap sheet.

I spent too long musing. For the next thing I knew, the bandit chief grabbed Urna and hauled her to her feet. Then he held a blade against her throat. Me? I was still standing there with my arms folded, musing about what might have been.

"Now, here is how this is going to go," the boss said.

The right-hand man tilted his head back and brayed with laughter. I could not help but notice that he had several teeth. *Must invent toothpaste*, I told myself. Preferably before I invented lemonade.

That was about when I realised that perhaps I should have contributed to the discussion half a mile back down the track rather than abandoning it. Strutting about and delivering a one-liner from a two-thousand-year-old graphic novel, one said by a blue guy infinitely more powerful than me, turned out to be not quite as rewarding as I had thought. If I *had* thought about it – and I hadn't – I would have thought that dealing with a bunch of low-grade villains I characterised as bandits should have been easy compared to the challenges I had already successfully faced. But the bandits in question had decided not to play fair.

"None of your trickery, magician! You try to take my knife, like last time, and it might end up stuck in this pretty girl's neck! I'm holding it tight, see!" Bandit Chief told me.

My heart was slowly descending in my chest, although I took a soupçon of encouragement from his rather nervous-sounding tone. "The girl has a name," I said, trying to sound calm.

"Really."

"It's going to be all right, Urna," I said.

"Sure it is," Bandit Chief said. "Just so long as you do what I say. Now. Put your hands behind your back and let my colleagues here tie you up."

"You're too lazy to kill the one who does most of the work around here," I told him, racking my brains for an actual solution to the standoff. I could easily throw out my knives and stab both of the boss's henchpeople in their hearts. But that ain't me, and anyway, that scenario could end up with their boss putting his knife in Urna.

"Try me! You'll see how much I care about your fancy talk."

The right-hand bandit laughed again. It was not the kind of laugh that bore repeating. I ground my teeth and said, "You three probably had a hard upbringing. I get that. But sooner or later, the excuses start to rub off. You keep on trying to use them, but they just aren't there any more."

"What are you on about?"

"I'm saying that sooner or later, you have to stop blaming your evil ways on the bad hand the world dealt you, you know, the one like a foot, and admit that you have chosen to do evil of your own free will."

The bandit leader kept doing a strange side-eyed look to his right. I thought perhaps he was worried that Ronan might be somewhere around. But it turned out that he was looking for someone else. I heard a footstep behind me—

—and suddenly remembered that I was an idiot.

The gang was four members strong, not three. I was only looking at three-quarters of them. The other one—

A booted foot hit the back of my left knee, and I found myself falling forwards. I had hardly hit the snow when I yelled, "I'll swap her for the demon in a box!"

"Thanks, Edison," F3 said from my coat pocket, loud enough for all to hear.

I found myself looking up at the fourth member of the gang, a young man with a leering, gappy grin. "He's in my pocket," I said.

"Slowly!" the chief shouted. The fourth bandit beckoned for his prize with a mittened hand.

Slowly he said, and slowly I went. I tossed F3 up to the bandit, who almost fumbled the catch. "Careful!" the chief told him. "It stings!"

At that my heart rather sank. An attentive reader will know that F3 and I have frequently resorted to the trick of me handing him over, and him tasering my enemy at an opportune moment. It seemed that rumours of F3's ability had spread throughout the criminal fraternity.

"Only if you try to hurt him," I muttered, but my voice trailed off before I could be bothered to make an analogy with wasps.

"We can sell it in Trost," the fourth gang member said, turning F3 over in his mittens in a semi-tantalising way. But it was obvious from where I was lying that my omni was not going to get an angle to stun the guy through his heavy coat. And even if he did, the villain-in-chief still held a blade to Urna's throat.

"Don't get blood on his coat," the boss said. "We'll sell that in Trost, too."

I wanted to tell them that my coat was a unique piece, and that selling it in Trost would be a mistake because it would be recognised, and set the rest of the King's Magicians on them. But I couldn't muster the enthusiasm.

"Is it blue?" the guy holding F3 asked.

He meant my blood. "Yes," I admitted.

"No hard feelins. Coat off then like he said." He produced a knife from one of his pockets.

Whatever else I had to do, it had to begin with the bloke who was about to stab me with his steely knife. Of course, I could have stabbed him first, quite easily, just by tossing one or both of my daggers at him. But as I might have mentioned, that ain't me. Hurting undead is one thing. Hurting fellow humans is quite another. So instead of stabbing him in the heart, I flipped up his knife hand with the catalysts and launched myself at him. My calculation was that the boss wouldn't harm Urna as long as he thought his guy was winning the fight.

I grabbed the knife hand, and not knowing anything about hand-to-hand fighting, or any kind of fighting for that matter, I just concentrated on holding onto it for dear life. As long as I was hanging on to his knife hand, he would not be able to stab me with it.

"Luce, help him," the bandit chief ordered.

Rolling in the snow with the fourth bandit, I saw that the chief's left-hand woman had detached herself from the line and was heading my way.

Then Speckle intervened. She had turned herself around, and now gave the right-hand man a royal two-hoofed salute. He flew through the air and landed spreadeagled.

Urna took the chance to duck out of the stunned chief's grasp. With a twist and a wriggle, she left him holding only her coat.

Two other pairs of hands joined mine around the fourth bandit's wrist: they belonged to the family's mother and her son. Between them they began to peel the bandit's fingers off his knife's handle.

Then a fist wrapped in an elegant wine-red glove swung into view and connected firmly with the advancing left-hand woman's chin, whose owner went down like a sack of potatoes. Lexi gave me an "I'll deal with you later," stare and turned to face the ringleader.

That was when Ronan arrived. He came striding up the same track I had. As he passed the four-person struggle in the snow, he thumped the bandit on the temple, knocking him out cold.

Three pairs of arms and legs slowly disentangled themselves from the unconscious man.

Meanwhile, the boss was beginning to look a little undergunned, or underbladed, with only his little knife to fight with. For my friend the paladin pulled out his great sword without breaking stride. The boss looked about him. All three of his gang were out of the game. It was him against a guy twice his size with a blade six times the size of his.

Except suddenly he didn't have a blade any more. As Ronan bore down on him, the gang leader tossed his weapon aside. "I surrender!" he yelled. "I wasn't really going to hurt anyone."

Ronan said nothing. He merely looked at Urna, who had a bruised cheek.

"Oh that! I've got some arnica here somewhere for that. She'll be as right as rain in no time."

Ronan did not slow down.

The gang's leader fell to his knees in the snow and clasped his hands together in entreaty. "Spare me! I promise never to hurt anyone ever again!"

The paladin reached his target, raised his sword... and as I knew he would, stayed the blow. Just like Sir Lancelot, he had to accept that his opponent had yielded. Of course, the gang would do evil again. But we would have to deal with that another day, or someone else would. For now, we would take our horses, and theirs, and the family they had taken prisoner, and leave the criminal quartet to spend the rest of the winter on the mountain by themselves. They could cut their own trees, and smoke their own charcoal, and dig their own mine. At least the work would keep them warm.

At that moment, Edison Junior came staggering up through snow that was as deep as he was tall in places. He weaved his way between the other players in this scene as if they were in a freeze frame at the end of an episode of Police Squad. His destination, as we could all tell by the way he said her name, was Beckle – I mean, Speckle. The grey horse dipped her head for him to place a rosy cheek against it.

Ronan slotted his sword away; the gang leader still cowered at his feet.

Then the boy of the family unbarred the door of one of the storage sheds, and out came the old man who had tipped the paladin and me off about the other way into the Cursed Vale. Waving a stick, he looked about for someone to hit with it. But the drama was finished; the fighting was over. Instead of hitting someone, he spoke to me in words I could not understand.

Urna translated. "He asks if you ever made it over Running Edge."

"Yes. Yes we did," I said, and smiled. "I'll tell you all about it on our way down the mountain."

Kneeling down to pick up F3, I realised that there was a little spot of warmth under my glove: Hal's ring. Something told me that the magic it was alerting me to was deep underground, but that I could reach it via a labyrinthine series of tunnels leading from the nearby cave mouth. For a moment or three I knelt in the snow as an inner voice assured me that it would be simplicity itself to top up my batteries with a good charge of free magic in the mine. Meanwhile, a second and far more sensible voice told me *not* to say, "Let's have a look down there." Ever again.

It was a close-run thing, but eventually the second voice won. I kept my mouth firmly shut.

That was when Lexi reached down to help me up.

THE END.

341

562 Years Later

Yes, I'm the demon in the box.

Well, I'm not a demon.

And I'm not in the box.

I *am* the box.

But let's talk about you.

Let's talk about how you're going to get out of here alive.

In the dark.

In the deepest dark.

Quietly.

Silently.

Silently in the deepest dark.

*

F3 will return in *The Hollow Throne*.

About the Author

Your author is usually called Jit even though his real name is Jonathan. He lives in Norwich, UK, with his darling wife. When not writing fiction, Jit is an entomologist, as well as a butler to three cats.

Farewell Clyde: missing in action since 2015

Welcome Scully: joined the family in 2016.

If you go to *Goodreads* and type in *Jl Thacker*, you will probably find my author page.

By the Same Author

Edison Blue

Elsie Smith: Vampyre Hunter

1000:1

Shadowland books:

The Door into Shadow

The Factory of Souls

World's End

The Deepest Grave

Demon Hunter

The Tree of Life